COROMANDEL

Born in Ceylon, Owen Sela is an economics graduate of London University and a Chartered Accountant. He is the author of a number of novels including the bestselling *An Exchange of Eagles* and *The KGB Candidate*. He lives in Ontario, Canada.

OWEN SELA

Coromandel

To A[...]
With [...] affection.

Owen

HarperCollins*Publishers*

HarperCollins*Publishers*
77–85 Fulham Palace Road,
Hammersmith, London W6 8JB

This paperback edition 1997

1 3 5 7 9 8 6 4 2

First published in Great Britain by
HarperCollins*Publishers* 1995

ISBN 0 00 649021 2

Set in Sabon by
Rowland Phototypesetting Ltd,
Bury St Edmunds, Suffolk

Printed and bound in Great Britain by
Caledonian International Book Manufacturing Ltd, Glasgow

This is for
Sreela, Anima and Hiranya
and above all for
Smita

Chapter One

'A ship! A ship!'

Richard Darnell heard the faint cry and hurried to the front of the warehouse. He was not expecting a ship for months. The buying season was over; the first ships from England were not due till after the monsoons.

He heard the cry again as he pushed a wooden trolley out of the way, leapt over a fallen ladder, and strode out on to the factory house steps. He watched as a noisy horde of native men and children in multicoloured turbans and *dhotis* scurried along Drake Street to the Sea Gate in the East Wall.

Richard Darnell was the English East India Company's agent at Armagon, the smallest, poorest and most dilapidated factory along the five-hundred-mile strip of southeast Indian coast known as Coromandel. He was thirty years old and ten years in the East had burnt him as dark as any Indian. At six foot one inch and one hundred and seventy pounds, he was tall for an Englishman and lean for a European in India. His dark, curly hair fell in a thick mane to his neck. His face was a cleanshaven oval on which a knife scar stood out like a flashing strand of wire, illuminating a line from his left ear to his chin.

Darnell turned his dark, deep-set eyes eastwards, squinting at the sea roads where the ship had anchored. He recognized the *Unity*, a Company pinnace, which plied the coastal trade and carried mail between the Company's factories on the Coromandel coast. The Company flag – England's red, white and blue Union flag with thirteen red and white stripes – fluttered from its fore topmast and bowsprit. Sailors had already lowered the ship's boat, and a burly figure in knee-breeches, jerkin, ruffs and broad-brimmed hat was preparing to descend the rope ladder dangling above the waves. Darnell's face screwed up as he tried to identify the person.

'It's Cap'n Martin, the commandant at bleedin' Pettah-poli,' Ravi Winter said. Winter was Darnell's second at Armagon. Eight years ago, Darnell had saved him from being beaten to death by three Dutchmen and he'd remained with Darnell since. A Eurasian, he had inherited the dark good looks, flashing teeth and thick, curly hair of his Tamil mother, and the speech patterns of his English shipwright father. Despite the desiccating heat and stifling humidity, his cotton shirt was crisp and eye-achingly white, his pantaloons creased and thrust into gleaming, calf-length boots.

'What the devil does Martin want?' Darnell growled. Unexpected arrivals seldom brought good news, and he was annoyed that his eyes were becoming less sharp than Winter's. He strode down the steps, leaving Winter and the others to follow.

Armagon stood on a rise fifteen yards from the sea and was enclosed by a crumbling, twenty-foot-high wall built of earth, brick and laterite. It had originally been intended to house a garrison, so the wall had embrasures for guns and its parapets were wide enough to run a bullock cart between. A three-storeyed, blue and grey factory house, held together by peeling paint, sagging balconies and rotting window-frames towered over the centre of the enclosure. Its ground floor was a warehouse, its second floor Company offices and there was a mixture of living accommodation and offices on the third floor.

It had been a poor season and the warehouse was only half full. Except for the taffetas, silks and *mullmulls* that Richard Darnell had smuggled there three weeks ago from Vaidya, the cloth was of low quality. Cloth was the only

2

acceptable substitute for silver in Java, Sumatra and the Spice Islands, and without cloth no European nation could engage in the spice trade. Without the spice trade England, France, Denmark, Portugal and Holland would be destitute and most of Europe hungry each winter.

South of the factory house was a dusty *maidan*, where every evening the natives set up a bazaar, and across the *maidan* were four rows of single-roomed tenements where the native merchants, washers and peons lived. Three rutted streets lined with sewage and rubbish linked the factory house to the walls. Drake Street ran to the Sea Gate in the East Wall; Queen Elizabeth Street snaked between the dilapidated barracks and the native tenements to the Land Gate in the West Wall; Third Street meandered across the *maidan* to the Vaidya Gate in the South Wall.

Darnell strode out through the Sea Gate, across the crumbling roadway beside the docking pier. The sea-breeze snatched at his shirt and hair. The natives stood with folded hands raised to their faces as he stepped off the pier and hurried down to the beach.

The ship's boat was corkscrewing through the surf, Captain Martin hanging fiercely on to the gunnel with one hand and his hat with the other. Darnell tried to imagine what disaster could have brought him from Pettahpoli. An attack? A massacre? The onset of the famine that had devastated the Company's factories on the west coast of India? But the *Unity* bore no battle-scars, and Captain Martin wouldn't have brought news of a disaster in full dress.

The boat grounded in the shallows. Four sailors leapt into the water, hoisted Captain Martin on to their shoulders and carried him ashore. Martin was a large man. His fleshy cheeks were red from the exertion of the boat-trip and the wind. Sweat streamed down his forehead. Sweeping off his broad-brimmed hat he bowed, revealing greasy hair cut in three points and tied at the back with ribbon. 'Mr Darnell?'

Darnell nodded in response.

Martin opened the leather pouch strapped to his waist. 'I have a letter for you from His Excellency Mr Andrew Cogan, the Honourable Company's agent for Pettahpoli and principal agent for the Coromandel Coast.'

'I know who Andrew Cogan is,' Darnell growled. As a junior merchant in Java he'd roomed with Cogan, then an assistant warehousekeeper and determined to claw his way up the Company ladder and become a director. Darnell tore open the seals. The letter was dated two days ago: 23 February 1639/40. Cogan was scrupulous about observing the Company rule that all correspondence should carry both the calendar year and the civil year, which ran from Lady Day, 25 March, and was three months behind the calendar year.

Sir, Darnell read.

> You are hereby instructed to FORTHWITH accompany the bearer of this letter to the Honourable Company's establishment at Pettahpoli for the purpose of meeting with the governor and other representatives of the Dutch East India Company, and determining and agreeing a peace between the Honourable Companies to take effect immediately throughout the whole of Coromandel.
>
> By Order of the Council,
> ANDREW COGAN, *Principal Agent*.

Darnell clutched the letter tightly, as if the wind might snatch it away. His heart beat dully in his throat. His mouth was dry. If Cogan made peace with the Dutch, the Company would be finished, and with it the spice trade and England.

For twenty years the English and the Dutch had fought

4

each other over spices. Five years ago, the Dutch had driven the English from Java and the Spice Islands. Only by establishing themselves firmly in India could the English hope to survive.

Darnell thrust the letter at Ravi. 'A pox on the motherfickin' Dutch,' he roared. 'And a plague on all who would make peace with them!' He turned to Captain Martin. 'Tell Mr Cogan I'll see him dead before I talk peace with a Dutchman!'

From beside him, Ravi said, 'You 'ave to go to Pettahpoli, Richard. You can't disobey a direct order.'

'The devil I can't!' Darnell's face was flushed with anger. 'Don't you remember what happened the last time we had a truce with the Dutch?'

'Sure I do. They broke every article of the agreement and used it to steal our ships and destroy our factories. But you still 'ave to go to Pettahpoli!'

Captain Martin cleared his throat and said, 'The decision has been taken at the highest level, Mr Darnell. The presidency is sending Mr Ovington from Surat to meet with the Dutch and finalize the truce.'

'You must stop them, Richard,' Ravi cried. 'Ovington will listen to you! You've had more experience of the Dutch –'

'Better piss into the wind!' Darnell growled and shook his head. 'Cogan's been wanting this peace ever since he came to Coromandel. He's looking for six months or a year where he can trade freely, consolidate his fortune, and retire to run the Company from Leadenhall Street. And the Company'll do anything as long as it doesn't involve spending money or fighting.'

In the forty years since the English and Dutch Companies had been formed, the Dutch had prospered, spreading their trading empire as far as Japan, while the English Company's insistence that war and trade were incompatible had brought it to the edge of bankruptcy. But times were at last changing. The Dutch had overstretched themselves, and England now had access to the limitless silver of the New World. In three years, five at the most, the Dutch empire would start to come apart, then the English could wrest the East from the Dutch. So this was not the time to make concessions and talk peace, Darnell thought.

Ravi said quietly, 'If you don't go, Cogan'll destroy you.'

Darnell weighed up his options. He couldn't agree to a truce. How could he stop Cogan? If Cogan's summons had come a few weeks later he'd have had time to confirm the rumours about Prince Seringa. He recalled his meeting with the cloth-smuggler, three weeks ago. How much could he rely on what he'd been told? Could he risk his whole future and that of England on a smuggler's tale?

Captain Martin said, 'Begging your pardon, Mr Darnell, Captain Lawrence wants to leave with the tide.'

He had to make up his mind now, damnit. 'Tell Mr Cogan I cannot come,' he said firmly. 'Tell him I have pressing business that will make the Honourable Company a hundred times more profit than it has made in the last ten years. Tell him when I have finished my business there will be no need for a truce with the god-rotting Dutch.'

'I'll tell him,' Captain Martin said. 'If you're sure.'

'I'm sure.' Darnell held out his hand. 'God go with you, Captain.'

'And you, Mr Darnell, whatever you're planning.' He shook Darnell's hand, turned on his heel and marched to the boat.

'By the Cross, Richard!' Ravi Winter cried. 'What the devil are you goin' to do?'

Darnell stared thoughtfully at Captain Martin's re-treating figure. 'I'm going to Vaidya,' he said, 'to check on a cloth-smuggler's story.'

Ynessa da Soares knelt before the cross she and her father's managing clerk, Manuel Figueras, had fashioned from the branches of a tree and erected at the foot of the grave. 'Eternal rest grant unto thy servant, Don Rodrigo da Soares,' she prayed, 'and to those who died with him. Take them to your bosom and give them peace. Give them the new life your Son promised to all who believed in Him.'

She looked round the clearing, a small circle of grass and undergrowth on the edge of the forest, separated from the yellow-brown Pulicat–Celor road by palms and a screen of shade trees. The headman of Celor and his escort were squatting by the side of the road in the scrawny shade of their cart near her own bodyguard of five Portuguese mercenaries.

Her father, Don Rodrigo da Soares, had been head of the merchant house of da Soares, the largest merchant house in San Thome. He'd come to Celor five weeks ago at the invitation of the nizam of Kokinada, to bid at the pearl auction. He had bought the premier lot, the vendor's selection of the largest and best pearls. Two hours out of Celor he'd been murdered together with his escort.

Her fingers closed on the gold crucifix Rodrigo had given her when she'd received her first communion. Rodrigo had been the bravest, sweetest, most loving father a girl could hope for. She couldn't believe he was dead, that he was lying there beneath that mound of raw earth, murdered!

'It will be difficult for me to live without him,' she prayed. 'But this I will do. I will find the men who killed him. And I will deliver them to justice. That I swear upon these graves before you, Lord God Almighty Christ. I will not rest until those who killed my father and his companions are dead.'

She buried her face in her hands, a shapeless figure in a flowing black gown, her head and face covered with a black mantilla. She felt utterly alone; not even the presence of Manuel Figueras, whom she had known from childhood, eased that sense of isolation. She reminded herself she'd been trained for this since that day eight years ago when

Diego, her older step-brother, had drowned in a shipwreck off Diu. Then, ignoring convention, Rodrigo had brought her from the convent to the warehouse, where he'd instructed Figueras to teach her book-keeping and mercantile law, and engaged private tutors to teach her languages, history, geography and the principles of navigation.

Figueras placed a comforting hand on her shoulder. 'Come, Madonna,' he said, using his pet name for her. It went back to the time when she was three years old and Figueras would carry her round the warehouse on his shoulders. 'Let's go. There's nothing we can do here.'

She clutched Figueras's hand. She wished her fiancé, Joaquim Gonzaga, were here. Joaquim would know how to investigate Rodrigo's death. She stopped herself. Rodrigo had told her she must never believe that men could do things better, simply because they were men. She'd been trained better than Joaquim, and was more experienced than him, and Rodrigo was her father, not his. Finding Rodrigo's killers was the responsibility of the head of the House of da Soares, *her responsibility!* She would carry out that responsibility, with or without the help of Joaquim Gonzaga.

'Jesus, please help me,' she prayed. 'Give me the courage and the strength to find these men and I will never ask anything of you again.' Slowly she got to her feet. Rodrigo had always said he had *cojones*. She was a big, grown-up girl with *cojones*. She walked to where the village headman of Celor waited.

Mirza Baig got to his feet at her approach, an expectant smile on his face. He was fair-skinned and light-eyed, as if he'd had a European ancestor. Despite the heat he wore a waisted, scarlet jacket of English broadcloth over his sarong. Ynessa did not trust him. He had delayed their visit all morning on the pretext of waiting for the naik of the area, his cousin, Ali Baig, and had only agreed to show them the graves after Figueras had given him a gold *muhar*.

Ynessa took out another *muhar*. 'Who found the bodies?' she asked.

'One of the villagers, madam, but you need not concern yourself with him. Naik Ali Baig and I did everything that was needed.' He put his hands behind his back and swayed as if reciting a poem. 'When we got here all the men were dead, brutally slain by dacoits. We buried them, took their personal effects back to Celor and sent word to the nizam and to San Thome.'

It was all too tidy, Ynessa thought. 'Where were the bodies?'

'There.' Mirza Baig pointed to the clearing.

'Can you show me how they were positioned?'

'What is there to show? They were lying on the ground, all dead.'

Ynessa closed her fist over the coin. Mirza Baig was hiding something. She stared angrily over the mantilla at him. 'How were they killed?'

Mirza Baig paled, as if still shocked by the unpleasantness of his discovery. 'All were stabbed, except two who had had their heads smashed with clubs.'

'The oldest man, how was he killed?'

'Madonna, no!' Figueras grabbed her shoulder. 'It isn't necessary to –'

She twisted his hand away. Her eyes blazed at Mirza Baig. 'I want to know. Tell me!'

'Him cut here.' Mirza Baig fingered his throat. 'Here and here.' He touched his chest. 'This here,' he touched the site of the last wound, 'is cut to take pearls.'

The pearls, Ynessa knew, would have been in a soft leather bag fastened to the inside of her father's shirt. She wondered what her father had felt as the knives had plunged into his chest and cut his throat. Had he felt terror, pain . . . ?

Figueras touched her arm. 'Don't fret yourself, Madonna. He would have died quickly.'

9

He shouldn't have died at all, Ynessa thought angrily, her eyes suddenly brimming with tears. She visualized him standing before her and realized he'd been a man about her own height. Had death diminished him so? He'd been so large in life, a giant, filling rooms with his presence, dominating everything and everyone with his personality and intelligence. Why did you have to leave me, Father? she cried, silently. Her neck and back were cool with perspiration, her palms slimy with it. She wiped them on the front of her gown and asked Mirza Baig, 'Have dacoits attacked many travellers in this area?'

'No. This is the first time.'

'And since this attack have there been others?'

Mirza Baig's frown made him look anxious. 'No. No attacks.'

'How many dacoits were there?'

Mirza Baig flung out pudgy arms in helplessness. 'Alas, good lady, we do not know.'

And did not want to find out. Ynessa was now more certain than ever that Mirza Baig was hiding something. 'How did the dacoits travel?'

'We found signs of horses there.' Mirza Baig pointed to the forest north of the clearing. 'We couldn't tell how many. The earth was much churned up.'

It had rained since, Ynessa knew, and thought there was little point in looking now. 'Who else was at the auction?'

'Just local traders. People who come every time. I assure you, madam, none of them would have committed such an outrage.'

That was true. No pearl-dealer would kill to steal the prize pearls. They were easily identifiable and no one could get rid of them in Coromandel without being linked to the killings. 'What *feringhi* were there? How many Dutch, Portuguese, English?'

'There were no Portuguese apart from your father. There

was one Englishman from Gangapatnam, I think, or Armagon. He didn't buy anything.'

'How many Dutch?' Ynessa asked.

Mirza Baig hesitated. 'None.'

'Are you sure?' The Dutch were at war with the Portuguese and had besieged Malacca. Until five weeks ago the
Dutch had had a monopoly on this auction.

Mirza Baig looked down, avoiding her eyes.

So there *had* been Dutch at the auction. Ynessa gave
him the coin. 'Those pearls were worth a great sum of
money,' she said. 'A very great sum. I will pay half their
value to anyone who can tell me who killed my father and
his escort!'

Mirza Baig looked ashen. He chewed at his lower lip
and traced a circle with the toe of his slipper. 'Well, good
lady –' he began.

'Whoa! Whoa! Whoa!' A small man galloped into the
clearing and reared his roan up with much savage tugging
at the reins. He had a straggly, speckled beard, narrow,
bloodshot eyes, a bristle of hair and hollowed, pock-
scarred cheeks. The three men accompanying him drew up
a short distance away, in a line between the clearing and
the road.

Mirza Baig backed away from her, suddenly oozing
sweat and bending double with humility. 'Our naik, Ali
Baig,' he muttered and, turning to the newcomer, made
obeisance twice. 'Welcome home, cousin.'

Ali Baig's forehead narrowed in a frown. 'What are you
doing here? Who are these people?'

'They are relatives of Don Rodrigo from San Thome –'

'We are looking for the men who murdered my father,'
Ynessa said.

Ali Baig turned slowly towards her, peering at her closely
as if trying to penetrate her veil. Ynessa noticed his eyes
were small and bloodshot, like two red buttons. She wondered if he drank heavily. 'Your father was murdered by

dacoits,' he said. His voice grated, as if strained through cloth. 'There are no dacoits in Celor.'

'We wish to find the dacoits,' Ynessa said.

'I am already doing that. The nizam has offered a reward of ten gold *muhars*; as soon as the dacoits are found he will see they are suitably punished.'

'We could help. We have men –'

'There is no need for that. This is a local matter and must be dealt with by my people. I will send word as soon as we have found them.' He turned to Mirza Baig. 'Get back to Celor at once. There is work to be done,' he snapped.

Mirza Baig bowed repeatedly, scurrying to the carts as Ali Baig rode back towards his bodyguard.

'Do you believe dacoits would have taken only the pearls and left the money behind?' Ynessa called after Ali Baig.

He turned in the saddle. Again he stared at her, as if trying to penetrate the veil. Then he took a piece of areca-nut from a pouch at his waist and bit it. 'Who can explain what men do?' he said, shrugging. 'These men were obviously fools.' He spat out the sharp-tasting areca-nut juice. 'Only fools would have dared to kill the nizam's friends.'

Beyond Ali Baig, Mirza Baig's cart was moving to the road. Ynessa was losing her only means of finding who killed Rodrigo. 'We will recompense you amply for your hospitality,' she cried. 'And if you help us find the men who killed my father, we will pay you a large reward.'

'You cannot stay in Celor,' Ali Baig said. 'The fishing season has started and we do not allow strangers at this time –'

'We are not thieves!'

'Of course not. But strangers bring bad luck.'

Ynessa watched the group ride away after the cart, a thick, suffocating lump in her throat. If she couldn't get to Celor, she couldn't find Rodrigo's killers. 'A pox on their mothers!' she swore, slapping her hands together.

Figueras took her hand and walked her to where their horses were tethered. 'There is nothing more to be done here, Madonna,' he said. 'Let us go home.'

Ynessa squeezed her eyes shut against a sudden sting of tears. 'No,' she said, through rigid lips.

Figueras's large eyes were filled with sadness. 'You have a business to take care of, Madonna. And arrangements must be made for your wedding.'

Ynessa cast a long look at the grave. 'No,' she repeated. 'First we'll go to Gangapatnam and Armagon and find this Englishman. Then we'll come back here and get Mirza Baig to talk.'

Andrew Cogan walked slowly beside the long trestle-table in the Company dining room. The table groaned under sides of beef, venison and roasted suckling pig. There were loaves of freshly baked bread and cold cabbage cooked in pork fat, bunches of bananas, whole pineapples and enormous preserved fruit pies. Pitchers of claret and beer stood by each plate. From the hall outside came the sound of music mingled with the steady buzz of conversation. Satisfied that everything was in order, Cogan went into the hall.

All week, representatives from the twelve Dutch and seven English factories in Coromandel had been arriving. Stuart Ovington had arrived yesterday from the Company's presidency in Surat; and shortly after breakfast this morning, Willem de Groot, the Dutch governor of Coromandel, had arrived from Pulicat.

Cogan had turned fifty of his soldiers out of the barracks and lodged the Dutch there. He'd billeted the English on local merchants and given Ovington the spacious guest-quarters at the top of the factory house. The formal meetings would start at seven o'clock tomorrow morning. Tonight was the official welcoming dinner.

Kegs of ale and casks of claret, rhenish and malmsey

had been set up in the east corner of the hall. Ten soldiers from the Company band played a mixture of dulcet tunes. Company servants, in red and white striped tunics and turbans, roved the room serving chilli prawns, minced beef wrapped in pastry, and beer. Cogan looked at Englishmen mingling with Dutchmen and thought, *in four days there will be peace*. The only way the Company could become profitable and regain its share of the spice trade was by association with the Dutch. War was wasteful and expensive, and the time was coming when, in order to expand their trade, the Europeans would have to confront the natives. If this confrontation was to be economical and effective, the English and the Dutch must fight as allies instead of enemies.

Cogan looked benignly round the room. Three English merchants were laughing uproariously at jokes made by their Dutch counterparts. At the far end of the room, Stuart Ovington was in deep conversation with de Groot. The room was a babble of English and Dutch. It would go well, Cogan thought, and then he remembered Richard Darnell.

What the devil was Darnell up to? And what did he mean, he would make the Company a hundred times more profit than it had made in the last ten years? Darnell wasn't stupid. Darnell must realize that the fortune he'd made in Java was simply a matter of luck; and that his luck had run out. Cogan told himself he shouldn't worry about Darnell. He resolved that as soon as the truce conference was over he would have a word with Ovington about putting Darnell on a disciplinary charge.

Cogan picked up a pitcher of beer, shaking all thoughts of Darnell from his mind. He was sure they would have peace and profitable trade and then – he smiled quietly – a grateful Company would surely reward the architect of such a peace with a directorship . . .

*   *   *

The welcoming party was two hours old when Karel van Cuyler reached Pettahpoli. He had travelled from Sairin, ninety miles to the south, where he'd been cementing his friendship with the local naik, Ali Baig, so that, at the appropriate time, the natives would begin harassing the English.

Officially, van Cuyler was the envoy of the president of the Dutch East India Company in Batavia, sent to expedite the Coromandel truce. In fact he was an agent for the Coordinator's Office headed by Cornelius van Speult, dedicated to preserving and expanding Dutch hegemony in the East.

It was a job van Cuyler relished. He hated the English and had delighted in driving them from Java. He was preparing to do the same thing here. He had cultivated the friendship of local naiks like Ali Baig and financiers like Abdul Nana, and taken drastic steps to preserve the Dutch pearl monopoly at Celor. He was working with Ali Baig to persuade the nizam of Kokinada to close some English factories. He had come to Pettahpoli to ensure that de Groot did not give away forty years of Dutch sweat and struggle for a pathetic peace.

Van Cuyler stared at the English factory house, ablaze with the glow of lanterns. The sound of music drifted into the warm, night air. Cogan and de Groot were already celebrating their triumph. De Groot, he thought, was a lily-livered muckle, who couldn't see further than his nose and was concerned only with profits and easy options. He stroked the *sjambok* at his waist and thought, he had a few surprises for de Groot and Andrew Cogan.

'Whatever truce we sign we will never share our cinnamon with you!' Andreas van Stratten cried, gulping down more malmsey.

Cogan smiled politely at the chief merchant from Narsapur. Twenty years ago the Dutch had forced the Portuguese from Ceylon; now they controlled the highly profitable monopoly in cinnamon. 'We might trade your cinnamon for our mustard,' he said.

'Trade yes, share no!' Van Stratten hooted with laughter.

Suddenly the door to the room swung open. Karel van Cuyler stood there, large and dishevelled, his tunic and breeches flaked with dust, his small pig-eyes narrowed to puffy slits as he looked about the room.

Cogan's jaw sagged. He felt sick with fear. Van Cuyler was the butcher of Java. Seven years ago he had organized the massacre of seventeen English merchants at Japara. If any one man could be held responsible for forcing the English from Java, it was Karel van Cuyler. And now he was here, with his *sjambok* – that vicious combination of whip and cudgel made from elephant hide – dangling from his waist, ready to fight the English again.

Cogan moved mechanically towards van Cuyler. He had to get the man out. The mere fact that he was here was proof the Dutch weren't negotiating in good faith. He became aware of de Groot walking beside him.

'I see you already know our presidential envoy.'

Cogan snorted with disgust. 'From Java!'

'Much has changed since then,' de Groot said. 'His wife had a lot to do with it. She was –' De Groot shrugged as they came up to van Cuyler. He clicked his heels and said, 'Excellency, may I present Mynheer Karel van Cuyler, the personal emissary of our president in Batavia. Mynheer van Cuyler is committed to peace. Through his good offices, the agreement we negotiate will be speedily approved by our president in Batavia.'

It couldn't be true, Cogan thought. Van Cuyler would never work for a peace with the English.

Van Cuyler was looking down at him and bowing. 'I am greatly honoured,' he said with the heavy lisp Cogan remembered. 'And I want to assure you, Excellency, that Java was a very long time ago. I give you my word that I now seek nothing more than peace between our Companies.'

Cogan stepped back as van Cuyler spread out his arms. 'What say you now, Excellency? We become friends. *Ja*!'

'*Ja*,' Cogan muttered tightly, as he allowed himself to be embraced.

Van Cuyler peered over Cogan's shoulder, his sharp eyes scanning the room. All the English agents were there, and all the Dutch. But there was one person missing; a man van Cuyler was determined to find. Because the other reason he'd come to India was to kill Richard Darnell.

Chapter Two

Richard Darnell and Ravi Winter led their horses up the barely visible jungle track. The hot season had begun and, though it wasn't yet midmorning, the March sun was fierce, sucking up the moisture from beneath the close-pressed trees, making the air dank and oppressive. They had been travelling in Vaidya for three days and had reached the Tiretani foothills, a region of dense jungle and narrow winding trails. Leaves and undergrowth snatched at their clothes and their bodies.

Vaidya was a large strip of land on the southern part of the Coromandel coast, ruled by Raja Railoo Venkat. Its northern province, also called Venkat, was thirty miles from their factory at Armagon, and ruled by Railoo's cousin, Prince Seringa. Forty years ago the Portuguese traders had enraged the Vaidyans by attempting to forcibly convert the population to Christianity. Since then Vaidya had banned all trade with Europeans.

At Darnell's insistence the company had twice approached Raja Railoo for permission to open a factory in Vaidya. Both requests had been summarily rejected, forcing Darnell to continue smuggling cloth from Vaidya, since the region produced the best and cheapest cloth, and it had been the only way he'd been able to show a profit.

Three weeks ago, a smuggler had told Darnell that twenty thousand Mughal troops under Crown Prince Aurangzeb were fighting their way across the arid Deccan plain towards Vaidya; that Prince Seringa had sent his army against them and hadn't been able to stop the advance. Which meant that Vaidya was in imminent danger of being invaded, an event Darnell believed would make Prince Seringa extremely receptive to an English offer of trading rights and the building of a factory-fort in exchange for the use of English guns in defending Vaidya.

'Bleedin' 'ell!' Ravi said hoarsely, staring at a thin dust cloud rising above the trees. 'I think we've found 'em.' He jogged forward, yanking at his horse's reins. The horse followed without enthusiasm.

Ravi had refused to let Darnell travel alone. Until convinced otherwise, the Vaidyans treated all Europeans as cloth-smugglers. Ten weeks ago, two Danes caught smuggling in southern Vaidya had been dragged over thorns, beaten with cords, branded and had their legs crushed under the wheel of a cart.

Darnell pulled his horse up the rise. In front of him, the tangled green and brown web of jungle swept down to a narrow earth and mud trail twisting between the foothills. The trail was covered by a long line of soldiers.

They were travelling in orderly columns, without the usual rag-taggle of camp-followers. They wore a standard uniform of dappled green and brown, which from time to time made whole sections of the troop invisible. They had no scouts, which meant that the army was Vaidyan and travelling in home territory. There were walking wounded and wounded on litters, and they were coming from the north-west, the direction of the Deccan. He had found Seringa's defeated army, Darnell thought. The smuggler had been telling him the truth.

'Bleedin' 'ell!' Ravi whispered. 'Them troops give me the heebie-jeebies. Now that you've seen 'em, let's go home.'

Darnell said, 'You go on ahead. I'm going down to find out more about those soldiers.'

'Why d'you 'ave to do that?'

'I need to find out how badly they've been defeated, and what Seringa's plans are.'

'What's it matter 'ow badly they've been defeated?' Ravi

cried. 'They've been defeated – that's enough. You go down there and they'll cut your bleedin' goolies off.'

Darnell smiled. Switching from English to fluent Tamil, he asked, 'Why? I don't have any cloth, and I look as Indian as they do.'

Ravi had to admit that was so: dressed in *kamis*, pantaloons and sandals, a grubby turban pulled low down on his forehead; and with his hollow cheeks, broken nose and the thread of a knife scar under the black stubble on his jaw, Darnell looked more like a Pathan warrior than an English merchant. 'You've gorn crazy about buildin' factories in Vaidya,' Ravi complained.

'We'd be crazy *not* to build them here.' One factory in Vaidya would produce more profit than all seven English factories in northern Coromandel. If he succeeded in building that factory, the Company would have to protect those profits by putting more men and ships and guns into Coromandel. If he succeeded in building that factory, within eighteen months he'd recover the fortune he'd lost four years ago.

Ravi asked, 'How're you goin' to get down there and talk to them soldiers?'

Darnell pointed. On the trail ahead of the soldiers, a man was unloading bright yellow king coconuts from a cart and stacking them beside a makeshift stall he'd built by the roadside. 'I'm going to buy that man's stock and sell coconuts. Now, you get back to Armagon.' He climbed into the saddle and kneed his horse off the trail.

'No! Richard, wait! You can't – don't be stupid! *Richaaarddd!!*' Ravi Winter slapped his thigh in frustration as the top of Darnell's turban became a fast diminishing blob beneath the thick green curtain of jungle.

Darnell squatted by the roadside, holding up a bright yellow king coconut, calling '*Thambili, thambili*,' in high-pitched, ululating Tamil. It had taken him five minutes and three *pagodas* to persuade the coconut vendor to sell his stock and allow him to help resell the coconuts to the soldiers. 'Very good, very cool, very refreshing. Only one *fanam*,' Darnell called. Between serving customers he studied the narrow trail in front of him, choked with carts, horses and soldiers.

The soldiers were moving in something between a march and a shuffle. Many of them were barefoot. Some had bandages wrapped round elbows and knees and others, healing leaves stuffed into open wounds. Litters bearing wounded swung busily, the groans of the injured mingling with the steady creak of axles and the whinny of horses. There were archers, spearmen and pikemen divided into separate groups. There were men carrying *lathis* and others carrying the round-edged battle-axes known as *tabars*. Darnell noted that every man wore the slightly curved, double-edged dagger known as the *khanjar*, and carried a *shamshir* or light sabre.

It was hot and the men were thirsty. Soon the ground in front of the stall was littered with severed yellow and white tops of coconut, and the sheet between Darnell and the vendor was heaped with a growing pile of coins.

'Coming from far, master?' Darnell asked one soldier.

'Far enough.' The soldier snatched the outstretched coconut, threw a coin on the sheet and went to join his comrades.

'Hurry up you lazy lout. I'm thirsty.' A soldier held out a coin in a grimy hand.

'So sorry, master,' Darnell apologized, slicing the top of a coconut and handing it over.

He studied the faces of the soldiers; dusty, sweaty faces, drawn with fatigue, the eyes beneath the turbans reddened from dust and lack of sleep. They were the faces of soldiers everywhere, hard, tired and watchful.

Darnell had to find someone willing to talk soon. The pile of coconuts behind him was diminishing fast.

'*Thambili! Thambili!*' he called, 'Very good, very refreshing!'

He spotted a soft-eyed young man at the back of the crowd who was looking longingly at the coconuts. He had a round, innocent face; the puppy fat on his cheeks barely shaded by soft stubble. His thick, liver-coloured lips were as cracked and dry as a parched river-bed.

Darnell smiled and held out a coconut to him. 'Take it. You can pay me later.'

The young soldier pressed his hands against the side of his grubby trousers. 'I don't know if I will ever pass here again . . .' He was obviously tempted.

'Take it, brother, and give alms for me when you get home.'

The young man hesitated. He pressed his cracked lips together and the sting made him decide. 'Truly, I will.' He took the coconut and drank greedily and gratefully.

Darnell let him enjoy the relief for a moment before moving closer to the young man. 'Whose army are you?' he asked casually.

The young man stopped drinking and wiped his mouth with the back of his hand. 'We are the army of Prince Seringa. Our commander is the Venerable Bharatya.'

A cart rumbled by, four soldiers hanging on to its sides. 'Where are you coming from?' Darnell asked. He tried to appear merely polite, as if the answer were unimportant.

'The Deccan.'

Darnell cut a coconut for himself, and said, 'Oh yes. Where in the Deccan?' It was a vast place. Darnell had crossed it once and the journey had taken three weeks.

'Chitaldroog.'

Two hundred miles west of Vaidya. 'How long have the Mughal been in that part of the Deccan?' Darnell allowed a note of curiosity to enter his voice.

'Since December. Prince Aurangzeb means to take all the Deccan and then take Vaidya.' The youth raised the coconut and drank, the liquid sloshing noisily inside the fruit.

He said, 'We would have defeated them if they hadn't brought in ten thousand fresh troops from the north,' and wiped his mouth with the back of his hand.

'Ten thousand!' Darnell exclaimed. 'That is truly a huge number! It is no shame to be defeated by such a large force.'

'We were not defeated,' the young man said, fiercely. 'We're returning home for the hot season.'

'Yes, of course.' There would be no more fighting till September. Darnell asked, 'What about the Mughal?'

'We expect them to attack after the monsoon. But they won't succeed. We've left troops in the hill forts on our western border. In those mountains one hundred men can easily hold off a thousand.'

'True,' Darnell murmured, 'true. You're going home to Venkatapur?'

'Yes. We will be there in three days.' The young man put down the coconut and sighed. 'There are rumours we will be sent to garrison our northern border with Kokinada. Our commander Bharatya feels that, rather than attack from the west, Aurangzeb may make for the coast and join up with the nizam of Kokinada.'

That was very likely; and the nizam would be a willing ally. Twelve years ago he had attempted to invade Vaidya and been badly defeated. 'Where in the north?' Darnell asked.

'I think, Madera.'

Darnell's heart sang. Madera was a spit of land four miles south of the Kokinada-Vaidya border. Formed by the silt of two rivers flowing into the sea, it was surrounded on three sides by water and joined to the mainland at its northern end. Easily defended and equidistant from the heartland of Vaidya and the English factories in Kokinada, uninhabited except for a small fishing village at its south end, it was the perfect site for a factory. The only road from Kokinada crossed two bridges directly opposite Madera. If

23

Seringa gave the English permission to build a factory there, the road and the bridges would be covered by English guns and any military advance into Vaidya easily stopped. 'How many of you will go to Madera?'

'I don't know. Perhaps five hundred or a thousand.'

Darnell thought: even five thousand wouldn't be enough against a combined Mughal-Kokinada army. A foreign alliance was Vaidya's only chance. Darnell had to ensure that that alliance would be with the English. His own future and that of England and the Company depended on it.

Perched high in the saddle, naked except for a dazzling white turban, *dhoti* and riding boots, Prince Seringa Venkat rode furiously along the broad, tree-lined avenue that led from his palace to the Tiretani road. He'd been fretting with impatience since he'd heard his army had reached Tiretani, a three-day march away. He was anxious to learn the condition of his soldiers and to see his commanders, Bharatya and Dorai Ghosh, who were his dearest friends.

He pressed his head against the horse's neck, urging it forward. A large tiger's eye glinted in the centre of his turban, and another in the middle of his chest. The mottled shadows of the cassia trees made dizzying mosaics as he sped towards the plumes of dust rising ahead of him, blurring the shapes of men, horses and carts. Upraised pikes, spears and pennants striped the moving cloud.

He slowed to a trot as he reached the advance guard of pikemen, raising his left arm in a gesture that was a mixture of salute, greeting and encouragement. Where were Bharatya and Dorai Ghosh? When he'd last heard from the battle-front, they'd been safe. There'd been no major battles since so nothing could have happened to them, he told himself. Both men were experienced soldiers.

Seringa pulled to the side of the road and squinted through the throat-scraping dust. He hoped nothing had happened to Ghosh. Dorai Ghosh was his closest friend.

They'd been brought up together here in the palace of Venkatapur, studied together, played together, fought together. Throughout their lives they'd been inseparable. Seringa searched the faces of the passing soldiers. Ghosh would not be distinguishable by his dress; he insisted on wearing the same uniform as his men, sharing their hardships and living exactly as they did. That was what Bharatya had taught them.

Bharatya was a Hindu priest, the creator of a philosophy of militant Hinduism. It was he who had, under Seringa's father, trained the Venkat army. Ghosh and Seringa had been sent to his monastery when they were eight. There Bharatya had taught them how to read and write, and later taught them history, geography, mathematics, military tactics, religion; all the skills necessary to rule a province. Everything he was, Seringa owed to Bharatya.

As if thinking of him had conjured him up, Seringa saw Bharatya emerge wraith-like from the dust, shaven head bare, lithe upper body gleaming with sweat. Bharatya's right arm and the right side of his chest were ribbed with old sword-scars; a chain of wooden prayer-beads was wound tightly round his neck. A sabre and a *khatar* hung from his narrow uniform trousers. A large cylindrical shield and a fearsome double-headed battle-axe were fixed to his saddle. Despite the heat and dust he rode erect, looking about him with an expression of serene alertness.

Seringa leapt off his horse and threw himself face down in the dust. Bharatya was his teacher, his *guru*, his second father. The tramp of feet and the thump of hooves grew louder. Dust stuck to Seringa's face and beard and irritated his nostrils. Then a hand caressed the back of his head and he looked up into Bharatya's lean, high-cheek-boned face. His sun-browned skin seemed stretched and translucent.

'How many times have I told you not to do this?' Bharatya asked, his voice soft and melodic but carrying strongly against the steady rumble of traffic. 'You are the ruler of

Venkat and my sovereign. It is I who must make obeisance.'

Seringa stood up and reached forward to stop Bharatya making obeisance. Bharatya steepled his hands before his face and bowed his head over them.

Seringa copied the gesture. 'How was it in the Deccan?' he asked.

'At the beginning we won.' Bharatya told him how they had harassed the Mughal with surprise attacks and ambushes; how they had wrecked bridges and sabotaged the Mughal supply lines. 'But they had an endless supply of reinforcements,' Bharatya said. 'It was too much for us and with the hot season due –'

'It was a good decision,' Seringa agreed.

Bharatya said, 'My men now hold the western passes and the hill forts. When the Mughal gets there he will find that even an army of ten thousand won't pass.'

'Crown Prince Aurangzeb might well bypass the hill forts and join up with Kokinada.'

'I've thought of that. We'll have to stop him at Madera,' Bharatya said.

They mounted their horses and moved into the crowd. 'Where's Dorai?' Seringa asked.

'He was supposed to join us last evening, but we had a message he'd been delayed by a skirmish and would come here direct.' Bharatya pointed over his shoulder. 'Some of his men joined our rearguard today.'

'You go on to the palace,' Seringa said, not allowing himself to frown or show his worry. 'I'll find him.' He moved into the throng, and soon he was among the carts carrying supplies and the stragglers, who were almost invisible amidst the head-high column of dust. His hair and beard were thick with it. Where was Ghosh? Had he been hurt in this skirmish? Killed? Seringa shouted an enquiry to a carter and then to a passing soldier, but both were part of Bharatya's contingent and knew nothing about Ghosh. He pressed on through the grainy, yellow-brown dust cloud, telling himself Ghosh was too strong, too clever, too well-trained, too brave to die. As boys, it was Ghosh who'd been quicker on his feet and more vicious in attack.

The column had thinned to a trickle; just when Seringa had nearly given him up he saw Ghosh riding alone at the end of it, a red scarf over his nose and mouth as protection against the dust. 'Dorai!' Seringa called, 'Dorai!' He urged his horse forward.

Ghosh turned and lowered the scarf. His normally trim moustache was bedraggled, his cheeks covered with heavy stubble. His eyes were steeped in shadow and he slumped in the saddle as if dragged down by a heavy weight.

'Dorai! Are you hurt?' Seringa asked anxiously, flinging his arms about his friend.

Ghosh broke the embrace brusquely. 'I'm all right.' His face was drawn and set in an expression of exhausted flatness. A mess of dusty black curls hung down to his shoulders. His dirty knee-length tunic bore the marks of sword-cuts at chest and shoulder. 'Why did you do this, Serai?' Ghosh cried. 'Why did you allow Bharatya to order us back?' His voice shook with emotion.

'Bharatya didn't consult with me. In any case it was the right decision.' Seringa placed a hand on Ghosh's shoulder. 'Now, you need to rest. Let me take you home.'

Ghosh twisted his shoulder from under Seringa's hand. His eyes flashed with anger. 'This is all your fault,' he cried. 'We could have defeated the Mughal if you'd had the guts to overthrow Railoo.'

'Railoo is my cousin and our raja. I have sworn an oath of loyalty to him and –'

'You promised your father on his deathbed you wouldn't overthrow Railoo, and you don't want to have to kill Railoo's wife and sons.' Ghosh spoke in a mocking, keening lilt.

'I'm a soldier,' Seringa grunted. 'I do not fight women.'

He turned angrily to Ghosh. 'Those are perfectly honourable reasons.'

'A plague on your honour! If we had Railoo's army with us we could have defeated the Mughal and taken Crown Prince Aurangzeb prisoner!'

'God willing,' Seringa said.

They rode on together in silence. Ghosh slumped in his saddle, his chin touching his chest. After a while he asked, 'So what do you propose we do now?'

The sarcasm of Ghosh's tone reminded Seringa of the way he'd picked fights when they were boys. He said, 'Bharatya's forces are already defending the west. We must find a way to defend the north.'

'The north? The Mughal is in the Deccan and the Deccan is in the west!'

'I think Aurangzeb will bypass the west, go straight through to the coast, join up with Kokinada and attack us from the north.'

'Then we're finished,' Ghosh said. 'We can't hold back an invasion from the north without more troops.'

'As soon as you're recovered I want you to visit Madera and lay out plans for building a large barracks there.'

'That's nonsense, Serai! Madera is too small a battlefield. We'll be jammed right against the Mughal, and with their superior numbers they'll massacre us. Our only chance to defeat the Mughal is *before* he gets to Kokinada!'

Chapter Three

The road between Armagon and Pettahpoli was a strip of packed sand rutted with the passage of carts. For ninety miles it ran through unchanging scenery: palm trees and narrow, white beaches on the right, palm trees growing out to scrub and jungle to the left. Every twenty miles or so there were huddles of wattle-and-daub huts with roofs of coconut thatch, and fishing villages on the beach standing protectively over neatly laid out rows of canoes.

Darnell rode steadily, fighting sleep and the ache that covered his entire body. He'd been travelling for five days, his body riddled with stiffness from riding ten hours a day. He had to reach Pettahpoli before Cogan finalized the truce. If the English wanted control of Coromandel, the Dutch could not be allowed to share in Vaidya. The Dutch should not even *know* of Vaidya until after Darnell had finalized a trade agreement with Seringa and obtained permission to build a factory at Madera. Darnell rode past a small temple, whose guard walls were partly submerged in the sea. He was four hours from Pettahpoli. He tried to avoid thinking what would happen if he failed to reach Pettahpoli in time: the end of the Company, the servitude of England to the Continental powers, the end of his merchanting career and his love affair with the East.

All he'd ever wanted was to be a merchant and trade in the East. The twin ambitions had grown out of and been fuelled by the experiences of his father and Alban Cormac. His father had been a jobbing merchant for the Company, buying odds and ends at Company auctions for resale to the public. It was humiliating work, requiring his father to bootlick every Company flunky so he could have the favour of buying surplus Company goods. Listening to his father being sworn at by agents half his age, Darnell had resolved that one day he would be a director of the Company and rich; and that no one would humiliate him as they had his father.

Alban Cormac had been one of Darnell's teachers at Merchant Taylors' Grammar School in London. Cormac had sailed on the early Company voyages. It was he who had filled Darnell's head with wondrous tales of Java and the large group of islands between Celebes and Guinea that traders called the Spice Islands. Darnell relived these tales over and over, playing in his father's storehouse with his older brother Roland and his younger sister, Caddy. The storehouse was a fascinating place for a child, filled with crates and barrels and racks, with numerous places to hide. Darnell had loved its smells: hemp and tar and oil and cloth and metal and spices. Each commodity had had its specific odour, fevering Darnell's imagination with visions of ships and sun-bright seas, of coral islands, vividly coloured birds, mysterious, remote strands of golden beach, scorching heat and exotic, foreign people.

When Darnell was fourteen he'd been apprenticed to John Aldworth, chairman of the Company's Rials Committee, which acquired the silver the Company needed to finance its trade. Darnell had spent the next four years learning book-keeping, maritime law, mercantile law, languages, navigation and geography, and making himself indispensable to Aldworth. Soon he was accompanying the elderly merchant to St Malo, Amsterdam, Middleburg and all the other places where they traded silver. But as his apprenticeship neared its end, he realized that, without capital of his own, he could never become a merchant.

The year was 1629. At the time the Company distributed much of its dividend in pepper, a system which Aldworth and many other merchants opposed because the worth of the dividend depended on the price of pepper, which in turn depended on the total amount of pepper imported by all the European traders, not only the English. Darnell hit on the idea of using their silver agents to provide estimates of pepper stocks. He organized a system of couriers so their information would be up-to-date, and had Aldworth and his friends form a syndicate and buy all the Company's pepper – an arrangement the shareholders approved because it gave them dividends in cash instead of pepper. The syndicate acquired a monopoly in pepper and, because of Darnell's information system, bought the pepper at a price that made them immense profits. Aldworth gave Darnell a thousand pounds and offered him an associateship, but Darnell refused. He wanted to go to the East, where he believed his fortunes and those of the Company lay. Two months after the pepper coup, he sailed to Java.

He found the land as lush as Alban Cormac had told him it would be, with harvests three times a year, wonderful corals, strange fish, and jewels as large as eggs. He also found the English cowering and timorous, crowded into the factory town of Bantam, while with great energy and flamboyance the Dutch enlarged their sumptuous capital, Batavia.

'You don't understand,' his housemate Andrew Cogan had said. 'The Dutch have ten times as much capital as us, and ten times as many ships and men and guns. They've already driven the Portuguese from Java, Sumatra and the Spice Islands. They're getting into the Indian trade, they've taken Ceylon from the Portuguese, and they have a monopoly on cinnamon.'

'We must stop them before they turn on us,' Darnell had said, but neither Cogan nor anyone else had listened; not even when, under Cornelius van Speult of the Dutch Coordinator's Office, the Dutch began to attack English factories and ships, intriguing with the natives to destroy English settlements.

'My father says no one listens to you because you're neither rich enough nor old enough,' Robina Jearsey had told him. Robina was all of sixteen years old and the daughter of Bantam's senior merchant. She believed she was in love with Darnell.

'How old?' Darnell had asked. 'How rich?'

'Old, older oldest; the oldest merchant in Bantam,' Robina had laughed. 'Or the richest.'

Darnell had settled for becoming the richest, and set out to learn how the other merchants made their money. He'd watched what they did and listened to their conversations. He found they were a lazy, greedy, selfish lot whose idea of trade was to send their *gomastahs* into the interior to select their purchases, and to make their profit by selling those goods to the Company at an inflated price.

Darnell realized that, if he bought goods direct, he could make the *gomastah*'s profit as well as the merchant's, and set about learning native languages and making journeys to the interior. At the end of five months he began to trade, going into the interior and buying his stock directly from the farmers. The merchants and the *gomastahs* protested; but when Darnell threatened to reveal their incompetence and deceit to London they left him alone.

Nevertheless, a year later, he hadn't made the fortune he needed to persuade the English to fight the Dutch. The Dutch harassment continued, and Robina and her family had followed the example of other English merchants and left Java for India's Coromandel coast.

Then had come the letter from John Aldworth. England was negotiating a peace with Spain. If that peace happened, the Spanish silver market would be transferred to London; there'd be a glut of silver from the New World and the price of silver would plummet.

Might? If? Darnell had realized that if it *did* happen and someone sold silver short – promised to deliver silver on a certain date in the future at a price agreed now – that person would make a fortune. An immense fortune! A fortune large enough to make him the richest English merchant in Java. But did he dare take such a risk? If he lost he'd not only lose everything, he'd be made bankrupt, jailed and expelled and never work with the Company again. It was too great a risk, Darnell thought; but would he ever have another opportunity like this one? He had to risk it. Darnell had to act blindly now or lose his chance.

Darnell had gone to the council and offered to sell them all the silver they wanted at thirty per cent below the current market price. Afterwards he'd made the same offer to individual merchants and, as silver was the currency of the East Indies, had no difficulty selling as much silver as he could promise. When he closed his account he found he had contracted to deliver nineteen thousand pounds of silver, eight times the amount of money he had.

The months that followed were filled with tension. Every time there was a ship, Darnell hurried down to the harbour. He read letters from home avidly and sat in bars for hours on end, talking to seamen and ships' captains. Then a Portuguese brigantine brought the news: Spain and England were no longer at war. The Spanish had moved their silver market to London and, with the Anglo-Spanish peace, vast amounts of silver were reaching London from the Americas, forcing the price of silver down and down and down.

The next ship brought Darnell's certificates of purchase. Darnell had made a profit of over fifteen thousand pounds; he was now the richest English merchant in Java.

He became known as the Silver Fox, and took to wearing a silver earring. He bought his own ship, the *Silver Rial*, and set up his own factory on the island of Sera Baru. And this time, when he called on the English to resist the Dutch, they listened.

Darnell armed his ship and sank a Dutch frigate. The action gave encouragement to the English and in no time at all they were firing on Dutch ships, raiding Dutch factories and out-trading the Dutch. The English exodus stopped; the Dutch grip on the spice trade loosened. The Dutch made a truce.

For two years the English flourished. Then, Karel van Cuyler and Cornelius van Speult, with the secret support of the Compagnie, started to break the truce. They had natives make unprovoked raids on English factories. They ravaged the farms of English suppliers. They intimidated native merchants, stole goods off English ships, and artificially pushed up the prices of trade goods so the English couldn't buy them. The climax of their campaign came when van Cuyler arrested seventeen English merchants on the island of Japara, charged them with rebellion and shot them.

The terrified English fled. In vain Darnell appealed to them to stay and fight, appealed to the Company for more ships, more men and more guns. The rush to India became a rout. The Dutch sailed the Java Seas unchallenged, and one day Darnell returned to his factory at Sera Baru and found his guards killed, his brother Roland murdered, and his factory sacked by van Cuyler.

He'd gone after van Cuyler, stalking his ship, the *Prinsen*, remorselessly. When he'd found it, he'd raked it with cannon fire till the vessel was little more than a hulk. He'd boarded it, transhipped his goods and left it to drift, while he sailed to India from waters that were now owned by the Dutch.

He'd gone to Gangapatnam, where he'd found Robina grown into a beautiful woman of twenty. He'd married her and settled in Gangapatnam, but found trade impossible without access to spices. He bought more cannon, enlarged the holds of the *Silver Rial* and began smuggling.

For eighteen months he'd been gloriously successful and become enormously rich. Then Ravi Winter had been caught with a cargo of cloves out of Macassar, and the

Dutch had threatened to execute Winter and the crew unless Darnell paid his entire fortune in ransom. Darnell was left penniless. He'd taken employment with the Company which had sent him to Armagon, the most dilapidated and unprofitable station on the Coromandel coast.

Madera would change all that, Darnell thought now. Madera would be the biggest and richest and most profitable factory in all of India and, as architect of the agreement with Prince Seringa, he would be agent of that factory. He would be rich again and have immeasurable power; power to change and shape the Company; power to change its destiny and, with it, the destiny of England and India. It was a heady thought! But first he had to get to Pettahpoli in time.

Karel van Cuyler was drowsing as he listened to the English and Dutchmen around him discussing the truce. Thirty of them were crowded into the committee room of the English factory at Pettahpoli; the twelve delegates to the Executive Committee facing each other across a long baize-covered table, four writers seated behind each delegation, scrupulously writing the minutes in English and Dutch. Little boys waved fans made of horsehair and native peons stood against the lime-green walls, ready to carry any urgent messages. The session had been in progress since the end of *siesta* and, despite the efforts of the boys and the open windows, it was hot and close and everyone sweated.

Van Cuyler thought the past four days' meetings had gone extremely well. He'd steered de Groot away from sharing factories and shipping, and joint purchases of cloth. He'd ensured that the English could not open new factories without Dutch consent. He'd established short-term borrowing facilities for bullion. The talks were in their final stages, and the agreements would be signed at the end of this meeting. Van Cuyler let his head droop and dozed.

'Anyone in breach of this agreement shall be brought

before a tribunal of both Companies, which tribunal shall have in its sole discretion the power to imprison, fine, dismiss and hold any person found guilty of such breach, personally liable for all damages the tribunal shall deem to have been caused thereby.'

Van Cuyler came bolt upright. Andrew Cogan was rolling the words off his tongue as if they were marbles.

'In the event of the individual not being able to pay such damages in full, his Company shall pay whatever balance is due.'

Van Cuyler had to stop Cogan incorporating this clause into the agreement. He looked quickly round the room. Everyone was totally absorbed in Cogan's speech. He couldn't tell what they would decide if he forced a vote.

Cogan continued. 'The tribunal shall be composed of three persons who shall be officers of either the English or Dutch Companies. One member of the tribunal shall belong to the same Company as the accused. The other two members of the tribunal shall be members of a Company other than that to which the accused belongs. If the accused . . .'

If Cogan's clause was passed, it would be too dangerous to implement his plans for harassing the English and driving them from Coromandel. He'd be liable for arrest, summary trial, imprisonment, fines and dismissal. He'd be tried by Englishmen! Van Cuyler pressed his hands between his thighs to stop himself jumping up. He had to control his anger and his fear. He must at all costs *appear* to be reasonable. Cogan had sat down and de Groot was getting to his feet.

Van Cuyler jumped up and bowed to de Groot, twisting his mouth into a smile. 'With your permission, Excellency, and your forbearance,' he bowed deeply to Andrew Cogan, 'this clause is an insult to every Englishman and every Dutchman. We are all men of honour. We are signing this truce with full knowledge of what it contains and with every intention of fulfilling it to its smallest detail. To impose sanctions as our honourable friends suggest . . .' Van Cuyler stopped and shook his head as if shocked beyond reason. 'My friends, just as we trust each other in business matters, we must trust ourselves to be honourable in this.' He looked round the table. The Dutch merchants seemed to be in agreement, and some of the English, including the Englishman from the presidency in Surat, were nodding. He'd made the right approach, van Cuyler thought as he sat.

Cogan was on his feet. 'I agree completely with everything our honourable friend here has just said.' Van Cuyler let his breath out softly between his teeth. 'But,' Cogan continued, 'we must make provision for those who come after us and may not have the knowledge we have. Sanctions will make it necessary for these persons to learn of these provisions.'

Van Cuyler got up again. 'I fear my friend is not being completely truthful. I believe my friend is more concerned about the past than the future.' He smiled. 'I believe my friend is concerned that the events that occurred in Java and the Spice Islands a few years ago might repeat themselves.'

Cogan had the grace to blush. 'I admit that is a matter of concern.'

'Let it not concern you any more, my friend,' van Cuyler cried. 'Many bad things happened in Java . . . terrible things . . . Terrible things were done *by* and *to* each of us.' Van Cuyler paused and looked round the room. He had the full attention of all the delegates. In a low voice he added, 'What is important is that we have all learned from that experience. We are all better people, more honest, more honourable. We do not need punishments and threats to tell us how to behave.'

De Groot said, 'I favour Mr Cogan's amendment, in case people haven't learned, or have forgotten.' He stared directly at van Cuyler.

Van Cuyler felt a blind rush of panic, followed by the familiar pain slicing through his head. De Groot was a cowering lickspittle who was selling the empire for quiet and private profit; Cogan a conniving alleycat determined to weaken the Dutch. He pressed the depression in his forehead. With de Groot and Cogan in agreement he couldn't defeat the proposal; but he could modify it. He said, 'The procedure is too cumbersome. Each Company should try its own people.' That left him in with a chance. Van Speult and others could be prevailed on to influence a Dutch tribunal and –

Cogan said, 'We need judges who are seen to be impartial.'

De Groot twisted his fingers together and stared straight ahead of him. 'Agreed,' he said.

Van Cuyler fought to control his temper. De Groot was such a fool. He wanted to grab hold of de Groot's scrawny neck and wring it like a chicken's. He savoured the imaginary snap of breaking bone and said, 'The tribunal has too much power. The punishments are too severe. People should not be punished for carrying out their patriotic duty.'

Cogan was looking at him with barely concealed surprise, and de Groot said, 'The patriotic duty of everyone here is to keep the peace.' He sighed and pushed away the ink-stand in front of him. 'Mr Cogan, we have no more amendments. When will the agreement be ready for signature?'

'As soon as the writers have finished copying out and translating this clause. Meanwhile . . .' He rang a little bell and the door opened. Company servants came in carrying trays of malmsey and beer.

Van Cuyler gathered up his papers and rushed from the room. Rage boiled through him. The pain in his skull was unbearable. De Groot and Cogan had outwitted him and now he and the Empire were finished. He raced across a large hall. There was a door to his right. He opened it and stepped out on to a balcony. The air outside was still and turgid. Sweat rolled down his forehead and along his cheeks. He started to feel sick as his anger gave way to the nausea of failure.

Achieve, achieve, achieve! His father's death and Uncle Hendrijk had shaped his life for him and made him focus on a single ambition – taking the place that would have been his father's on the committee that ran the Compagnie, the Lords XVII.

His father and his Uncle Hendrijk had settled Batavia. His father had been its first governor and, after his death, Uncle Hendrijk had brought him up so that he could be the worthy successor to Nicholaas van Cuyler, the first governor of Batavia.

From the time he was five he'd been forced to compete, first with Uncle Hendrijk's sons, then with all the other children at school. Though he'd always worked hard, he'd rarely succeeded. Van Cuyler shuddered as he remembered Uncle Hendrijk's anger at his failures and the countless times he'd been beaten, locked in his room, made to stand for hours in the garden in the winter cold, sent to bed without supper.

When he was eleven, he'd discovered he was bigger than other boys and could use his size to force others to help him. Thereafter, the gruesome punishments stopped and his next three years at the *académie* had been an unqualified success. Later, as an apprentice to the Compagnie, he'd taken the coveted van Daarlen prize by leaving an emerald brooch in the desk of his closest rival and having him arrested for theft. Van Cuyler's heart warmed as he remembered how Uncle Hendrijk had enjoyed that triumph, and how for the first time in his life he'd felt loved.

Life had been easier after that. As a young merchant he'd bullied and cheated his way to success. Finally Uncle Hendrijk had arranged for him to be sent to Java as assistant supracargo in charge of four coastal ships.

Three years' experience, Uncle Hendrijk had said, three years seeing how the money was made and he would make supracargo. Two years more and he'd be deputy governor or given the governorship of a group of islands. With that experience he could return to Amsterdam, ready to become a committee member and then a Compagnie lord.

Java had been wonderful, at first. As the son of Nicholaas van Cuyler, all doors had been open to him. Within a year he'd become a supracargo, with charge over a dozen ships, and in the following two years, due to his habit of ensuring his profits increased every month, supracargo of the entire coastal fleet. He fell deeply in love with the governor's daughter, Annatjie van Helden, and married her. He was expected to become deputy governor in a few months; and with the English on the run everywhere in the East Indies, his happiness had been complete.

Then Richard mother-fickin' Darnell had rallied the English. Dutch ships had been sunk and Dutch settlements sacked. Darnell and the English had bribed natives, underpriced sales and overpriced purchases. Within a year the English had begun out-trading the Dutch.

Van Cuyler's profits had turned to losses and, as chief supracargo, the Compagnie held him responsible. Every loss of stock, cargo, trade deal, ship or settlement became a black mark on his record. Even Uncle Hendrijk had not been able to help, and within eighteen months he was reduced from supracargo to warehouse assistant, condemned to spend years in the East if he was to regain his former status. The dream of returning to Holland and taking his father's place among the Lords XVII seemed unattainable.

But Uncle Hendrijk had intervened again, and at his urging, Cornelius van Speult had taken him into the Coordinator's Office. With the secret help of the Compagnie they had fought the English. They had been successful beyond their wildest expectations. They had driven the English from Java and the Spice Islands. Van Cuyler had become chief supracargo again. There was even talk of him being appointed governor of Batavia. Then had come Darnell's barbarous attack on the *Prinsen*, and for a long while afterwards, van Cuyler's life had been finished.

Pushing the bitter memories to the back of his mind, van Cuyler forced himself to look at the street beyond the factory house. The English called it King Charles Street after their sovereign. It was full of Indians milling amongst lumbering carts and pack-laden coolies. A naked *sannyasi* with dust-matted hair and shiny begging bowl stood stock-still halfway down the street. Urchins danced around him, sniggering at his exposed private parts.

Van Cuyler's breathing had slowed and his heart stopped its mad pounding. All was not lost, he told himself. He simply had to be more careful in meeting and instructing his native agents. Coromandel would be Java all over again, he promised himself. The Dutch would win again.

The balcony jutted over a stone-flagged pathway; he heard footsteps and voices immediately beneath him. He leaned over to see who the visitor was. Then he heard the voice, strong, arrogant and imperious: 'I don't care what Andrew Cogan's bloody doing. I've been riding my boots off for five days and I will see him now!'

A giant shiver ran through van Cuyler, all the way from the base of his spine to the centre of his brain. He knew that voice as well as he knew Uncle Hendrijk's house on the Rijkstraat. Richard muck-fickin' Darnell!

A red mist floated before his eyes as he eased the pistol from the holster at his waist. He was on board the *Prinsen* again, feeling the lopsided tilt of the ship, hearing the moans of the wounded. He smelt gunpowder and smoke and once again cursed Darnell, whose ship had been far better armed with twelve-pounders and mortars, and whose fire had been so damnably accurate.

41

Once more he recovered consciousness in Annatjie's lap, a shaft of sunlight singeing his face, and Annatjie, his darling Annatjie, pressing a wet rag to his forehead. 'The bridge collapsed,' she was saying. 'It's lucky you were thrown clear.'

A shadow was blocking out the sun. He was turning his head and looking into the barrel of a pistol. Darnell was staring down at him from behind the gun, those startlingly deep, blue-black eyes filled with hatred. 'You burnt my fort,' Darnell said, thickly. 'You killed my brother.' Behind Darnell the English sailors were bouncing across the net between the ships, carrying the last of the goods he had taken from Darnell's fort at Sera Baru. 'You stole my goods. You've forced me out of Java.' Darnell's voice had been flat but his tone so cold and menacing that, despite himself, van Cuyler had trembled.

Darnell had spat at him, and, too late, van Cuyler had twisted his head to avoid the saliva spraying his cheek. 'If you could fight, I'd kill you,' Darnell had said, and walked away.

Van Cuyler remembered the hatred flaring through him as he'd lain helpless watching Darnell go, remembered Annatjie wiping the saliva from his face. If he could have moved, if he hadn't been so ill ... then he'd realized that Darnell was leaving them on a badly damaged ship without sails or rudder and called, 'You can't leave us like this! We have little food or water! If you leave us, we'll die!'

Darnell had turned. 'If you die, it is your *karma*.' Darnell had climbed over the netting and gone.

By the third day their food had run out and all the wounded had died. Despite frequent dousing in sea-water, everyone's temperature soared and their eyes turned to puffy slits which they could hardly open against the glare. No one had had the energy to haul the dead away; they'd sat amongst bloated corpses, smelling the odour of putrefaction and clinging to their metal cups and their constantly diminishing supply of water.

Annatjie had lain across his lap, her face blistered and shrunken, her skin as wrinkled as that of an old woman. He'd let her lie there, unable to move her and unwilling to let her go. Her belly had swelled and her mouth sagged open, discharging a yellow mucus. He'd given her his ration of water and listened to their empty cups rolling against the deck until, four nights later, a Dutch caravel had loomed out of the darkness and taken them aboard.

It had taken Annatjie's body five months to recover from the burns and the dehydration. Her mind had still not recovered. He'd taken her home where she would have better doctors and could be with her family.

After six months, Uncle Hendrijk had told van Cuyler there was nothing more he could do for her, and that he should return to the East and resume his career. For the first time in his life, van Cuyler had argued with Uncle Hendrijk, but Annatjie's father had intervened and persuaded van Cuyler to return.

Now, he occasionally received long, rambling letters from his wife, while her father wrote telling him she was putting on weight again and looked forward to his return as a candidate for the Lords XVII.

Van Cuyler peered over the balcony. He was trembling, his body soaked in sweat. Any moment now Darnell would appear from underneath the balcony and go up the steps. His mind was racing; he was shaking with pent-up fury. He would take his revenge now, at no matter what cost to himself. He dabbed his face dry, licked parched lips and, with slow deliberation, pointed the gun at the steps Darnell would climb.

Darnell came out from beneath the balcony, his lean figure unmistakable in its customary white cotton, towering over a soldier. His black hair cascaded untidily down to his shoulders. His deeply tanned face was thin and even more predatory than van Cuyler remembered. Van Cuyler took a deep breath, wrapped both hands around the pistol, and aimed it at the centre of Darnell's head. *For you, Annatjie*, he breathed. *For you!*

Chapter Four

Van Cuyler looked along the dull metal line of the gun barrel. He had his enemy in his sights. When he pulled the trigger, the gun would kick. Powder would sear his cheek. He would be momentarily blinded by flash and smoke, the ball would smash into Darnell's skull, crushing bone, tearing tissue, rupturing blood vessels and brain. He saw blood erupting, brain matter spewing . . .

A sound behind him brought him abruptly back to his senses. *Gott im Himmel!* What was he thinking of? He must be mad! If he killed an Englishman in an English fort he'd be hanged. He couldn't let that happen. Apart from wanting to live, that would give Darnell the final victory. Quickly he started to put the gun away, moments before a voice called out, 'Ah, there you are!'

Van Cuyler whirled, pushing the gun the rest of the way into its holster. Marcus van Damm, the agent for Poonmalli, the second largest Dutch factory after Pulicat, stood in the doorway. Van Cuyler felt his heart beating as if he'd been running. He breathed deeply in an effort to get himself under control. 'I needed some air,' he said before van Damm could ask. 'The heat in that room –'

'Yes, yes, I know.' Van Damm smiled. He was a short, pot-bellied, jovial man of forty, with a neat, pointed beard, rubicund cheeks and a tentative way of standing, as if at any moment he might break into a jig. Despite the heat he was formally dressed in stockings and trunks, with an embroidered doublet over a silk tunic and ruff. 'It's over now. The treaty's signed. They're starting the speeches and the toasts. It is a momentous day for us.'

'Yes,' van Cuyler said. 'So it is.' He followed van Damm through the balcony doors.

The hall inside was a large bare room separating the conference room from the offices of the agent and senior merchants. Its half-panelled walls were painted cream. Oil paintings of the sea battle at Swally and the East India docks in Blackwall were fixed on two opposite walls. During the day, van Cuyler supposed, eyeing the desks stacked against the walls, the English Company's writers and junior factors worked here. Now the room was full of bucolic, cheery men and native stewards, who, under the watchful eye of a red-and-blue-uniformed Englishman, were dispensing jugs of claret and ale.

A red-faced de Groot was hoisting his puny frame on to a chair, helped by a Dutch agent and an Englishman. As de Groot began his speech, a soldier hurried across the room to Cogan and spoke to him, pointing urgently at the private offices. Cogan frowned, looking quickly at Ovington and de Groot before following the soldier out.

Van Cuyler knew exactly who was waiting for Cogan in the office, and wondered what news Darnell had brought that was so urgent. More importantly, how could he find out?

Darnell stood in Cogan's office, staring over the factory house walls at the pulsating mass of Pettahpoli. The sun was setting and the streets teeming with life. A mass of bodies swathed in turbans and *dhotis* and brightly coloured saris clogged King Charles Street, moving slowly around stalled carts and lurching *howdahs*. The evening air was rich with the smell of spices and frying ginger. Wisps of smoke from cooking fires filtered the vivid orange sky. A rainbird called from its nest in the roof.

'Goddamn it Richard, this had better be important!' Cogan bustled into his office, rattling the inkwells on his desk.

Darnell turned from the window. As over the years he'd fulfilled his ambitions, Cogan had grown larger and redder. His face reminded Darnell of a veined cheese, crumbling with age. His narrow mouth was tightly clamped and the small, blue, pip-like eyes stared irritably.

'It's damned important,' Darnell said. 'At last we can get into Vaidya and build a factory there!'

'Is that where you've been? Bloody, poxwobbled Vaidya?' Cogan's voice rose to a shriek. 'You're damned lucky I haven't charged you with insubordination. If we weren't friends –'

'We can build a factory in Vaidya,' Darnell insisted. 'We can be the first Europeans to trade with Vaidya. We will be rich. The Company will be rich.'

Cogan flung his stumpy body into the chair behind his desk, the chains of office on his mauve, silk doublet jangling against his brooches. 'Those god-rotting Vaidyans don't want to trade with us,' he said in a strained voice as he mopped his face. 'Their god-rotting Raja – whatsisname Railoo – has twice refused us permission for a factory.'

'Railoo doesn't matter any more,' Darnell said. 'What matters now is that Vaidya needs us as much as we need them.'

'What matters is that they're all god-rotting Hindus and think that if an Englishman's shadow falls on them, they'll go to hell! You know what they call us, Richard? They call us *pariahs*.'

The right word was 'outcasts' but Darnell didn't correct Cogan. Instead, he began to tell him what had happened in Vaidya. Cogan's small eyes remained immobile beneath the sandy eyebrows as Darnell talked.

'Quite honestly, Richard,' Cogan said when Darnell had finished, 'I think this whole Vaidya thing's exaggerated. I don't believe the profits are there in the first place.'

'What the devil do you mean, exaggerated? You've always said Vaidya produced the best and cheapest cloth!

47

That their *beteilles*, *mullmulls*, *dimitys* and *pintados* were the embroidery of heaven!'

'True,' Cogan said, 'true,' and sighed as if he regretted his enthusiasm. 'But what about the *real* profits from that cloth? We've got to put in a whole lot of effort and a cash investment of – I don't know – over a thousand pounds. And there's no guarantee we'll see any of it back. There's no guarantee their cloth comes up to sample. There's no guarantee we'll be able to sell it.'

'There's no guarantee you'll draw another breath, Andrew,' Darnell said, unable to keep the hardness from his voice. 'You turn down this factory now and you'll lose us the last chance to establish ourselves in Coromandel and rid ourselves of the mother-fickin' Dutch.'

'You don't have to worry about the Dutch, Richard.' Cogan's tone was treacly with amusement. 'As of this evening we're at peace with the Dutch. The treaty has been signed, sealed and delivered.'

'You're a fool, Andrew! It'll be Java all over again!'

'No,' Cogan said. 'Not this time. This time we've included harsh penalties in the agreement.'

Penalties wouldn't work, Darnell knew, but Cogan would never believe that. He had too much invested in the Dutch truce, whose success would bring him huge rewards. Cogan would now never approve the factory in Vaidya, and without Cogan's approval, Darnell couldn't approach Seringa or build the factory. 'Andrew, this is our best chance! You've got to –'

Cogan shook his head firmly. 'Vaidya's too risky an enterprise to ever succeed.'

Darnell's heart sank. Cogan was obviously determined to stay with the Dutch treaty. But why not bypass Cogan and talk to Stuart Ovington? Ovington had been in India six years. He'd been second in council in Broach, then agent at Chaul, then assistant secretary, from which post he'd risen quickly to deputy president. He seemed both

48

ambitious and shrewd, which meant he could grab at the chance to increase his standing through initiating a highly profitable factory and turning round the Company's fortunes. On the other hand, he could turn out to be nothing more than a bureaucrat and refuse to overrule Cogan.

Darnell thought if Ovington refused, the matter was over. Then he thought, if he didn't talk to Ovington, the matter was over anyway. He said, 'I want to see Ovington.'

A flicker of uncertainty crossed Cogan's face, and he tightened his grip on the edge of the desk. 'You can't. Stuart's playing host to our Dutch allies. You can see him tomorrow.'

By tomorrow Cogan would have had time to persuade Ovington not to approve the factory. Darnell said, 'I want to see Ovington now.'

'Don't be silly, Richard. This'll keep till tomorrow.'

'It won't. We have very little time. If this factory is going to work for us, we must get to Seringa before the Dutch. If you won't get Ovington here, I'm going in there to tell him you refused to let me consult him on a trade agreement with Vaidya.'

'You go in there and I'll have you arrested!'

'Do that and I'll have the Company investigate your joint ventures with the Dutch!'

'I never . . . You bastard!' Cogan stared angrily at Darnell. Then he marched to the door. 'I'll get Ovington for you. But don't think he'll like your factory any more than I do.' He slammed the door as he went out.

Van Cuyler sipped claret and moved restlessly about the room. He drank little and so was an anachronism amongst both the Dutch and the English merchants, who usually began drinking in the morning, drank heavily with lunch and then again with dinner. It was not unusual for a man to drink three flagons of claret in a day and as much malmsey, madeira, beer and geneva as he could hold.

From his chair in the centre of the room, de Groot was talking of the wonderful new unity that would prevail, and of the increased profits and prosperity in store for each and every one of them. He spoke of the war for a free Netherlands, and said their common enemy now was Spain. 'We shall have peace and we shall have prosperity,' de Groot was saying. 'Our ships will control the Far East, yes even beyond the Japans.'

Cogan came back into the room, red-faced and frowning. He marched up to Ovington and took his sleeve. For a few moments the two men whispered together. Then they strode out of the room towards Cogan's office.

Something *very* important was happening, van Cuyler thought. Darnell had brought some *very* important news. Van Cuyler edged towards the balcony doors. He had to find out what had brought Darnell to Pettahpoli. He opened the doors and stepped out on to the balcony. The sun had set and a refreshing sea breeze cooled the sweat on his face and brow. Immediately in front of him Pettahpoli spread in a sea of tiny coconut-oil lights. He looked to his left where Cogan's office was. If only he could get there and hear what was being said.

He looked behind him at the hall. De Groot was still speaking and everyone else was milling around and drinking hugely. He walked to the end of the balcony. Beyond the fort's walls the beach was dark, the sea dappled with reflections from the ships in the roads, the ships themselves towering like speckled houses above the water. Van Cuyler leaned over the edge of the balcony and looked.

The windows along the wall were open for coolness. On the other side of the balcony rail was a small ledge that ran all the way along the side of the building. Van Cuyler wondered if he should climb over the balcony and sidle along the ledge. He looked behind him again. Everyone was still inside the hall, and de Groot was still talking about the Japans. Van Cuyler swung one foot over the balcony rail.

Below him there was nothing. His palms sweated, even though it was cool out on the balcony. His heart raced, its thumping filling his chest. He swung his rear foot over and edged on to the ledge. *Gott im Himmel*, it was narrow, just wide enough for his boot. The sea breeze suddenly seemed as fierce as a gale. With his back to the wall, his sweating palms pressed to it, he sidled sideways. *Scheit!* This was crazy! There was nothing below him except dark, empty air. He pressed his palms into the wall, its roughness giving him the illusion of something to grip. He moved one foot to the left, then the other, sucking in his stomach and pressing the small of his back to the wall. He forced himself not to think about the emptiness below, or the breeze snatching at his puffed sleeves and blowing him off the ledge. He forced himself to concentrate on moving one step at a time. The voices became louder. He edged closer. Running beside Cogan's window was a rain-gutter. He reached for it.

Ovington was a tall, sad-faced man, with a long jaw and jet-black eyes ringed with dark circles. His dark hair rose in a high pompadour from a wide forehead. He was formally dressed in tights, an embroidered silk tunic, doublet and ruffles. The heavy chain and seal of the presidency sagged about his neck. Emeralds, rubies and amethysts glittered on his fingers. 'What's so damned important about Vaidya, Mr Darnell, that you had to interrupt my evening?' he snapped.

'Profits!' Darnell said. 'Profits greater than anyone's ever imagined.' He walked to the mildewed map of southern India that hung between the shelves to the right of Cogan's desk.

'Coromandel,' Darnell said pointing to the south-eastern part of the coast, 'divided into the kingdoms of Kokinada in the north, Vaidya in the south.' He lowered his finger.

51

'Northern Vaidya, known as Venkat, and administered by Prince Seringa on behalf of his cousin, Raja Railoo. Venkat shares a common border with Kokinada.'

Darnell placed his finger inland. 'The Deccan, where Seringa's troops have been fighting the Mughal. After the monsoons are over, the Mughal will resume their march on Vaidya. They can move in from the Deccan across these mountains to the west of Vaidya. Or they can march up the coast, join up with Kokinada, and invade Vaidya from the north.'

Darnell circled his fingers over the mountains to the west of Vaidya. 'Seringa can easily repulse the Mughal *here*.' Darnell moved his finger to the Vaidya-Kokinada border in the north. 'Defeating the Mughal will be almost impossible *here*. The terrain is flat with little cover, and Seringa will not be able to overcome the Mughal's numerical superiority.'

Again Darnell ran his finger along the map, south down the coast from Kokinada. 'This is the Kokinada-Vaidya road, the only invasion route the Mughal can take. And here,' he pointed to the spit of land on which Madera stood, 'right opposite Madera, the road narrows and crosses two bridges. The guns of a fort here could easily destroy those bridges and stop the Mughal army. Those guns could even *destroy* the Mughal army.'

Ovington listened with growing interest. This was a fantastic opportunity that would turn the Company round and enable it to regain control of the spice trade. If he initiated it, there was no doubt that he, not Lawrence Thackeray, would be made president of the Company in India. But could Darnell do it? He had rallied the English in Java and, until that unfortunate incident with the Dutch, been one of the richest merchants in Asia. Ovington studied Darnell's lean, predatory face with that ribbon of white scar running down one side. The face of a buccaneer, he thought, a merchant adventurer . . .

Cogan interrupted his thoughts. 'Building a factory in Vaidya will be a breach of our agreement with the Dutch,' he pointed out.

Darnell asked, 'You think if the Dutch knew about this, they would get your permission before talking to Seringa?'

'Our alliance with the Dutch must be the cornerstone of our policy in India,' Cogan insisted. 'It is our only means of safe trade and expansion.'

'If the Dutch get into Vaidya before us, they will spit on your treaty and bury us.'

'The Company has forbidden alliances with natives,' Cogan said.

'Not in a situation like this. Not in a situation where the alliance is necessary to save the Company.' Darnell turned to Ovington. 'As soon as the Dutch hear of Seringa's defeat, they will be in Vaidya, offering their support and their guns in exchange for trading rights and permission to build a factory at Madera.'

Ovington said, 'You're probably right, Mr Darnell. But making an alliance with Seringa, building this factory, leads to many other things, new things. It will lead to a fundamental change in the way we do business in the East. Have you thought of that, Mr Darnell?'

Darnell had, but wasn't sure he could share his thinking with Ovington. The changes following an agreement with Vaidya would be fundamental and far-reaching. The Company would have to make alliances with natives. The Company would have to fight, and spend money defending its trading rights. The Company would have to prevent others getting trading rights. The Company would have to expand. The Company would have to build a political and trading empire.

'You're right, Mr Ovington. Building a factory in Vaidya is the first step in driving the Dutch from Coromandel and regaining the spice trade,' Darnell said.

Ovington looked interested, so Darnell continued, 'The

profits out of Vaidya will be enormous, so enormous that the Company will have to fight to protect them, so enormous that the Company will be able to afford an army to protect those profits. As our profits increase we will need to take a greater part in native affairs, make more alliances, prevent other Europeans making similar alliances. We will expand throughout India. We will become the dominant European power in India. We will control the cloth trade and then we will take the spice trade back from the Dutch. Vaidya,' Darnell finished, 'is the beginning of the end for the Dutch.'

Van Cuyler seized the gutter like a drowning man grabbing a spar. He was shivering from the effort of controlled movement, and drenched with sweat. Once or twice his sliding foot had sent stones pattering to the path below; he had frozen with fear, unable to move quickly or hide, certain that he would fall or be seen. But his perilous journey had been worth it. As he'd drawn nearer, the voices had become clearer; he'd heard almost everything Darnell, Ovington and Cogan were saying. And, as he clung wearily to the gutter, he was already planning what he should do about it . . .

Something clattered against the side of the building and bounced on to the path below.

'What the devil's that?' Cogan cried.

'There's someone at the window!' Darnell rushed to the open window and looked out. To his left, the lights of the ships, directly ahead of him the lights of the town, and to his right a narrow ledge running the width of the building, a rain-gutter and an empty balcony. Cogan and Ovington joined him.

'Can you see anything?' Cogan asked.

'No,' Darnell said slowly. He stared at the gutter again, at the lights of the town, at the dark emptiness below.

There wasn't anything to be seen, and yet . . . Shutting the window firmly, he tried to concentrate on what Cogan was saying. 'Quite honestly, gentlemen, I don't see the point of continuing this discussion when in its directive of 18 February 1628/9, the Company has prohibited the creation of any new establishments without written permission from London.'

Cogan had spoken with authority but Darnell knew the Company had previously approved factories *after* they had been built. 'The Company's always made exceptions,' he said. 'Metchapollam, Armagon . . .' He looked quickly at Ovington. Ovington could override the Company's directive and give him interim permission.

Cogan smiled and shrugged. 'All we know is what London has written,' he said, softly. He let the sentence hang there, delighting in his triumph. He rummaged in his desk and pulled out the directive. Ovington took it.

'Getting permission from London will take a year,' Darnell cried. 'It'll be too god-rottin' late.'

Ovington read the directive and shook his head sadly. 'I'm sorry, Mr Darnell.' The slump of his shoulders clearly showed there was nothing more he could do.

Darnell said, '*You* could authorize an exception!'

'I don't think so. I'm not even sure the President could.'

'We have to meet with Seringa in days!'

'I know. I'm sorry. If there was a way . . .'

Ovington looked down again at the directive.

Darnell couldn't let everything go like that. Damnit, he'd build the fort himself! He stopped, feeling wildly excited at the thought. What if he did build the fort himself? All he needed was money – the Company could lend him that. There was nothing in the directive banning the Company from *investing* in a fort, nothing banning it from *lending* money. He said, 'I'm going to build the fort privately.'

Ovington jerked upright. Cogan's face flushed, his eyes narrowing. 'Where will you find the money?' Cogan asked.

'The Honourable Comp'ny'll lend it to me. There's nothing in the directive that prohibits it lending money.'

'I don't know –'

'That's an interesting idea,' Ovington said softly. 'There's nothing in the directive that prohibits us from investing in a fort . . .'

'How will you repay the loan?' Cogan asked, his voice rising sharply.

'Simple. When we get approval for the fort, the Company will adopt it.'

'And if the Company doesn't adopt it?'

Darnell looked from Cogan to Ovington and back again. 'How much difficulty do you think I'll have selling that fort to the Dutch or the Portuguese or even the Danes?'

'You wouldn't! No, Richard. I won't countenance this –'

'I'm satisfied.' Ovington spoke over Cogan's objections. 'As soon as I get back to Surat I'll place your proposition before the Council. Meanwhile, Mr Darnell, talk to Seringa as soon as you can.' He smiled and put his arm around Darnell's shoulder. 'You've had a long journey. Now please join us for some refreshment.' He eased Darnell before him to the door.

The hall was noisy and crowded and smelt strongly of alcohol and sweat. Men milled about, red-faced, bearded and boisterous, drinking copiously and chewing at hunks of roast beef and slices of mutton pie. A group of English merchants saw Darnell and surrounded him. These were men he'd known and traded with at various times in his career: some were old Java hands, some friends, all rivals. They talked about commodities, the coming monsoon, the prices of copra and jute.

Ovington had climbed on to a chair and was coughing into his fist. 'Today marks a significant development in the history of our two great Companies,' he began, speaking first in English and then in Dutch. 'From today hostility is replaced by cooperation. From today we show the world what can be achieved by friends working together.'

Darnell knew that Ovington was merely acting. It was Vaidya, not the truce, that would make India safe and profitable for the English. Because of Vaidya, the Dutch would be out-traded, their hold on India and the Eastern empire prised open; the Dutch empire folded up like a used rush mat.

Best of all, the Dutch empire would be replaced by an English one, an empire that would be the largest the world had ever seen. Darnell looked round the room at the other English merchants. They and their sons would inherit that empire. What began with Vaidya would go on for centuries. Though the Mughal stood on Vaidya's western border, the Mughal empire was crumbling; when it did it would be other foreigners who would hold India together. If the English held Vaidya, those foreigners would be English! His heart beat excitedly at the prospect. The English could take India – if they had the courage, the fortitude, the wisdom – and if it was their *karma*.

He knew it was his *karma* to build the first factory in Vaidya. Why else had he gone smuggling cloth in Vaidya? Why else had he come to India?

'And now gentlemen, let us drink to peace between our countries – perpetual peace!' Ovington had finished his speech and all around the room flagons were being raised and people were crying, 'Peace! To peace!'

Darnell kept his glass by his side.

'You do not believe in peace, mynheer?'

Darnell turned. The speaker was Marcus van Damm, a Dutch merchant with whom he'd occasionally done business. 'I do not believe this treaty will bring peace,' Darnell said.

'Why is that?'

'We had a similar treaty in Java, mynheer.'

Van Damm blinked in puzzlement, and Darnell remembered he'd always been an India trader. 'What happened in Java?'

'All that happened in Java,' a voice behind them said in sibilant Dutch, 'was that we got rid of a number of thieves, pirates and scoundrels!'

Darnell stiffened. It couldn't be! It was impossible! But that lisp? It had to be! He whirled. Karel van Cuyler stood two feet away from him, massive and slablike as ever. He still weighed over two hundred pounds and had a menacing breadth of shoulder. His small, dark eyes glittered in his full-cheeked, oval face, and the flicker of the torches made the dent in his forehead seem alive. He wore a tunic of brown calico with amethyst cuffs and buttons. A short dagger was stuck in his waistband, beside a holstered pistol and his favourite *sjambok*. His thick brown hair and beard were close-cropped and a scrappy pigtail twisted rigidly between his shoulder-blades.

'I should have killed you,' Darnell ground out, the burnt hulk of his factory at Sera Baru and the bodies of his guards flashing before his eyes. He felt a wave of savage fury as he saw the blood-spattered body of Roland, his pathetic, drunken older brother, who had attempted to fight van Cuyler off and had had the top of his head blown away by a pistol ball for his pains.

He should have killed van Cuyler when he'd caught the *Prinsen*, Darnell thought, dropping a hand to his knee within easy reach of his right boot where he carried one of his knives. But one didn't kill a defenceless man. One didn't kill a man in front of his wife. If it had been only van Cuyler, he'd have left him to rot on the *Prinsen*; but because of the woman and the crew he'd sailed west until he'd found a Dutch caravel and informed them of the whereabouts and the condition of the *Prinsen* before altering course for Gangapatnam in India. Afterwards he'd heard that the caravel had discharged its cargo before searching for the *Prinsen*; because of that delay, many of the *Prinsen*'s crew had died.

'In Java we were driven out by blackguards who didn't keep their word,' Darnell said. It was the wrong place for a quarrel, but he wasn't going to back down.

Van Cuyler said again, 'All we did was free Java of smugglers, pirates and rogues!' He was arrogant, almost sneering.

'The English only took back what was stolen from them by liars!'

They'd moved within touching distance of each other, shoulders hunched, heads thrust forward, hands hovering over their knives.

'Stop this at once!' Ovington strode between them, followed by de Groot, Cogan and a Dutchman with a battered face.

'This is an occasion of peace!' de Groot cried.

The big Dutchman eased van Cuyler backwards, talking to him slowly and urgently.

'If you fight here I'll have you arrested,' Cogan snapped, pushing Darnell away. 'You'll be the first person to be charged with breaching the truce.'

Darnell let himself be pushed back. His mind raced as he watched his enemy striding briskly away. There'd been something triumphant about his manner, Darnell thought now, and for some reason he remembered again the noise outside the window. It wasn't possible . . . But one thing was certain. If van Cuyler had been sent to India, it could only mean that, despite the agreement the Dutch had signed, they were determined to expel the English from Coromandel. The English needed that fort in Madera more than ever, Darnell thought. Thank the Lord the Dutch didn't know about it yet.

Outside, King Charles Street was deserted, except for the night-watch and scavenging pi-dogs. Darnell walked carefully in the centre of the road, avoiding the sewage piled about its edge. The night air was cool, carrying the smell of rotting fruit and the light perfume of jacaranda. This was the only time the coast was pleasant, when the sun's fire had died and the sea winds blew.

He found himself walking towards his sister's house, and felt expectation bubble within him at the thought of seeing Caddy and his four-year-old son, Crispin, who'd been living with her since Robina's death a year ago. Remembering Robina brought a tightness to his chest. Her death of a flux had left Darnell inconsolable. For three months afterwards she had come to him every night in dreams, as if unable to leave him. Then she had gone. He'd felt totally alone and lost; it was only Crispin's need of him that had kept him struggling on. *Karma*, Darnell thought angrily, always goddamned *karma*. Where did we go wrong, she and I?

He stopped before the bungalow where Caddy and her husband Davey lived, surprised at having reached it so soon. Caddy opened the door, the shadow of her dark eyes magnified by the flicker of the oil-lamp, a sweaty hank of tousled hair shading one cheek. The lamplight turned her pale skin orange. 'Richard! What are you doing here?' She almost dropped the lamp in her effort to hug him.

Darnell threw his arms around her. Caddy was his favourite sibling. Five years younger than him, as a child she'd been his pet. Then, as they'd grown older, she'd become his friend and confidante. Eight years ago she had joined him in Java, fallen in love with Davey Wheaton and married him.

'Why didn't you tell me you were coming?' she asked.

'Because I didn't know.' Caddy had inherited their father's large bone-structure and had grown bigger with each of the sons she'd borne. Darnell ran his hands along her face, sweetly oval once, but now large and comfortable and motherly. 'It's good to see you. How're the children? Crispin?'

'They're fine.' She pulled away from him. 'Have you just got here? Have you eaten?' She led him through the reception room to the back veranda which overlooked the rear compound and the separate kitchen standing away from the house for fear of fire. Caddy lit more lamps, poured out beer, shouted to the servants to bring chicken, *chappatis* and salad. Lamps flickered on in the kitchen. Shadowy figures rustled through the compound.

Davey Wheaton came out of the room further along the veranda that he used as an office. He was a plump, balding, slightly bewildered-looking man, dressed in an open tunic, pantaloons and slippers. He threw Darnell a shy smile. 'You've been talking with the Dutch?'

'Yes.'

'Caddy looking after you?'

'Of course.'

Davey shifted from one foot to the other. 'Then I'll – if you'll excuse me – work.' He scurried back to his office. He was a hardworking and quietly ambitious man, making up in shrewdness and diligence for what he lacked in imagination. He made good money and kept Caddy and the boys in comfort. Caddy was shepherding servants on to the veranda with his food, and Darnell started to eat. 'How's Crispin?' he asked again.

'He's well. But he misses his mother. And he misses you, poor tyke. I do all I can but . . .' Caddy's voice trailed off, emphasizing the impossibility of replacing a mother in a little boy's life.

'It'll be over soon,' Darnell assured her. 'Can I see him now?'

'No. It's late and he'll be too excited to get to sleep afterwards. You can see him tomorrow.'

'I'm leaving early tomorrow. I *have* to,' he said quickly as he saw the expression on his sister's face. 'It's very important.' He told her about Seringa and the fort.

Caddy shook her head. 'You're mad! You risk your life

smuggling cloth from Vaidya and now you risk everything again to build this goddamn fort. You've got a son, Richard. You've got responsibilities. When will you grow up?'

'We need that fort if we're to stay in India. We need that fort if we're to regain the spice trade.'

'*We* need nothing,' Caddy snapped. '*You* need that fort.'

'We *all* need it. Without that fort we're finished here –' He shrugged. 'Finished everywhere. Where d'you think we'll go if we're driven from here by the Dutch? England? What will Davey do there? And you? There's nothing like this anywhere else, and certainly not in England!'

'And you?' Caddy asked. 'Would you go back to England?'

'No,' Darnell said, and stared past her into the garden. Fireflies danced over the grass. 'After running a factory here, I couldn't simply buy and sell from a small office in London. When I go back, I'll be a director. There's so much in the Company that needs to be changed, and the Company must have people who've lived and worked here running it. I must be able to do that, I must be able to change things...' His mind drifted, thinking of the changes: better conditions of employment, contracts for the weavers, capital for Indian factories...

'You're just talking,' Caddy said. 'No one's going to drive us from Coromandel.'

'Van Cuyler's in Pettahpoli,' Darnell said. 'I met him at the factory house.'

'Oh my God!' Caddy's hand darted to her throat and her eyes suddenly brimmed with tears. 'Richard, for God's sake, leave him alone! Do you hear me? Leave van Cuyler alone! What happened at Sera Baru is over. Nothing you do to van Cuyler will bring Roland back.'

Darnell reached across and patted her arm. 'The fort in Vaidya will save us from the Dutch,' he said, deciding he wouldn't worry Caddy by telling her what had happened at the factory house, or that he still meant to kill van Cuyler. 'And as soon as the fort's ready, I'm going to have Davey and Crispin and all of you move there. We'll all live together, make our fortunes together –'

'How long will it be?' Caddy asked.

'Six months.'

'Don't make it any longer, Richard, please. Crispin needs a home. He needs to be with you. And you need a wife.'

'After I build the fort,' Darnell said. 'I promise.'

Caddy stared at him thoughtfully, then shrugged and stood up. 'I'd better get Crispin for you,' she said.

Early the next morning, Darnell walked through the purple pre-dawn light to the barracks where he had stabled his horse. The noise of his boots on the brick-pave sounded unnaturally loud. Around him houses slept, slatted wooden shutters fastened against the dawn. Dogs scavenged amongst the rubbish on the street. The wind off the sea was chill and made him turn up his collar and walk faster.

Pettahpoli was built like all English forts – the factory house in the centre housed the administration offices and agent's quarters; brick-paved streets, with wide channels of deep sand in the middle for the passage of carts, radiated out to walls that were twenty foot high and two yards wide with emplacements for cannon. The streets were lined with shops, houses and warehouses, great brooding shadows in the half-light. The barracks stood by the west wall, a wide, three-storeyed building with large open verandas on every floor. To its right were the stables, long, low and red-roofed, with a muddy exercise yard and the rich smell of horse dung. Just outside the door a small fire glowed. The dark figure squatting in front of it got to his feet as Darnell approached.

'You want horse? You going back to Armagon, Darnell sahib?' The man steepled his hands before his chest in greeting.

Darnell returned the greeting. 'Yes, Tambipillai.' Tambipillai was the chief syce, a scrawny bow-legged man of about forty, with a crumpled, weather-lined face. He shouted orders to the grooms inside, then poured some *cha* into a metal beaker and offered it to Darnell.

Darnell took it and sipped gratefully. It was made the Indian way, boiled many times over and sweetened with molasses. It warmed his stomach and took away the morning chill.

They walked together to the stable entrance as two grooms led his horse out. Darnell noticed the stalls next to the one he'd used were empty. 'What's happened to them?' he asked Tambipillai.

'Dutchmen!' Tambipillai sniffed contemptuously. 'Left last night. Came here shouting and bawling and waking everybody up. Move arse black bugger, they say. Get horses, *jaldi, jaldi*, right away. They did not even give us even a small *pagga*.'

Darnell felt a sudden sense of alarm, a sinking feeling in his stomach. 'What did these Dutchmen look like?'

'There was the one with the hole in his head.' Van Cuyler, no doubt about that!

'And the one with the face trampled by a horse.' The chief body-guard!

'Three others, all soldiers.' Tambipillai knelt with his hands out so Darnell could mount.

'Where were they going?'

'Didn' say, Darnell sahib. Jus' wen', like wind.'

Darnell thought again about the stone clattering against the side of the building, and his rush to the window with Cogan and Ovington. It couldn't be, Darnell thought. There was no way for anyone to get outside that window. There had to be some other reason why van Cuyler had left. He mounted his horse, tossed Tambipillai five *fanams* and rode slowly to the factory house.

Accompanied by a soldier, he went up to the hall on the

64

second floor and went out on to the balcony. Between the balcony and Cogan's window there was a ledge.

Ignoring the soldier's startled glance, he climbed over the balcony. Below him was the unyielding stone-paved path leading to the main entrance. He thought of falling and felt his breath catch. He stepped on to the ledge. For a moment he teetered and thought he would fall. He inched sideways. The ledge was just wide enough for his feet; if he moved slowly and carefully he could edge up to the window of Cogan's office. There was a rain-gutter by the window, he noticed, wide enough for a man to shelter behind.

He edged back to the balcony, sweating. Van Cuyler must have been crazy to do it, but he was sure he had. He recalled van Cuyler's triumphant air. Van Cuyler was on his way to see Seringa.

Darnell climbed quickly back over the balcony rail. He was in a race with van Cuyler. He had to reach Venkatapur before van Cuyler did.

Chapter Five

The dawn sun was sullen, an angry, bruised red lanced with purple stripes of cloud. Beneath it the sea was leaden and heavy, moving with the mailed menace of a coiled snake. A flotilla of fishing boats swept shorewards on the incoming tide. Darnell and Ravi Winter stood halfway along the spit at Madera, peering through a telescope and holding on to a plumb line.

'By now van Cuyler will be days ahead of us,' Ravi Winter grumbled. 'We should 'ave gone on to Venkatapur.'

It was six days since Darnell had left Pettahpoli and he and Ravi were on their way to Prince Seringa's capital. Darnell had insisted they stopped at Madera to survey the spit, make drawings of the site and get the approval of the fishermen to the building of the factory. It would demonstrate that the English were serious, painstaking, responsible and caring. Darnell hoped Seringa would be more impressed with that than the expensive presents the Dutch would bring – and which the English could not match. He began to pace out a large square near the middle of the spit.

Madera ran north to south, parallel to the coast and separated from it by a river that flowed into the sea at Madera's southern tip. It was one and a quarter miles long, and tapered from a width of six hundred yards at its north end to less than ten yards at the mudflats that covered its southern extremity. Two wooden bridges joined Madera to the mainland. The bridge at the northern end linked Madera to the coast road, and a second bridge, about two thirds of the way down the spit, joined Madera to a low-lying marshy island in the middle of the river. The island itself formed part of the coast road and was joined to the mainland by two further bridges. The river side of the spit was covered with clumps of fruit trees and vegetation. A ribbon of beach and rows of palm trees lined the coast. At the south end of the spit, about half a mile before the mudflats, was a fishing village.

Darnell shivered in the cool morning breeze and looked at the square he and Ravi had paced out. Each side was about a hundred yards long. It was located near the centre of the spit and almost directly opposite the island. The ground was well compacted here, and both road bridges would be within easy reach of the factory's cannon. Building the factory so far down the spit left an open space to the north, which would remove all risk of a surprise attack and be easily defended by the factory's cannon. No enemy could approach across the mudflats to the south, and any hostile force attempting to cross the river or land by sea could be easily disposed of. The site was near to impregnable. Now if only they could build on it. Darnell looked at the fishing boats crowding in the shallows before the village. 'Let's get to know the villagers,' he said and marched towards the beach.

The fishermen were twisting the third boat ashore when Darnell and Ravi reached them. Cheerfully they made room, and Darnell stepped in beside Ravi to help. Each boat was made of three logs caulked and bound together, with a narrow slot for the mast. Darnell marvelled that they fished all night in craft as frail as these. Push, pull, push, pull; Darnell was getting the rhythm of it. The men and boys sang as they manhandled the boat up the beach in a series of sigmoid slides. One more push and the boat was beyond the waterline. Darnell turned and grinned at Ravi and went back to help with the other boats.

By the time they had finished, a watery sun had risen, covering the beach with a soft, hesitant light. As the fishermen walked back to the village, their catch dangling, gleaming and silvery in small nets, a man in his late thirties, with thick, curly black hair liberally sprinkled with grey thanked them for their help. 'My name is Naidu,' he said. 'I am the fisher-chief of Madera.'

Darnell introduced himself and Ravi. 'We're from the English factory at Armagon.'

A portly man from the village joined them. Naidu introduced him as Ponappah, the village headman. Ponappah's moustache was freshly oiled and a large brass medallion gleamed on his soiled white tunic. 'What are you doing here?' he asked.

'We're travelling to Venkatapur to get permission from Prince Seringa to build a factory here.'

Without ceremony Naidu said, 'Prince Seringa will not allow you to build a factory here.'

Darnell told Naidu of the threat from Kokinada and the Mughal and how the guns of an English fort would stop an advance into Vaidya. He said, 'When I see Prince Seringa I want to tell him you and your people do not object to our factory.'

Naidu and Ponappah looked at each other. 'What will your factory do to our fish?' Ponappah asked.

'Nothing, except give you a large market for your fish right here.'

'And will your price be better than we get from the merchants in Ankulai?'

'It'll have to be. There will be so many more of us.' Looking from Naidu to Ponappah, Darnell said, 'Once we build the factory, all of you will earn far more money than you do now. Those who fish will have a large market for their catch. Those who do not wish to endure the dangers of fishing will be able to work on our *masoola* boats, moving goods and people between the factory and our ships. And for those who do not wish to go to sea at all, there will be more than enough work on land. We will pay

68

you in *pagodas*, and silver and gold *muhars*.'

Ponappah said, 'That seems good – if you speak the truth.' He shrugged in unison with Naidu. 'Prince Seringa will know if you speak the truth or no. He will tell us what to do.' He took Naidu's shoulder and, bowing curtly, turned and walked towards the village.

Darnell and Ravi hurried along the beach to the spit. If they left now they could get in two hours' travelling before noon. They reached the middle of the spit, and stared around it. They couldn't see their horses! They'd left the animals tethered in the grove, and while one animal could break free, it was unlikely that all three would.

Hearts pounding, they ran to the grove, smelling first the tangy odour of offal, then the hot, sweet stench of blood. The whirring, darting specks between the trees became flies buzzing over three dark mounds.

Ravi cried, 'Lord a'mighty!' his face going a milky brown.

Darnell stared at the horses lying on their sides, their eyes open and their throats cut. 'God rot the muck-fickin' Dutch!' he swore. Now they'd never get to Venkatapur.

They ran back to the village. Unless the fishermen helped, they'd have to walk the fifteen miles to San Thome, catch a ship to Armagon and get fresh horses; by which time van Cuyler would have met with Seringa and got the permissions.

The village was a collection of thatched huts spreading from a rondel of trampled earth. They ran to the largest hut. Naidu and Ponappah sat just inside before a mat spread with *sambals*, fish curry and a heaped dish of rice. Darnell told them what had happened. 'We need your help to get to Prince Seringa,' he pleaded.

Naidu washed his fingers and got to his feet. 'Alas! We cannot help you. We are poor people and have no horses.'

'You can get horses in San Thome,' Ponappah advised.

By the time they did that, they'd have lost van Cuyler. Darnell asked, 'How do you get your fish to Ankulai?'

'We have a cart,' Naidu said.

'Good. We'll hire your cart to take us to Venkatapur.'

'Impossible! How will we get our fish to Ankulai?'

'We will pay you for your catch while we have the cart.'

Ponappah and Naidu exchanged glances before Ponappah said, 'You won't want to ride in our cart. It is old and not in a good state of repair. It won't get you to Venkatapur.'

'We will pay you for two days' fishing for each day we have the cart,' Darnell said.

Naidu and Ponappah spoke to each other softly. Then Ponappah cleared his throat and said, 'Naidu must travel with you, to bring our cart back. And you must pay three days' fishing, not two.'

Darnell made a quick calculation and said, 'Agreed.' He thought, if they travelled with Naidu dressed like natives, they'd lumber right through the ambush that van Cuyler would undoubtedly have set for them.

Van Cuyler stopped beneath the bo-tree whose massive roots spread like a shady tunnel over the junction of the north-south coast road and the trail leading inland to Venkatapur. He'd gone straight from Pettahpoli to Pulicat where he'd collected bales of Chinese silk, brocades, satins and velvet, some sugar, tin, Japanese copper trays and fifteen fine swords. Then he'd set out for Venkatapur. The presents and supplies for the journey had filled three carts and van Cuyler had picked van Roon, Ginsel and Beck to accompany him, together with four other soldiers and a dozen bearers, camp servants and cooks. They'd been travelling for two days, and had broken camp before sunrise that morning to cover as much distance as possible before the sun became too hot. While van Cuyler had travelled slowly with the presents, he'd sent van Roon ahead with Ginsel to find Darnell.

He turned at the sound of hooves and glimpsed van Roon and Ginsel scudding between the palms at full gallop. 'Have you found him?' he asked as van Roon reared his horse to stop.

Van Roon's battered face was wreathed in a smile. He told van Cuyler they'd seen Darnell and Winter surveying the spit and when they had gone to help the fishermen, he and Ginsel had killed their horses. 'You can forget about Darnell, now,' van Roon said. 'For sure.'

Van Cuyler said, 'Darnell won't be that easy to get rid of.' He told van Roon Darnell would hire or steal transport from the villagers. 'While we go on ahead,' he told van Roon, Ginsel and Beck, 'this is what I want you to do.'

Darnell, Ravi and Naidu left after a hurried meal of rice and fish. The cart was an unpainted wooden platform barely large enough for four people, attached to a rigid axle drawn by a single bullock. Its roof and sides were covered with thatch. Darnell and Ravi put on turbans and *kamis* over pantaloons and boots, and lurched up the coast road with majestic slowness. At the giant bo-tree they turned inland. Venkatapur was four long days away. Darnell wondered how van Cuyler would set his ambush.

They passed ribbed paddy-fields and thick sugar-cane-groves; slopes covered with peas and courgettes and clusters of fruit trees: mango, pineapple, papaya, grapefruit, and the inevitable coconut and palmyra palm. There was more than enough produce to support the factory, Darnell thought.

They joined a group of travellers going part of the way. The travellers told Darnell they hadn't seen any *feringhi*. The heat and the steady rocking of the cart lulled Darnell to sleep. He woke with the clip-clop of hooves in his ears.

It was definitely a horseman, two horsemen at least. He

reached under his *kamis* for the gun strapped to his waist. The sound of hooves grew louder. He saw that Ravi's hand was also under his *kamis*. Motherfickin' Dutch, Darnell thought and wondered if they would dare attack with so many witnesses.

He leaned forward and looked out of the back of the cart. Two horsemen were riding level with the rear of the convoy, their heads moving from side to side as they looked closely at the travellers. Darnell recognized the Dutchman with the battered face who'd been at Pettahpoli. He nodded to Ravi and mouthed, 'Dutch.'

Where was van Cuyler, Darnell wondered? Ahead or behind? How many other Dutchmen were nearby? Darnell eased the knife from its scabbard and thought Ravi and he could take the two Dutchmen. But what if there were others?

The Dutchmen drew closer. They were still peering into the carts. Should he seize the advantage of surprise and attack them? Better to let them make the first move. Ravi was loading his gun. Darnell gestured to him to put it away.

'If them bastards find us they'll kill us,' Ravi protested.

'Relax and look as Indian as you can,' Darnell said. 'They'll never think to look for us here.' He slumped against the side of the cart as if exhausted. Ravi looked at him angrily, then put away the gun and did the same. The Dutchmen drew level with the cart. Their bodies obscured the light. Unwinking blue eyes in a battered face stared at Naidu. Then a lowered head was thrust into the cart.

Darnell repressed a start and looked drowsily at the Dutchman. He let his mouth sag. The Dutchman looked from him to Ravi and back again. Their eyes met and for a moment Darnell thought he saw a glimmer of recognition. He moved his hand under his *kamis* as if to scratch his belly and took hold of the gun. He imagined he saw the Dutchman nod, then the head was withdrawn. Darnell watched as they inspected the next cart, and kept looking till they were gone.

The next morning Darnell, Ravi and Naidu left the other travellers and journeyed alone through forests of ebony and silver-streak birch. The trees were brilliant with parrots, and shrill with the rapid chatter of mynahs. Gradually the trees grew closer together and the undergrowth more dense. The trail narrowed and disappeared; Naidu navigated by the angle of the sun.

Darnell was still thinking about the Dutch. Surely if they had been recognized, they would have attacked by now; recognized or not, wouldn't van Cuyler have set an ambush? Darnell peered out at the close-knit tapestry of trees and leaves.

Suddenly weird, high-pitched shrieks rang out. Something hit the roof with a series of thuds. The cart shook. Darnell dived for the floor, reaching for his knife, and Ravi crashed on top of him. Darnell took out his knife, his heart beating wildly.

Naidu's laugh broke the tension. 'Monkeys,' he called back to them. 'We must have got too close to their lodge.'

Darnell pushed Ravi away and sat up, his heart still pounding. Goddamnit, it could so easily have been Dutchmen.

He climbed out on to the seat beside Naidu. The trail was barely visible and the trees beside it so close together that if a Dutchman were a foot away they wouldn't see him. They had to keep a watch, take turns walking ahead of the cart. 'If we do that, van Cuyler'll be toasting scones in Pulicat a month before we get to Seringa,' Ravi protested.

'You may be right,' Darnell said. 'But until we're out of this jungle we'd better be careful.'

'Might as well turn back,' Ravi said. 'At this pace we'll get nowhere.'

Darnell ignored him and walked ahead. The grass was

soft under his boots, the air close and clammy. The trapped heat did not allow sweat to evaporate and it streamed down his face. After forty minutes he changed places with Ravi.

They travelled slowly all morning, with Darnell and Ravi alternating approximately every forty minutes. On his third shift Darnell saw the trail ahead of him curve sharply round the foot of a hill, the curve, the slope and the trees obscuring all sight-lines. An ideal place for an ambush, Darnell thought. Asking Naidu and Ravi to wait ten minutes before moving on, he plunged into the trees.

The spaces between the trees were thick with undergrowth. The rustling sounds of the forest intensified. Within moments, Darnell was suffocating in clammy, oppressive air. He peered through a dismal grey half-light. Everything seemed dank and threatening; the forest filled with sounds of a savage underlife. He could no longer see the cart.

He worked his way up the hill, slashing at creepers, finding his way by the steepness of the slope. He peered carefully about him for snakes, drew down the sleeves of his tunic and fastened up his collar.

Something trampled through the undergrowth behind him. Darnell whirled and stood still, knife thrust out in front of him, heart pounding in his ears. This was wild country, the haunt of bear, cheetah and leopard and, though the scent of man would normally keep them away, there was no guarantee. The rustling stopped and Darnell moved on, stooping forward as he fought the hill. His face streamed with sweat. The constant stooping and the steepness of the hill made his legs ache. The humid air made him pant. Then the slope started to flatten and movement became easier. He straightened up gratefully and moved through thinning jungle to the edge of the treeline. He stopped with a start and ducked back into the forest. He had almost walked into three Dutchmen!

Two of them, the slim one with the squarish brown beard and the large one with the battered face, stood on the crown of the bend looking towards the area from where the cart would come. Round the curve to the right, a stocky, red-bearded Dutchman knelt by a partly buried barrel of gunpowder. A trail of powder led from the barrel to where the other two Dutchmen waited. Darnell realized they were going to detonate the gunpowder as the cart completed the second part of the turn.

He had to warn Ravi and Naidu, but already he could hear the swaying jingle of the bells tied to the bullock's neck as they approached the corner. There was no way he could get back to them in time.

He ran back to the edge of the forest, crouching as the trees thinned, moving awkwardly on his haunches. Darnell's mind raced. The jangle of the cart's bells was growing louder. He could hear the creak of its body and the thump of its wheels in the ruts. The Dutchmen had disappeared into the trees. He had to act *now*.

Frantically he pulled out his pistol, rested the barrel against the tree and took careful aim. He had to get it right. A miss would serve as a warning and end with their being outnumbered, outgunned and killed. He steadied the barrel with his left hand, and breathed in deeply. And fired at the barrel of gunpowder . . .

There was a blinding white flash and a hot, smarting sensation against his cheek. His ears reverberated with the double bang of the shot and the explosion. A great orange ball of flame erupted out of the ground, mushroomed and expanded, ribboned with whirling stripes of black timber and human flesh.

Darnell saw the two surviving Dutchmen rush into the road and stand confused, unable to decide whether the explosion had been an accident. As the sounds of the explosion died, a wild chattering of birds and a massive rushing sound like a river overflowing its bank filled the air.

The two Dutchmen started to run towards the horses, but Darnell drew his knife and ran into the road to stop them. He hurled it at the smaller man; the knife caught him high in the throat and stuck. The man reeled, wrestling with the embedded knife, his feet stuttering in shallow circles. Blood trickled over his closed fingers and Darnell saw his eyes roll up as his legs splayed out from underneath him and he fell.

The brute-faced man rushed at Darnell, his gun drawn, his face contorted. Darnell leapt at him, kicking, and managed to knock the pistol away. But the man's fist caught him in the stomach and Darnell was lifted back on to his heels. Another blow caught him in the body. Massive arms were crushing him, his elbows were being pressed into his ribs. His face was pressed against the man's chest. Darnell wriggled, twisted his head and gasped for air. Dragging himself into a sitting position, Darnell's attacker drew a knife.

Darnell gulped air. He watched as the blade glinted above him. In a second the knife would plunge deep into his chest. He flexed his muscles, as if their strength alone would prevent the knife killing him. Something flashed. Darnell gritted his teeth.

Suddenly the man swayed sideways. Another blurred flash. A liquid, choking sound. The man's mouth was sagging open, his shoulders slumping; he was falling forward, his knife scraping the ground by Darnell's head. In a grey blur Darnell saw Ravi, pistol gripped in one hand, lean forward and drag the man off. Then Ravi was stooping down and helping him to his feet. 'By the flippin' Cross!' Ravi gasped, 'that were bleedin' close.'

They roped the Dutchman to a tree and lit a fire near his feet. 'Your name,' Darnell asked.

'Van Roon,' the Dutchman replied surlily.

'How far ahead is van Cuyler?'

Van Roon said nothing. Darnell picked up a firebrand, pressing it swiftly against van Roon's cheek. Van Roon twisted his head, swearing in pain and surprise. There was a smell of burning flesh and his cheek turned black.

'The next time it'll be your eye,' Darnell said, picking up a fresh firebrand. He held it near van Roon's cheek so he could feel the heat.

'They're about half a day ahead,' van Roon said hastily.

'How many men with him?'

'Six, and three carts.'

'How many more are there of you?'

'We're the only ones.'

Darnell was inclined to believe van Roon. Van Cuyler couldn't have travelled with more than a dozen people. Darnell weighed the chances of a surprise attack on van Cuyler. 'Far better,' Ravi said, 'to get to Venkatapur before he does.'

Darnell asked Naidu if he knew a short-cut.

'Not for carts,' Naidu said.

'Flippin' 'ell, man, we don't need carts. We got the Dutchmen's horses.'

'In that case,' Naidu said, 'I know a short-cut over the mountains.'

They released van Roon and told him to start walking. If he left now he would have cleared the jungle by nightfall, and someone on the coast road would no doubt help him get to Pulicat. Van Roon strode away. Long after he was lost in the trees they could hear his cursing.

Chapter Six

Darnell and Winter followed Naidu's directions and a day and a half later, after crossing a plain dotted with grazing sambhur, reached Venkatapur.

The city was a convoluted huddle of buildings, some brick with red-tiled roofs, the rest mud with thatched roofs, all of them flanking narrow, twisting bazaar streets crowded with palanquins, litters, wagons, carts and masses of scurrying people. To the east rose the broad stone spire of a temple, and on a small hill in front of them, preceded by a broad avenue lined with cassia trees, stood Prince Seringa's palace.

It was an impressive structure of solid granite, three hundred years old, close-pillared and low-roofed. The walls at each of the compass points were wider, deeper and longer than the others, and were the only walls with gates. As they approached, soldiers in marigold and black uniforms came out of the open north gate and stood in a row across the gateway. Darnell told the soldiers who they were and that they had come to see Prince Seringa. The guards asked them to wait.

Two hours passed. Their shadows shortened. The sun dried their mouths and their skins. The castle walls shimmered in the heat. The guard was changed. At last a group of six soldiers marched up and beckoned them inside.

They followed the soldiers along a stone-flagged path across a vast, open courtyard. Ahead of them was the public audience chamber, a low, wide granite pavilion that was open on three sides and whose slab roof was supported by triple rows of pillars.

To their left was a small temple, standing on its own stone platform and on their right was a wooden platform with tethering pegs used for punishments. On a parade ground beyond the punishment area, soldiers drilled.

Accompanied by the shouts of the drilling soldiers, they went up the steps of the audience chamber. In the middle was a stone platform with a throne and, behind it, a massive pair of iron gates set into a high dividing wall. Six bearded guards stood beside the gate carrying bared *tulwars*. Four others swung it open. They went through the gates into a covered, stone passage and their escort fell behind them as they marched with hollowly echoing footsteps. At the far end of the passage, a tall, lean, moustached figure in the marigold and black colours of the palace appeared. He was in his late twenties, with a square, regular face and large, black eyes that were as soft as a woman's. He was paler than most south Indians, his skin burnt the colour of milky coffee instead of black. His turban was freshly wound and, like his uniform, did not have a crease out of place. The buttons of his jacket were small tiger's eyes, Darnell noticed, and the hilt and leather scabbard of the *khatar* at his waist were scarred and dulled with use. 'I'm Dorai Ghosh,' he announced, 'commander of Prince Seringa's army. Please follow me.'

Turning on his heel he hurried them along a pillared veranda surrounding another courtyard, then led them up a flight of stairs to a room on the first floor. It was large with an uneven stone floor, rock walls and windows that were gaps in the rock. The room was cool and there was a surprising amount of light. 'Prince Seringa will send for you when he is ready,' Ghosh said, and left.

Darnell paced restlessly about the room. Having reached Venkatapur before van Cuyler, he was eager to use the advantage and close the deal before van Cuyler arrived.

'For God's sake, stop that pacing, or I'll never finish

these drawings,' Ravi cried. He was seated at a trestle, which, with a square teak wood table, low ebony sofa and chairs, comprised the furniture in the room. Before him were a portable writing tablet, inks and paper and a partly finished sketch of Madera.

Darnell grunted and continued pacing. The late afternoon sun cast long, silver rays through the gap in the rock that served as a window. It was nearly four o'clock, almost four hours since they'd arrived at Venkatapur.

'Sit,' Ravi said, not looking up from his drawing. 'Relax. Enjoy the view.'

Darnell sat, and poured himself some sherbet from the beaker on the table. Seringa's people had fed them lentils, rice and tomatoes baked in banana leaf, and brought them endless beakers of sherbet; but all requests to hasten their audience with the prince had fallen on deaf ears.

'What do you think?' Ravi asked and held up his drawing. It depicted a view of the fort from the bridge on the Madera road. Four ponderous cannons loomed on the wall of the fort. It would certainly show Seringa what he meant, Darnell thought. If he ever got to see Seringa.

'Seringa's goin' to love these,' Ravi forecast confidently. 'Things aren't so bad.'

'They will be,' Darnell said, gloomily, 'when van Cuyler gets here.'

The sun had sunk below the level of the window and half the room was in shadow when two soldiers flung open the door once more. Ghosh came in wearing a fresh uniform. 'Prince Seringa will see you now,' he announced, turning smartly on his heel and striding from the room.

Darnell and Winter hurried after him. Unusually for an Indian, Ghosh walked with brisk, regular strides, as if he were on a forced march. He led them along the veranda and into an unkempt garden. Wild marigold and bougainvillaea creepers tumbled over thickets of thorn and twined around mango and cassava trees. Hibiscus bloomed amongst wild daisies and ragweed and the occasional tall rhododendron. They reached a tall, stout gate in the middle of an eight-foot-high wall. Six turbanned, bearded soldiers stood before the gate with drawn *tulwars*.

They swung the gates open at Ghosh's approach, and Darnell and Ravi found themselves in another, more orderly garden, with neat flower beds and gravelled paths. In the centre was an open, circular pavilion, whose eight slender pillars supported a tiled canopy roof and linked a curving balustrade. In front of the pavilion three fountains cascaded into a stone pond. Above the line of the balustrade, Darnell saw a swarthy, white-clad figure seated facing the pond, a massive tiger's eye glinting in the middle of his turban. Prince Seringa!

Darnell felt his mouth go dry as they went up a short flight of damp, cement steps into the pavilion. The rear half of the interior was a curved three-foot-high dais. Prince Seringa sat on a wide marigold and black sofa in the middle of the dais, one foot curled under him, the other braced on the floor.

He was a compactly built man in his late twenties, with a round, thoughtful face, a heavy black beard and vivid, dark eyes. He had exceptionally well muscled shoulders and biceps. He wore a sleeveless white tunic and a simple white *dhoti*. A second tiger's eye hung round his neck to match the one on his turban. They were the largest stones Darnell had ever seen.

Prince Seringa obviously used the pavilion as a working place and private audience chamber. To his right was an inlaid, rolltop writing desk, and to his left, a carved ebony cabinet with drawers. Below the dais were rows of benches that reminded Darnell of choirstalls. A man of about fifty, with a tuft of greying hair in the middle of his shaven head, and ash daubed across his forehead, sat on one of the benches.

Ghosh stood to attention and bowed. 'Your Highness, I beg leave to present the English from Armagon.'

Darnell moved beside Ghosh, and lowered his head over steepled hands.

'Welcome to Venkatapur,' Prince Seringa said, his voice surprisingly deep. 'You have already met Dorai Ghosh, my army commander.' He pointed to the other man. 'This is my *guru*, Bharatya.'

Guru meant mentor, guide and leader as well as teacher. Darnell looked at Bharatya more carefully. He was a small, tightly muscled man with smooth, nearly translucent, sun-browned skin and a thin, ascetic face. He wore a coarse cotton *dhoti* and a necklace of wooden beads. Ugly fronds of sword-scars snaked along his right arm from the silver amulet on his wrist to his bare chest. A teacher and a soldier, Darnell thought, and, eyeing the beads and the ash with dismay, a Hindu conservative who would be opposed to dealing with foreigners.

'You may begin,' Seringa said.

Darnell's breath caught. His thoughts raced. He would have no second chance.

He introduced Winter and himself by name. Indians expected lengthy, circumlocutory preliminaries and thought *feringhi* directness uncivilized. But there was no time for digression. He had to reach agreement with Seringa by this evening. If he launched into the preamble Seringa expected, he would lose nearly an hour, and everything would be delayed until tomorrow or the day after, by which time van Cuyler would have arrived. Seringa, Bharatya and Ghosh were looking at him expectantly.

Darnell cleared his throat and said, 'We live in times of war and threats of war, of rebellion and famine. We are taught that strife is part of human existence and whatever happens is *karma*. But *karma* can be changed. The Hindu sage Agastya advised: "Go and wake up your luck".'

The three Indians, their eyes fixed on him, had barely

moved in their seats. Agastya had got him their attention, Darnell thought, pleased at the unexpected reward from all his reading of Indian philosophy. He said, 'If you wake up your luck you could stop Kokinada and the Mughal invading Vaidya.' He stopped and waited for one of the Indians to ask how.

The fountain's steady gush filled the silence. Crows cawed harshly among the low palmyras. On the balustrade by the entrance, two thrushes fought noisily over a twig. Darnell's chest tightened with tension. Finally he said, 'Let me show you how.' He'd raised his voice, but even to himself it sounded more blustery than confident.

He beckoned to Ravi to stand up and unroll the map of Madera and show his sketches. Bharatya and Ghosh crowded round Seringa as the three of them studied everything carefully. Darnell pointed to the map of Madera and the sketch of the fort from the coast road. 'If you gave us permission to build a factory in Madera, those guns will cover the bridges on the coast road. We could stop an invading army. Or destroy it.'

Seringa sucked in his breath quickly, as if the thought of destroying the enemy filled him with excitement. 'Your guns can do that?'

'Yes.'

'Show us how,' Ghosh demanded.

Darnell led them on to the steps and loaded his pistol. Ghosh watched closely as he set the lock to half-cock, rammed the cartridge down the barrel, poured powder into the priming pan and set the lock. He waved Ghosh back and walked down the steps. In front of him the fountains streamed cool, translucent columns. Water dampened the steps. Darnell looked past the fountain at a palmyra palm. It had no nuts, but he thought he could shoot a branch off. Focusing on the branch he told them what he was going to do.

'No.' Ghosh stepped beside him and pointed to the

plaster statue of a laughing warrior on the further side of the fountain. 'Shoot that.'

Darnell saw Seringa nod his permission, and he took aim. The figure was about two foot high, a portly dwarf with a triangular hat and a wide smile holding a curved sword across his ample belly. Darnell brought the barrel into line with the belly. If he was right in estimating the gun's kick, it would shoot off the head. He inhaled deeply, exhaled and pulled the trigger.

The pistol kicked against his wrist. The flash and the explosion were matched by loud exclamations from the Indians. The statue's head disappeared in a puff of white plaster. Darnell lowered the smoking pistol. Seringa, Bharatya and Ghosh looked awestruck. 'Our guns at Madera will be much bigger,' Darnell said. 'Each will weigh about three thousand pounds, and fire about ten pounds of shots. You can imagine what that will do to a tightly packed army.'

Seringa led the way back inside the pavilion, stroking the giant tiger's eye that hung from his neck. The stone was the symbol of Vaidya and had been his grandfather's. It was a reminder of his solemn oath to place the interests of Vaidya before everything else. He climbed the dais and sat. Was breaking ancient traditions of Vaidya the best he could do for Vaidya? Was that right or merely convenient? The *feringhi* betray and corrupt and eat your soul, his grandfather had said. Seringa turned to face Darnell. 'Vaidya does not need foreigners to defend it,' he said. 'Vaidya can defend itself. There will be no factory at Madera.'

Darnell's heart stuttered with shock. Seringa had been enthralled by the demonstration. He couldn't refuse permission now. 'Why?' Darnell asked. 'Why?'

'Vaidya has never treated with foreigners. That has been our custom since Vaidya was founded.'

That was the opinion Darnell had expected from Bharatya. If Seringa shared it, then everything was lost. Doggedly

Darnell launched into the argument he'd rehearsed. 'Much has changed since the founding of Vaidya. One hundred and twenty years ago India was divided into hundreds of separate kingdoms. Now all of India except the Deccan and Coromandel are united under the Mughal. One hundred and twenty years ago the only foreigners in India were a few travellers. Now they are here in their thousands. They have settled and built factories. They live and trade here. The welfare of their countries depends on their trade with India. The foreigner will not leave India. The foreigner will stay here and play an increasingly large part in the life and development of India. The foreigner will grow stronger and richer, as will those who work with him. Those who do not –' Darnell shrugged. 'The law of history is that the weak are absorbed or destroyed, like all those Indian kingdoms of one hundred and twenty years ago.'

All the time he'd been speaking, Seringa had been switching his gaze to Bharatya, checking his *guru*'s reaction to Darnell's words. Darnell realized that though Seringa would make the final decision, that decision had to meet with Bharatya's approval.

Seringa said, 'We will not break with our traditions. If it is our fate to be vanquished, let it be as it is written.'

'Have you thought that it might also be written that you will ally yourself with foreigners and grow stronger and more powerful?' Darnell paused and looked swiftly at Bharatya and Ghosh. Bharatya had a patient look of detached interest. Ghosh was staring stonily ahead of him. 'If you ally with us you won't lose your independence or your freedom,' Darnell said to Seringa. 'Instead you will become stronger and richer and more able to fulfil your destiny. You will become even greater than the Vaidya of old.'

For the first time Bharatya spoke. 'Will you not attempt to make us Christians?'

Darnell remembered why Vaidya had originally

excluded foreigners. 'No,' he said, 'we are not Portuguese. Our Christianity does not require us to force anyone to convert. I swear to you, we will not forcibly convert any Vaidyan.'

'How do we know you will keep your word?'

'I will write that in our agreement. Together with a guarantee that there will be no churches or schools except for the use of those already Christian. Anyone found proselytizing will be fined a minimum of one thousand *pagodas* and expelled from the settlement.'

'Will we be allowed to practise our religion in our way?'

'Of course,' Darnell said. 'I'll put that in the agreement too.'

Bharatya still looked uncertain. The future of Vaidya rested on Bharatya trusting the English. Darnell said, 'You will have the right to build two temples at Madera. That will also be in the agreement.'

Bharatya continued staring at Darnell. Then he asked, 'What do you want in exchange for protecting us?'

'The exclusive right for twenty-five years to trade, first in Venkat, then, as it becomes possible, in the whole of Vaidya. Permission for two more factories in the next three years. Power to enforce our laws in our territories and to levy duties. The grant of lands to support our establishments.'

'How many foreigners will live in your factory?'

Darnell hesitated. Too few and Bharatya would think the English unable to defend Madera. Too many and he'd worry about being corrupted by foreign ways. He said, 'At the beginning about sixty. Then, as the fort grows larger, about four hundred.'

He saw Bharatya frown, as if intimidated by such a large number. He said, 'The increase from sixty to four hundred will take time. Your temples will have been built and you would have taken the necessary steps to reinforce your way of life long before then.'

'Why should we need to reinforce our way of life?' Ghosh asked.

'Because it is impossible for our two peoples to come together as one,' Darnell said. 'The best we can do is help each other over certain matters. For the rest, we must each develop and grow separately. We are from different castes. We have different *karmas*.'

Bharatya gave him a thin smile. 'What is your business?' he asked.

'I work for the Honourable English East India Company, which is an association of London merchants trading to Persia, India and the East Indies. They send two or three voyages a year, each consisting of three to seven ships. They try to sell English goods and buy spices, indigo, salt-petre, silk, ivory, drugs and sugar which they then sell at a profit in England and on the Continent.'

'But from India you buy cloth?'

'That's right. We exchange the cloth we buy in India for spices in Java and Sumatra, which enables us to reduce the amount of silver we would otherwise need.'

'How much profit does your Company make from the business of cloth and spices?'

'Sometimes as much as two hundred and fifty per cent, sometimes less than five. Sometimes, the Company even makes a loss. It all depends on supply, demand, prices, the mix of goods, what the Dutch and Portuguese have sent to Europe, the winds around Africa, the monsoons, how many ships return home and in what condition – and whether the gods smile on the venture.'

Bharatya leaned back, looking awed and a little nervous at having to control a people who were so rich and strong. Darnell hoped he wouldn't choose the easy option and exclude them from Vaidya; that he was shrewd enough to understand that in the end one could only accommodate strength, not overcome it.

Bharatya asked, 'How will we benefit from your trade?'

'Your people will make four times as much as they do now,' Darnell replied. 'In addition to the profits of trade, the building of the fort and supplying the people living in it will give your people more work and wealth. To help you and us, we will assist you with developing your agriculture and creating new industries in woodworking and shipping. By the end of three years, trading with us, you and your people will be ten times as rich as you are now!'

Seringa said, 'We have no need of such wealth.'

'We all need money,' Darnell said softly, 'you most of all. Money is more than the ability to buy goods. It is with money that you buy soldiers and build armies. It is with money that you launch wars and recover what was stolen from you. Money is power. If you don't make money, soon others will be richer and more powerful than you.' He walked up to Seringa. 'How much do you think Kokinada makes from twelve Dutch, seven English and four Portuguese factories? How much more money will he have in six months? A year? What does he do with his money? Spend it on gambling and dancing girls or soldiers and weapons? Money buys armies, armies take territory and make more money. It is as simple as that.'

Ghosh said, 'We can defend Vaidya. I have reconnoitred the area round Madera and we can keep Kokinada out quite easily, and in the hill country of the west we can hold out against the Mughal for ever.'

Darnell thought Ghosh was proud of his military skills and his army, and would have to be dissuaded without disparaging either. Keeping his voice low and steady, Darnell said, 'Your army is strong and brave and fights well. But you are ranged against huge forces. The Mughal reserves of men and materials are vast. They could bring twenty or thirty thousand troops against you, and the battle you fight in Madera will be on Vaidyan soil. The area of the battle and the land surrounding will be laid waste.' Darnell paused and added, 'Your land, your people.'

Bharatya asked, 'How do we know that once you have built your factory you will use your guns to fight Vaidya's enemies?'

'We wouldn't have a choice,' Darnell replied. 'The trading rights you give us are too valuable to let them be controlled by others. Whatever we may feel about defending Vaidya, we will fight to protect those rights.'

Bharatya turned to Seringa. 'I believe a foreign alliance is something we should consider. I know it is against our traditions and the ways of your father and grandfather, but times have changed. We are facing a war we have to win.'

Bharatya had decided! Darnell's heart leapt.

Then Ghosh said, 'If we are entering into this alliance so that we may win, the foreigner must supply us with guns and the training to use them. Without that we will only be dependent on a foreigner's promises and goodwill.'

Darnell felt himself going pale. So that guns could not be used against them, the English, Dutch, Portuguese and Danish had agreed not to supply guns or training to Indians. There was no way he could honour a promise to arm the Indians.

But the Indians didn't know that, and this was a promise he could avoid keeping. By the time the Vaidyans realized they wouldn't have any guns, the fort would be built and the English impossible to dislodge. He looked from a no longer soft-eyed Ghosh to Seringa and Bharatya. Seringa was staring intently at Ravi's sketch of a cannon, Bharatya looking expectantly at him.

From beside him Ravi whispered, 'Go on, tell 'em yes. They'll never know till it's too late.'

But Darnell had made up his mind. 'No,' he admitted. 'I cannot agree to supply you with guns. Even if I did, the Company and the other *feringhi* would stop me doing so.'

'It means you do not trust us,' Ghosh cried.

'It means that if we armed you, then the Dutch will arm

Kokinada, and before any of us know what's happening, Kokinada's army of twenty thousand men equipped with cannon and muskets will be marching against yours, and all of India will erupt in violence.'

Ghosh looked away angrily, but Darnell went on quietly. 'I promise you this, though. If any European supplies Kokinada or the Mughal with guns, we will supply you and train your army in their use.'

Bharatya and Seringa exchanged glances, and Bharatya made a quick chopping motion with his hand. Seringa stood up and said, 'It is late. We will continue this discussion another time.'

Darnell bowed his head over steepled fingers as Seringa passed and murmured, 'As Your Excellency wishes,' his mind a maelstrom of emotions as he wondered whether his honesty had cost him the fort.

A cool morning breeze blew between the granite pillars of the audience chamber. Karel van Cuyler saw the look of appreciation on Prince Seringa's face and felt the tension seep out of him like water. The gifts he had brought, the bales of Chinese silk, brocades, satin and velvet lay scattered in slashes of wild colour on the pale marble steps of the platform. Above them, glinting menacingly on the jewelled carpet that covered the dais, was the pile of swords. Seringa took one from its scabbard and pranced across the dais, thrusting and parrying.

Van Cuyler had reached the palace an hour previously. To his surprise he'd been kept waiting barely twenty minutes before being conducted to the audience chamber across the courtyard from the main entrance. While soldiers had helped his men unload the carts, others had laid the jewelled carpet along the top of the dais, and covered the throne with cushions and a second carpet. Soldiers and clerks had filed into the area before the throne and squatted on the stone floor. Soon afterwards, servants in the marigold and black palace uniforms had appeared and stationed themselves strategically on the dais and among the audience, waving fans of peacock feathers. Twelve well-nourished men in their forties, identically dressed in marigold tunics, turbans and white *dhotis* had taken their places in two rows of six on either side of the dais. Then Seringa himself had arrived, resplendent in a white and gold embroidered *achkan*, trousers and slippers, with the largest jewel van Cuyler had ever seen stuck in the middle of his white silk turban. Seringa had been accompanied by two men who now sat on stools on either side of Seringa. Seringa introduced them as Bharatya, some kind of priest, and Dorai Ghosh, the commander of Seringa's army. Seringa said, 'We thank you for your gifts. We welcome you to Venkatapur.'

Van Cuyler said, 'We have come to help you. We have been deeply concerned at rumours that your enemies are massing against you, that you may soon be under attack from the west and the north. We have come to offer you our help in defeating your enemies.'

'How exactly will you help?'

Van Cuyler started in surprise. It wasn't Seringa who had spoken but Bharatya. He looked at the priest more closely. The man had sword-scars on his right arm and the right side of his chest. Van Cuyler masked his surprise with a smile that included both Seringa and him. 'We will begin by building a factory at Madera. That way, Dutch guns and Dutch troops will prevent any invasion from the north.'

The priest was about to say something, but Seringa interrupted. 'You will use Dutch troops to help us?' Seringa's tone was incredulous.

'Yes. We Dutch do not do anything by halves. If we promise to help you we will help you with everything we have.' He moved his eyes slowly from Seringa to Bharatya and Ghosh. 'Ours will be a total alliance. Your enemy will be our enemy. Your friend, our friend.'

'What is the price of this friendship?' Bharatya asked.

'Price?' Van Cuyler felt uneasy at Bharatya's bluntness. 'There is no price on our friendship. But so that our alliance will not be an economic drain on us, we do ask for the right to trade exclusively with Vaidya for a period of twenty years. If our relationship proves satisfactory, we would wish in the next two years to build three more trading establishments. We will require grants of land to support our establishments and the right to impose duties and our own laws in our territories. We will pay you a guaranteed sum of three hundred pounds a year on account of your share of duties.'

The Dutch terms were better than the English, Seringa thought. Last evening, Bharatya had addressed the council and told them a foreign alliance was essential for Vaidya's survival. Bharatya had said they needed to abandon the strict traditionalism of the past, that if their religion was worth anything, it would survive and overcome this association with foreigners. He'd told Seringa his duty now was to make the most advantageous deal.

Bharatya asked, 'Will you force us to become Christians?'

'No,' van Cuyler said immediately. The Bible decreed that each people was wonderful in its own way and had its proper and separate tasks. There was to be no mixing of races, and the Dutch had never attempted to convert natives or allowed them to participate fully in their church.

The Dutchman's reply was too quick, Bharatya thought, and asked, 'Will you undertake not to build churches and schools other than for your own use? Will you undertake that anyone attempting to convert Vaidyans to Christianity will be punished and expelled from your factory?'

Van Cuyler thought this was something better settled by a *predikant*. But he was not going to delay agreement over technicalities. 'Yes,' he said.

Bharatya nodded his approval.

Ghosh asked, 'Will you provide us with guns and the training to use them?'

Van Cuyler looked down to hide his shock. He wondered if the Vaidyans had asked Darnell the same question and how Darnell had dealt with it. He decided that his inability to deliver the guns didn't matter. By the time the Vaidyans realized he had lied, the fort would be built and the Dutch firmly established in Vaidya. He told himself what mattered now was that the Vaidyans heard what they wanted to hear. 'We will supply you with all the guns and training you want,' he said.

Ghosh flashed him a brilliant smile, then leaned across and spoke to Seringa, who nodded vehemently and smiled. Seringa cleared his throat. 'We are most grateful for your presents, and even more grateful for your offer to help us.' He turned to his councillors. 'We are happy to announce that Vaidya will, for the first time in its history, enter into an alliance with a foreigner. The terms of that alliance will cover the grant of certain lands, the payment of certain taxes and the construction of a factory at Madera.' Seringa stopped as a collective sigh ran through the councillors.

Bharatya leaned forward, caught Seringa's sleeve and whispered something. Seringa began to speak again. 'We have an English delegation here who we will summon to this place now. You will each be given the opportunity to offer us your best terms. Whoever does so will get our approval to build the factory at Madera.'

Darnell fairly bubbled with relief as, surrounded by soldiers, he and Ravi hurried out of the main palace buildings alongside a high wall. He'd been testy since his meeting with Seringa the previous evening, and all morning had been sending messages asking to see Seringa. Now at last they were being taken to him.

They emerged through a narrow gate on to the parade ground in front of the barracks. The audience chamber to his right was filled with people, the floor covered by a marigold and white tapestry. Unlike last evening's affair, this was going to be a formal meeting. Darnell walked faster, almost running across the parade ground and the wide expanse of the punishment area, his boots skimming over the uneven stone of the courtyard. The soldiers dropped behind as he and Ravi climbed up the broad steps of the audience chamber.

Seringa sat on the throne at the back of the chamber. As before, Bharatya and Ghosh were seated on either side of him. The throne platform glittered under a covering of thick carpet studded with tiger's eyes. A pile of swords stood at the base of the throne. Twelve men sat immediately below the platform, and the area in front of it was filled with seated clerks and soldiers. Servants with fans stood among the audience and behind Seringa. Ahead to the right, metal gleamed. Seated on a trestle with chest pieces gleaming darkly and helmets on their knees were six Dutchmen; and bigger than all of them, solid and menacing, his squint fixed ferociously on Darnell, was Karel van Cuyler!

Darnell's heart pounded. His mouth went dry. He felt the blood drain from his face. He walked up the narrow central aisle and took his place before the platform. He steepled his hands in front of his chest and greeted Seringa, Bharatya and Ghosh. Everything was over. He had lost!

The three Vaidyans looked at him impassively, not acknowledging his greeting. Then Seringa spoke. 'These are Hollanders,' he said, pointing at the Dutch. 'They have also offered to befriend us and build a factory at Madera.'

Darnell switched his gaze to van Cuyler who was looking steadily at him, a gleam of quiet triumph in his small, close-set eyes.

Seringa explained the terms that the Dutch had offered.

'We have decided that whoever makes us the best offer will be allowed to build at Madera.'

Darnell felt an insane anger flare through him. He wanted to draw his knife and leap on van Cuyler, to press his pistol against that close-cropped head and pull the trigger. He forced himself to look at Seringa, Bharatya and Ghosh. He had to leave his anger at van Cuyler till afterwards. What he had to do now was convince Seringa to give him the permission.

But that was impossible. The Dutch were richer and more powerful and could out-bid him. He ran over the Dutch offer again. Guaranteed payments, three settlements, the provision of guns, troops and training. He said, 'We too will offer you a guarantee of three hundred pounds against duties, and reduce the term of our agreement to twenty years.'

'That is the same offer as the Dutch!' Seringa sounded surprised.

'Not the same,' Ghosh snapped. 'The Dutch are giving us guns, troops and training.'

'They won't.'

'What the devil do you mean by that?' Van Cuyler flushed angrily.

'The Dutch lie!' Darnell insisted again.

Van Cuyler hesitated, hands looped into his belt, dangerously close to his dagger and *sjambok*. 'Watch your tongue, English, or I'll cut it out.'

Seringa raised his hand abruptly for silence and turned to Darnell. 'Why do you accuse the Dutch of lying?'

'Because they will not send their troops against Kokinada. The biggest Dutch factory in India is at Pulicat – in the kingdom of Kokinada. The Dutch have eleven other factories there. Do you believe that anyone with such substantial interests in Kokinada will fight the nizam for the sake of one factory in Vaidya?'

'You have factories in Kokinada too.' Van Cuyler spoke coldly.

'Seven factories, the largest of which is only half the size of Pulicat. But in any case, we haven't promised to use our troops against Kokinada.'

'We damned well will,' van Cuyler cried. 'We will do whatever is necessary to save Vaidya.'

'But you will not send Dutch troops against Kokinada, and you will not supply cannon or training because, like us, you are bound by the agreement between all the European companies prohibiting the sale of arms to Indians.'

'We have abandoned that agreement,' van Cuyler cried. 'We have permission from Batavia. We can supply cannon. And we will fight Kokinada.' Van Cuyler decided he would forge the authority if he had to. He turned to the throne, large beads of sweat rolling down his reddened cheeks. 'Don't you see, once we have built the factory in Madera it will become even bigger than Pulicat. More and more of our trade will shift to Vaidya from Kokinada and Vaidya will become more important to us than Kokinada.'

Darnell saw that Seringa and Ghosh wanted to believe that, and that van Cuyler would give them guns and troops and training. Unless he did something, the Dutch would get the fort. 'How long will it take before Vaidya becomes as important as Kokinada?' he asked. 'How long will it take you to build twelve factories in Vaidya? And what will you do if meanwhile Kokinada invades Vaidya? Whose side will you take?'

'What about your factories?' van Cuyler demanded. 'Will you abandon them for the sake of trading in Vaidya? In Java you English abandoned your local allies and fled. You will not keep your word.'

'*Bas*!' Bharatya called. 'Enough!' He stared angrily at both of them, his fingers toying with the beads at his neck. 'We have heard too much from both of you and do not know who to believe. Until we know which of you is telling the truth,' he continued in a calmer tone, 'we cannot grant permission to either of you.'

'I –' Darnell began, but Bharatya cut him off with a gesture.

'If you were both Vaidyans,' Bharatya went on, 'we'd know very quickly. We have certain tests we use to determine who is telling the truth.'

'Put us to the test,' Darnell said.

Bharatya looked at van Cuyler.

'Yes,' van Cuyler said. 'Do that.'

Bharatya said, 'The tests involve physical danger. If you fail you could die.'

'We'll do them,' Darnell and van Cuyler said together.

'In that case, go to your quarters and prepare yourselves. Tomorrow, before sunrise, you will be brought here for your examination.'

Chapter Seven

The soldiers arrived shortly before sunrise, the light from their flaring torches throwing smoky shadows on the rock walls and the corridor roof. Darnell marched out of the courtyard accompanied by high-pitched wailing music and the throbbing of drums. Once more, he was led along the veranda and the tunnel and out through the gate at the rear of the public audience chamber. The courtyard beyond was full. Torches bobbed and weaved, illuminating a mass of shadowy bodies with turbans and shawls pressed about head and shoulders, warding off the evil spirits that brought the morning chill. There were men in unfurled *dhotis* and women in flowing saris. Vendors moved through the throng with flaming torches fastened to trays of *dosai* and *vade* and green and yellow sweetmeats. There was an excited hubble-bubble of sound that died to a murmur as Darnell and his escort were spotted.

Some of the soldiers rushed ahead, swinging the flats of their swords to clear a way for Darnell. Darnell became aware of a press of shadowy faces and staring eyes that were wide and curious and, in a strange way, friendly. A vast stage had been built over the punishment area. Accompanied by another discordant wail of music, and surrounded by a military escort, van Cuyler emerged from the area near the barracks.

They met at the foot of the steps. Like Darnell, van Cuyler wore an open shirt, breeches and boots. His face was still puffy with sleep, but as their glances locked, his eyes blazed with hatred. Immediately, soldiers moved between them. Darnell was led up the steps and made to kneel on the left. Then van Cuyler was brought up and made to kneel on the right.

At the end of the stage directly opposite them, Bharatya waited with five other bare-bodied priests, all with shaven heads, ash-smeared faces and wearing thin *dhotis*. Along the stage to their left, Seringa sat on a throne above tiers lined with benches filled with councillors and courtiers. To their right was a small altar with a two-foot-high statue of Shiva emerging in a cloud of fire from the cosmic pillar the Hindus called *lingam*.

No sooner had Darnell and van Cuyler knelt than Bharatya and the priests started to chant, circling a brazier set in the middle of the stage, throwing twigs, cooked rice, liquefied butter and coarse sugar on to it. After each offering, the fire sputtered and smoked. There was a smell of hot oil. Bharatya took a vessel containing water, rice and flowers and offered it to a palely rising sun. He joined the priests and they walked around the statue, chanting and placing metal receptacles of water on the steps of the altar. Bharatya went to Seringa and returned with a gold coin which he placed at the feet of the idol.

The ceremony went on, the sky turning a silvery grey as the sun rose behind a bank of cloud. A pale white light crept across the stage, first mingling with and then evaporating the pre-dawn purple.

Suddenly four of the priests were standing before Darnell. From behind the priests, Bharatya called, 'You will now submit yourselves to the first ordeal. You will place the rice that is offered you in your mouth, chew it five times and expel it into the bowls. The one whose rice is dry will be shown to have lied.'

Darnell felt his mouth go dry as the priests beckoned him and van Cuyler to stand, then took them by the hand and led them to Bharatya.

Bharatya stood with his eyes turned up into the tops of his lids. He stared at them blindly, then raised seemingly sightless eyes to the sky. 'Sun, moon, wind, fire, Swarga,' he called, 'earth, water, virtue, Yama. Day, night, dusk and dawn, you know these men's deeds and whether their actions be true or false.'

Darnell felt an involuntary shiver prickle the hairs on the back of his neck. One of the priests nudged his elbow. A shaven-headed acolyte in a grey cotton robe stood before him holding up a bowl of brown rice grains. With the priests watching closely, Darnell took a handful of grain and thrust it into his mouth. The rice trickled over his teeth and into the space at the bottom of his gums. Each grain was hard and dry and small and threatened to choke him. He squeezed his cheeks together to force saliva into his mouth. It was no good.

From the corner of his eye he saw van Cuyler chewing mightily and sucked his own cheeks together again. His mouth was as dry as paper. His cheeks started to hurt with a strange drawing sensation. He tightened his jaws to keep the dry rice in his mouth. The acolyte was holding a second bowl up to him. The rice felt as hard and gritty as when he'd first put it into his mouth. Darnell spat it out.

Head bowed in reverence, the acolyte passed the bowl to a priest, who closed his eyes and held it up to Bharatya. Bharatya looked into the bowls carefully, prodding the chewed rice in each bowl with the nail of his first finger. Perhaps van Cuyler too had had trouble producing saliva.

Finally Bharatya turned from the bowls to face Seringa. 'The rice in both bowls is wet,' he called. 'Both men tell the truth!'

Darnell's body went limp with relief as a vast, expectant murmur ran through the crowd.

Bharatya turned back to Darnell and van Cuyler. 'Are you both willing to undertake the next ordeal?' he asked. He raised his voice so that it carried to the back of the crowd. 'I ask you now, will you both face the ordeal by fire?'

Fire, Darnell wondered. How much worse would fire be than dry rice? He recalled Bharatya's warning that there would be physical danger, and his gloomy prediction that if Darnell was wrong he could die! He glanced sideways at van Cuyler. Van Cuyler looked as nervous as Darnell felt. Darnell decided he had no alternative. He said, 'I will.'

Van Cuyler coughed. 'I also will do it.'

They squatted on either side of the steps while the priests, helped by soldiers, laid out eight circles of earth along the stage in rows of four. A ninth circle was laid directly in front of them. Bharatya used tongs to pick up an eight-inch-long iron rod and heat it in the brazier.

When the circles were laid, Bharatya handed the tongs to a priest and walked round the circles, praying at each and blowing incense. Darnell watched the iron rod glow red hot. What, he wondered, would Bharatya do with it? Liar or not, the rod would sear anything it touched. His heart thumped painfully as two priests came up, led him to the first circle and made him stand in it, facing Seringa.

The circle was about one and a half feet in diameter, the gaps between the circles about three feet. A priest took Darnell's hands and dipped them in a mixture of curdled milk and wheat flour that stuck to his hands in a white, soggy mess. Bharatya came up and said, 'When you are ready, you will take the rod and walk quickly through each circle, stopping momentarily in each. I will be at the ninth circle and will take the rod from you. If the rod does not burn your skin, you will have told the truth.'

Darnell stared at the iron bar, now a glowing red cylinder. The priests were wrapping his hands with leaves, making them feel swollen and clumsy. He knew the rod would burn through the leaves in seconds. There was no way he could succeed in this test. Then, as the priests bound the leaves with stalks of grass, he realized that van Cuyler too must fail.

Bharatya came and stood in front of Darnell, his eyes

swivelled into the top of his head once more.

'Oh fire!' he called to the sky. 'You know the secrets of men! Reveal the truth to us!' He reached behind him, took the tongs from the first priest and put the red-hot bar of iron in Darnell's hands.

Darnell heard the hiss of sizzling leaves and felt the heat against his palms. He had to move and move quickly. He stepped out of the first circle and walked to the second. A smell of burning stung his nostrils. He walked to the third circle. The smell grew stronger. Ash fluttered from inside his palms. He reached the fourth circle. The heat was searing his skin now. He moved more quickly, almost breaking into a run. The end of the rod was turning white. His hands grew hotter. The sixth circle. The heat was scorching his palms in a constant, piercing sting. The seventh circle. His palms felt skinned. The heat burned his skin in a steady, raw smart. He wanted to drop the rod. He didn't think he could reach the eighth circle. He forced himself to jog, to keep his hands clenched. He reached the circle and stood there. Bharatya was beckoning him on to the ninth circle. He covered the distance in a frantic leap. Bharatya took the rod with his tongs. The pain didn't diminish. Bharatya hurled the rod on to a bed of straw by the circle. The straw erupted into flames.

As the priests extinguished the flames, Bharatya pulled the grass bonds and burnt leaves from Darnell's hands. Darnell felt the sweat trickle down his cheeks, the shirt adhere to his body. The rod had burnt through the leaves. They were black and had flaked away. Beneath the ugly black stripe on his palms, oily skin gleamed. Bharatya removed the last of the leaves, placed grains of boiled rice in Darnell's palms, and made him rub them together.

Darnell did. The effect was oddly cooling.

Bharatya stooped low, examined the skin on Darnell's palms and stepped back.

Darnell waited, barely breathing. Had he passed the test or not?

Bharatya took a deep breath and threw his head back. 'This man does not lie,' he called.

Van Cuyler was drenched in sweat. As the priests came for him, he got to his feet, shambled to the first circle and stood with his palms out. The mixture of milk and flour felt cool. It was a thick enough insulation, he thought, as they bound the leaves. He told himself there was nothing magical about the ordeal. Everything depended on how hot the rod was, how fast it burned through the leaves and how quickly he moved.

Bharatya was standing in front of him, chanting, then he was holding out the glowing rod. Van Cuyler took it and concentrated on moving, smoothly and easily and quickly. He reached the second circle, the third circle, the fourth circle. This was easy. He felt nothing but a warm tingling in his palms. Fifth circle. The rod was hot and he was leaving a thin trail of ash. Sixth circle. His palms were smarting. Seventh. His palms were on fire. He ran. Eighth. He couldn't hold the rod any more. He had to drop it. He sprinted to the ninth circle. It didn't matter about the fort. Nothing mattered except ending the savage smart in his hands. He hurled the rod on to the bed of straw. The straw flamed.

Sweat streamed down his face. He tried to keep his hands from shaking as Bharatya tugged away the leaves. There was a black scar across his palm. Had he failed? He had no doubt he was burned. Again Bharatya provided boiled rice, then stooped over, examining van Cuyler's palms. There were flecks of white where the rice had been crushed and a faint shine where he'd rubbed it into the skin.

Bharatya picked at the white flecks, checking if they were rice or skin. At last he threw his head back and called, 'This man also tells the truth!'

The crowd murmured loudly. Darnell watched van Cuyler swagger back to his place, grinning and waving to the Dutchmen gathered at the foot of the stage.

Bharatya was circling the brazier as soldiers manoeuvred two waist-high rattan baskets on to the middle of the stage. Seringa stepped down from the throne and walked with measured tread to the baskets. A priest opened the first one and there was an instant, frightening hiss.

The crowd gasped.

Seringa dropped a coin into the basket, then moved to the second one. Two acolytes lifted the lid. There was the same, savage hiss. Seringa dropped a coin into it and walked slowly back to his place.

Solemnly Bharatya announced, 'Both these men have told the truth. We will put them to a final test: the ordeal of the cobra.'

The crowd let off a huge collective sigh of awe.

The cobra was the deadliest of Indian snakes. Between five to ten feet long, its dark yellowish-brown coils making it virtually invisible in its normal habitat, it killed thousands of Indians every year. There was no antidote to its sting and its venom acted swiftly, paralysing and killing within minutes of an attack.

Ravi leapt on to the stage beside Darnell, the skin on his face stretched, his dark eyes hot and feverish. 'It's time yer stopped this bleedin' heathen nonsense,' he cried.

Darnell said, 'I can't. Not if we want the fort.'

'Let the goddamn fort go. It's not goin' to be much use when yer's dead.'

Darnell looked across at van Cuyler, who was staring straight ahead. He couldn't give in to van Cuyler, he couldn't lose to the Dutch. More than that, he couldn't shame the English by publicly declaring himself a coward and a liar. 'I have no goddamn choice,' he said.

'Of course yer has. Yer can walk, can't you? Get on yer trotters and walk.'

It wasn't as simple as that. As his teacher Alban Cormac had said, for an Englishman there were many things worse than death. 'I won't be a coward,' he said. 'And I won't back down to god-rottin' van Cuyler and the muck-fickin' Dutch.'

'There'll be other times,' Ravi said. 'Lots of other times when we'll whip 'em.'

Darnell shook his head. An Englishman did not walk away. Better, he thought, death than dishonour.

'Don't be bleedin' stupid,' Ravi cried. 'Yer life's worth more than this. Yer've got a son to bring up. What's goin' to happen to that little tyke if yer gets stung by a cobra?'

'He wouldn't want a coward for a father,' Darnell said firmly.

He looked across at van Cuyler. The Dutchman must be experiencing the same fears. He stared at him, willing the Dutchman to weaken.

Van Cuyler kept staring straight ahead, ignoring the sweat soaking his tunic and armpits. Everyone knew how deadly cobras were; Darnell wouldn't be stupid enough to go through with this. He must know the snake had no way of telling who had lied and who told the truth, that the snake was tetchy and dangerous and would react to any intrusion of its domain with an attack. He remembered that Darnell had a family. He wouldn't risk his family's future on this. Van Cuyler looked across at him and stared into those strange, midnight-blue eyes. Darnell's gaze was level and unwavering. Damnit, Darnell was going to do it, he realized with mounting alarm.

'The snake knows all,' Bharatya cried. 'The snake will tell us which of these men lie.' He fixed his gaze on Darnell and van Cuyler. 'You will each approach the baskets and, after being blindfolded, take out the coin which you have seen our ruler Prince Seringa place in each basket. The snake will not attack the man who has told the truth.'

Darnell turned to stare again at van Cuyler. Van Cuyler wasn't giving up. Instead he'd had two of the Dutchmen join him on the stage with their knives drawn. If he got stung, the Dutchmen were going to bleed him.

Darnell turned to Ravi. 'I want you to come with me,' he said, 'and while I reach for the coin, I want you to heat your knife in the brazier and prepare to bleed me.'

'That'll never work with a cobra!' Ravi protested.

Darnell pointed to van Cuyler. 'As long as he thinks it will, we'll have to try too.'

Bharatya beckoned van Cuyler forward. Van Cuyler got to his feet. He was pale, his face shiny with sweat.

'You're taking a big risk, Dutchman,' Darnell called.

Van Cuyler turned. 'Are you crazy enough to die for this fort, Darnell?'

Darnell's lips curved in a tight smile. 'I won't die!'

Head high, van Cuyler marched up to Bharatya. One of the priests rolled up the right sleeve of his tunic. Bharatya opened one of the baskets and allowed van Cuyler to look inside.

Darnell watched closely, hoping he might see something that would help him outwit the snake. Bharatya and the priests pulled a blindfold over van Cuyler's eyes. Darnell's heart sank. It was a game of chance, and all the odds were in favour of the snake.

Bharatya chanted. The crowd went very still. Then Bharatya lifted up the cover of the basket.

Van Cuyler leant forward slightly, groping for the basket. His hand skirted the rim, then, as he got his bearings, plunged in and down. A small smile creased his face. He'd got the coin. His elbow bent. His hand was coming up and out. Then his face reddened, he grimaced in pain and leapt back, hand clasping his forearm, gold coin protruding between his fingers.

He scrabbled frantically at the blindfold as the Dutchmen ran up to him. Holding up the coin weakly, van Cuyler allowed himself to be led away.

Darnell's heart was tripping madly. From beside him, Ravi said, 'You can still walk away. They can't give the fort to van Cuyler 'cos 'e's been stung.'

And they wouldn't give it to him if he didn't try. There was a chance, he told himself, a small chance, that he could succeed. If he was fast enough and lucky enough. If it was his *karma*.

'Let the fort go,' Ravi pleaded. 'It's not as important as your life.'

Van Cuyler had almost done it, Darnell thought. He *could* do it. He had to believe that. 'If I'm stung,' he said to Ravi, 'you'll be there to bleed me.'

'It's not much good against a cobra,' Ravi repeated.

Bharatya was beckoning to him. Darnell stood up. The Dutchmen were huddled around van Cuyler, knives glinting, the stage by their feet spotted with blood. Bharatya opened the second basket and let Darnell look.

In the darkness inside he could see the muddy coils of the cobra. He peered more closely. The gold coin sat in the middle of the creature's body, well away from its head. He heard a stirring and a hissing, saw the cobra's speckled hood puff up and sway, and then, as it did not see any threat, deflate.

Darnell branded the location of the coin on his brain, visualized his arm streaking down in the centre of the basket, whipping back, straight out with the coin. He could do it. There would be no problem. Bharatya rolled up his sleeve and Darnell stooped to allow the priests to blindfold him. He focused his mind's eye on the coin, on the vision of his arm going down into that gloomy cavern, on his fingers closing on the coin and snatching it up, fast, moving away as quickly as the snake itself.

The blindfold felt hot and sticky. He was surrounded by darkness and heat. He heard Bharatya say, 'Snake, you are the symbol of life. Settle the doubtful question which now concerns us. Tell us if this man tells the truth or not!' Speaking softly he added, 'Proceed when you are ready.'

Darnell's hand flashed down. He'd gone straight down the middle of the basket. His fingers opened and closed. He felt something oily and cool and scaly brush his fingertips, heard something rustle in the basket. Where was the coin? He moved his hand in a circle, not daring to press further down, not willing to bring it up without the coin.

His fingertips brushed the snake again. There was no help for it. He had to go lower. He pressed. The snake's body was solid. He heard it move, felt the coin brush his fingers. He thrust down. Grabbed it. It slipped. His fingers groped, found it again.

He whipped his hand back, straight up, as he had visualized. There was a violent hiss and a snapping explosion of pain in his hand as he tore it away. He held up the coin. The crowd roared. He told himself the snake had missed, that he'd only ripped his hand on the basket, but as he tore away the blindfold he saw two swollen circles the size of small coins on his wrist. He clamped his arm above his wrist as Ravi grabbed him.

Swiftly Ravi took Darnell's hand and made two cuts above the sting. Blood welled up within the white slashes, then spread to cover the wrist. Ravi placed his mouth on the cuts and sucked. Darnell felt a moment of light-headedness. Then Ravi drew his head away and spat through bloody lips. Darnell's mouth closed on the wounds. The blood tasted salty against his tongue. He sucked and spat.

They took it in turns for five minutes, sucking, spitting and sucking again, the continual harassment of the wounds preventing the blood from clotting. The cuts and the stings started to hurt. Darnell felt a great lassitude seep through his body. Ravi cut strips from a kerchief and bound the wounds tightly. Bharatya beckoned them away from the bloodied stage to a clear space near the brazier.

Van Cuyler was already there, leaning for support on one of the Dutchmen. Bharatya placed his hands on both their shoulders. 'Both men have told the truth,' he cried, 'or both have lied. The snake's wisdom will reveal all. One of these men will die.'

Darnell sat on his heels. His arm hurt. He wasn't feeling any worse or any better. The day had turned quite humid and he'd begun to sweat again. The sweat would bring more poison out. He looked up at the sun, silvery behind grey cloud, but still warm enough to sear his cheeks.

Van Cuyler squatted across from him, staring at the stage, head lowered, no longer defiant. Another Dutchman stood over him, reading aloud from a Bible. 'I am the Resurrection and the life. Whoever believes in me shall live, even though he dies.' Darnell shut out the words. He would not have that kind of consolation.

He looked up. A little boy of about nine, wearing a white and gold embroidered tunic and a white turban with a small tiger's eye was squatting at the foot of the tiers, staring at him. The child had Seringa's round face, almond-shaped eyes and protuberant jaw. It was strange, Darnell had just been thinking of his own son. Darnell smiled at the boy and the boy smiled back shyly. Taking his bullet-bag from Ravi, Darnell rolled a bullet across the stage towards the boy. The boy grabbed it, studied the bullet carefully, and frowned at Darnell.

Darnell rolled a second bullet. Then a third. He thought that if he had to die, what better way to go than playing with a child? He signalled to the boy to roll one of the bullets back, and as Darnell leaned sideways to catch it, the boy laughed.

Bharatya turned at the sound. Young Arjuna was playing with Darnell. A man who chose to die playing with a child must have a clear conscience. He looked at van Cuyler. In contrast to Darnell, the Dutchman looked craven. He looked back at Darnell and Arjuna again, and then turned to Seringa. It was the sign he had been waiting for.

Seringa too had noticed. He raised his hand slightly, the first finger crossed against the third. Bharatya sent the priests with beakers of water to Darnell and van Cuyler and watched carefully as both men drank. Moments later, van Cuyler gasped, swayed and fainted. The Dutchmen milled round him. 'He is not dead but sleeps,' Bharatya called. 'Take him to his room and let him sleep. He will wake in three hours and be fully recovered.' He watched the Dutchmen bear van Cuyler away.

Darnell looked up. Seringa and Bharatya were standing in front of him. 'Most of the poison was drawn from the snakes before they were brought here,' Bharatya said. 'So if you've survived this long, you will live.'

Darnell looked at the space where the Dutch had been. 'How did van Cuyler –'

Bharatya smiled. 'The truth was revealed to me and I decided to change his *karma*.' He edged Seringa forward.

'You shall build your factory,' Seringa said. 'We will finalize the details tomorrow. But you must begin building in three weeks.'

'Three weeks,' Darnell repeated, his euphoria fading at the impossible task. 'Why three weeks?'

'Because word will get out and obstacles will be raised. There may even be a pre-emptive strike by Kokinada.' He smiled. 'In any case, we need the factory by the time the monsoon ends.'

'I understand.' But three weeks was impossible. Ovington wouldn't have reached Surat, and it would be three weeks at least before he heard from the council.

'If you have not started building in three weeks, we will have to make an arrangement with the Dutch,' Seringa said and, taking his son by the hand, walked away.

Chapter Eight

Cogan's office was long and rectangular, and filled with furniture. A row of chests stood beneath the grimy window, through which Darnell could see the *Santa Maria*, the ship that he'd been fortunate to catch in San Thome. The wall behind him was blocked by dusty cupboards whose ivory inlay was stained yellow from sunlight. A pile of grubby Turkoman carpets covered the space between the cupboards and the three hard leather chairs with sun-bleached backs that stood before Cogan's large desk. The desk-top was covered with untidy piles of ledgers and diaries. Darnell remembered Cogan had always kept things to himself, never delegating responsibility.

Cogan crouched behind the desk, puffing out his veined cheeks as he listened to what had happened at Vaidya. The room was hot and airless. The grey curls at the back of Cogan's neck sagged under the weight of his sweat.

'It's a fantastic deal,' Darnell said. He wished he knew what Cogan was thinking. 'We'll have exclusive trading rights for twenty years and an option to build three more factories. Seringa will find us the materials and labour we need to build at Madera. All we have to do is turn up with the money and start building.'

'We haven't got a thousand pounds,' Cogan said.

'We don't need all the money now, Andrew. All we need is an advance of two hundred pounds.'

'Seringa wants the factory completed as soon as possible, preferably before the monsoons?'

'That's right.'

Cogan frowned through the window at the sky. 'The

monsoon will be starting in six or seven weeks,' he said. 'You're going to need the thousand pounds by then.'

'Yes, and by then we'll have heard from Surat –'

'Ovington has only just reached Surat.' Cogan spoke slowly, as if lecturing a child. 'Even if the council meets with him right now – and we have no reason to assume they will – we won't hear from them for another three weeks. If the council approves the fort, it will take another four weeks to receive any money.' He leaned back in his chair and looked directly at Darnell. 'So what you're asking me to do is to advance you two hundred pounds now and a further eight hundred over the next two months.'

'You can always raise that money from the *chittys* right here in Pettahpoli.'

Cogan leaned forward across the desk. 'Let me make this very clear, Richard. Until the council approves Ovington's proposal, I won't advance you a *fanam*.'

'Lord Almighty, Andrew!' Darnell jumped to his feet. He pounded his fist in his palm and strode to the window. 'We can't wait for council approval. If we don't start building in three weeks, Seringa will make a deal with the Dutch.'

'A thousand pounds is a lot of money. Seringa could find the Dutch have the same problem.' Cogan threw Darnell a faint smile.

Darnell wasn't sure if Cogan meant to be consoling. He said, 'We can't gamble on that. Once the Dutch get into Vaidya, we're finished here, and in the spice trade.'

'Oh, it may not be as bad as that. We do have an agreement about new factories, you know.'

'Which the Dutch will ignore as they did in Java.'

'We have sanctions.'

'Which are worthless because the Dutch will prevaricate and postpone and appeal to Amsterdam and London. For heaven's sake Andrew, we've been through all this before! By the time your tribunal finds the Dutch guilty of breaching the agreement, they'll have built three factories in Vaidya and be ready to tear up the peace agreement.'

'I don't agree.' Cogan sighed and straightened his shoulders. 'In any case, what the Dutch might or might not do is not my concern. My concern is that I can't advance you anything until Surat or Ovington or London authorizes me to. And it's no good flinging up your hands in horror. If Surat or London refuse permission, I'm the one who'll be in trouble for authorizing the investment, not you.'

Darnell sat opposite Cogan and tried to speak calmly. 'Look, Andrew,' he said softly. 'This could be the most important deal of our lives, the most important deal in the Company's history. This deal is going to turn the Company round and, for the first time since we lost Java, it'll show profits. We'll both be rich men . . . very rich men.'

Cogan leaned back in his chair and stroked his chin. Darnell felt pleased he was giving the making of money the attention it deserved. He went on. 'You will make more money out of Madera than you do here. You can retire and rejoin Ann and your sons in England. As the man who turned the Company round, you'll be a director. You can send the boys to Rugby or Harrow and never have to worry about school fees again.'

Cogan smiled at the idea. He looked out of the window and his mouth twisted. 'Are you sure you're talking about me?'

'Of course I'm talking about you. If we pull this off, you're the one who'll get all the credit.'

'Don't try to befaddle me, Richard! We've known each other too long. You want this fort so *you* can be the richest man in the Indies, again.' Cogan leaned forward and slapped the desk. 'You want this fort so *you* can go back home and run the Company.'

Darnell said, 'If you give me the money, I'll give you a note agreeing to your being the first agent of Madera.'

Cogan pressed his lips together as he considered the

offer, then he shook his head. 'I don't trust you, Richard. Besides, if I approve the advance I will be in direct breach of a written Company order prohibiting the creation of new establishments without written permission from London.'

'That order has always been breached in exceptional circumstances, Andrew. The Company will understand.'

Cogan shook his head. 'No.' He bent down over his books. 'I think you'd better meet with Seringa and ask him for more time, and then return to Armagon and wait to hear from Ovington.'

Darnell walked slowly over to the pile of carpets and picked up his saddle-bags. Coromandel, his future, the Company, Davey Wheaton, Caddy, her boys, Crispin – all of them were finished. 'I've given Seringa my word,' Darnell said.

'That was foolish.'

'I'll borrow the money from one of the *chittys* in Pettah-poli and build the fort myself,' Darnell said.

Cogan looked up at him. 'Don't be damned silly, Richard. No one'll lend you the money. You've got nothing and your word's not good enough any more.'

Karel van Cuyler sniffed with disgust as he hurried his troop of four soldiers and their laden pack-horse through the narrow spaces between the squalid hovels of Sairin. Chickens squawked out of his way. Goats ran bleating before him. He ducked and twisted his head to avoid the face-ripping timbers protruding from the thatched roofs. Holding his breath against the reek of dung, which the villagers used for their floors and to repair their walls, he cantered into the open compound before Naik Ali Baig's brick-built house and stopped.

Ali Baig's guards lounged on the dust-blown veranda that ran along the front of the house. 'Hulloa sahib,' they cried in Hindi. 'How goes it with you? You come quickly. We tell Naik Ali Baig you come. He coming soon also.'

Naik Ali Baig was the cousin of the nizam of Kokinada. Three months ago, van Cuyler had come across a Dutch survey of the district, which, if shown to the nizam, would have revealed how much Ali Baig was cheating on land taxes. Van Cuyler had presented the survey to Ali Baig and promptly turned him into a loyal, ruthless and greedy ally.

Van Cuyler dismounted, his hand on his dagger. On his first visit the men had loosed a pit mongrel on him to see how fast a *feringhi* could run. Van Cuyler had ripped the dog's snout open with his dagger, stabbed it in the chest on its second pass, then kicked its ribs in. Both dog and men had learned that the Dutch did not run.

Ali Baig appeared at the front of the veranda, burly and beetle-browed, with grey speckled hair that stood up from his forehead like a coxcomb. A three-strand pearl necklace sagged across his chest. He wore a knee-length Persian-style *camise* pimpled with jewelled brooches. Beneath the *camise*, pyjama trousers were stuffed into knee-high boots. 'Hulloa, Dutch,' he called. 'You been gone a long time. I thought you'd forgotten us.'

Van Cuyler stepped on to the veranda. At five foot ten he was five inches taller than Ali Baig and looked down at the patches of bare scalp on top of the naik's head. 'I've brought you some wine.' He watched Ali Baig's narrow eyes fix themselves on the soldiers rolling two hogsheads of claret on to the veranda. Though his religion forbade alcohol, Ali Baig drank heavily.

The soldiers left the barrels on the veranda and returned to the horse. Van Cuyler watched Ali Baig walking round the barrels as if checking them for leaks. 'Wine?' he muttered, talking to himself. 'Two barrels?'

'It's French claret. You'll like it.'

'Two barrels.' Ali Baig raised his head abruptly and shouted, 'Ibrahim! Ibrahim!'

One of the men on the veranda rushed up.

'Give this to the men,' he said sarcastically. 'Tell them

it is a present from our generous fucking Dutch friends.'

Van Cuyler forced himself to remain calm. There had to be a reason for Ali Baig's rudeness. 'You should drink some yourself,' he called. 'Then you'll know exactly how generous we are.'

Ali Baig brushed past him, striding into the house. Van Cuyler followed him into a room at the side of the house. The room was small, shaded by windows half shut against the glare, with bare walls and a floor covered with rush mats. The only seating was cushions piled against the wall. Van Cuyler groaned inwardly. He'd been riding for four hours. Ali Baig pointed to a pile of cushions opposite him. Van Cuyler sighed and sat. 'That was excellent wine,' he said. 'You'll not see its like in Coromandel. Why did you give it to your men?'

'They deserved it.' Ali Baig's eyelids drooped balefully. He poured geneva from an earthenware flask into a goblet. A servant boy came in with a cup of steaming coffee which he gave to van Cuyler. Ali Baig drew at his hookah; the sweet smell of hashish permeated the room.

Van Cuyler decided not to pursue the matter of the wine. Ali Baig would tell him what was wrong, soon enough. 'Are you well?' he asked.

'What do you care about my health? What does it matter to you if my guts melt or I have the pox?'

'All right, I don't give a shit about your health or your pox. I came here to ask you to do a job for me.'

'A job like Celor?' Ali Baig laughed bitterly. 'How many people do you want me to kill this time for thirty pounds?'

Accompanied by Ali Baig and eight men, van Cuyler had followed the Portuguese from the pearl auction at Celor, the *kohl* that he'd used to darken his hair and beard becoming runny in the heat. The five Portuguese had been brightly illumined shades in the light of their camp fire when they had rushed in. '*Goondas!*' van Cuyler had shouted. 'Give us the pearls and we won't harm you!'

The oldest one, the merchant who'd bid successfully for the prize pearls, had clutched at his chest, his hand closing over the pouch of pearls pinned to his undershirt. The hand had felt bony and fragile as van Cuyler had grabbed it. All he'd wanted was to take the pearls and scare the Portuguese away from Celor. Celor was a Dutch monopoly and contributed hugely to the Dutch profits from Coromandel. He'd wanted it to stay that way. 'Give me the pearls and I won't harm you!' he'd repeated.

'No!' The merchant had stared at him, wide-eyed, arms across his chest. Then, 'There's dye running off your beard!' he'd cried in surprise. And, as if encouraged by that, he'd yelled, 'The Dutch! We're being attacked by the heathen Dutch!'

A growing ball of panic had filled van Cuyler. He couldn't afford to have the nizam find out the Dutch had robbed his visitors. He'd grabbed the merchant's hands. 'Give me the pearls!'

'No! No! The Dutch! The Dutch! We're being attacked by the dung-eating Dutch!'

Van Cuyler had plunged the knife into the merchant's throat. 'Kill them!' he'd shouted to Ali Baig. 'Kill all of them!'

Van Cuyler remembered the knife shuddering against his wrist, heard the chicken-bone snap of gristle as it plunged into the Portuguese merchant's throat. God knew he hadn't wanted to kill the merchant! But he'd been forced to! *Forced to!*

His whole body was shaking and he hugged his knees to stop it. The room was full of the sickly sweet smell of hashish. Ali Baig passed him the mouthpiece of the hookah, looking at him with an expression that was almost compassion. Van Cuyler inhaled gratefully and felt his inner trembling ease. 'I paid you twenty pounds more than we agreed,' he said.

'And kept the pearls! How much are those pearls worth,

Dutch? Twenty pounds?' Ali Baig reached into his *camise*. 'Here, I'll give you forty pounds for those pearls. What do you say, Dutch?'

Van Cuyler held on to the hookah and inhaled again before he spoke. He felt supremely confident. 'If I weren't a friend, I'd say yes.'

'You would –' Ali Baig looked surprised. Then he laughed. The Dutchman had smoked too much hashish. 'All right. Give me the pearls, the prize pearls.'

'Forty pounds would be forty times what they're worth.' His head was clearing now. He was feeling calm, already forgetting the horror of Celor.

'Don't try to fool me, Dutch. Those pearls are worth a thousand pounds if they're worth a *fanam*.'

'And your neck. Don't you realize those pearls have no provenance? That whoever is found selling them will have his hands cut off for theft and his head pounded in a mortar for murder?'

Ali Baig hadn't thought of that, but if it were true, why had the Dutchman kept the pearls?

Van Cuyler was saying, 'Those pearls are worthless. Whoever sells them will have to account for where he got them. Only the murderers of the Portuguese would have those pearls.'

'So what will you do with them?'

'Sell them quietly, one at a time, as and when I find persons who won't require provenance. Then, I promise, you'll get your share.'

Ali Baig decided he'd have to trust the Dutchman. He said, 'You cheat me and I'll come after you. Even into Pulicat.'

Van Cuyler thought there was little chance of that, but he said, 'I know.' The hashish was making him drowsy. He said, 'I've got a job for you, bigger than Celor. I will pay you forty pounds plus all the cloth you can steal.'

Ali Baig looked uncomfortable. Nothing was for nothing; if van Cuyler was offering so much, the job had to be very dangerous. Still, he had to find out. 'What do you want me to do?'

'I want you to seize all their goods and drive the English from Armagon.'

He'd been right. Van Cuyler wanted the world for his money. 'No,' Ali Baig said vehemently. 'No, no, no!'

'Why not? You've nothing to be afraid of. Armagon is the weakest factory on the coast. It doesn't have more than a dozen soldiers and its walls are like paper.'

'The nizam wants the English in Armagon!'

'So tell him the English abused your people, that they didn't pay their taxes.'

'But the English don't abuse their workers. And they've paid their taxes.'

'Raise taxes so high that they can't pay!'

Ali Baig thought about that. 'Who'll pay the taxes when the English leave?'

'We will. I'll give you a note confirming that.' Ali Baig was going to do it, van Cuyler thought with relief. Darnell would lose his only means of financing the fort, which meant in four weeks' time, Madera would be Dutch and Darnell hopelessly defeated. He stroked his beard to disguise his pleasure and said, 'You can keep everything you take from the English. All their cloth. All their liquor. All their trade goods.'

With the voyages from England due, Ali Baig knew the English warehouses would be full with nearly eight hundred pounds' worth of goods. Even if he sold them at a discount he'd be rich. It was a tempting thought. 'What about the abused weavers?' he asked.

'I'll produce them.'

Ali Baig looked mollified. Then he said, 'I don't want cloth, I want cash. Who'll buy the English cloth?'

'You might find some merchants or ship captains –'

'No. You will buy the English cloth.'

Van Cuyler thought not. The Dutch had little need for cloth, and de Groot certainly would not buy stolen English cloth for fear of breaching the truce. He said, 'You will get a better price elsewhere.'

'That's possible. But the price I get from you will be certain.'

There was a hardness in Ali Baig's face and a firmness in his tone that made van Cuyler think he'd reached a sticking point. He thought that if the goods were discounted highly enough, de Groot could be persuaded to buy the English cloth. 'We'll buy them for a hundred pounds,' he said.

'Those goods are worth at least six hundred.' Ali Baig shook his head. 'Three hundred.'

De Groot would never go that high. 'Impossible.'

'Then I won't do it.'

'Two hundred.'

Ai Baig shook his head again.

'In gold.'

'Silver.'

'Done.'

'And two hogshead of geneva.'

'One.'

'Agreed.'

Van Cuyler stretched his numbing legs and laughed. 'My friend, we have an agreement.'

By late afternoon Darnell had begun to believe Cogan was right. Even at eighteen per cent, not one of Pettahpoli's five native financiers wanted to lend him money to build a fort.

He returned despondently to Caddy's and spent the afternoon playing with Crispin. His last hope was Abdul Nana.

In the Company's record book, Nana was listed as an arrack supplier. In fact he owned two bars and three brothels and invested the cash surplus from these and other enterprises in money-lending. Abdul Nana's money-lending business centred on those poorer merchants and farmers who the more established financiers considered were too risky to lend to. Abdul Nana shared his competitors' views and took brutal steps to ensure his loans were repaid.

Shortly after sunset, Darnell left for the waterfront to find Abdul Nana. The area outside the Sea Gates, thronged during the day with carts and coolies and heavy loads being moved to and fro, was pocked with light from the dismal doorways of houses huddling in the shadow of the giant warehouses. Furtive figures scurried between the patches of light. Women in tight blouses and knee-length sarongs sidled in and out of the light, the garish scent of their perfume mingling with the sickly smells of hashish, *ganja*, coffee and rotting fish. The narrow path between the houses was slippery with mud and refuse. Darnell kept his hands close to his knife as he walked.

He climbed on to the veranda of Diego's, the largest and most popular bar on the waterfront. Shadowy figures sat at tables surrounded by the fireflies of pipes, hookahs and small native *beedis*. Voices babbled in counterpoint to the steady rumble of the sea. Darnell brushed aside serving wenches and strode to the large room at the back.

It was hot, smoky and noisy. Men sat at unpainted tables fixed to the floor, and women bearing trays of food and brimming tankards pushed their way round the room. Music from a sweating four-piece Portuguese band bounced off the walls and made his eardrums flutter. Diego, a short, round-shouldered Portuguese with a drooping moustache and a red shirt open to his belly presided over the scene from behind a large bar at the back, sweating profusely as he humped beakers of ale on to a tray. Smoke from the cooking fire behind the bar assailed Darnell's nostrils, bearing with it smells of curry and frying garlic.

Darnell's nose wrinkled and his eyes smarted as he reached the bar, ordered port, and asked where he could find Nana.

'Not here. Try one of the native bars.' Diego thumped a mug of port before Darnell.

Darnell finished his port quickly and left. The veranda outside was blessedly cool.

'Mizzer Darnell! Mizzer Darnell!'

Darnell recognized the scrawny, bow-legged figure of Captain Sen stumping across the veranda, stained white cap thrust over the back of his untidy, speckled curls, *khatar* and fighting iron dangling from the belt of his grubby calico breeches.

'Come and have a drink, Mizzer Darnell. I know where this rascal of a Portuguee has some fine double-distilled arrack.' He laid a surprisingly large hand on Darnell's shoulder.

Darnell moved away. 'No thanks, Sen. Right now I've got some business to do.'

'All right then, we talk bizness. Good bizness.'

Darnell resisted. Sen was a country ship captain, sailing a leaky schooner, the *Hughli Star*, from various ports in Bengal to the Red Sea. The last time they'd discussed 'bizness', it had cost Darnell four days and a hundred pounds and left him with the grandfather of all hang-overs. 'Another time, Sen. I'm busy now.'

He found Abdul Nana in the fourth bar he visited, seated at the back with eight of his followers, four of whom, with their scarred faces and *tabars* placed arrogantly on the table, looked like body-guards.

They turned like hostile dogs at Darnell's approach. As Darnell introduced himself, Nana stared at him, a fat, round man who, except for a thin dusting of fuzz above his eyes, seemed completely hairless. His head shone. His cheeks shone. The rolls of fat round his neck shone. He wore a long striped burnous and a fez and his podgy hands glittered with rings. A flagon of toddy stood on the table before him, and beside it a dish of goat meat.

Nana pushed the man nearest him away and waved to Darnell to sit beside him. He offered Darnell some goat meat. The meat was chilli-hot and highly spiced, and Darnell accepted a glass of toddy gratefully, drinking the cool, milky liquid, and feeling it warm his stomach at the same time as it quenched the burn in his mouth.

His mouth full, Nana asked without preamble, 'What do you want?'

Darnell said, 'I want to borrow a thousand pounds for three to six months.'

Nana chewed thoughtfully. His skin, Darnell noticed, was more pale brown than black, and his eyes were surprisingly light. 'That is the story of life,' Nana said. 'Everyone wants to borrow money.' He shouted to a waiter to bring more goat meat and toddy. 'What do you want this money for?'

'To build a factory. We need to complete this factory as quickly as possible, before our agreement with the Dutch is fully implemented.'

'Why won't the Company put up the money?'

'It's the end of the season and none of our factories has much cash.'

The thin fuzz on Abdul Nana's forehead knitted in puzzlement.

Darnell went on. 'The agreement with the Dutch prevents us from building new factories. It was signed last week, and we only realized afterwards that if we wanted to build another factory without Dutch approval we'd have to build it now, before the monsoons.' With repeated telling the story came out fluently.

Nana looked at him sharply. 'Why isn't the Company borrowing from your chief merchant or the big lenders here in Pettahpoli?'

'It is the end of the season and they too are short of cash.'

Abdul Nana asked, 'Why are you looking for this loan and not Mr Cogan? Why are you looking for this loan in bars and not at the Company offices?'

'The new factory is my responsibility,' Darnell replied. 'I like to do business fast, even if that means meeting in bars.'

'Where is this factory being built?'

'Near the Vaidya border.'

'When will you need the money?'

'I'll need two hundred pounds tomorrow, the rest in equal instalments over nine weeks.' Darnell's heart sang with relief.

Abdul Nana squeezed his eyebrows together. 'I will want Company guarantee, your guarantee, guarantee of Mr Cogan and all English council people in Pettahpoli.' He wiped the sweat from his fingertips on his *dhoti*.

Darnell's mouth went dry. He drank some toddy. 'You can have my personal guarantee, but the council doesn't give personal guarantees. You know that.'

Abdul Nana's smooth face was expressionless. 'You give me Company guarantee then, and your guarantee.'

Darnell licked his lips before he spoke. 'There's a problem with the Company guarantee,' he said. 'It will have to be signed at a special council meeting in Surat and getting it there and back will take at least a month. We must start building next week.'

'Mr Cogan and English council can give guarantee until you get guarantee from Surat.'

Darnell smiled, and hoped his smile was convincing. 'We have a problem with that, too. Mr Cogan and the English council are not authorized to give guarantees. Only Surat can do that. We'll only need the money for a few weeks,' Darnell said, speaking quickly, 'until the paperwork between Pettahpoli and Surat has been sorted out.'

Nana studied him carefully from beneath lowered lids. Then he said, 'I'm afraid that is not good enough. What is important is that my money is safe. And without a Company or council guarantee it is not safe.' He shook his head. 'I think, my friend, you'd better try elsewhere.'

Darnell walked despondently towards the fort, telling himself he was not defeated, that somehow he would find the money. Timana Chitty, his chief merchant at Armagon, would be good for fifty pounds, and he and Ravi Winter could find a similar amount. That still left a shortfall of –

A hand reached out of the darkness and grabbed his shoulder.

'By the Cross!' He'd been so involved with his problem he'd forgotten where he was. 'Bastard!' he shouted, reaching for his knife.

'Mizzer Darnell,' Captain Sen breathed out of the darkness. 'Now can we talk bizness?' His cap glimmered faintly in the gloom, matching his peak-toothed smile. He kept his hand on Darnell's shoulder.

Darnell straightened up, heart pounding, his body covered in sweat. 'You should be more careful grabbing people in the dark,' he warned. 'The next time I might shoot first.'

'Next time I'll be more careful.' Sen released his shoulder. Though he smelt worse than in Diego's bar, he walked with no more than his customary roll. 'What're you doing with a shark like Abdul Nana?' he asked. 'He'll chop you into little pieces and eat you with his *chappati*.'

'I need money,' Darnell said. 'Why else would I talk to Abdul Nana?'

They walked a few yards in silence. Finally Sen asked, 'How much money? Maybe I kin help.'

Darnell felt a wave of affection for the old rogue. 'That's very kind of you, but it's too much money.'

'Not much, too much, enough, who knows? How much money you want, Mizzer Darnell?'

'A thousand pounds.'

To Darnell's surprise, Sen did not seem put out by the amount. 'That is not impossible,' he said.

'The devil you mean "not impossible"?' Darnell asked, running the words together in his excitement. 'Where would you get one thousand pounds?'

'I could sell my ship.'

'But seriously?'

Sen stopped and looked at Darnell. 'But seriously, Mizzer Darnell, we could do business and you could make one thousand pounds.' He looked over his shoulder. 'Let's go see if we can get that Portuguee bastard give us some of his good arrack.'

At Diego's they sat on a now almost empty veranda while Sen gave the serving wench twenty *fanams* and told her not to let Diego palm her off with any of his cheap arrack. Then he turned his attention to Darnell. 'Them Dutch bastards double-crossed me,' he said.

Sen had had a deal with the Dutch in Binlipatam to buy their entire stock of *sallores* and *guzzees* – turkey red and coarse cottons – which sold best in Arab and African markets. The Dutch, however, learning of the war in Persia and expecting prices to rise, had refused to deliver the cloth. Sen now had a large order he could not fulfil, and would be liable to heavy damages. 'Typical muther-fuggin' Dutch trick,' Sen finished.

Darnell frowned. He couldn't see how he could make a thousand pounds out of Sen's difficulty.

Sen said, 'Mizzer Darnell, at Armagon you have the worst cloth in Coromandel. Only people who buy it are Arabs. I would like to buy all your cloth.'

'That's impossible!' To avoid being cheated, and to ensure that it always had a supply of cloth, there were a million regulations preventing private sales of Company cloth to natives.

'Why impossible? You sell your cloth to me, I sell cloth to

Arab peoples, you happy, me happy, Arab peoples happy.'

'You know the Company won't let me sell you all our cloth.' Even if he ignored Company regulations and sold Sen the cloth, it wouldn't fetch more than six hundred pounds.

Sen shook his head as if bewildered. 'No, Mizzer Darnell, you wrong. Company stop other people. Company not stop you. You Company *bahadur*. You famous man. Company let you sell cloth and build your fort, and give you nice present afterwards.'

If only that were true, Darnell thought. The serving wench came with two glasses and a beaker of water. Sen sniffed the glass appreciatively. 'This the real stuff, Mizzer Darnell. You smell, you see?'

Darnell sniffed. It was true. The liquor didn't have the sharp, acidic stench of the cheaper arrack. He took a sip and thought over Sen's suggestion. With six hundred pounds from the sale of the cloth, borrowings from Timana Chitty and his own investment, he could just about finance the fort. But what about the Company? What about Cogan? What about closing down Armagon on his own initiative and building at Vaidya, contrary to the directive of 18 February 1628/9?

Sen asked, 'How much stock you sell me, Mizzer Darnell? I give you good price, bes' price.'

Darnell said, 'I have some muslins and fine cloth from Vaidya.'

'I buy them. I buy everything from you Mizzer Darnell. How much?'

'A thousand pounds,' Darnell said. Once he began building at Madera, he'd be in so much trouble that the closing down of Armagon and the Company's directive would scarcely matter.

Captain Sen laughed and clapped his hands. 'Mizzer Darnell, I thought you was my friend. You no got thousand pounds' worth of cloth at Armagon, even if you smuggle from Vaidya every day. I give you bes' price. Four hundred pounds.'

'You're a thief, Sen,' Darnell cried in mock anger. 'You would see me and all the English at Armagon starve so you can make your miserable little profit.' He drank more arrack. 'Nine hundred pounds. That is my last price.'

They bargained vigorously for the next hour, eventually agreeing a price of six hundred pounds.

'I want cash,' Darnell said. 'Not pro notes. Not loans on the security of your brother's wife's jewellery, or even on your brother's wife.'

'I unnerstan', Mizzer Darnell.'

'Cash,' Darnell repeated. 'Any currency will do; but it must be cash.'

'All right, Mizzer Darnell,' Sen agreed, 'but in two weeks.'

'I want the money before then.'

'Ten days bes' I can do, Mizzer Darnell.'

Ten days was cutting it very fine, but if Sen would deliver the cash, then his problem was solved. He repeated, 'It must be cash, Sen, for the whole amount.'

'Yes, Mizzer Darnell. You go to Armagon and get cloth ready. I be there with the *Hughli Star* in ten days.'

'You try to shortchange me on the cash and I'll cut your balls off and make you eat them.'

Sen laughed. 'Is good, Mizzer Darnell, that I not holy-holy Hindu vegetarian.'

Chapter Nine

Darnell knew something was wrong the moment he rode into Armagon. It was gone four o'clock and the short evening was just beginning. The settlement's three rutted streets were deserted. The native bazaar to his left, normally a hubbub of trinket vendors, gram sellers and men selling fruit, vegetables, *dosai*, sherbet, cloth, chicken and mutton was empty. The long row of brick-built rooms where the washers, peons and servants lived was shut fast, its long veranda devoid of women and bawling, half-naked children. The rows of clothes-lines before it, normally a-flutter with yard upon yard of freshly washed cloth, gleamed blankly in the sun.

Darnell urged his horse to the flat area of bare earth before the factory house known as the factory square. A lone sentry stood outside the factory house. As Darnell stopped, a manservant trotted down the steps and seized the horse's bridle. 'Hulloa, sahib! You come back. Is good, is good.'

Darnell dismounted. 'Where's everybody?'

'Everybody gone with Winter sahib to workshop in barracks.'

What the devil was Ravi doing there, Darnell wondered? Leaving the servant to take care of his horse, he hurried into the factory house. The hallway inside was cool and dark. The familiar warehouse smells of new cloth, sandalwood and spices seeped out from the open door across the hallway. Inside the warehouse, his chief merchant, Timana Chitty, stood amidst barrels of pepper and shelves piled high with cloth. 'Just the man I want to see,' Darnell said, beckoning to him to follow him to the main offices upstairs.

The main offices were a series of partitioned rooms separated by a corridor. They occupied the entire floor. Darnell's office was to the right, with a large window facing the sea. The window was closed and his chair, desk and papers were covered with a thin layer of dust. He flicked at the dust with his hat and sat. Timana Chitty stood at the door, hands shyly steepled before his chest. Darnell waved him to a chair. He shouted for Rawlins, the young writer who'd come out from England four months earlier. He hurried in, his freckles inflamed by the sun. Darnell sent him to fetch Ravi, then turned to Timana Chitty. 'We're going to build a new fort in Vaidya,' Darnell said abruptly.

Perching uncertainly on the edge of his chair, Timana Chitty nodded approval. He was a great black pudding of a man, swaddled in a white turban, tunic and *dhoti*, his red and blue chief merchant's sash wrapped proudly round his ample waist. 'Vaidya, very good for business. Good for cloth.'

'We need money to build the fort,' Darnell said. 'How much can you raise?'

'How much you want?'

'The fort will cost about a thousand pounds.'

Timana Chitty shook his head in large semi-circles. His cheeks and eyelids drooped with the pain of his refusal. 'Most sorry, sahib. I cannot lend such a sum at the moment. At the moment everything out on stock: Company stock, people's stock, some farmer's business.' He shrugged. 'When the voyages come, perhaps, but even then, soon after voyages people borrow more money for more stock.'

That was the truth. People borrowed to buy stock, repaid their loans when the voyages arrived with money from England, then borrowed again for the next season's stock. Timana Chitty wasn't a big enough financier to have two hundred pounds spare after he'd made the seasonal loans due to his regular customers. But, Darnell thought, Timana Chitty came from a family of money-lenders. Money-lending was a function of his caste. 'Couldn't you borrow the money from your family?' Darnell asked.

Timana Chitty pinched his cheeks together as he considered that. Each member of the family worked his own territory, and the family rarely combined as a single unit. 'It will be difficult,' he said. 'But I will try.'

'We'll need the money in ten days,' Darnell said.

Timana Chitty shook his head. 'That is impossible, Mr Darnell,' he said softly. 'Very, very impossible.'

Ravi Winter pushed into the room. His hair hung in damp streaks, his tunic and breeches were filthy, and great rivulets of sweat ran down his face. 'Thank God you're back, Richard,' he cried. 'Ali Baig's goin' to attack us!'

'What the devil's got into Ali Baig?' Darnell dismissed Timana Chitty with a wave.

'I don't know. 'E came here coupla hours ago with about thirty of his men, arrogant as Lucifer. Wouldn't even get off that bag o' bones 'e calls a 'orse. 'E asked for you and when I told 'im you was away, 'e said we'd better pay the taxes we owe.'

'We don't owe any bloody taxes!'

'Right. We've paid everything we owe and paid Ali Baig his *bakshee*.'

'So what the devil does he want?'

''E says these are new taxes. 'E wants an eighty per cent surcharge on the value of all the goods in the fort.'

'Eighty per cent! I'll see that scum-sucking fornicator in hell before I pay him a *fanam*!' Darnell slammed the side of his hand on the desk.

Ravi grinned. 'I thought you'd say that. I told 'im we didn't 'ave the money to pay 'im and even if we did, we wouldn't. 'E said, unless we did, 'e was goin' to come back and take all our goods.'

Darnell thought of the goods he had promised Captain

Sen disappearing together with the finance for the fort. 'Was Ali Baig serious?'

'Cross me heart, 'e was. I sent one of the lads after 'im and, sure 'nuff 'e's camped about two miles from 'ere wi' about a hunerd an' fifty men.'

Ali Baig was serious then. Even if his men were poor fighters, they outnumbered the English fifteen to one and those were impossible odds. 'What're you doing to defend the fort?'

'I've sent the washers and traders away and told the others to stay in the lines. I've got some of the soldiers making ammunition – we've got less than ten rounds a man. I'm also having the cannon made ready. The only working one's on the sea wall,' Ravi said. 'I've 'ad a plat-form built an' hitched to a train of bullocks. It should be ready any time now. As soon as it is, we'll move the cannon.'

Darnell got to his feet. 'I'll come and help.'

'We need every pair of 'ands we can get.'

Young Rawlins knocked and came in. 'Beg pardon, Mr Darnell, there's a party of Portuguese merchants in the square, asking if they can stay the night?'

'They can't,' Darnell said, 'but I'll see to them.'

He hurried down the front stairs. The Portuguese stood grouped in a weary semi-circle at the foot of the factory house steps; five young men flanking an elderly merchant and his son. Each of them had pistols and daggers and the young men carried swords. Their clothes and horses were covered with dust. The horses' heads drooped with fatigue.

'*Boa noite*, senhor,' the older man said. 'I am Manuel Figueras. We are merchants from San Thome, members of the House of da Soares. We seek your hospitality for the night.'

'For your own sakes I must refuse you,' Darnell said. 'We are about to be attacked by natives. You will be safer continuing your journey south to San Thome.'

'How do we know these natives won't attack us as we leave here?'

Darnell started in surprise. The voice was a young woman's. Figueras was not travelling with his son but with his daughter! Darnell looked more closely at her. The face under the shadow of the large hat was smooth and hairless, and he could make out the swell of breasts beneath the lines of the loose leather doublet and grey silk tunic.

'The natives' quarrel is with us. They want to seize our goods for what they claim is unpaid taxes. If you leave now –'

'We saw the native force as we rode here,' the woman said. 'That is why we came here, to seek the protection of your walls and cannon.'

'We are outnumbered fifteen to one,' Darnell said. 'It would be safer if you continued your journey south,' he repeated.

The woman turned and carried on a whispered conversation with Figueras. Then she dismounted in a swift, flowing movement and came up to Darnell, walking with an easy litheness and a jangle of spurs. Her yellow breeches were thrust carelessly into expensive knee-high boots, and a knife and a pistol with a worn butt hung from the broad leather belt at her waist. She wore little jewellery, a ring and a gold crucifix on a thin gold chain round her neck. She stood in front of Darnell and tilted her broad-brimmed hat back to see him better.

Her face was an etching in sandstone: snub-nosed, level-eyed, dimpled and oh so alive! Her skin was pale brown and smooth. Her eyes sent a quiver of excitement through him. They were deep, dark limpid pools that reached to infinity. Darnell thought he could drown in those eyes and rapidly checked himself. She couldn't be more than nineteen, and she was Portuguese. Darnell avoided looking at her eyes. A captivating dimple divided her chin and another sat on the soft bloom of her cheek. Darnell felt his breath catch.

'I am Ynessa da Soares,' she said. 'And you are . . . ?'

'Richard Darnell. I am the agent here.'

'Senhor Darnell, we have decided to stay. Despite what you say, we believe we will be safer inside your fort than on the road. At least here we have the protection of your soldiers, your walls and your cannon. If the natives were to attack us on the road –' She shrugged helplessly. 'Seven of us wouldn't have much chance against a hundred and fifty natives. Besides, two of our horses are lame and need new shoes. The rest are too exhausted to go much further.'

Darnell looked at the horses. The woman spoke the truth. He said, 'You and your party may stay *menina* – at your own risk.'

She turned and gestured to the men to dismount. 'I place my bodyguard under your command, senhor. They will help you with your defence.'

Darnell took a deep breath. 'You will find accommodation on the topmost floor of the factory house,' he said and, ordering the men to follow him, marched quickly towards the Sea Gate.

It was strange that any woman, let alone a young and beautiful Portuguese woman, should travel unchaperoned with six men. Even more strange that she should control those men. She was quite clearly the daughter of the da Soares merchant house. But for a Portuguese woman – for any woman – to have such authority was incredible. Darnell remembered her eyes and felt a curious warm shiver. He forced his attention on the top of the sea wall, where soldiers and coolies were milling round the cannon. Further along the wall, carters pushed and pulled reluctant bullocks up steep steps. He hurried to the Sea Gate.

The stone steps beside it were broken and loose in their sockets. He went up carefully, followed by the Portuguese.

The wind whipped his face and snatched at his tunic and hair as he reached the top. A soldier stood at the join of the north and east walls with a spyglass, surveying Ali Baig's troops.

Karl Eckaerts, the commander in charge of twelve ragged soldiers, broke away from the crowd round the cannon and shambled towards him. 'Good to see you, Mr Darnell. You're just in time to help us move this mother.'

Eckaerts's tunic was unbuttoned and his trunks hung outside his boots. As usual he smelt of stale wine. Darnell introduced the Portuguese, and Eckaerts sent them to join the crowd round the cannon. 'This'll have to work, Mr Darnell,' Eckaerts said. 'We've had no time to make up more ammunition.' He walked Darnell to the cannon.

The cannon sat in a raised embrasure overlooking the sea. Soldiers and coolies were packed around it, trying to roll the cannon on to a board angled against the rear of the embrasure, and then down on to the top of the wall. Further along the wall, bullocks stood ready to tow the cannon to an embrasure on the land wall. It was the quickest way to move the gun – and the most dangerous. The gun and its carriage weighed nearly three thousand pounds; if the gun came down the board too fast, it would launch itself on to the compound twenty feet below. Eckaerts pointed out the winch that would control the descent, and Darnell checked the attachments, the tension of the chains, and the ropes Eckaerts had put in as extra security. Everything looked good.

He saw Ravi in the middle of the crowd, pointing and shouting. 'All ready,' he cried from below.

'Mr Darnell, sir, could you acquaint me with what is happening?'

Darnell recognized the quavering tones and spidery figure of Archibald Quince. As far as Darnell knew, Quince did not appear on any Company register. He'd been at Armagon when Darnell arrived, and said he'd been there when Armagon was founded. He traded a little and lived off his profits. He had no family, and Darnell had never queried his position with Pettahpoli or Surat, and had allowed him to continue living at Armagon, as he always seemed to have done.

'I knew there was something wrong when Mr Winter wanted every pair of hands on the sea wall,' Quince said. Despite the heat he wore a dark tunic, ruffles, trunks and stockings. He began to roll up his sleeves. 'I'll do my best to help.'

'Move it lads, move it,' Ravi called out from below. 'Heave! Heave! Heave!'

Darnell left Quince and joined the soldiers and coolies crowding round the cannon. He grabbed hold of the wooden frame and heaved. 'One, two, shift! One, two, shift!' The gun was ten feet long, half of it resting on the wooden four-wheeled carriage. Darnell's muscles tautened. Sweat trickled into his eyes. 'One, two, shift! One, two, shift!' Everyone cheered as with a cracking, scraping sound the cannon moved.

'Hold it!' There was a frantic heaving and scrabbling as they tried to line up the cannon with the board. 'Push! Push! Lift! Lift!' Darnell ran with the others to the front of the carriage and pressed his shoulder to the wooden wheel. The cannon began to trundle down the board. The chains holding the towing rings rattled. 'Lock it! Lock it!' Eckaerts shouted. Men flung their weight on the handle of the winch. The chain clattered and stopped. Then slowly, agonizingly, with a whining scrape from the winch, the chains unwound and the cannon rolled slowly down to the wall.

Darnell skipped to the next embrasure and jumped down to receive the cannon. The gun had to be turned at right-angles so it could be lined up with the yoked bullocks further along the wall. Everyone bent. 'One, two, altogether now, heave!' The gun moved sixty degrees to the wall. They bent and heaved again. One more heave and it would be aligned with the bullocks. Darnell stood aside.

'It will be an honour to take your place, sir,' Quince's voice suddenly piped up, and he thrust himself into the mass of heaving bodies.

'Thank you, Mr Quince,' Darnell cried, and ran along the wall to where the soldier was watching Ali Baig's troops.

He took the spyglass and looked. Ali Baig's rabble were filtering on to the esplanade before the west gate in a steady stream. A few of them were mounted on scrawny horses and wore scraps of body armour. Most of them carried *lathis*, the others a haphazard assortment of pikes, spears and *tulwars*. Darnell couldn't see Ali Baig. A cart with tree-trunks for use as battering rams lurched through the mob. He made a rough count of the men. About ninety. The rest were obviously coming with Ali Baig. They'd attack in about an hour, he reckoned.

The men had chained the gun carriage to the six bullocks, and were inching it along the top of the wall, the carters urging the bullocks with loud slaps and cries of '*Jukmuk*.' The cannon was a demi-culverin, capable of firing nine pounds of shot. Three or four rounds from it among Ali Baig's rabble would send them scampering back to Sairin, Darnell thought.

Suddenly the huge cannon started to tilt. The rhythmic chanting of the soldiers and coolies turned to shouts and screams as an awful sliding sound filled his ears, accompanied by the rumble of falling stone and the startled, agonized bellowing of bullocks. Horrified, Darnell saw the earth wall break under the cannon, saw men try to hurl themselves away from the falling rush of earth and stones. As he stared helplessly, the carriage slewed sideways, sweeping earth and stones before it in a wild, gigantic slide. For an agonizing moment the bullocks strained to hold their footing. Then, legs still splayed, they were dragged inexorably downward, heads lifted above the dust, eyes rolling in panic. The carriage and the bullocks were plunging downwards; finally the gun broke free with a horrendous crack, gouging its path before sliding to a halt, its barrel buried in the earth. The carriage too tumbled to a standstill, one miraculously unbroken wheel turning slowly above the dust. There was a terrible silence. Darnell began to run.

Dust was everywhere, thick and blinding. Peering through the cloud, Darnell could see men picking themselves up or standing about, dazed, while others slid down the pile of rubble. The bullocks bayed. Darnell looked anxiously about him for anyone injured.

'Help me! Someone please help me!'

Tunic held in front of his face, Darnell followed the sound.

The voice, weak and rasping, came from behind the upturned gun carriage. Quince's voice. Darnell groped his way to it. The carriage lay on its side, tilted at an angle along the slope of the rubble. A white-haired head and a pair of thin arms stuck out from beneath one end of the carriage, stockinged legs from underneath the other.

'Help! Help!'

Darnell struggled up the pile of rubble, grabbed the end of the carriage and heaved. It moved. The rubble beneath him shifted. Quince gave a shrill scream. Darnell lifted again, and shouted urgently, 'Move man, get out!' He heard scuffling beneath him.

'Goddamn it sir, I cannot move! I seem to be stuck!'

Darnell looked down. Quince was lying on his back, the edge of the carriage above his grotesquely splayed hips. He wasn't stuck, he was crippled.

'Help!' Darnell shouted. He couldn't take the weight of the carriage much longer. He would have to let the carriage down on the elderly merchant. The weight dragged at his hands. The carriage was going. He didn't have enough leverage. The carriage was slipping through his hands.

'Right, Mr Darnell!' Eckaerts, Winter and two soldiers lurched out of the dust. The soldiers jammed themselves under the sliding carriage and the pressure on Darnell's back eased. 'Come out of there!' Eckaerts dragged out Quince. Then the soldiers pushed upwards and jumped. The carriage crashed to the ground, throwing up earth and dust.

'You all right?' Ravi kept asking. 'You all right?'

Darnell's palms were bleeding and his arms felt as if they had been put through a mangle. 'Yes,' he breathed as two more soldiers appeared with a litter and lifted Quince on to it. Through the dust he saw the da Soares woman and Figueras, kneeling beside a coolie. As he watched, the woman tore a strip off her shirt and bandaged the coolie's leg, then ordered her Portuguese to carry him to the barracks. She stood up and moved towards another fallen figure.

Eckaerts came up to them. 'Sorry, Mr Darnell. The load must have been too heavy for the wall.'

They walked to where the cannon lay buried in rubble. It would take days to get it clear and on to the west wall. He'd have to surrender the fort to Ali Baig, Darnell thought. His despair made him angry.

Something moaned. He looked down at a hideously twisted bullock's head. Large, bovine eyes rolled up over a mouth flecked with froth and blood. The rear of the animal's body was flattened and lifeless and two legs were bent at right-angles. Darnell took out his pistol, knelt down, pressed the weapon to the animal's ear and fired. The bullock's head jerked under the impact of the ball. Blood spouted on to Darnell's breeches. The rolling eyes stilled and air guffawed out of collapsing lungs. Darnell stood back and wiped his hands on the front of his breeches. 'See to the animals,' he told Ravi. 'Shoot those who are too badly hurt.'

'We haven't enough ammunition,' Ravi said.

'Do it,' Darnell ordered.

Eckaerts asked, 'What are we going to do, Mr Darnell?'

Darnell remembered the Dutch ambush on the way to Venkatapur. 'How much gunpowder do we have?'

'Three barrels.'

'And grenades?'

'Half a dozen.'

'Fit the gunpowder barrels with cloth covers and place one in front on the *maidan*, one beside the road from the Land Gate and one in the middle of the factory square. Then clear the barricades from the west gate and bring the grenades with you to the factory house. Go quickly! Do it now!'

Eckaerts left at something between a shamble and a run. Darnell yanked up the ends of his tunic and wiped his face. When he looked up, Ynessa da Soares was striding towards him through the thinning dust, followed at a respectful distance by Figueras.

He looked like a conquistador, Ynessa thought, standing astride the dead bull, his face and rolling mane of hair covered with dust. His raised tunic revealed a narrow waist and a stomach alive with muscle. His body would feel solid and hard, she thought, and was amazed that she could think such things at a time like this. It was the devil, she told herself. Bishop Ephraim and Mother Anastasia had warned her that the devil would tempt her at the most unexpected moments. Jesus, Mother Mary, forgive me, she prayed silently and called, 'Senhor Darnell, I want to talk to you.'

Darnell let the tunic fall over his naked stomach. He was exhausted and irritable. He had to check on the wounded, change his clothes, and check that Eckaerts had fixed the gunpowder barrels properly. 'Later, *menina*,' he said.

'No, senhor, now. I insist.' She stopped, staring in revulsion at the dead bull.

Darnell didn't move. If she insisted on talking to him now, let her do it here, standing beside the bull. That would keep the conversation short.

He was daring her to look at the bull, Ynessa thought. Damned men! All her life she'd had to deal with their pathetic attempts to demonstrate their superiority. In business they patronized her or avoided her; some tried to impress and others swore in front of her. Deliberately she fixed her eyes on the bull. She would not give him the satisfaction of seeing her faint. As she came closer, she raised her eyes and asked, 'What are you going to do now that you have no cannon?'

'We're going to fight,' Darnell said, disturbed that she had accepted his challenge and won.

'Wouldn't it make more sense if you negotiated a surrender?' She spread her arms out. 'Look around you. The walls of your fort are crumbling. Your cannon are rusty and need repair. You have few soldiers. You can't defend this place against a large native army. Better negotiate now and fight another day.'

Speaking softly, she added, 'I am concerned because our lives depend on your decision, senhor. I know it is hard for a man to think of surrender. But this time there does not appear to be an alternative.'

Darnell felt his skin crawl with irritation. This was none of her bloody business. 'Surrender is not an alternative,' he snapped. 'Ali Baig's claim for unpaid taxes is a pretext to allow him to seize our goods. Ali Baig wants to drive us from Armagon.'

'Why?'

'Because he's been put up to it by the nizam, or more likely the god-rottin' Dutch.'

'In that case, senhor, you must take your soldiers and mine, line them on the parapet over the Land Gate and have them pour fire on Ali Baig as he approaches.'

'We haven't enough ammunition,' Darnell said.

Ynessa frowned. 'Then you must send your men into the crowd and take this Ali Baig prisoner. Once you have him, his rabble will disappear.'

Or go berserk, Darnell thought. Then another thought struck him. He had to arrange some protection for this woman. The natives were no longer frightened of the Portuguese and what they would do to a woman once they overran the fort was unthinkable. He said, '*Menina*, I want you to go right away with your men to the factory house and stay there on the topmost floor until this is over.'

'No,' she said. 'You haven't enough soldiers. We will stay with you and fight.'

'You will not,' Darnell snapped. 'This is my fort. You will do as I say.' He turned to Figueras. 'You heard my orders. Take the senhora away.'

'But, but –' She beat her fists in frustration. '*Estupido*! You will be the death of us all!'

Darnell hurried to the barracks where Ravi was treating the injured. Apart from Quince who had a fractured thigh, no one else was seriously hurt. Darnell spoke to the injured and went to his apartment in the factory house.

The windows were shut, the apartment smelt fetid, and it was so hot he immediately broke into a sweat. He went through the apartment opening windows. Light flowed over fly-spattered walls, revealing the rush matting, the settle, the four stools, the massive cupboard and the bookcases in the lounge; the large, rectangular bed with the thin mattress in the bedroom. The *Ramayana*, which he'd been reading before he left, lay open on the bedside table. The bureau in the corner of the room was open, his account books lying flat on the flap as he'd left them. He picked up the water jug from beneath the washstand, poured water into the washbowl and doused his face. Then he stripped off his tunic and sponged his body and arms.

The water felt good. Leaving the water to dry on his body he took a fresh tunic and pantaloons from the court cupboard in the corner of the room, peeled off his boots and trousers and slumped naked on the bed. Why was Ali Baig raiding Armagon when he knew the English couldn't pay, and knew he risked reprisals or the English abandoning Armagon and leaving him with an untenanted fort and no taxes? Had Ali Baig gone mad?

Mad as a fox, Darnell thought. Ali Baig didn't want an eighty per cent surcharge. He was imposing a tax the English couldn't pay so he could drive them from Armagon. Which meant someone had indemnified Ali Baig against the loss of taxes and his *bakshee*. The Dutch, Darnell thought; the Dutch were behind Ali Baig's raid.

But why would the Dutch go to such lengths to force the English from Armagon? It had no strategic importance and was in a state of gross disrepair. Whatever profits it did make came from smuggling. The Dutch, sensible, practical and profit-conscious, would have to be paid to take over Armagon.

Bloody, god-rottin' van Cuyler, Darnell thought. This was exactly how he had operated in Java. Van Cuyler had set up Ali Baig to raid Armagon so he couldn't finance Madera! Darnell dressed, loaded his pistol and checked the draw on his knife. Taking a last look around the room, he went out, his expression grim with hatred. Van Cuyler would not win this time . . .

Eckaerts was waiting on the factory house steps with the grenades, hollow iron balls the size of a fist, filled with gunpowder and threaded with short fuses. He carried them in a leather pouch decorated with the picture of a one-legged grenadier. Together he and Darnell went to inspect the barrels of gunpowder, Darnell checking that the cloth covers would break easily. Climbing the wall, they saw that Ali Baig's rabble were gathered in front of the Land Gate, preparing to use the battering rams.

Returning to the factory house, Darnell had Eckaerts assemble the soldiers and all the English on the steps in a forward-facing echelon, Darnell, Winter, Eckaerts, Rawlins and James Ellwood – the factory merchant – in the middle, the soldiers spread out around them with muskets at the ready, acrid smoke trickling from their smouldering slow-matches. Then Darnell signalled for the Land Gate to be opened.

The mob poured in. Ali Baig and two other men on horseback rode down the west road, surrounded by the jeering rabble. The drooping helmet and ill-fitting breastpiece made him look even more like a barrel. His eyes were bleary and red-veined and the grey beard around the betel-stained mouth was straggly and punctured with a rash of festering pustules. He rode uncomfortably, stumpy legs sticking straight out in front of him in the stirrups.

Darnell waited until the mob had reached the factory square before he nodded to a soldier. The soldier put his match to the touch-hole of his musket and fired into the air. 'All of you stop!' Darnell roared.

The crowd stopped.

Darnell had instructed the soldier to fire a second shot before roaring, 'What you are doing is illegal! The nizam will punish you!'

'We have come to take what is ours!' Ali Baig cried. He waved the crowd forward.

'Wait!' Darnell applied a slow-match to the grenade's fuse. It sparked and sputtered, took hold and burned fiercely. Darnell hurled it at the gunpowder barrel on the *maidan*. The grenade bounced against the side of the barrel and rolled. Oh God, he'd missed!

Darnell reached for a second grenade. With a vivid white-orange flash, the grenade and gunpowder exploded.

The barrel flew apart, hurling staves through the air. A yellow ball of flame mushroomed and flared and flaming debris flew along the street. The crowd screamed and scurried back towards the Land Gate.

'We have more barrels like that in the square and by the road,' Darnell cried. 'If you approach our warehouse you will all be blown up!' He took out another grenade and held it over his head.

Ali Baig spoke to the men nearest him. Riding straight into the people at the west gate, they brought their *lathis* crashing down indiscriminately on heads and shoulders, forcing the crowd back towards the factory square. Another group of men ran to the tenements. Ali Baig edged his horse ahead of the group and stopped in the middle of the square. 'We have come to take what is lawfully ours!' he cried hoarsely, signalling to the mob to advance.

'You are breaking the nizam's *firman*,' Darnell called. 'The nizam will punish you for breaking his law.'

'This is lawful,' Ali Baig cried. 'Taxes have not been paid.' He looked around him and then, as if unable to find inspiration from his surroundings, repeated, 'We have come to take what is ours.'

'If you take our goods we will bring soldiers from Pettahpoli and recover everything you have taken,' Darnell shouted. 'We will impose taxes on Sairin until you have compensated us three times over! We will make Sairin the poorest village in Coromandel!'

'You English are too frightened to do anything!' Ali Baig called and spat.

'We will destroy Sairin with our guns!' Darnell shouted. 'You will no longer be naik; your Dutch friends will not save you. They won't even pay the full price for the cloth you're stealing.'

'The Dutch pay better than you English!' Ali Baig replied.

'So the Dutch *are* paying you to steal our goods and drive us away! They will betray you!' Darnell shouted.

'The Java seas are full of fools like you who trusted the Dutch!'

There was a sudden hubbub of cries and shouts from the native lines. Accompanied by the high-pitched shrieks of women, a circle of men emerged from the rows of fast-shut rooms, dragging a struggling man. A nervous crowd of local men and women followed and were kept back by waved swords and flailing *lathis*. As they entered the factory square, Darnell saw that the man being dragged so unceremoniously was Timana Chitty.

Chitty's tunic was torn and there was a swelling above his left eye. His hair and *dhoti* were covered with dust and the men kicked and cuffed him as he struggled. There were tears of rage and fear in his eyes as he was dragged through the mob.

Ali Baig cried out: 'This is the man who is the cause of our misfortunes, a thief and the son of a thief.' Ali Baig paused while Timana Chitty was spreadeagled across the barrel of gunpowder.

'It is because of this man's thieving that we have been compelled to take action against our English friends. It is because he failed to keep proper accounts that the taxes due to us have not been paid. Timana Chitty has driven a wedge between us and the *feringhi*. Through his negligence he has forced us to seize the English goods.'

A clever move, Darnell thought, turning the dispute into one between natives and only indirectly involving the *feringhi*. Stakes were quickly hammered into the ground and Timana Chitty's arms and legs bound to them.

Ali Baig turned to face Darnell. 'Now,' he called, 'explode your barrels of gunpowder.' He waved to the mob. 'Take everything from the warehouse.'

Darnell lifted the grenade above his head. The mob started to move forward and stopped. Darnell knew that if he threw the grenade near the barrel, both grenade and gunpowder would explode, killing Timana Chitty and many of Ali Baig's men. The explosion would drive them back with so much carnage that Ali Baig would not be able to force them to attack the factory house. Darnell reminded himself it was not property that was at stake, but the future of England and the Company; that Ali Baig's men were soldiers and had to expect to die. But Timana Chitty was not a soldier. Timana Chitty was a Company servant. He could not save the Company without killing Timana Chitty. Out of the corner of his eye he saw Eckaerts hold up his slow-match to light the grenade's fuse.

'So the Dutch are paying you to steal our goods and drive us away!' Darnell's words reverberated in Ynessa's brain like a cannon blast. If the Dutch were paying Ali Baig to steal Darnell's goods, couldn't they have paid Ali Baig to kill Rodrigo? The Dutch had wanted to protect their monopoly but couldn't take direct action for fear of upsetting the nizam. So what better solution than have Ali Baig do their dirty work for them? That was what Mirza Baig might have told her had Ali Baig not intervened. That was why Ali Baig had driven them away from Celor.

Ali Baig had killed Rodrigo for the Dutch! Ynessa felt certain of it. She stared down at Ali Baig, her body shaking with anger, burning with a terrible flash-fire of fury. It was all she could do to keep from screaming, from smashing her fist through the window. That man down there had killed her father!

She took the pistol from her waist. She would kill him! But if she did that she'd never know who was behind Ali Baig. Besides, murder was a mortal sin, for which she would go to hell for all eternity. She had to prove Ali Baig killed Rodrigo. She had to find out who his Dutch accomplices were. She had to make Ali Baig confess! With a gun pressed to his head, Ali Baig would talk.

Figueras loomed beside her. 'Madonna, what is it?' She was breathing hard and soaked in sweat.

'This nonsense has gone far enough,' she snapped. 'I'm going down there. Have the men cover me from the window.'

Figueras protested. 'Madonna, you can't – don't be –'

She pushed past him and went out.

Outside, Darnell was holding a grenade with an unlit fuse over his head, shouting, 'Get away from the square or you will all be blown up!' The mob was shouting back, not totally frightened, not totally hostile. Darnell's eyes widened in surprise as he saw her. Holding the pistol in front of her, she ran down the steps.

The crowd parted before her in shock. She ran right up to Ali Baig. 'Stop it!' she cried, levelling the pistol at him. 'Cease this obscenity at once!'

Silence descended like a curtain. Ali Baig fixed her with bloodshot eyes and chewed a corner of his lip. Then he spat out a red stream of betel, threw his head back and laughed. 'Ignore the tart in man's clothes!' he called. 'Move into the warehouse. Take all the English goods.'

Ynessa's finger whitened round the trigger. 'Son of a pig! Stop everything or I'll put a ball between your stupid eyes!'

Ali Baig's face flushed. All movement in the crowd ceased.

Ynessa felt a wild, victorious surge. 'Now you lily-livered bastard,' she called, 'tell me what happened in Celor. What did you do for the Dutch there? How did you kill my father? Who were the Dutchmen involved?'

Ali Baig's mouth dropped open. The blood drained from his face. He looked about him as if checking if anyone else had heard. Then he bared his broken teeth in an obscene grimace. 'Stupid, foreign bitch!' he shouted. 'You're mad!'

'I will count to five before I shoot. *Ek, do, teen . . .*'

Darnell wrenched a slow-match from Eckaerts and, holding his pistol in one hand and the grenade in the other, ran down the steps. The Portuguese woman had *cojones* as big as cannonballs. She had Ali Baig shaking with fear and the mob paralysed. He should have listened to her when she'd told him to isolate Ali Baig. He ran up behind her and pointed his gun at Ali Baig. 'Set my merchant free now or you're dead meat!'

'And before you think of doing anything stupid, look up at the factory window,' Ynessa added.

Ali Baig looked from the two pistols pointed at him to the guns trained on him from the factory window. Dead meat was right. He called an order over his shoulder. Timana Chitty was released and, clutching the front of his *dhoti*, scurried quickly back to the safety of the tenements.

'Now,' Darnell said. 'Get the hell out of here!'

The white flash almost blinded him. A loud rushing sound filled his ears. The raindrops hit him with the force of cannon-shot, spattering on the ground with loud smacks. His face and hands stung. Within seconds his shirt was stuck to his body and his hair soaked. He saw Ali Baig's turban and clothes turn dark and heavy with water and the Portuguese woman's flesh peep through her tunic. The first cloudburst of the season, Darnell thought, as the slow-match in his hand fizzled and died.

Ali Baig's mouth twisted into a grin. 'The English guns are useless,' he shouted above the patter of the falling rain. 'Seize the woman! Rush the warehouse! Take the English goods.'

Ynessa felt bodies slam into her. Hands grabbed her arms and pulled them apart. She fought to hold on to the gun. Her hand was forced back against her wrist, her fingers prised away. Pain shot up her arm. The gun sprang free. Then there were hands all over her, tearing at her tunic, pawing at her breasts. She was surrounded by excited, unshaven faces and an overwhelming smell of sweat and stale hashish. She tried to push but the bodies formed an unyielding wall. The front of her tunic ripped. Hands dragged at her boots and breeches.

Then there was the chopping sound of metal smashing into flesh. A man's face exploded like an overripe orange as a gun-butt smashed into his cheek. She came aware of Darnell beside her, swinging his pistol like a madman, of other soldiers beating at the mob with their muskets.

Darnell was clubbing another man. She saw his knife flash, and then she was released. She fell against Darnell who grabbed her round the shoulders and whipped his knife round in a furious semi-circle. A man spun away, a ribbon of blood spouting over his face and beard.

'Run!' Darnell gasped, turning her round. 'Get back to the factory house!'

She ran across earth that was already turning to mud. Ahead of her three soldiers were crowded into the doorway of the factory house. Their muskets belched orange as they fired. Smoke filled the doorway and the sharp crack of shots was followed by shouts of anger and fear. Then Darnell was beside her, pulling her by the arm up the factory house steps. He pushed her before him, past the soldiers and into the hallway that was filled with men and smelling of sweat and damp cloth.

Darnell turned and ordered another salvo. The rain drummed on the roof.

Ravi Winter forced a path through to them. 'We've got to give up the goods, Richard. We haven't got enough ammunition to keep 'em out.'

Darnell went to the doorway and looked. The mob was crowding around Ali Baig and his lieutenants, ten yards from the factory steps. As suddenly as it had started, the cloudburst had stopped. Ali Baig was having all the luck today, Darnell thought.

'Seize the English goods!' Ali Baig roared.

The crowd started to move forward.

'Open the warehouse doors,' Darnell ordered James Ellwood. 'Get everyone upstairs,' he called to Ravi. 'Keep your soldiers on the stairs,' he ordered Eckaerts. 'Kill the first man who tries to come upstairs.'

He ran and joined the soldiers crowding the stairs as, with whoops of triumph, Ali Baig's men rushed through the hallway into the warehouse. Some of them looked at Darnell and the soldiers crowded on the stairway, then deciding the risk of storming it wasn't justified, ran on into the warehouse. Carts clattered outside and more men rushed in, colliding with those hurrying out.

He could go after Ali Baig and recover the cloth, Darnell thought. He could appeal to the nizam for punishment and compensation. But none of that would happen quickly, and certainly not before Captain Sen arrived to collect his cloth. None of it would happen before Seringa's ultimatum for the construction of Madera expired.

It took the mob half an hour to ransack the warehouse and load up the carts. 'We've got what we came for,' Ali Baig cried as he wheeled his horse round and rode out of the fort. 'Consider your taxes paid!'

Darnell watched him go from the top of the factory house steps, his mouth tasting acrid from tension and defeat. Everything was over! He had lost the chance to build at Madera! Van Cuyler and the mother-fickin' Dutch had won. He wondered if it was worth returning to Pettah-poli and pleading with Cogan.

'I'm sorry you've lost all your goods.'

It was the Portuguese woman, her hair still bedraggled and her tunic torn and bloodstained. 'Are you all right?' he asked mechanically.

'Yes, senhor. I'm only angry that damned swine Ali Baig has got away.'

'What were you trying to do?'

She tossed her head angrily. 'Ali Baig helped to kill my father! I wanted to make him confess so I could find out who his accomplices were and who ordered him to kill my father.'

'How was your father killed?' Darnell was curious.

She blew her nose and wiped her eyes with the back of her hand. 'My father was Don Rodrigo da Soares, the founder of our merchant house. Seven weeks ago, at the invitation of the nizam of Kokinada he attended the pearl auction at Celor and bought the prize pearls. He and his escort were murdered soon after he left Celor.'

'How do you know Ali Baig murdered your father?'

'You say Ali Baig is connected to the Dutch; I know the Dutch want to keep their monopoly of the auction at Celor.'

'And you think the Dutch –'

'Yes, senhor.' She told him of her visit to Celor, how Mirza Baig's story of dacoits hadn't rung true, and how Ali Baig had avoided helping with the investigation and refused to let her stay in Celor.

The woman's story made a horrible kind of sense, Darnell thought. It was the sort of thing the Dutch would do: the sort of thing Karel van Cuyler would do. 'Don't you have any brothers who will find your father's killers?' he asked.

She flung her shoulders back. 'My elder brother is dead and I am the oldest in the family. I have twin brothers aged seven and a sister aged eight.'

So much love, he thought, so much loyalty. Her father must have been quite a man. And this was some woman. He asked, 'What would you have done if Ali Baig had confessed?'

'Made him reveal who the Dutchmen were, and handed Ali Baig over to the nizam for punishment. Then I would have confronted the Dutch and recovered the pearls they stole from my father.'

'How do you know they still have the pearls?'

'There's nothing else they can do with them. The pearls are readily identifiable and have no provenance. If they try to sell them, they will reveal their involvement in the murder.' She made to move past him. 'Thank you for your help, senhor.'

Darnell caught her arm. 'Wait.' A crazy, convoluted plan was forming in his head. If van Cuyler were behind the killing of the Portuguese, then he would still have the pearls. Van Cuyler wouldn't trust Darnell, and certainly wouldn't deal with him, but what if van Cuyler *had* to deal with him? What if he offered de Groot a vast sum for the pearls? Or better still, de Groot and all the other Dutch merchants at Pulicat? He asked, 'Are you sure the Dutch still have the pearls?'

'They couldn't sell them, senhor. Of that I am certain. What are you thinking?'

'I was thinking it might be possible to get into Pulicat and recover your father's pearls. How much would those pearls be worth to you?'

'Oh, senhor, if you could do that, if you could bring me evidence of who had Ali Baig kill my father –' She sighed. 'I will give you half the value of the pearls. That is two thousand five hundred *escudos*, nearly five hundred pounds.'

That settled it. If he got the pearls he'd have the funds for the fort and be able to tie van Cuyler to the murder of Ynessa's father, which would finish van Cuyler in India. He said, 'I'll need about twenty pounds' worth of gold and all the coin you can spare.'

She looked at him with a surprise which quickly turned to excitement. Her eyes sparkled, she lifted her head and flung her shoulders back. 'All right,' she said, and paused a moment. 'Will you tell me how you will get the pearls?'

'Yes, *menina*, but first I have to think a little more.'

Chapter Ten

Railoo's private audience chamber reminded Seringa of a tomb. Lit by tiered brass lamps and small windows set high in the stone walls, with a bare stone floor and rock walls that greedily absorbed light, the long, narrow room was dark and forbidding. Even sound died. Seringa's footsteps gave off a muffled echo as he walked up to the throne at the far end of the room.

Railoo slouched on a gem-studded throne beneath the marigold and crimson silk umbrella of state. He wore a large pearl in the centre of his turban; his tunic, pantaloons and turban were of cream silk and decorated with rows of pearl buttons. In that light the gems had a cold glitter, and his clothes the appearance of a shroud.

Slowly Seringa knelt and pressed his forehead to the cold, stone steps. Even though they were cousins and were meeting in private, Railoo insisted on being formally greeted. It was a kind of revenge, Seringa thought, for all the humiliations he and Ghosh had inflicted on Railoo when they were children.

He was surprised at how old Railoo looked. His skin was greyish and pitted with old acne scars, his shoulders were rounded. A paunch pressed out the waist of his pantaloons. His thin moustache was flecked with grey, and the lips of his narrow mouth cracked and reddened from chewing betel. He looked a decade older than his twenty-eight years. Seringa found it difficult to imagine the age difference between them was only four months.

'It is always a pleasure to see you, cousin,' Railoo said, indicating to Seringa he could stand. Railoo's voice was high-pitched and rasping, and was irritatingly reminiscent of the sound of sandstone rubbed on glass. 'To what do we owe the pleasure of *this* visit?'

Seringa breathed deeply. He had come to inform Railoo of his arrangement with the English, and hoped to get Railoo's approval of the English fort. Vaidya needed that fort, and if Railoo opposed it he would have to be overthrown. Seringa prayed silently that it wouldn't come to that, and began with customary circumspection. 'I wanted to tell you of our campaign against the Mughal.'

Railoo smiled and shot a stream of red betel juice into the spittoon by his feet. 'A waste of time, cousin. The Mughal will never reach Vaidya. And if by some misfortune they do, my troops will deal with them.'

Railoo's untrained and ill-disciplined troops would be decimated by the Mughal, Seringa thought, fighting his irritation. Too much depended on this visit for him to let Railoo provoke him. He gave Railoo a brief account of their campaign in the Deccan.

A slab behind the throne opened and Bhagwan Dayal came into the room, slippers swishing as he walked up to Railoo and bowed. He was a stout, heavily moustached man and dressed like Railoo in a turban, tunic and *dhoti* of cream silk. Dayal had been an acolyte at Bharatya's monastery, and had taught Railoo, Seringa and Ghosh. He'd always protected Railoo against Ghosh and Seringa, and when Railoo had become raja of Vaidya, he'd repaid Dayal's care by appointing him chief councillor.

'Ah, Bhagwan,' Railoo crowed, 'I am so pleased you could join us. Seringa was telling us about his defeat in the Deccan.'

'It wasn't a defeat,' Seringa protested. 'We retreated because of the hot season.'

Dayal greeted Seringa with a broad smile and a swift steepling of palms, before sitting on one of the ebony couches beside the throne.

Seringa went on. 'My soldiers are home. I've left a force under Bharatya holding the hill forts on our western borders. Meanwhile, the Mughal are summering in the Deccan, poised to attack us as soon as the hot season and rains are over. At which time I fear Kokinada will invade us from the north.'

'Nonsense, cousin! You're talking like an old woman frightened of her own shadow.'

Seringa bit his lip and looked down. He saw that the strings of Railoo's leather sandals were spliced extravagantly with pearls. He said, 'It is because I believe Vaidya will be attacked on two fronts that I have come to propose an amalgamation of our forces, so that our combined strength will guarantee the safety of Vaidya.'

'Amalgamate!' Railoo shrieked with laughter. 'Did you hear that, Bhagwan? Amalgamate our forces! Surely, cousin, you're not serious. Who will command such an army? And to which of us will that army be loyal?'

'Besides,' Dayal added, 'there is no danger of an attack from Kokinada. We have a peace treaty –'

'Which Kokinada will tear up the moment it suits him. And if we are being attacked in the west, it will suit him very well.'

'Cousin, cousin,' Railoo cried, 'You're a soldier. Leave diplomacy to those who are experienced at it. Kokinada profits too much from peace to ever think of invading us. And as for the Mughal, the heat and the rain will decimate them and the Maratha guerrillas finish off what's left.'

'And if that doesn't happen?'

'Then Kokinada will join us!'

Seringa stared at his cousin in astonishment, but Dayal explained that Kokinada was a Sunni Muslim and the Mughal were Shi'ites.

'They hate each other more than they hate us Hindus,' Railoo finished. 'So if the Mughal attacks us, Kokinada will help us fight them.'

Railoo and Dayal had to be crazy to believe that, but Seringa realized they *wanted* to believe it: it was the perfect excuse for doing nothing. He said, 'I am more cautious than you, cousin, and more exposed to an attack by Kokinada. So I have taken special steps to defend Venkat against an attack from the north.'

Railoo's face darkened. 'What special steps?'

'I have given the English permission to build a fort at Madera.'

'How dare you!' Railoo's face contorted with fury. Betel juice dribbled down his chin. 'Only I can make agreements with foreigners!'

'There was no time to talk to you –'

'Serai, I am ashamed of you,' Dayal cried. 'Foreigners defile us and make us unclean. We have never before permitted foreigners to live among us.'

'Kokinada and the Mughal will make us far more unclean than the English.'

'Perhaps,' Dayal murmured. 'And then, perhaps not. But this is no excuse to bring foreigners into Vaidya.'

'I will not allow this!' Railoo shrieked. 'You must cancel your agreement with the English at once!' Railoo was pounding his thighs and stamping his feet in fury. Seringa knew that once out of control, Railoo would do anything, even order Seringa's execution, despite the certainty that that would start a civil war. Hastily Seringa started to make obeisance, a gesture that had pacified Railoo since childhood, then just as abruptly stopped. If he placated Railoo now, he could lose the English, Venkat and Vaidya. 'I'm afraid that's impossible,' he said.

'Impossible! I am ordering you to do this, Serai! Ordering you! Do you hear me? I am your raja and I am ordering you!' Railoo's eyes were wild and bloodshot and the front of his tunic was covered with red betel spray.

Seringa steeled himself to go on. 'If I were to cancel my agreement with the English, we would risk retaliation.'

'Nonsense, Serai,' Bhagwan Dayal said. 'We've refused the English permission before and they've accepted the situation gracefully.'

'No more,' Seringa said. 'We can no longer ignore the *feringhi* or prohibit them. The *feringhi* are determined to trade with us, and they will do so whether we wish to or not.' He told Dayal and Railoo how he had been approached by both the English and the Dutch. 'They will not take a refusal. Only the fact that one of them is now "protecting" us has stopped the other from forcibly settling a factory on our territory.'

'You should have fought them, Serai,' Railoo taunted, 'as you fought the Mughal.'

Seringa bit back a sarcastic retort about the fighting capacity of Railoo's army. 'We are powerless against a *feringhi* attack,' he said. 'Their guns make them thirty times as strong as we are. If we didn't make an agreement, they would have established themselves by force.'

'But they should talk to me, not you! I am the raja of Vaidya! Have them come back and talk to me!'

'That will be impossible. They begin building in two weeks.'

'They mustn't! You must stop –'

Dayal asked, 'Why did you choose the English? Did they offer you more money?'

'No. They were the more honest.' He told Dayal and Railoo of the ordeal Bharatya had organized for the English and the Dutch.

'So on the basis of these tests, you decided to trade with the English, even though the Dutch offered you better terms?'

Dayal turned to Railoo. 'It seems we must negotiate with the Dutch. Otherwise our cousin Seringa will grow too rich and too powerful and we will owe allegiance to him.'

'Yes,' Railoo chortled. 'We'll do that. What a splendid idea, Bhagwan. Make the arrangements right away. Go now and do it.'

'You mustn't do that!' Seringa cried. 'That will only start a civil war in Vaidya!'

'You're talking nonsense, cousin. You're simply jealous because we'll make a better arrangement with the Dutch than you have with the English.'

'Listen to me! The Dutch and English hate each other. They fought with each other all the way to Venkatapur. If we let both the English and the Dutch into Vaidya, they will continue to fight and draw us into their conflict.'

'That's impossible!' Railoo said. 'We're cousins and you have sworn allegiance to me.'

'On the contrary, it is very possible, if the Dutch support you and the English support me.'

Dayal said, 'So you want us to do nothing while you steadily grow richer and more powerful than us. We won't do that, Serai.'

If Railoo and Dayal brought the Dutch into Vaidya, that would make civil war inevitable, Seringa thought, and lay Vaidya open to centuries of alien rule. He'd have to assuage Railoo's greed and jealousy, for the sake of Vaidya. He said, 'If all that concerns you is the size of my fortune, I will give you half my additional revenues. But you must undertake not to make any approach to the Dutch.'

Railoo and Dayal exchanged glances. Then Dayal said, 'All right.'

'And we want sixty per cent of your revenues,' Railoo said. 'Not fifty.'

Seringa wasn't fooled: both Dayal and Railoo were too greedy to abide by such an agreement. As soon as they saw how things were working out with the English, they would talk to the Dutch. He said, 'We will sign the agreements before I leave,' and was filled with sadness. Railoo would make a deal with the Dutch, Railoo would do nothing about the Mughal or Kokinada. Railoo had become too dangerous; he would have to be overthrown. Atman, help me, he prayed silently, smiling at Railoo.

Chapter Eleven

Ynessa slumped in the saddle as they rode beneath the arch of St Francis's Gate into the bustle of San Thome. She hated wearing gowns and mantillas and she hated riding side-saddle. But four miles before San Thome, she had stopped and changed and begun to ride as a lady so that her dress and demeanour would not outrage the Catholic priests of San Thome and her future mother-in-law, Donna Isabella Gonzaga.

Twelve weeks ago, at one of the most magnificent balls ever given in San Thome, Ynessa had been betrothed to Joaquim, the twenty-four-year-old head of the House of Gonzaga, the richest merchant family in San Thome after da Soares. Everyone had said it was *bellissima*, a match made in heaven. But then Rodrigo had been murdered and a week afterwards Donna Isabella had visited, severe and haughty beneath her mourning clothes, to express her sympathy and set out her dictate of how the dynasties of Gonzaga and da Soares would be run. The wife of a Gonzaga would not work in business, nor would she wear men's attire. Ynessa would no longer swear or shout and behave in the unacceptable manner Rodrigo had tolerated. She would move to the Gonzaga mansion immediately after the wedding to take up the traditional duties of wife and mother. Joaquim would run the combined houses of Gonzaga and da Soares until the twins came of age when they would receive a third of the new, larger venture.

Encouraged by Bishop Ephraim, the Gonzaga chaplain who had arranged the marriage, and still befuddled by grief, Mama had agreed; it had taken all Ynessa's skills of negotiation to be allowed to visit Rodrigo's grave in Celor to find out how and by whom he had been killed. She shuddered at the thought of living in the Gonzaga household, dancing attendance on Donna Isabella, looking after Joaquim and bearing him sons. That arrangement would be the death of her.

She'd grown up with the business. Since she was eleven the warehouse had been an extension of home. Many of her happiest hours had been spent working with Rodrigo and Figueras. She remembered how, four years ago, she'd forced them to divert the House investments from pepper to sisal, and how, when the pepper market had collapsed, Rodrigo had given her the office next to his. Da Soares was *her* business. She had helped Rodrigo build it. She couldn't leave it.

That wasn't what Rodrigo had wanted for her, and that wasn't why Rodrigo had built the House of da Soares. He'd never have agreed to give it to the Gonzagas, or agreed to her spending her life as a prisoner in the Gonzaga household. She'd persuade Joaquim to accept a compromise, she decided. Joaquim loved her and knew she would be unhappy living with his mother and doing nothing but woman's work. And Joaquim knew how good she was in business, that she had been Rodrigo's most trusted aide.

'Hai! Hai!' 'Kadale, kadale, sherbet!' 'Dosai!' 'Machli!' 'Behega! Behega!' the hawkers' cries flooded her brain. Startled, she realized they'd ridden past the Rua Igreja da Rosario and San Thome Cathedral, and were alongside the ten-foot-high walls of the Estado India – the inner fort comprising barracks, government storehouses, powder magazines, the captain-general's house and offices. The ladies of San Thome were setting out to do their shopping, and gaily coloured palanquins surrounded by uniformed retinues of West African slaves thronged the streets. Ynessa lowered her veil, not wanting to be recognized and delayed, and turned into the Praca das Flores which was lined with flowers and the mansions of Portuguese merchants. The da Soares mansion, halfway down the street, was the largest.

Ynessa felt a wave of tiredness as she saw its three-storey central tower surrounded by the two-storey wings that occupied the space of six normal-sized houses. Home, she thought, staring at the familiar pillared veranda standing well back from the street, and feeling the sense of freedom she'd experienced on the trip from Celor evaporate. Home meant responsibility and problems. She reined before the iron gate, slid out of the saddle into the arms of her escort and thence on to the pavement.

Her legs felt spongy, and she was boiling beneath the stifling gown and veil. Servants opened the gate. She walked across the narrow, paved courtyard, then up the steps to the veranda. Mama waited at the top of the steps, a small, shrivelled figure in a black gown and mantilla. The twins, Paolo and Juan, stood next to her, along with eight-year-old Katerina. Ynessa tore off her veil, ran up the steps, and flung her arms about her mother.

Mama felt smaller; there were new lines in her olive-skinned face. Her eyes were wider and larger, and bright as if with fever. Ynessa kissed them all, asking the twins if they'd behaved themselves, and Mama led them solemnly to the parlour off the veranda where the family usually gathered.

It was a cosy room, with a cane settle, chairs and table, and a leather armchair where Rodrigo had always sat. Ynessa felt tears spring to her eyes at the indentations in the leather seat. She wiped her face and blew her nose. For the sake of Mama and the children she had to be strong. They stood grouped round the settle, as if waiting for her to do something. 'Let me tell you about Celor,' she said straight away, and realized that Mama was waiting for her to sit in Rodrigo's chair. It was her way of acknowledging that Ynessa had taken her father's place.

Ynessa eased herself into the chair and sat leaning forward, elbows on her knees. Gathering the children to her, Mama sat on the settle opposite. They waited in silence for Ynessa to speak. Ynessa cleared her throat. 'I visited Celor,' she said, looking at Mama. 'Our father is dead. I visited his grave and placed a cross on it. As we were informed, he was murdered and the pearls he was carrying were stolen.' Seeing the pain in Mama's face, she added, 'They told me he died quickly, without any pain.'

Mama bowed her head. Her lips moved in silent prayer as her fingers skimmed over a rosary. 'By dacoits?' she asked.

'No – yes!' Ynessa decided not to worry Mama with everything that had happened and what she had arranged with Darnell.

Mama's fingers flew faster over the rosary.

'A hunt for the dacoits has been organized,' Ynessa said. 'I will be informed when they are found.' She paused and added, 'I might have to return to Celor. I've agreed to help find the people who killed our father.'

Mama said, 'Perhaps Joaquim will go instead.'

Ynessa didn't think so. Joaquim had pleaded he was too busy with the affairs of the House of Gonzaga to accompany her to Celor.

'Donna Gonzaga, Bishop Ephraim and Joaquim have been to see me,' Mama said. 'It is not fitting that you should expose yourself to these dangers and trouble yourself with the business. It will be best if you were to marry Joaquim next month.'

She wouldn't, Ynessa determined. There was much to be discussed; she *had* to find Rodrigo's killers.

Mama sighed. 'It will be good to have a man in the family again.'

Ynessa stifled an angry comment. Rodrigo had been dead only seven weeks and already Mama was talking of getting another man into the family! She wouldn't have it! She wouldn't ... She looked at her mother. Mama must still be in shock. Ynessa took a deep breath and said, 'Let's not rush any decisions, Mama. There's much to discuss.'

'What's there to discuss? You're betrothed to Joaquim. It makes no difference if you marry him next month or in four months' time.'

'All the –'

'He's such a good boy,' Mama sighed. 'You can't imagine how helpful he's been while you've been away. He's visited us three or four times and been overseeing Alvarez at the warehouse.'

'Whatever for?' Alfonso Alvarez, whom she had left in charge of da Soares, was as experienced as Figueras. He had no need of Joaquim's help. And by his own account, Joaquim should have been too busy with the affairs of the House of Gonzaga to have the time to check on Alvarez.

Mama was smiling. 'Joaquim wanted to be sure nothing went wrong while you were away. He's such a nice man, so thoughtful and considerate. You don't know how lucky you are that your father arranged for you to marry him. Now child, you must get some rest. I'm sure Joaquim will call this evening and you must eat and sleep and be re –'

Ynessa got to her feet. 'I'm going to the warehouse as soon as I've bathed.'

'But you've only just got here!'

'I've got work to do,' Ynessa said, striding from the room. She had to find out what Joaquim had been doing at the warehouse, and think of something to bring Mama back to her senses.

The warehouse was in the northernmost part of the fort, a vast two-storey cavern with its own docks and piers. Every foot of the huge space was covered with piles of wooden crates, bales of cloth and racks of barrels. In the spaces between, clerks worked at desks. Overseers in grubby white overalls and pantaloons ran along the aisles and clambered over crates. Coolies sweated and heaved.

Carters plodded through the building, loading and unloading goods. Six cranes stood at various points against the walls, three of them working now, swinging huge bundles of crates in their nets. Ynessa felt a catch in her throat as she remembered the energy and pride with which Rodrigo had organized the building of the warehouse, and how they'd argued about the move from the old warehouse in the middle of the docks.

Ynessa went up the polished wooden stairs. A long Oriental runner spread up the stairway and along the balcony, which ran all the way above the storage area and led off to offices and locked storerooms. She stopped and looked down at the warehouse. The constant activity excited her, and she loved the amalgam of smells, the tang of the sea mixed with new cloth, nutmeg, pepper, sandalwood, sweat, wood polish, dung.

A clerk hurrying by saw her and stopped. 'Welcome back, *menina*.' Ynessa smiled in response and continued along the balcony, passing doors which opened on to rooms full of industrious clerks. Alvarez's door was open too. He sat at his desk poring over a ledger. Her heart pounded as she paused outside the closed door of Rodrigo's office, hoping for an insane moment that if she flung it open she'd find him there. Biting her lips, she marched to her own office. Joaquim was seated behind her desk earnestly studying the da Soares journal, in which every transaction of the House was recorded.

'What're you doing here?' Ynessa demanded. 'Why are you examining our journal?'

Joaquim put down the journal hurriedly and came round the desk, his lips parted in a dazzling smile. 'Ynessa, *minha querida*, I'm so glad you're back!' His voice was a bear's murmur. Ynessa shivered at the sound of it. 'I've missed you so!' He held out his arms to her.

Joaquim was so handsome that just looking at him made her breathless. His face was a perfect oval. His skin, beneath the neatly tapering beard, was smooth and copper-toned. She admired his delicately arched eyebrows and the piercing quality of his dark eyes, the thoroughbred flare of his nostrils and the way his jet-black hair hung down to his shoulders. She told herself she'd always loved him.

Four years ago, aged sixteen, she'd rouged her cheeks, put *kohl* on her eyes and nearly died with longing each time he'd walked near her in the *paseo*. Joaquim hadn't even noticed her, and she'd been madly jealous of every girl he walked with. But Joaquim hadn't married any of them and, four months ago, Bishop Ephraim had brought a marriage proposal which Rodrigo had, after discussion with her, accepted.

She still couldn't believe that Joaquim loved her, that a man who could have any woman he wanted had chosen to marry her. She folded into his arms and closed her eyes as he kissed her forehead and cheeks, inhaling the male smell of him, enjoying the roughness of his beard against her face. His strong arms enfolding her made her feel secure; the hardness of his body through the cool silks he wore sent little thrills along her fingertips. She ran her lips along his cheek and then he was kissing her on the mouth. She let him take her lips and run his tongue over them. *Oh Joaquim, you are so wonderful*, she thought.

Joaquim pulled away and stood back, allowing her to lean against his locked arms. 'I missed you so much,' he said, his eyes boring into hers. 'So much!'

Ynessa realized that she'd been so absorbed in what she'd been doing the past three weeks, she hadn't had time to miss Joaquim. And she still wondered why he'd been so interested in the da Soares journal. His mouth closed on hers again; once more she surrendered to his kiss. His hands stroked her neck and she felt a surging wave of desire as he pressed his body against hers. She wanted him to kiss her and spread her and feel him and . . . She twisted her head away and pressed her arms against his shoulders. Her breath was coming in rapid gasps. Her face and cheeks were hot. She wriggled out of his arms and sidled between him and her desk. 'What are you doing here?' she asked, annoyed at the quaver in her voice. 'Why were you examining our journal?' she demanded again.

Joaquim laughed, a strong, confident laugh that made her feel he knew how much he'd excited her. 'I was just helping you, my sweet, making sure no one was taking advantage of your absence.'

'You really needn't have bothered. Alfonso Alvarez is most competent: he's been with the House twenty-two years.'

'It was no trouble. And there's no harm in keeping an eye on our business, is there?'

Hating his proprietorial tone, she went round behind the desk and sat down.

Joaquim looked down at his hands, admiring the flash of rubies and sapphires on his fingers. 'Tell me about your journey,' he said.

Ynessa told Joaquim of her visit to Celor, her subsequent visit to Gangapatnam, what had happened at Armagon, and finally about her arrangement with Darnell.

Joaquim's eyes widened in horror. A slow flush rose from his neck to his forehead. 'Are you crazy or stupid or what? You could have been killed, or worse!'

'I had to find out if Ali Baig killed Rodrigo! And –'

'Gallivanting all over the country with six men! Rushing into a native crowd? Threatening a man with a gun?' Joaquim shook his head and clicked his tongue in disgust. 'Believe me, Ynessa, this nonsense has got to stop. Bishop Ephraim and I have arranged with your mother that we will get married next month. So you can put all this out of your head, right this minute. This is a man's job – I'll take care of it.'

'You mean you will hunt down my father's killers?'

167

'As head of the House of Gonzaga—da Soares, I could do no less.'

'Excellent.' There were things in the investigation a man could do better. 'When do we start? How soon can we return to Celor?'

Joaquim cleared his throat. 'I will start by making representations to the nizam of Kokinada and ensuring that no effort is spared in bringing these dacoits to justice.'

'Dacoits!' Ynessa cried. 'Haven't you listened to what I've been telling you?'

'I've heard, and it isn't enough to convince me to leave everything and go charging off to Kokinada threatening the nizam's cousin and the Dutch.' Joaquim sounded as if he were talking to a three-year-old. 'It's quite obvious —'

'Obvious fie! You weren't in Celor or Armagon! How can you see what was obvious and what wasn't?'

'It's precisely because I wasn't there that I can see things more clearly. Listen to me, Ynessa. Your problem is that you're too involved in this whole business to think straight. It's absurd to think the Dutch would have risked the nizam's wrath by murdering Rodrigo, that anyone else who attended the auction would have killed him over pearls that were worthless to them. There's no doubt that Rodrigo was killed by dacoits. If we put sufficient pressure on the nizam, he'll find out who they were.'

'You put pressure on the nizam,' Ynessa said. 'As soon as Darnell brings me the evidence, I'm going to find the men who killed my father.'

'Darnell's another example of how insensible you've become. Darnell's a liar and a cheat who's fooled you into giving him money. You'll never see him again.'

She felt her temper rising at Joaquim's unfounded criticism of Darnell. 'I know Darnell, you don't,' she snapped. 'Darnell's an honest man. He'll come here with the pearls.'

'He won't. Why should he risk his life stealing pearls for

you when he could keep them? Why should he settle for half when he can keep everything?'

Not Darnell, Ynessa thought with a horrible sinking of her heart. Darnell wouldn't. But maybe Joaquim was right – why shouldn't he keep them?

'Forget Darnell,' Joaquim said, 'forget the money you gave him. You'll never see or hear from him again.'

She remembered Darnell charging into the mob after her, remembered the sudden tenderness in his glance when he'd seen her crying on the steps of the factory house. She looked straight at Joaquim. 'If Darnell gets the pearls, he'll bring them to me,' she said. 'You'll see!'

'If he brings you the pearls it will be because he's thought of another way to cheat you.'

'Stop talking nonsense!' Ynessa cried. 'Going after Ali Baig was my idea! Sending Darnell to steal the pearls was my idea!'

'That's what *he* made you think, my sweet.' Joaquim tilted his head back and looked down at her along the line of his nose.

She suddenly realized how stupidly arrogant he looked, how stupidly arrogant he *was*.

He was still speaking complacently. 'You don't know how clever men like that are. One day you'll realize how he's manipulated you and you will thank me for stopping you.'

'Stopping me?' Ynessa glared at him. Her voice was dangerously low and quivered with anger. 'You won't stop me doing anything. Now, leave Darnell alone, and leave me to find Rodrigo's killers – and we'll leave our wedding till that's over.'

'But – but –'

'Enough buts, Joaquim. You can't get married without me, and I'm not getting married till I've found Rodrigo's killers.' She picked up the journal from her desk. 'Now, I've got work to do.'

He took the journal from her hands and put it back on the desk. He pressed her fingers to his lips. 'Ynessa, Ynessa, why are we quarrelling like this? Let's find Rodrigo's killers together. Let's act as if we are lovers, not enemies.'

For a moment she felt a warmth come over her at his sudden meekness, but then she reminded herself that only seconds ago he'd been an arrogant, patronizing male *fidalgo*.

'Let's do some business together to prove we're friends,' he went on. He kissed her hands again.

'Business?' Ynessa drew her hands away.

'Business,' Joaquim smiled. 'I'm about to corner the market in indigo. And because we're friends and are going to be married soon, I'm going to let you join me. In two months we'll triple the size of Gonzaga–da Soares!'

Ynessa felt sick with horror. 'How much have you invested in indigo?'

'As much as I could borrow and the House of Gonzaga could spare. I need to buy more indigo. With another fifty thousand *escudos* I will have total control of the market so that the price of indigo will be what I say it is. Put up the fifty thousand *escudos*, Ynessa! Together we'll make a fortune.'

Ynessa shook her head. The market for indigo, used mainly for dyeing cloth, was well past its peak: everyone who'd needed to switch to indigo from woad and logwood had already done so. There was now an over-production of indigo, and the market was drifting into a slow decline. 'What do you know about indigo?' she asked.

'Enough to know that demand is growing, that by cornering the market now –'

'Get rid of your indigo before you make a loss you can't afford. Get rid of it before you destroy the House of Gonzaga.'

'Don't you tell me what to do! Gonzaga is my business.' Joaquim's forehead and cheeks were flushed and there was an ugly curl to his mouth. Abruptly he smiled; a tight, hard smile that had no humour. 'Don't be frightened, Ynessa, *cara mia*. There will be no loss. Instead, in one move I'll triple the profitability of the House of Gonzaga! And you will do the same for da Soares too, if you will put up the fifty thousand *escudos*.'

Ynessa's hands felt cold. Was it a coincidence that fifty thousand *escudos* was almost exactly the amount of spare cash the House of da Soares had available? Was that why Joaquim had been snooping round her office? She thought Joaquim was reckless, greedy and a bad businessman; but he was her future husband. She couldn't refuse him without wounding his pride. But to give in to him would mean ruining the House of da Soares, killing the dream that had been Rodrigo's and now was hers. In a low voice she said, 'The House of da Soares does not wish to invest in indigo.'

'Does not wish . . .' His eyes had a wild, maniacal look, and for a moment Ynessa thought he would strike her. 'You can't refuse me. You're going to be my wife. In a few months I'll be able to invest as much as I like on whatever I like.'

'In a few months,' Ynessa said tightly, thinking she had to find a way to keep Joaquim's hands out of the da Soares treasury. 'But for the present the House of da Soares will not invest in indigo.' She got to her feet. 'Now please go, Joaquim. I have work to do.'

'You're asking me to leave! How dare you?' He moved across the room towards her.

'We'll speak later,' Ynessa said, looking blindly down at the journal. She kept looking at it until she heard the door close.

Chapter Twelve

For five miles the massive star-shaped walls of Pulicat had dominated the bare landscape. Now, as he rode up to the Land Gate, Darnell felt his heart sink; faced with the vast strength of the Dutch, his whole plan seemed far too simple to succeed.

Pulicat was defended with eighteen-foot-thick walls, topped with parapets and embrasures for cannon and musketry. It had four land and two sea bastions, each mounted with four cannon; eight demi-cannon and four culverin lined the walls. There were four Land Gates and two Sea Gates, each protected by a guard of fifteen men. The gates were solid wood, reinforced with iron bands. Soldiers patrolled the walls, and the roof of a large barracks loomed over the west wall.

Darnell rode beneath the wooden portcullis of the Land Gate. Breaking out would be as difficult as breaking in, he thought. His horse's hooves made a peculiar, hollow, drumming sound. He was riding over the notorious Pulicat bear-pit, filled with pointed stakes. If his plan didn't work, he could well end up there, or be made to ride 'the horse' – a high, narrow wooden triangle, to which a man was chained for days, with his legs spread apart and weighted with lead pellets, so his body weight rested on his crotch. After two days most men died; all were seriously incapacitated.

Darnell told the guards who he was and that he wanted to see Governor de Groot. The signing of the truce had made the guards friendly, and they directed him straight away to the Compagnie offices in the Centraalplein.

Inside the fort, checkerboard houses freshly painted in grey and white lined eight paved streets and interconnecting alleys radiating from the Centraalplein. The streets, crowded with carts and coolies, were like those of any other large factory, except for the sombre, dark clothes of the Dutch, scrupulously dressed in doublets, breeches, stockings and folded-down lace collars – and the flowers. Darnell thought their love of flowers was the only decent thing about the Dutch. Each grey single-storey house had window-boxes and its own small garden filled with flowers. They made the fort less forbidding and the Dutch more human.

Darnell rode into the Centraalplein. The two-storey, brick St Pieterskerk, with its stepped, tiled roof, stood beside the two large houses where the writers and junior factors lived. The Centraalplein was dominated by the Compagnie house and the armoury, the former painted cream, the latter yellow, both built in the massive Dutch style with heavy stone walls, tiny, narrow windows and red-tiled roofs like a *hausfrau*'s bonnets. Darnell went over his plan for the hundredth time since he'd left Armagon. It was a good plan, he reassured himself, and it would work. Of course there were unknowns – everything depended on whether he had read de Groot and van Cuyler correctly – but what plan was perfect?

Two Dutch soldiers approached. Should he abandon the plan, make this trip a mere social visit? But he knew it was too late for that and unthinkable. As the Dutchmen reached him, he dismounted and asked to see Governor de Groot.

Karel van Cuyler sat in de Groot's office, toying with a quill and staring angrily at de Groot. He ignored the papers de Groot pushed across the desk at him. Following the success of Ali Baig's raid, he had obtained a loan from Abdul Nana for the full cost of the fort in Vaidya.

'I cannot approve this loan,' de Groot said. 'Five

thousand *guilders* – one thousand pounds – is beyond my authority; and in any case, if we are building a new factory, we must get approval from Batavia.'

'There isn't time,' van Cuyler hissed. The quill snapped. He made to throw it away and controlled himself. Forcing himself to be calm, he placed the broken quill on the desk. 'Within two weeks we must go to Seringa and offer to replace the *scheithaus* English. If we don't, we will lose Vaidya. Worse, the English will have Vaidya.'

De Groot appeared perplexed. 'But you tell me the English haven't the money.'

'They haven't the money *now*! That doesn't mean to say they won't have it in a month.'

'I've heard from Cogan,' de Groot said. 'He is positive the English aren't building a fort in Vaidya.'

'Cogan lies! The only thing stopping the *scheithaus* English building a fort in Vaidya is lack of money. But let us not concern ourselves only with the bloody English. Seringa will make a deal with anyone who will give him guns. There are others who will do that – the Danes, even the French.'

'That is possible,' de Groot agreed. 'But not, I think, very likely. It is the end of the season and no one has any money. So Seringa will have to wait.' He leaned across the desk. 'I understand the seriousness of what you are saying, mynheer, and I want to help you. But we will lose nothing by doing things in the proper order. Rather than borrowing from natives at extortionate rates, let us get approval and money from Batavia.' He pushed the papers closer towards van Cuyler.

You blathering half-witted gilly, van Cuyler thought, and said, 'We cannot wait. And we mustn't underestimate Darnell. All he needs is front money of two hundred English pounds and –'

There was a brief rap on the door. De Groot's writer came in. 'I'm sorry to disturb you, Excellency, but the

English agent from Armagon is downstairs and seeks to meet with you as soon as is convenient.'

'Darnell!' van Cuyler and de Groot said together, and stared at each other in surprise.

'Do you know what he wants?' van Cuyler demanded.

De Groot shook his head.

Van Cuyler was beginning to wonder if de Groot had a secret liaison with Darnell, if Darnell had discovered his link to Ali Baig . . . 'How many people are with him?' he asked the writer.

'He's alone.'

Alone! Van Cuyler couldn't think why Darnell would have come to Pulicat alone.

De Groot said, 'If we have finished our business, mynheer, I will see Darnell straight away.'

'Of course, mynheer. Of course.' Van Cuyler jumped to his feet and hurried to his own office next door. Locking the door, he sidled into the narrow space between a document cupboard and the wall adjoining de Groot's office. Through the hole he had drilled in the wall he could see de Groot seated behind his desk rearranging his inkwells. He pressed his ear to the wall and heard de Groot cough.

De Groot's office was typically Dutch, crammed with large pieces of solid furniture strategically placed to block any breeze. The walls were panelled. An oil painting of an East-Indiaman hung behind de Groot's desk, just below the Compagnie's coat-of-arms. The painting was dramatic, a ship keeling before a storm. Darnell wondered if it was that love of adventure that had brought de Groot to the East.

De Groot himself looked most unadventurous in the dark tunic, cotton ruff and dark trunks that made up the unofficial uniform of the Compagnie. Unlike other governors, he wore no medals; only his ring of office. His grey hair hung straight over his ears from the bald spot on the crown of his head; his pointed beard was neatly trimmed. He sat behind a vast desk, empty of everything except an ink-stand and a broken quill.

He gave Darnell a cheery smile. 'It is a great pleasure to see you, Mynheer Darnell. How is my friend Mynheer Cogan?'

'Extremely well and prosperous the last time I saw him.'

'For which we thank God.'

'And *karma*,' Darnell said.

De Groot looked at him sharply. The Dutch did not approve of any God other than their own. 'What brings you to Pulicat?' he asked Darnell.

Darnell said, 'We are seriously concerned about the truce. Indeed, we feel it might already be broken, that Java is being repeated.'

'There is no repetition of Java,' de Groot snapped. He pressed his hands together. They were small and clean, Darnell noticed, with polished nails. He said, 'We too are concerned about the truce. It is our understanding that you are building a factory in Vaidya.'

Darnell was glad he had anticipated de Groot's concern about Vaidya. He said, 'We have always contemplated building a factory in Vaidya – just as you have.'

De Groot acknowledged the point with a stiff nod. 'It is my understanding that the construction of your factory is imminent.'

Darnell shrugged. 'It would be – if we had permission from Prince Seringa . . .'

'So you don't have permission from Prince Seringa.'

Darnell looked blankly at de Groot, then past him at the Compagnie's coat-of-arms. 'Not exactly,' he said.

De Groot leaned forward and rested his elbows on the desk. 'Let me make myself very clear, Mynheer Darnell. Under our agreement, you may not build any new factories without our approval. We have not given approval for the building of a factory in Vaidya. In fact, we have not been asked for such approval. Any building in Vaidya will therefore constitute an irrevocable breach of our truce.'

Darnell asked, 'If you were to be asked for such approval, would you give it?'

It was de Groot's turn to look away. He said, 'That would depend on whether we were permitted to share in the factory.'

Good, Darnell thought, but not good enough. It wouldn't take long for the Dutch to turn an Anglo-Dutch enterprise into a Dutch one – as they had done in Java. Besides, the whole point of the factory in Vaidya was to drive out the Dutch, not encourage them to share in English profits. He said, 'Before we can even think of a joint enterprise in Vaidya, we must be reassured that we have a truce here in Kokinada.'

'Of course we do,' de Groot said.

Darnell told him about Ali Baig's raid on the factory and Rodrigo's murder.

De Groot shifted irritably in his chair. 'These incidents have nothing to do with us,' he said sharply. 'They give you no excuse to breach the truce. Ali Baig is not Dutch and, as far as we know, the Portuguese merchant was murdered by dacoits.'

A faint colour had risen to de Groot's cheeks, and there was indignation in his crystal blue eyes. Darnell couldn't tell if de Groot's emotion was genuine. He said, 'That is not the belief of the Portuguese who have found a connection between the Dutch and Ali Baig.'

'Then you must place the evidence before us, and we will have the perpetrator brought to justice.'

'The Portuguese are not party to our agreement.'

De Groot frowned, and Darnell went on, 'The Portuguese believe that the prize pearls were taken by the Dutch and are here in Pulicat. That is why I am here. To ask for your cooperation in finding them.'

'My cooperation? What are you suggesting, mynheer? That I act on this Portuguese fantasy?'

Darnell's heart beat faster. This was when he would find out if de Groot was working with van Cuyler – and, if he was, whether de Groot would betray his partner. He said, 'Mynheer, I am asking that you make a thorough and careful search of this factory, because if you find the pearls and provide evidence identifying their possessor, you will be entitled to a reward of five hundred pounds.'

De Groot sank back in his chair. In a small voice he said, 'But that is almost the value of the pearls.'

De Groot would do it for the money, Darnell thought. Fighting to keep his face impassive, he said, 'The House of da Soares is concerned with justice, not profit.' He leaned forward. 'In fact, I can make you an even better offer.'

'Better?' de Groot repeated faintly.

Darnell nodded. 'Because of the troubles in England between King Charles and Parliament, there is a huge demand for stones of all kinds. The Honourable Company is desperate for good stones. I am desperate for good stones. I will pay one thousand pounds for these pearls. No provenance is required.'

De Groot began to twist his fingers together. 'And you have the money?'

Darnell picked up his saddle-bag and placed it on the desk. Slowly he took out the sacks of coin he'd had made up in Armagon. The sacks were canvas and secured with heavy seals. Each contained as many small coins as Timana Chitty and everyone at Armagon had been able to muster, mixed with the twenty pounds' worth of gold Ynessa da Soares had advanced. The sacks settled on the table with a solid, satisfying clink. 'I have the money in gold,' Darnell said. 'Hungarian *ducats* and double *pistolets*.' It was unlikely de Groot would have come across those coins; their strangeness would account for any unfamiliarity in size or weight.

He held his breath as de Groot fondled the sacks. De Groot asked, 'How do you have this money when you say Ali Baig raided your factory?'

'Ali Baig only took the cloth from our warehouse. We had soldiers on our stairways preventing him getting into our offices.'

De Groot said, 'As I'm sure you know, mynheer, the sale of jewels and precious stone without permission from Batavia is forbidden. Any breach of that regulation is punished with flogging, imprisonment, and quite often the horse.'

'I know,' Darnell replied. 'But these stones are not Compagnie property. If they are here in Pulicat they were obtained by murder and by theft. I am certain the Compagnie would not wish to profit from such crimes.'

De Groot sat back, looked down at his chest and ran his fingers through his beard. He was choosing, Darnell knew, between the reward and the consequences of involving the Dutch in murder. Darnell said, 'If the Portuguese convince us you are protecting a criminal, we will abrogate the truce.'

De Groot looked up sharply.

Darnell went on. 'In fact, protecting such a criminal could be dangerous, if the Portuguese place their evidence before the nizam.'

De Groot looked uncertainly at Darnell. 'What do you want me to do?' he asked, his voice suddenly hoarse.

'First of all, you must talk with your council. Then you must make sure every Dutchman in this fort knows about the pearls and the reward.'

'I will do that right away.'

'Next, you should search every inch of this factory.'

'That will not be easy, or quick.'

'But you must do it. Once everyone knows of the reward, the person who has those pearls will not be able to entrust their custody to anyone. Nor will he be able to leave them outside his personal control. I don't believe your task will be too difficult.'

'Perhaps not.' He leaned back in his chair. 'Is there anything else you wish to discuss?'

'Yes,' Darnell said. 'I wish to replace the cloth I lost. I'll buy as many *salampores* and *guzzees* as you're willing to sell.'

De Groot said, 'Let me take you to our main warehouse. Abu Murad, our chief merchant, will find you what you want.'

The cloth warehouses were a series of linked, low-ceilinged rooms built into the fort's north wall. Here, piled bale upon bale, were the largest quantities of *chucklees*, *moorees*, *cossos*, *calicoes*, brown and white longcloth, chintzes and *eckbarees* that Darnell had seen. Sweating labourers in loincloths and turbans sorted the bales into piles, while others packed them for shipment. Nearest the door, Darnell spotted a quantity of *pintadoes* painted in the distinctive gold and red of the north, and further in the warehouse some *palempores* – thirty-six-yard-long chintz bedspreads.

A round-bellied man with a greying, spade-shaped beard, dressed in white pantaloons, embroidered jacket and cap, stopped giving directions to the coolies and turned to be introduced to Darnell. Having told Abu Murad what Darnell wanted, de Groot left to meet with his council.

Murad sprang into action, badgering the coolies and assistants to bring cloth for Darnell's examination, kneeling and unrolling bales himself, shouting to the coolies to bring more cloth and constantly importuning Darnell to feel the material.

Darnell looked at the cloth. Much of it was similar to what Ali Baig had stolen, but there was nothing he could positively identify as Company property. He kept looking, hoping he would find something.

* * *

Van Cuyler crawled out from behind the cupboard and lay flat on the floor. He was drenched in sweat and he could hardly breathe. Darnell, de Groot and the confounded Portuguese would crucify him. He was ruined, together with the Dutch empire.

He stood up and paced frantically round his office. He had to stop them. Somehow he had to stop them, for his sake, for Annatjie, for Holland! Also for Uncle Hendrijk, who had devoted his life to making him worthy. He thought of the exclusive Valck Academie and the apprenticeship to an assistant governor of the Compagnie that Uncle Hendrijk had arranged. He touched the dent above his left temple where Uncle Hendrijk had once hit him. Even that was so he could become worthy.

He *couldn't* fail. He wouldn't allow himself to fail. He was a van Cuyler. But how could he succeed against such impossible odds?

He sat down at his desk, clutching his head in his hands. He would hide the pearls! But where? If de Groot and all the Dutch were looking for them, there was no safe place in the fort. And that *scheithaus* Darnell had been right. Anyone he entrusted them to would claim the reward or sell them to Darnell and betray him. God take Darnell and de Groot and the Portuguese to hell!

He would kill Darnell. Darnell was alone in a Dutch fort. There would be plenty of opportunities ... He stopped that thought abruptly. Killing Darnell would endanger de Groot's truce and wouldn't stop de Groot's search. In fact, to protect the truce, de Groot might investigate the killing and discover that arraigning van Cuyler for murder was as good a way as any to get the reward.

How about a partnership deal with de Groot? But if de Groot knew he had murdered the Portuguese, incited Ali Baig and had the pearls, he would have him tried for murder and a breach of the truce and again claim the reward himself. He spat. De Groot had no need of him.

Sell the pearls to Darnell, he thought. No! That was stupid! Any idiot could see that Darnell would use the evidence to hang him. What could he do? He *had* to find a way to stop Darnell and the hunt for the pearls.

A thought struck him. Where had Darnell got the thousand pounds he had offered de Groot? He'd said the Portuguese were putting up only five hundred pounds, which meant Darnell was putting up the rest. But if Darnell had five hundred pounds, what was he doing looking for pearls when he should be building a factory in Vaidya?

Hungarian ducats *and double* pistolets! Darnell's voice rang in his ears. Where would Darnell get hold of five hundred pounds' worth of *ducats* and *pistolets*? Van Cuyler recalled the last time he'd seen a double *pistolet* had been six years ago in Surat. As for a Hungarian *ducat*, he hadn't seen one since he'd come East! Darnell's money must be salted. Which meant Darnell had no intention of paying the reward, or buying the pearls. So what *was* he trying to do? Van Cuyler wondered what he would do if he were Darnell . . . In time he had an idea, and a little while afterwards, a plan.

Darnell lunched with de Groot and the members of the council on soup, mutton pie, rice pudding, cheese and beer. He hadn't found any Armagon cloth at Pulicat, and concluded that van Cuyler must have sold it to Binlipatam. He asked where van Cuyler was now; de Groot told him that van Cuyler frequently ate alone.

The council were most interested in the pearls and the reward and decreed that a detailed search of the factory would be held the next morning. Immediately after lunch, Darnell went to the room in the barracks de Groot had given him. Removing his shirt and boots, he lay down on the narrow soldier's bed.

The room was dark and stifling. Warm sweat formed between his back and the sheet. The sounds of movement and conversation around him faded as the fort and barracks sank into afternoon torpor. He could do nothing but wait. The next move was up to van Cuyler. Van Cuyler *had* to move: he was well and truly boxed in. Darnell tried to think what van Cuyler would do.

'*Estupido*! You will kill all of us!' He heard Ynessa's voice as if she were in the next room, and realized that with the heat and the silence he had drifted off into a shallow sleep. He recalled how vulnerable Ynessa had looked after she'd been attacked by the mob, the way her face had puckered when she'd confronted him over his strategy at Armagon. He imagined the candescent glow of her eyes when he gave her the pearls. Her eyes! He felt himself melt as he remembered their depth and their reflecting darkness. *Estupido!* He must be out of his mind. Ynessa was Portuguese and Catholic and beautiful and rich and probably already betrothed. There could never be anything between them. He must stop thinking of her. He must simply deliver the pearls, take his money and build his fort. *Estupido! Estupido! Estupido!*

He slept and dreamed that van Cuyler was chasing him with a butcher's knife, that Ynessa was standing in front of him removing her clothes, that van Cuyler was running between them. He saw Ynessa take out a pistol and point it. Her dress was torn. She was looking at him, her eyes large, deep pools. He had a knife in his hand. He was moving after van Cuyler . . .

Darnell sensed rather than saw his door open. Quickly he rolled to his feet, grabbing the knife from beside his pillow. A pinch-faced urchin with matted hair, a tattered shirt and grubby pantaloons stood hesitating inside the door. For a moment Darnell thought he'd come to steal. Then the boy said, 'You Misser Darnell you come wi' me.' His bright eyes darted round the room. He raised a hand to his lips. 'Come quietly. Now.'

It had happened, Darnell thought. Van Cuyler had acted. Was the boy leading him into a trap? Had van Cuyler decided to end it quickly and murder him? He threw on his tunic, pulled on his boots and put the knife into its sheath. The only way to find out was to go with the boy. He strapped the pistol to his waist, draped the ends of the tunic over it and followed the boy out.

They went on to the empty parade ground. The heat was stunning, rising in steady currents from the baked earth. Within moments, Darnell was bathed in sweat, his throat as parched as if he had eaten sand. Around him the streets were deserted. Nothing moved except an occasional pi-dog searching for a scrap of shade. Darnell followed the boy to the cloth warehouses, their bodies casting tiny shadows about their feet.

The warehouses were closed, a drowsing native soldier sprawled before each door. The boy kicked a pi-dog out of the way and led Darnell to a flight of steps cut into the wall beside the warehouses. He pointed up at the wall. 'You go up. You see fren'. Go *jaldi jaldi.*'

Darnell hesitated. The steps, narrow and almost vertical, with rough handholds cut into the wall, were a precarious route. If he climbed the steps it would be difficult to see who was at the top, or resist an attempt to throw him off.

'You go up. You see fren'. Now.'

The boy's voice was bright, alive, encouraging. It seemed unlikely that he'd be an accessory to murder, Darnell thought, but then perhaps the boy didn't know. Slowly he edged up the wall. He looked up. The sun, bisected by the wall, shone straight into his eyes. He couldn't see if anyone was at the top. He stopped as his head drew level with the top of the wall, checking there was no one there before reaching up, grabbing the top of the wall and pulling himself up. He crouched as he twisted his feet under him, looking to right and left. Waves of heat rose off the top of the wall. It was deserted. He looked rapidly from side to side. The wall was about eighteen foot wide and paved, with a railing on the inside and a head-high parapet on the outside, broken by gun embrasures. Van Cuyler could have set an ambush in one of the embrasures.

'Misser! Misser!'

Darnell looked down. The boy was gesticulating that Darnell should walk away from the sea. Darnell stood up slowly, his right hand hovering near his pistol. Tentatively he walked along the wall, checking each embrasure as he went. Empty, empty, empty. His heart beat thickly, and there was a bitter taste of fear in his mouth. The gaps in the embrasures revealed an expanse of sun-parched grass, stretching to a dense grove of palms. A ribbon of golden beach unravelled endlessly beside a somnolent, sun-bright sea.

Something moved. His heart fluttered. He drew his pistol. In the sixth embrasure he found Abu Murad huddling in the skeletal shade of the walls.

Abu Murad threw him a shy smile, displaying a gold tooth. 'Is very hot,' Abu Murad remarked inconsequentially as Darnell climbed into the embrasure.

Darnell looked back at the fort. Apart from the pi-dogs and a few soldiers loitering in the doorways of buildings, it still seemed deserted. He turned to Abu Murad. 'What do you want?'

'You want buy pearls. I have pearls. You want see?'

So van Cuyler had fallen into his trap, Darnell thought; but clearly van Cuyler had also set his own trap. 'I want to see,' Darnell said.

Abu Murad reached under his tunic and brought out a small bag. Opening it, he took out a tiny saucer. Slowly he emptied the bag. Eight silver-white pearls rolled into the saucer. Darnell noticed how easily they moved. He took the jeweller's glass Abu Murad was holding out and looked. These were Orient pearls, the most valued in the world. Each pearl was translucent, as if lit by a warm flame inside. They were the best of their kind, each pearl perfect, *and* they were perfectly matched. These were the prize pearls of Celor.

'Is nice,' Abu Murad breathed. 'Is very good. Is bes' pearls in all Coromandel.'

Darnell couldn't take his eyes away from the pearls, brilliant and glowing.

'I give you good price. You buy seven thousand five hundred *guilders*, one thousand five hundred pounds. You give money, I give pearls, we are both happy men, no.'

The price was high but he was expected to bargain. 'I don't have one thousand five hundred pounds,' Darnell said.

Abu Murad stopped smiling. 'These bes' pearls. Seven thousand five hundred *guilders*,' he repeated.

'No,' Darnell said. 'Five hundred pounds. Two thousand five hundred *guilders*.'

Abu Murad struck his forehead with the heel of his hand and hissed as if he'd been hit in the stomach. 'Seven thousand five hundred *guilders*,' he said again. He pulled out another bag containing a mixture of pink and black pearls. 'For that, I give you these also.'

'I don't want these other pearls,' Darnell said. 'I'll give you five hundred pounds for these.' He tapped the bag of prize pearls with his finger.

'No. You take all.' Abu Murad was insistent, and suddenly Darnell knew what van Cuyler intended to do. He was going to catch him dealing in precious stones and kill him during the arrest. That way he could keep the prize pearls and get rid of Darnell and the offer of a reward. Darnell wondered if he should close the deal with Abu Murad and have de Groot attend the exchange. But in that case van Cuyler wouldn't show and de Groot would just claim the reward. What if de Groot set up an ambush? Van Cuyler too would be lying in wait, and the chances of one not discovering the other were minimal. He'd have to trap van Cuyler without de Groot, Darnell decided, by springing the trap himself. That would heighten the risk of arrest, but there was no alternative. He'd play hide and seek with van Cuyler. At worst that would give him at least the pearls. If everything worked, he'd have van Cuyler too . . .

Darnell said, 'Even if I had seven thousand five hundred *guilders*, I wouldn't give more than three thousand five hundred for those pearls.'

Abu Murad beat his forehead in despair and put the pearls away. Darnell turned to step out of the embrasure.

From behind him, Abu Murad said, 'Where you going? You stay here. You my fren', I give you good price for pearls. One thousand two hundred pound.'

'Eight hundred pounds,' Darnell said, climbing back into the embrasure. 'For all the pearls.'

Abu Murad patted the parapet beside him. 'Come, sit. We talk.'

Forty minutes later he had agreed a price of four thousand five hundred *guilders* – nine hundred pounds – for all the pearls.

Abu Murad said, 'You meet me here, five o'clock. You bring money. I bring pearls.'

Abu Murad was so decisive, Darnell felt sure he had been ordered to set up the meeting for precisely that time. By five o'clock the light would be starting to fade. Van Cuyler must mean to spring his trap then. But the fading light would also help Darnell reverse the trap. 'All right,' he said.

Darnell watched Abu Murad go, sidling furtive and crab-like between houses, his portly figure soon lost between the roofs of the shuttered buildings. He wouldn't make the exchange at five o'clock here, Darnell decided. He would make it somewhere else, somewhere van Cuyler wouldn't find him.

He began to walk inland along the wall, searching. Inside the fort there were too many places for concealment; getting out would be a problem too. He turned along the west wall. The land to the north and west had been cleared, leaving wide esplanades of parched grass. The whole area was too exposed for a meeting.

At the end of the west wall Darnell turned towards the sea. Though he could feel the sun burning his skin, his body felt cool from the sea breeze. Below him was a fruit grove which spread all the way down to the beach and was separated from the esplanade by a high wall that looked like a trail of white ribbon. He decided to take a better look. He climbed down the wall and walked to the Sea Gate.

Two sentries sitting in the shade of the arch gave him a desultory wave as he went out. Outside the Sea Gate was a boatyard with a dry dock for careening and repairing ships, a wharf almost as wide as the fort and capable of unloading four ships at once. Between the wharf and the fort was a terrace of beaten earth extending to the fruit groves. Darnell walked along it, squinting at the sun, allowing the rough breeze to dry the sweat from his tunic. Where the terrace ended he turned and walked through the fruit groves till he came to the ten-foot-high wall separating it from the esplanade. He knew what he would do.

Van Cuyler sat on a cushion in the small room Abu Murad used as an office, and tried to find a comfortable position as he listened to the chief merchant's account of his meeting with Darnell. When he'd finished, van Cuyler said, 'I want four of your men to go with you. They must not be seen by Darnell and must simply observe both of you. If Darnell refuses to make the exchange on the north wall, you must use one of these men to get a message to me. If you can't talk to them without Darnell knowing, you should look at them and scratch your nose like this.' Van Cuyler showed him. 'Then the men should watch where Darnell is meeting you and one of them must come and tell me. Do you understand all that?'

'Yes, yes. It will be no problem.'

'You must be very careful,' van Cuyler warned. 'Darnell mustn't know he's being followed.'

'Of course, of course.' He started as the door was flung open and van Roon strode in with two Dutchmen.

Van Cuyler spoke to them in a Javanese dialect unknown to Abu Murad. 'I have discovered that Darnell is going to make a deal in illegal stones with Abu Murad,' he said. 'I want you at the armoury at half-past four, fully armed. First of all we will kill Abu Murad, and make it look as if Darnell murdered him in a dispute over the stones.'

'And Darnell?'

'Darnell will die resisting arrest,' van Cuyler said.

Van Roon's broken face split in a huge grin of anticipation.

Shortly after five that evening, Darnell climbed the steps to the top of the north wall. A cooler breeze than the afternoon's snatched at his tunic and tousled his hair. He kept one hand on his pistol, just in case van Cuyler had planned something unexpected.

Abu Murad was waiting in the same embrasure in which they'd met that afternoon, his smile more constrained. He took out the sealed bags of stones from beneath his jacket and looked questioningly at Darnell for the money.

Darnell held out his hand for the stones. 'I didn't bring the money in case you were tempted to take it and keep the stones.' He examined the bags closely through Murad's glass. They were the same pearls he had been shown that afternoon. Knotting the bags with a tight double-hitch that would take Abu Murad a while to unravel, he returned the bags. 'Wait for me there,' he pointed across the fort to the south wall. 'In the third embrasure from the east wall.'

Murad said, 'Is not necessary. I wait here. You bring money.'

'You meet me there,' Darnell insisted. 'On the south wall in the third embrasure from the east.' He crossed his hands in front of his chest.

Abu Murad opened his mouth to say something, but thought better of it and brushed past Darnell as he left.

Darnell watched him walk hurrying along the middle of the street towards the Centraalplein. He didn't stop or talk to anyone and just once blew his nose. Abu Murad had come alone and no one had followed him. How long a leash had van Cuyler given him, Darnell wondered?

By the time Darnell had made his way round the fort wall, Murad was waiting for him in the embrasure. 'I'm not taking delivery of the stones inside the fort,' Darnell told him. 'I want you to take the stones outside the fort for me.'

'Why outside? Why we not do business here?'

'Because if I am found with the stones I go to jail. You've got to take the stones outside the fort for me. There.' Darnell pointed to a banana grove below them and described its precise location. 'I will meet you there, and this time I promise I'll bring the money.'

'This time no money I go home,' Abu Murad said. Again Darnell watched him until he disappeared from view along the road leading to the Sea Gate. Again, Abu Murad spoke to no one, nor did anyone follow him. His cold seemed worse. He blew his nose twice before he'd reached the foot of the steps.

Darnell waited ten more minutes, then walked to the Sea Gate. The sun was setting. Outside the fort the strollers on the terrace had diminished to a few stragglers. An hour previously he'd collected his horse from the stables and ridden out of the Sea Gate with a change of clothes and the sacks of coin in his saddle-bags. He'd ridden along the beach by the terrace, crowded then with Dutchmen and their wives strolling on the sand, some of the men paddling in the shallows while the women held their boots. He'd ridden into the grove, tethered the horse in a clump of jak trees, and returned to meet Abu Murad.

Now, as he walked along the terrace, the setting sun threw ripples of orange and red across the sea and the air had the raw salt stench of an incoming tide. He jumped off the terrace and walked quickly through the grove, ignoring the fine sand creeping through the soles of his boots.

The short twilight was filled with dying shadows. He looked up at the fort walls to see if he was being observed. A lone sentry stood on the ramparts, gazing out to sea. Darnell scurried between the palms. It seemed ages before he reached the jak trees.

His horse whinnied as he approached. He spoke to it softly, patted it, put away the feed-bag and led the animal to the banana grove where he'd asked Abu Murad to wait. Tethering the horse to a tree, he went in.

The grove was filled with a dim, shadowless light that took away all depth. There was no sign of Abu Murad. Darnell wondered if Abu Murad had gone home as he'd threatened, if he'd come to the right grove, if his manoeuvring had been observed and he'd walked into a trap. His heartbeats filled the silence. Abu Murad *had* to be here. For van Cuyler's plan to work, he had to exchange the stones.

Walking to the edge of the grove, he peered out. Evening was rapidly turning to night, and he could see nothing but a tangle of undergrowth and the darkening shadows of trees. Where the devil was Abu Murad? He heard a soft rustle behind him and whirled. Abu Murad emerged from the half shadow of the adjacent bamboo grove, then solidified into a silent, white-clad shape, his face split by a rigid smile.

'Where the devil were you?' Darnell demanded in a harsh whisper.

'There.' Abu Murad pointed to the bamboo grove. 'I make sure all is safe. All this dangerous for me also.' Abu Murad sounded peeved.

'Are you alone?'

'Yes.' Abu Murad sniffed nervously. 'Why?'

'I thought I heard something.'

Abu Murad swallowed, then raised a hand, closed his eyes and made a show of listening. 'Is nothing,' Abu Murad said, opening his eyes. 'You have money? You want pearls?' Abu Murad held out the stones.

Darnell took the pearls and passed him one sack of coins. 'Don't break the seal till I tell you.' Darnell looked quickly at the pouches. The knots were unbroken. He put them into his pocket. Holding out the second bag of coins he suddenly swung it with all his might, hitting Abu Murad behind the ear with the heavy sack. There was a solid clunk and Abu Murad's knees crumpled. He fell softly, face forward on to the sand. Darnell knelt and made sure he was breathing, then rolled him on his side so his nostrils wouldn't be blocked by sand. He picked up the sack Abu Murad had dropped and hurried out of the grove.

'Ah, there you are!' Van Cuyler sat comfortably on a chestnut hunter beside Darnell's horse, a pistol in his hand. He had van Roon and two soldiers with him; all were armed with knives and muskets. Van Cuyler said, 'We've got you dead to rights, Darnell. You've been dealing illegally in precious stones. Give them to us.'

Darnell darted back into the trees, fumbling for his pistol as he ran. He heard van Cuyler shout, 'Get him!' followed by the sound of a pistol shot and the whizz of a ball tearing through the trees. He darted past Abu Murad's prone figure. From behind him came the sounds of pounding boots and the rasp of clothing and buckles. He ran into the bamboo grove.

Darnell knew he couldn't hide in the grove for long. The soldiers would come after him and van Cuyler could quickly summon more soldiers. With more men combing the grove for him, he'd have no chance of escape. Standing behind a tree, he looked back. He could see two of the soldiers clearly silhouetted against a flaming backdrop of trees. They were coming into the grove, waving their muskets. Shooting the nearest one in the shoulder, Darnell ran through the back of the grove, across an open space and into a clump of papaya.

A shot crashed through the trees. Van Cuyler called, 'Come on out, Darnell. You can't escape.' Darnell listened to the crashing of undergrowth as the second soldier searched for him. Somehow he had to get back to his horse. He glimpsed the soldier crossing the open space and moved deeper into the grove.

Pressed sideways against a tree, he watched the soldier slow and look round hesitantly, first to the left, then to the right. Darnell stepped out from behind the tree, knife in hand. The soldier saw him and raised his musket; at the same instant Darnell flung the knife, catching the man in the throat and cutting off his frothy gurgle almost as soon as it started. The man dropped the musket and fell. Looking up, Darnell saw van Cuyler and van Roon coming after him. Hurriedly he turned and darted out of the grove towards his horse.

He sprinted, zig-zagging round the trees. He heard the rapid pounding of hooves, then van Cuyler's horse loomed out of the shadows. Darnell's back flamed as van Cuyler's *sjambok* landed across his shoulders once, then again. Darnell felt as if his tunic had been split open and his back sliced with a red-hot knife. He ran, but van Cuyler drew level easily and hit him across the face. 'There's no point running! I've got you dead set.' Van Cuyler levelled his pistol.

With all his might, Darnell flung a sack of coins at van Cuyler. It hit with a ringing thump. Van Cuyler gasped and swayed, but regained his balance, and lashed out with his *sjambok*. Darnell jumped back quickly allowing the tip of the lash to hiss past his nose. Leaping forward, he pulled van Cuyler's foot, drew his empty pistol and smashed the butt into the side of van Cuyler's knee.

Van Cuyler cried out and beat down at Darnell with his *sjambok*. Again the pain blazed along Darnell's back, but Darnell hammered at van Cuyler's knee again then, as the *sjambok* swung down, turned his back and pulled van Cuyler's flailing arm over his shoulder. With a great cry and creaking of leather, van Cuyler overbalanced. For a moment Darnell felt an enormous weight on his neck and shoulder. Then van Cuyler curled through the air and crashed on to the sand with a massive expulsion of breath.

Darnell jumped on van Cuyler's stomach, running across his face and using him as a launch to leap into the saddle. He turned the horse round, kicked his heels into its flanks, and urged it forward. The horse took off, surging across the sand towards van Roon who stopped running and drew his knife. Driving his heels in harder, Darnell pulled van Cuyler's empty pistol out of its saddle-holster, rode straight at van Roon, and flung the pistol at his face. Van Roon cried out and dived to the ground. Darnell thundered past him through the trees.

He let the horse find its way through the grove, urging it on with heels and hands. They twisted round this way and that, leaning precariously as the huge animal tried to keep its footing in the soft earth. Then the wall loomed in front of them, white, high and solid. Darnell felt the animal falter, booted it and leaned forward, bunching the reins. 'You can do it,' he murmured into the animal's ear. 'You can do it,' running his hands along its head, encouraging it, willing it.

The wall drew nearer and seemed to grow higher and more solid with each stride. Darnell gave the animal a quick rake with his heels, gathered up its head, launched it. He felt the huge shoulders below him bunch. Then they were flying at the wall. There was a moment of utter silence. Darnell glimpsed patches of exposed brick and the twilit sky between the horse's flattened ears. He felt the wind catch his sweating body and a moment of exhilarating weightlessness. Then they were crashing down on the other side and his pelvis rushed to meet his neck and he had to hold himself in the saddle and gather the horse and keep it moving forward till they were cantering across the esplanade away from the fort, tasting the bitterness in his mouth and hearing his heart beat as loud as the hooves beneath him.

Chapter Thirteen

Ynessa's office was an unusual combination of sitting room and work area. She'd designed it herself. It was brighter than most business offices, with pale aquamarine walls complementing the deep olive of the leather-topped desk, the lemony-yellow cushions of the settle and the two armchairs at the end of the room. Her desk and all the furniture was made of pine, the lightness of the wood emphasized by a Chinese silk carpet in pale blue and yellow.

Her desk was covered with papers. With three ships – half the da Soares fleet – in at the same time, the past week had been a constant bustle between docks and warehouses, with barely time to sit in one place before rushing to the other.

The mid-morning sun streamed through the window. Sweat trickled between her shoulder-blades and beaded on the dimpled flesh below her nostrils. The build-up of heat was nearing its peak and only a shred of breeze trickled through the open windows. She wiped sweat from her forehead and added a row of figures.

Jaime Figueras, Manuel's son, knocked and entered. He was fourteen and had joined the House two months ago as a junior writer. He had his father's doleful features but right now his face was animated. 'Beg pardon, *menina*, there's an army deserter outside who insists on seeing you.'

'Have Alvarez see him.' The Portuguese army treated its men abominably, and many simply walked away with only the clothes they stood in. Some came to the House of da Soares looking for work.

'He insists on seeing you, *menina*. He says his name is Darnell and he is –'

'Darnell! Why didn't you say so, you idiot? Bring him here at once!' Jumping to her feet, she swept her papers into a drawer, straightened her tunic and dabbed her face and neck with a handkerchief. She rushed to the windows and opened them wider. She wished her tunic wasn't so damp with perspiration. Her heart was beating rapidly and she told herself it was simply anticipation about the news Darnell would bring. She was betrothed and had no interest in Darnell. She'd thought of him, true, but that was only because he was bringing her the evidence that would hang Rodrigo's killers. She dabbed her face again and put some cologne behind her ears and on the inside of her wrists.

Jaime Figueras knocked on the door again. Richard Darnell shambled through, his tunic and breeches filthy and stiff with salt, his boots striped white with it. His hair was matted, his chin covered in a heavy growth of beard. He seemed leaner, his shoulders and ribs sticking out from under the tattered tunic; his cheeks so sunken it gave his blue-black eyes a hollow stare. A vicious red weal stretched diagonally across his forehead, and there were cuts on his hands, some of them weeping yellow pus. 'Oh, Senhor Darnell,' Ynessa cried. 'What's happened to you? Let me send for our chirurgeon –'

'Later. I have a lot to tell you, *menina*.' Incredibly he grinned, his teeth flashing white against the dark of his beard. He reached inside his shirt, unpinned two pouches and spilled their contents in a sparkling shower on her desk.

The pearls gleamed against the olive-green leather, those from the first pouch a uniform off-white, the others a rainbow of colours. Ynessa bent down and looked closely at the white pearls. They were flawless and glowed with an internal fire. She had no need for a glass to know they were the prize pearls of Celor!

She turned and looked at Darnell, her heart cartwheeling with excitement. He'd done it! He'd got the pearls and found Rodrigo's killers! She reached out and threw her arms around him, pulled his head to hers and kissed him. His lips were stiff and dry, then suddenly they were moist and moving and his arms were round her and he was kissing her with a fierce passion. A warm flame of desire flickered about her loins. He smelt of salt and sweat and she wanted him to keep holding her and pressing her to him –

She couldn't! She mustn't! She was engaged to Joaquim Gonzaga . . . Pushing against Darnell's arms, she broke his grip and ran behind her desk. Her heart was tripping. She placed the back of her knuckles against her mouth so he wouldn't see how fast she was breathing. 'Thank you, Senhor Darnell. I am so grateful, so overcome –' She couldn't think of what to say. 'Before we do anything else we must get your wounds treated. Wounds become sour so quickly in this climate. It won't take long and –' She sat down and looked at him.

She was stunningly beautiful, Darnell thought, the sheen of the green silk tunic and yellow pantaloons highlighting the dusky smoothness of her skin. Beneath the loose clothes he could make out a strong, slender body, with a waist that was high and narrow and solid legs that were disproportionately long. His body still flamed from her kiss and he wanted her as he'd wanted no other woman before. But she was Portuguese and Catholic and much younger. Calming his own uneven breathing he said, 'Let me tell you about the pearls.'

He told her how he had met with de Groot, and about his subsequent confrontation with van Cuyler and his escape from Pulicat. He told her how he'd ridden most of the night after leaving Pulicat and been surprised that van Cuyler hadn't given chase. When the road had ended at an estuary, he'd realized why. Unless he chose to swim there was no way forward. He would have to ride back to Pulicat.

Then he'd spotted the fishing boats, not beached but thankfully moored where the river met the sea. He'd crept past the fishermen's huts to the river and stolen a boat. He'd pushed it out of the estuary and, once he'd rowed it far enough into the sea, hoisted sail. There'd been a good wind which had swept him briskly south. His *karma* had been good and he'd come ashore a few miles north of San Thome, where some villagers had given him a ride to the fort.

Ynessa couldn't believe what she'd heard. He'd lied, he'd stolen, he'd fought, he'd risked his life over and over again – and escaped. Only the sight of him sitting there in his salt-stiff clothes with his face scarred and his hands cut to ribbons convinced her it was true. You're an incredible man, Richard Darnell, she thought, with *cojones* like melons. And stopped herself. She shouldn't ever include Richard Darnell and *cojones* in the same thought. She scribbled out a provenance, divided the pearls into two and pushed one pile towards Darnell. 'Your share.'

Darnell put the provenance away, scooped the pearls into one of the pouches and pinned them to his shirt.

Ynessa wanted to hold him again, to help the chirurgeon bind his wounds. She gripped the pouch with her share of the pearls. Better to concentrate on what had to be done. 'I want you to write me an account of –'

'But first a favour.'

'Of course! Anything!'

'I want to buy five hundred pounds' worth of assorted *guzzees* and *sallores* for delivery in ten days. I will pay you when they are delivered. I've already contracted to sell all of it.'

'I'll see how much we have.' Ynessa took a huge ledger off one of the shelves on the far wall and stood studying it. 'I can let you have four hundred pounds' worth at cost.'

Darnell nodded. That would more than take care of Captain Sen.

She walked briskly to the next office and came back a few minutes later with a contract note. When they'd signed it she said, 'Now I want you to write me a sworn account of what happened at Pulicat.'

Darnell shook his head. 'A sworn account won't do you any good. All I can swear to are my dealings with Abu Murad. As far as I *know*, van Cuyler had nothing to do with the pearls.'

'But he was there. You saw him. He tried to arrest you.'

'Arrest me, yes, in pursuit of his legitimate duty preventing the sale of stones.'

'The stones were not his.'

'The pearls were not his. The other stones were Dutch.'

'That makes no difference. Make your statement. Abu Murad will say he got the pearls from van Cuyler.'

'If he lives to make the statement.' He told Ynessa about van Cuyler being responsible for the deaths of seventeen English merchants at Japara. 'If he feels threatened by Abu Murad, van Cuyler will kill him.'

'How do you know so much about van Cuyler?' Ynessa asked.

He told her about Java.

She stared at him, her brain reeling. A merchant with his own factory at – she made a quick calculation. Darnell couldn't have been more than twenty-five then! He'd had to have been very shrewd and very lucky. *By God, I think I could love you, Richard Darnell*, she thought, then stopped herself. It was impossible. She had to concentrate on the matter in hand.

It was frustrating to be so near to unravelling the truth and yet so far. She told Darnell about Mirza Baig and her visit to Celor. 'I want you to come with me to Celor and tell Mirza Baig what you know,' she said. 'The fact that we have the pearls, and know of the link between van

Cuyler and Ali Baig will frighten Mirza enough to make him talk. Then we can take his evidence to the nizam and have him make Ali Baig talk.' She brought her palms together sharply. 'That's how we get van Cuyler.'

It was a good idea and probably would work. But Darnell had only ten days before he had to start building at Madera. He said, 'I'm sorry, *menina*, I haven't the time to accompany you to Celor.'

He wanted money, Ynessa thought, and felt disappointed. She said, 'I'll make it worth your while. I'll pay you more than your Company does.'

'It isn't a question of money,' Darnell said. 'I have work to do.'

'Work? At that flea-pit of a factory? I'll pay you four times as much as you earn there!' Her voice was shrill.

'It's not to do with Armagon,' Darnell said. 'I'm building a fort at Madera.'

She stared at him, wide-eyed. The Vaidyans were Hindu conservatives and feared contamination from outsiders. 'How did you get permission from the Vaidyans?' she asked.

'I convinced Prince Seringa a factory at Madera was a necessity.'

He had a mocking smile on his face, and for a moment she thought he was teasing her. She asked herself if Darnell was the kind of man who could persuade the Vaidyans to let him build a factory, and concluded he was. So, after all these years, Vaidya would be open to foreign trade. Incredible! Darnell was going to build an English factory at Madera . . .

The sweat chilled along her spine. An English fort at Madera would draw the *entrepôt* business away from San Thome. She asked, 'How does building the fort stop you from travelling to Celor with me?'

'I have to start building in the next ten days. Otherwise Seringa will offer the fort to the Dutch.'

A Dutch fort at Madera would be the worst possible disaster. The Portuguese were in a state of war with the Dutch, and while the English would simply draw away business, the Dutch would prevent ships calling at San Thome, cut off its food supplies, harass its inhabitants and force its abandonment. She had to inform the merchants' council. The Portuguese had to do something about Madera.

There was an alternative to the Dutch and an English fort sucking away San Thome's business, she thought. The Portuguese could work with the English and use the English fort as an opening into Vaidya. That would strengthen San Thome *and* increase the Portuguese influence in Vaidya, and both the English and the Portuguese would prosper. That is what Rodrigo would have arranged. But how could she persuade the English to let the Portuguese trade from their fort?

Do something for them, she heard Rodrigo say. *Put them under obligation.*

She asked, 'Is this why you need the pearls? To finance your fort?'

He nodded.

'Our merchants' council can help you finance it,' she said.

Darnell's mouth tightened. 'No. The fort at Madera must be English. That is what Prince Seringa wants. It is what the Honourable Company wants.'

Ynessa sensed there was something wrong. If the English Company was financing the fort, why did Darnell need to use the pearls? 'Will the money from the pearls be enough for you to finance the fort?'

'No.' Darnell explained that the fort would cost over a thousand pounds.

'Where will you find the rest of the money?'

'I'm hoping that by the time we need it, the voyages will have brought us money from England.'

'Well, if you need any help,' Ynessa said, 'I'm sure our merchants' council will be pleased to give it.'

'I'll bear that in mind,' he said, almost too politely.

There was still something not quite right about the fort. 'Will you bring settlers to Madera from many English forts or just from Armagon?' Ynessa asked.

'Initially, just from Armagon.'

Now *that* was unusual. Armagon hadn't enough settlers; she wondered why, with such a magnificent opportunity for trade, the English weren't settling Madera from all their establishments. The English reluctance could be Portuguese good fortune, she thought. The English would need a larger infrastructure than the settlers at Armagon could provide, and the only other people who could provide that quickly enough were the Portuguese.

There was more she had to learn about this fort, but, Ynessa decided, for the moment she'd asked enough questions. She would keep a check on what was happening at Madera and try to get Darnell under obligation to her. 'Let me get you some refreshment,' she said, 'and have our chirurgeon look at your hands.' She walked to the door. 'We have a ship sailing north in an hour. If you wish I will arrange a passage for you to Armagon.'

'*Menina*, I would be most grateful . . .'

Ali Baig pushed his way to the front of the veranda as the Dutchmen galloped into his compound, scattering dust and chickens. Three of them formed a loose semi-circle as van Cuyler dismounted and strode across the compound. The Dutchmen had drawn their muskets and lit their slow-matches. They hadn't brought any presents and van Cuyler wasn't carrying anything except his *sjambok*. It obviously wasn't a friendly visit, and Ali Baig felt a tiny quiver of fear.

Van Cuyler pounded up the steps, his boots ringing on the dusty cement. His size was intimidating, but Ali Baig determined he would not show fear. 'What is the meaning of this?' he cried. 'Why have you come? Have you brought my money?'

Van Cuyler strode across the veranda and stood so close to him that Ali Baig could smell the meaty stench of the Dutchman's body. 'Inside,' van Cuyler hissed. His spittle dampened Ali Baig's forehead. 'We have to talk.' Pushing past him, the Dutchman marched inside the house.

Ali Baig looked from the Dutchmen with their muskets to his men waiting for orders. 'Wait here,' he snapped. 'I'll take care of him.'

Van Cuyler was standing in the small room where they had last met. Ali Baig found the goblet of geneva and poured some into a beaker. 'This is finished,' he said tersely. 'You should have brought me more of this.'

'I should have brought a noose to hang you,' van Cuyler said. 'You lied to me about Armagon. After a small skirmish you took over the fort! Hah! Bloody, good-for-nothing liar! You never went above the ground floor of the factory house!'

Ali Baig took another gulp of geneva. How had van Cuyler found out what had happened at Armagon? 'There was no need to go above the ground floor,' he said, trying to appear unruffled. 'All the cloth and goods were in the storehouse on the ground floor.'

'Darnell had twelve hundred pounds in gold on the first floor.' There was no reason for Ali Baig to know that Darnell had stuffed the bags with cheap coin and salted it with some gold.

'Gold?' Ali Baig's face paled. How had van Cuyler found out what Darnell had in the fort? 'You told me you wanted goods. You didn't say anything about gold. The goods more than satisfied the taxes I claimed.'

Van Cuyler's face was suffused with anger, his eyes large and bulging. 'Why didn't you tell me about the Portuguese woman?'

One of his men had sneaked to van Cuyler. He'd find out who and cut his tongue out. Van Cuyler had moved close to him again, towering, intimidating.

'The woman was of no importance. Just a silly little draggle-tail in need of a good jigging.'

'She was Rodrigo's daughter. She accused you of murdering Rodrigo.'

'So what. She can't prove anything.' Ali Baig backed away to his hookah. His hands shook slightly as he took a dried tobacco leaf from a pouch by the hookah, filled it with *ganja* and lit it.

'The woman can hang you now.' Van Cuyler told him how Darnell had come to Pulicat and stolen the pearls.

Ali Baig stared at van Cuyler, amazed. None of this could be true. Van Cuyler was simply constructing an elaborate stratagem to cheat him of his share of the pearls. 'If Darnell stole the pearls,' he asked, 'why haven't you gone after him and got them back?' That would show van Cuyler he couldn't be cheated with elaborate stories.

'The pearls aren't Dutch property. I can't send Dutch soldiers after them without someone finding out about Celor.'

All right. So Darnell had the pearls. But what difference did that really make? Darnell wouldn't be able to sell the pearls without a provenance. And perhaps at some time they could come to an arrangement . . .

Van Cuyler interrupted this thought. 'Darnell will get together with that Portuguese woman and use those pearls to hang us!' he hissed.

Van Cuyler's words were like a brace of arrows through his brain. 'But why? What does Darnell care what happened at Celor?'

'Because Darnell hates me and will do anything to ruin me. And now he hates you. Your raid on Armagon ruined plans he had for a fort in Vaidya.'

'I didn't know –'

'Darnell doesn't care about that.' He told Ali Baig about Annatjie and the destruction of the *Prinsen*.

Ali Baig looked down angrily as the tobacco leaf burnt down to his fingers. Grinding it out, he said, 'I want nothing to do with this. Nothing. This is between you and Darnell –'

'It's too late,' van Cuyler spat. 'You're too far in.'

Ali Baig hung his head in his hands. How had he allowed himself to get involved in this? He was now caught between the Dutch and the English, an accessory to murder, guilty of directly breaching the nizam's mandates.

Van Cuyler said, 'There's one way you can save us. You must raid Armagon and recover the pearls.'

That was impossible! He had no reason to raid Armagon again; even if he had, prising the pearls from Darnell was likely to be dangerous and difficult. Darnell was a resourceful man, ruthless and efficient – and a killer.

'And kill Darnell!'

Ali Baig looked up in astonishment. Van Cuyler was mad. Even if he could kill Darnell, he'd have to answer for the killing to the nizam. And while the English might not do too much about the loss of goods, they would certainly seek punishment and compensation for the murder of one of their agents. 'I can't,' he said flatly. It was van Cuyler who had got them into this mess. It was up to him to find a way out.

'If you don't, you're worse than dead. Darnell will take the pearls to the woman and they will tell the nizam about you.'

'Why me? There's no link between the pearls and me. The only link is between you and Abu Murad.'

'The woman has already accused you of killing her father. By now Darnell suspects a link between you and me. They will have the nizam arrest you so that you can tell them about me.'

Van Cuyler's theory made a horrible kind of sense. 'So

why can't you do something? You're at risk too.'

'Not as much as you, my friend. You see, I can always return to Batavia . . .' He bent forward, took a dried leaf from the pouch and lit it. 'Look at it this way. The English cannon is still buried in the sand. Without it they won't put up any kind of a fight. If you go in at night, you can seize the fort, seize Darnell, recover the pearls and be on your way home by dawn. You can always explain to the nizam you had information that Darnell was about to raid Sairin and kill you. There won't be any trouble getting people to swear to that, after you've dealt with Darnell.'

It was possible, Ali Baig thought. But the consequences were too terrible to think about . . .

'I will have the Dutch make a formal offer to the nizam to take over Armagon.'

That would settle the nizam, Ali Baig thought. All the nizam cared about was profits. He said, 'I want that offer in writing.'

'You shall have it, my friend. You shall have it as soon as you have agreed to go.'

'I agree,' Ali Baig said wearily. He couldn't think what else to say.

Ynessa worked late, methodically clearing her arrears. She heard doors open and close, voices making farewells. Figueras put his head round the door to say he was going home.

Much later there was a tentative knock on her door. Ynessa frowned. Alvarez returning to work? A messenger? Leaving the light burning on her desk she walked to the door and flung it open.

Joaquim stood there with hunched shoulders, as if he was fighting off a rain-shower. Beside him was Bishop Ephraim Salgado, the Gonzaga chaplain who'd arranged their marriage. Bishop Ephraim was a stout man, taller than Joaquim, clad in a purple cassock and deep purple sash. A tiny purple skull-cap perched on the back of his head, and a jewelled cross glistened above the silk sash.

Automatically Ynessa knelt and just as automatically Bishop Ephraim held out his hand. Ynessa drew the plump fingers close to her face and pressed her lips to the large amethyst on the solid gold ring. Bishop Ephraim rested his free hand on the top of her head and crossed her forehead with his thumb.

What could Bishop Ephraim and Joaquim want? Ynessa felt a wave of exhaustion wash over her. The last thing she wanted at the end of another long day was a new problem. But if she said she was going home they would insist on accompanying her, and coping with the two of them *and* Mama would be impossible. She got to her feet and smiled. 'How nice to see you both.'

'Your mother said you were working late,' Bishop Ephraim said.

Ynessa thought she would use their visit to discuss her continued employment at da Soares. She walked back to her desk rehearsing her arguments. She had eight years' experience of da Soares. She knew it better than Joaquim. Her presence would reduce Joaquim's burden and put her training and experience to the best use.

She watched Joaquim pull out a chair for the bishop. Joaquim was always subdued in the presence of Bishop Ephraim. As a simple priest, Bishop Ephraim had been the Gonzaga family chaplain, and had been in charge of Joaquim's education and upbringing; Joaquim was still like a little boy in the bishop's presence. She watched him wait for Bishop Ephraim to lower himself on to the green leather-cushioned straight-backed chair before seating himself.

Bishop Ephraim's boots were of a rare and expensive purple leather, and he wore a large, non-episcopal amethyst round his neck. She'd known the bishop since she was ten, and he'd seemed old even then. He was nearing forty now, and had a semi-circular crown of lank, grey-brown hair and a forehead striped with frown lines. He had a high-arched, aristocratic nose, a narrow, turned-down mouth and coarse skin. Bishop Ephraim worried Ynessa. She could never tell what he was thinking, and frequently caught him studying her with those mud-brown eyes of his, as if she were a valuable item of furniture.

'Would you like some refreshment?'

'No, my child.' Despite his high office, Bishop Ephraim's accent was common. There were rumours he was a church foundling, the oldest child of a poor family given to the Church so that his siblings could live.

'We are disappointed, my daughter,' Bishop Ephraim said, speaking with the ringing tones that compensated for his common accent. 'Disappointed and saddened that you have succumbed to the worst of all sins, the sin of pride. Pride was the sin of Lucifer, Ynessa. Never forget that. Never be proud.'

Ynessa felt the aquamarine walls of the office closing in on her. She was back in the classroom at the convent. Mother Anastasia was once again asking: *Ynessa, what have you done? Why have you been bad? Why have you nailed Jesus to the cross? It is your sin that has nailed Jesus to the cross. Your sin!*

Then, as quickly, she recovered her composure. She couldn't recall when or where she had been proud or overbearing. *Your conscience is your only judge,* she remembered Rodrigo telling her, no matter what any priest or bishop says. She steeled herself and asked calmly, 'When did I commit this sin, Father?'

'You have placed your opinion above that of others more knowledgeable and experienced than you. You have shown a dangerous tendency to disobey your future husband, the man who you will swear before God to love, honour and *obey*!' Bishop Ephraim lowered his voice. 'My child, for the sake of your immortal soul, I beg you, do not be proud. Do not be disobedient. Use this time to ask the Lord's forgiveness and to prepare yourself for the sanctity of marriage.'

'I still don't understand what you're talking about, Father. What have I done wrong?' Ynessa's fingers closed round the polished rock paperweight on her desk, as if it were a float carrying her through dangerous waters.

Bishop Ephraim folded his plump hands across his stomach. 'You have refused to help Joaquim, here, the man you have sworn to marry. You have dared to pit your shallow experience of business against the accumulated wisdom of the House of Gonzaga.'

'My experience is not shallow!' Ynessa cried. 'I have been working here since I was eleven! I was taught by my father! I helped him make the House of da Soares what it is. It was on the basis of that experience and my own knowledge of the indigo market that I refused to participate in Joaquim's investment. That is an unwise and foolish venture and will end in disaster.'

'There, my child, see how proud and wilful you are!'

'In refusing Joaquim, I only did what my father would have done!'

'What you *think* your father would have done. I knew Rodrigo well. He had the highest opinion of Joaquim's business acumen. He would have supported Joaquim in a way you have not. Listen to me, child –'

Rodrigo, Ynessa remembered, had always been wary of the Church's involvement in business. She spoke firmly. 'Like my father,' she said, 'I will not discuss business with the Church. So while you are here, Father, please confine your discussion to spiritual matters.'

Bishop Ephraim paused for a moment, then leaned across and whispered something to Joaquim. He turned back to Ynessa and smiled. 'My child, we will respect your decision. Joaquim has made alternative arrangements as far as the indigo investment is concerned in any case.' His smile broadened. 'Now, let us talk about your wedding.

You know your mother has agreed that you should get married next month.'

A chill settled on Ynessa's heart. 'I was aware the matter had been discussed.' She struggled to arrange her racing thoughts. She couldn't get married next month. She had to wait for Darnell to clear himself and help her find Rodrigo's killers. She had to devise a way of preventing Joaquim controlling da Soares. She had to see Darnell – no, Darnell was simply a distraction. The investigation and preserving da Soares were the only reasons for delaying her wedding as long as possible. 'The period of mourning will not end for another three weeks,' she said. 'I do not wish to dishonour my father by getting married before the mourning period ends.'

Bishop Ephraim and Joaquim exchanged glances. Joaquim bit his lip and turned away from the priest. 'Then you will get married immediately after the mourning period ends.'

'That too might be unseemly. We should get married in four months, as we've agreed.'

'That agreement was made before your father's sad demise.' Bishop Ephraim sighed and muttered and crossed himself. 'There is now great uncertainty as to the future of the House of da Soares, which, as you know, is one of the richest merchant houses in Portuguese India, whose dislocation will have serious consequences for everyone. That is why I have been asked to help bring this period of uncertainty to an end. The sooner the wedding takes place and the Houses of da Soares and Gonzaga are under unified control, the happier everyone will be.'

'By "unified control" I presume you mean that Joaquim will run both Houses?'

'Well, my child, he is older than you and there are things –'

'He is a man, isn't that it, Father? Isn't that the only reason why he should run da Soares instead of me?'

'That is how people look at it, my child.'

Anger rising, Ynessa turned back to more immediate concerns. 'Before I can get married I must bring my father's murderers to justice.'

'A very noble ambition, my child,' Bishop Ephraim said, 'and one I'm sure your prospective husband shares. This need not hold up the wedding, though. In fact, it is a reason for it to take place earlier. I know Joaquim will do everything in his power to find those evil men; you would be far more effective working together.' He looked at Joaquim. 'Isn't that so, Joaquim?'

'Yes, of course,' Joaquim said. 'I've already told you that, Ynessa.'

Ynessa was playing for time. All her instincts demanded that she should hunt Rodrigo's killers with Darnell, not Joaquim. She wondered where Darnell was and what he was doing; she wondered if he would have a way out of this dilemma. She said, 'I want to continue running the House of da Soares after the marriage. I have grown up in this business. I know it inside out and I'm very good at what I do. I will be a great help to Joaquim.'

Bishop Ephraim stroked his chin thoughtfully. 'That will cause consternation among the business community. And there will be rivalry between the Houses; even now you are divided about investment. In working against your husband you will be breaking the law of God. St Paul says –'

'I will be working for Joaquim,' Ynessa insisted. 'Joaquim will be the head of Gonzaga–da Soares.'

'Donna Gonzaga won't approve of your working,' Bishop Ephraim said.

'Isn't Joaquim head of the House of Gonzaga?' Ynessa asked defiantly. 'What do *you* say, Joaquim?'

Joaquim looked at Bishop Ephraim, then round the room. 'I don't know, Ynessa. My mother is old-fashioned: she would consider it a disgrace for a Gonzaga woman to work.'

Ynessa felt a flicker of contempt for Joaquim's weakness as Bishop Ephraim said, 'I will discuss it with Donna Gonzaga and let you know.'

Ynessa jumped to her feet. 'I will await your answer. Now, you must both excuse me. I have been here since seven this morning and want to go home.'

'Yes,' Bishop Ephraim said. 'You must be very tired. But you will come and see me when you have discussed the wedding with your mother?'

Ynessa wondered if Bishop Ephraim had already persuaded Mama to support him. 'I'll talk to my mother,' she said cautiously. 'I'll let you know what we decide.'

Chapter Fourteen

The fort was in chaos. Lines of goods and packages lay scattered from the sea wall to the docks. A cart with a broken carrying platform lay abandoned by the wall. Working by the light of smoky lanterns, men staggered to and from the dock carrying huge burdens, while heavily laden sailors clambered up long ladders trailing from the sides of the *Hughli Star*.

Ali Baig had appeared earlier in the day, threatening to take the fort and the pearls, and to kill Darnell and anyone else who got in his way. Without the men or arms to defend themselves against Ali Baig's 150-strong force Darnell had brought forward their departure for Madera.

He stood on the afterdeck with Ravi and Captain Sen making a final check. In four hours they'd loaded all the Company records, stores and provisions. The wounded Archibald Quince had been found a hammock below decks and the soldiers' families found accommodation in the fore-castle and on the main deck. Most of the natives had elected to move to Vaidya, and Timana Chitty had led them on board with his wife, five children and seven cousins. 'We should be finished in an hour,' Ravi said.

'In an hour this flamin' bloody ship sinks,' Captain Sen protested. 'Already we have too many people, too many things. We're only –'

Darnell clapped him on the shoulder and stepped on to the rope ladder snaking down the side of the ship. 'You'll be all right, Sen. Now remember, as soon as you hear a shot, abandon all loading and prepare to leave.'

'What about you?' Ravi asked.

'Don't worry. We'll be here.'

Darnell went down the ladder swiftly, pressing his face to the wooden side of the ship. Shadowy figures swirled in the torchlight on the dock. Darnell moved around them and hurried along the pitted trail to the fort.

The Sea Gate was dark and forbidding. Inside, Drake Street was in darkness. Darnell hurried along it, his eyes used to the dark now, avoiding pools of water and ruts. He crossed the factory square and hurried to the join of the north and west walls.

A pistol shot shattered the silence – the signal that Ali Baig's men were advancing. Darnell ran to the wall and up the steps. Eckaerts and his twelve soldiers waited at the top.

'Have the mines been put in place?' Darnell asked, and Eckaerts nodded.

Darnell went to the edge of the wall and looked. It was nearly one in the morning and very dark, except to the north-west where the coconut palms were lit by glowing torches. Darnell watched the lights dance through the trees, their progress accompanied by a faint clamour that grew steadily louder.

Ali Baig's men were approaching along a single track that ran through the coconut palms. The beat of their drums and their war-cry, a monotonously rhythmic chant punctuated with shrill ululations, grew louder. The torches made a dizzying spectacle as they darted among the trees, illuminating bark and throwing long, twisting shadows. As soon as the men came to the open space in front of the fort, they rushed forward and spread out. Bullock carts carrying battering rams raced to the front of the mob. Darnell saw a group of archers and another close-marching group carrying spears. The field became a mass of glistening bodies and turbaned heads irradiated by the glint of drawn swords and knives.

'Now,' Darnell called to the soldiers, their slow-matches

glowing brightly in the dark. Orders were whispered and repeated. There was a unified lifting of slow-matches, a hiss of sparks. Eckaerts's soldiers fired. Yellow flashes lightened the earthwork as the balls flew into the crowd. The boom of the muskets mingled with cries of pain, anger and fear. 'Stand back,' Darnell shouted. 'Retreat or you will all die!'

Arrows winged harmlessly through the night, falling well short of the walls. Below, a group of men were unloading a cart and forming two forcing parties. On the wall, guns were reloaded and more shots crashed out, followed by further cries of pain and anger. Darnell looked back towards the docks. Lights blazed on the *Hughli Star*. Everyone seemed to have boarded. He turned to Eckaerts. 'Go!' he cried. 'It's time.'

'Right you are, Mr Darnell.' Eckaerts hurried down the steps to light the fuses. Darnell ran back along the wall as the first wave of Ali Baig's men crashed against the fort gates.

The shock made the walls shake. Two groups of men were battering the gate in unison while a third group charged the middle of the gate with a cart. Darnell heard the gate splinter and knew it would give in minutes. He ordered the soldiers to fire once more; over the sound of the shots came the cries of the assault party, '*Haro, hara, haro, hara!*' followed by a tearing of splintered wood and a crash that shook the walls.

Darnell told the soldiers to fire again. He heard the gate give and, ordering the soldiers to abandon their posts, he too ran down the steps and waited for Eckaerts in the darkness, sweating, listening to the cracking of the gate, counting the soldiers as they went past. Where was Eckaerts?

They stood waiting impatiently. Crash! Boom! The cries of the assault party grew louder. One more assault and the gate would be smashed. 'Go,' Darnell ordered the soldiers. 'Go like hell for the ship.'

The soldiers turned and ran, their boots clattering against the brick pave. Where the devil was Eckaerts?

The elderly Swiss emerged out of the dark. 'Everything done good, Mr Darnell,' he announced with a smile.

'Let's go!' Darnell grabbed Eckaerts's shoulder and pushed him towards the docks. They set off at a rapid jog along Drake Street. As they reached the factory house, the gate crashed open.

'Move!' Darnell cried. 'As fast as you can!' Behind them the crowd burst in, yelling and whooping with triumph. Ahead of them the soldiers sprinted in an untidy mass.

'Run! Run for your lives!'

Muskets clattering in the dark, the soldiers ran. Snakes of torchlight reached along the walls of shuttered houses. Darnell ran beside Eckaerts, the old soldier drenched with sweat and panting stertorously. He took Eckaerts's musket; the tramp of feet and shouts grew closer. 'For God's sake, Eckaerts, move!'

But Eckaerts couldn't go any faster. The soldiers ahead of them had disappeared into the darkness. Darnell grabbed Eckaerts's hand and dragged the old Swiss after him. 'Not far, not far.' Behind Eckaerts he could hear the natives closing up on them, running silently now as they saw their quarry, torches held aloft, swords and daggers gleaming.

Eckaerts's legs were going. He was running splay-legged. Darnell glimpsed the open Sea Gate in front of them. 'Only ten yards. Move it, Eckaerts!'

'Can't!'

Darnell dragged Eckaerts to the Sea Gate. 'Go man, go as fast as you can.' He turned to face the mob. They were about twenty yards behind, a shapeless huddle of bodies, torches and gleaming metal. He raised Eckaerts's musket and fired into the middle of the crowd.

There was a howl of pain and a stuttering of feet. Hurling the empty musket at the onrushing men, Darnell turned and sprinted.

Eckaerts was a lone silhouette on the road. Darnell sprinted after him. Eight yards, seven, six, five. Eckaerts was running on to the dock. Darnell stopped and turned again. The mob, clearly visible in the light reflected off the beach, was closer. He fired his pistol, aiming again for the middle of the mob.

Again there was a cry of pain, and Darnell turned and sprinted for the dock, stopping, turning and firing Eckaerts's pistol before running across the boards, his feet pounding slowly on the vibrating wood.

Eckaerts had gone. Ahead of him the boards stretched on for ever. Behind him the pounding of feet grew louder and the dock began to sway with the weight of a hundred running men. Darnell willed himself to go faster, breath sucking in and out of his tortured lungs, arms and legs pumping. The relentless pounding of feet behind him drew closer, the men silent now, concentrating all their energy on catching him. A glimmer of light appeared between the end of the dock and the tall sides of the ship. The *Hughli Star* had already slipped her moorings and was easing away from the dock.

Darnell was sprinting now, his chest heaving, his legs pumping. Realizing what was happening, the men behind him began to shout. Darnell threw himself forward, his legs wheeling mechanically, his heart thumping as if it would burst. He was four yards from the end of the dock, the gap between the dock and the ship now clearly visible and wider. Three yards. Two. He could see faces looking down on him from the ship's rail, saw the ropes dangling down the side. One yard. His feet clattered over the boards. He reached the end of the dock going flat out, pressed down with both feet and jumped.

There was a moment of airborne stillness. Water glistened beneath him. The wooden sides of the boat fell away before his face. Ropes whistled through the air. Arms reached out desperately for him. His hands grabbed a rope and his palms burnt as he slid down it and stopped with a jerk that almost took his arms out of their sockets. Immediately, the rope was hauled up and he kicked forward, bracing his boots against the side of the ship. Hands grabbed him and drew him over the rail. He tried to walk on legs that suddenly felt like damp string, teetered and fell. He waved away the sailors who tried to help him up and lay there, panting as if his lungs would come out of his throat. Finally he staggered upright and walked unsteadily towards the rail, dimly aware of Captain Sen pushing through the crowd to him, of Ravi's helping hand.

'Eckaerts?'

'He's safe.'

Darnell reached the rail and hung on to it, staring back at the rapidly receding scene. The explosions began. The dock was the first to go, erupting in a mushroom of eye-tearing orange, the long wooden finger heaving, then twisting and scattering wood and men and the severed parts of bodies into the moon-silvered night. The sea came alive with splashes and then, as the remaining men ran back to the fort, the Sea Gate blew up, showering them with falling bricks and masonry. Amidst the frightened shrieks came the frantic neighing of horses. Ravi's house exploded, illuminating a surging crowd of men running back towards the Land Gate. The factory house went up in a flare of flying debris and leaping buildings. Fires started, casting elongated illuminations over running figures, revealing scores of others lying motionless and dismembered in sticky pools of blood. Screams drifted across the water accompanied by the harsh crackle of flames. A minute later the mine placed near the Land Gate exploded, and above the screams of the men came the baying of animals. Darnell became aware of Captain Sen standing beside him.

'I warned him,' Darnell said. 'I had to blow up the factory. Couldn't let it fall intact to the Dutch.' He watched as the acrid smoke swirled over the water, staring till

Armagon diminished to a glowing speck. Madera had been baptized in blood.

Ynessa sweltered behind the drawn curtains of her *tonga* as it sat stalled in traffic. She was returning home from a meeting of the merchants' council – the first time she had attended one – and felt disappointed at how mundane the proceedings had been: grants of *cartazes* and permits for arrack distilling, reports from the militia and the captain-general and the reading of the latest directives from Portugal.

Joaquim had not wanted her to attend. It would be less confusing, he'd said, if *he* were to represent the Houses of Gonzaga and da Soares, as he would do in a few months. But Ynessa had insisted that she go. As long as she was the head of da Soares she would represent her father's House. Besides, she'd been curious to know how the meetings were conducted, and concerned that Joaquim might commit da Soares to something as foolish as his indigo investment.

She pulled the curtains open. It was near noon and, with everyone going home for lunch, the street was jammed with stationary *tongas*, carriages, caleches and palanquins. 'What's wrong?' she asked the driver perched up front.

'A fight in the street, *menina*. The militia are clearing it up. We should be moving in a few minutes.'

Ynessa drew the curtains again and sat back. Mama had not taken kindly to her criticism of Joaquim. He was a nice boy, Mama had said, and still young. He would in time learn all about business. Rodrigo had once been like Joaquim and hadn't he done brilliantly afterwards? Mama said Rodrigo would never have agreed to the marriage had he doubted Joaquim's business skill; Ynessa must trust her father's judgement. She could not possibly break her engagement: that would anger the Gonzagas, the Church and make her the laughing stock of Portuguese India.

Everyone who was anyone had attended her betrothal two months ago. It had taken a great deal of persuasion to make Mama agree that, in respect to her father's memory, the wedding should not be brought forward. Now she had three months to find Rodrigo's killers.

The excuse of the mourning period had been enough to persuade Mama this time, but Ynessa would have to think up some new arguments soon. Because the terrible truth was that, the more she learned about Joaquim, the less she found to like. She was starting to realize her love for him had been nothing more than an adolescent infatuation. Already she was finding herself questioning his business acumen and his strength of character – she didn't like the way he seemed to defer to Bishop Ephraim so meekly. Whereas Darnell . . .

She mustn't think of Darnell. Darnell meant nothing to her and could never be allowed to mean anything. All that could come of an association with him was help in finding Rodrigo's killers.

Loud shouts from the street disturbed her thoughts and she drew back the curtains. Her heart stopped. She must be seeing things! For there was Darnell, his hands bound behind his back, his hair covered with dust, blood trickling down one cheek, towering over a group of soldiers and deserters who were dragging him towards the Inner Fort. Beating her fist on the side of the *tonga* she shouted to the driver to stop. 'Sergeant Ruiz!' she called as she got down from the *tonga*. Gonsalez de Gomez, one of San Thome's well-known jewellers, stood beside Sergeant Ruiz, his cheek stiff with dried blood. 'What's going on here?' she demanded. 'What are you doing with this man?'

'It's nothing to concern yourself with, *menina*. We have caught a jewel thief, that's all.'

'That's all! Do you realize who you have arrested, you foolish man? This is the agent of the new fort at Madera.'

Sergeant Ruiz flushed and looked perplexedly from

Ynessa to Darnell and back again. 'You are mistaken, *menina*. The man is a thief. He attacked Senhor Gonsalez here and –'

'Let me explain, *menina*.' Gonsalez sidled between her and Ruiz. 'This man came to my shop this morning to sell some pearls. He had no provenance and when I called the militia he knifed me and –'

'He lies,' Darnell called out. 'I had –'

'Didn't Senhor Darnell show you the provenance I gave him?' Ynessa demanded.

Gonsalez shifted uneasily sideways. 'He did, but I thought the provenance was forged.'

'Forged?'

'He also had some other pearls, which I know to be stolen from the Dutch.'

'*Know* to be stolen,' Ynessa repeated. 'Do you perhaps trade with the Dutch, senhor? Do you give aid and comfort to the muckel-faced besiegers of our brethren in Malacca?'

'No, *menina*, no. I thought –'

'If you thought at all, senhor, you would have realized that arresting Senhor Darnell could start a war with the English. Is that what your Dutch masters asked you to do?'

'No, *menina*! I have no dealings with the Dutch!'

'Then you wouldn't know if Senhor Darnell had stolen pearls from them or not.' Ynessa turned to Sergeant Ruiz. 'Release this man at once.'

'But Senhor Gonsalez –'

'Senhor Darnell is an honoured and trusted friend of the House of da Soares and I personally vouch for him.' She turned to Gonsalez, her tone loud and arrogant. 'Are you accusing a friend of the House of da Soares of theft?'

'Of course not, *menina*. I wouldn't –' Gonsalez made his mind up and glared furiously at Darnell. 'I've made a mistake,' he told Ruiz. 'Release the man.'

Darnell threw himself back against the hard seat of the *tonga* and rubbed the circulation back into his wrists.

'Thank the Lord you came along! I thought that bloody weevil was going to have me arrested and steal the pearls.'

Seated so close to him that she could smell his sweat and skin and hair, Ynessa suffocated with a forbidden excitement. 'What happened?' she asked, glad her voice sounded level.

Darnell told her that they'd arrived in Madera eight days ago, and he'd come to San Thome to sell the pearls. Gonsalez had been quite taken with the Celor pearls, and when Darnell hadn't been able to provide a provenance for the Dutch pearls, had threatened to have him arrested for theft if he didn't sell all the pearls at a very low price. When Darnell had refused, he'd sent for his *goondas*, and tried to rob Darnell. Darnell had cut Gonsalez and two of the *goondas* and escaped. Gonsalez had then got word to the militia who'd arrested him.

Ynessa watched the animation in Darnell's face as he spoke, attracted by the deep-down flaring of those blue-black eyes. You're a handsome devil, she thought: not pretty like Joaquim – how could you be with a broken nose and knife scar – but handsome in an earthier, stronger way.

He was saying, 'I don't know what I'd have done if you hadn't intervened.'

You'd have found a way out, she thought, and said, 'Where will you sell your pearls now?'

He held the pouch out to her. 'Would you like to buy them? All I'm asking is the six hundred pounds I need to finance the fort.'

Looking at him seated beside her, bedraggled, bleeding and defiant, Ynessa thought she would buy the pearls. It would be a good investment for the House and she wanted to help him ... Stop it, she told herself. He can never be anything to you. This is business. Ask yourself: is his proposition a good one? But wouldn't it be better if the fort was financed by the merchants' council instead of da

Soares? Then the Portuguese would have a long-term interest in Madera, a base in Vaidya, and both San Thome and Madera would become much more prosperous. So what should she do? Help Darnell, or manipulate him to accept help from the merchants' council?

She didn't like the idea of manipulating anyone. But Darnell was stubborn and obstinate. He'd refused to listen to that suggestion the last time they met. He didn't want anyone but the English to benefit from Madera. So if the Portuguese wanted to get into Madera, he had to be manipulated. 'No,' she said, firmly. 'The House of da Soares doesn't want the pearls.'

He said, 'But your father died for those pearls.'

'The House of da Soares has never traded extensively in gems,' she said. 'My father only attended the auction in Celor because of the nizam's invitation and to break the Dutch monopoly.'

'I see.' Darnell wasn't sure if she was lying. He said, 'I'll have to find someone else in San Thome who wants to buy pearls.'

'Apart from our house, the only people who can afford them are Gonsalez or the merchants' council.'

She was manipulating him, Darnell thought, and doing it very transparently. Well, goddamn it, he did not want the Portuguese and their confounded priests in Madera. More important, Seringa did not want them either: any mention of them would make him start dealing with the Dutch. Darnell said, 'If no one in San Thome wants the pearls I'll sell them elsewhere.' At worst he could do a deal with Abdul Nana. But that would be at a huge discount. And how long would it take?

Ynessa was reading his thoughts. 'If you decide to approach the merchants' council you will have your money in three days.'

It was irrelevant; he couldn't deal with the Portuguese. He wondered how long Ravi could delay payments and if the delay would send Seringa running to the Dutch?

'Why don't you like us?' Ynessa asked. 'Why don't you like me?'

Touched by the anger and the vulnerability in her voice, Darnell looked into her eyes, then took her hands and kissed each of them. 'I like you, Ynessa,' he said. 'Never doubt that.' He cleared his throat. 'And *I* do not dislike the Portuguese. But the Vaidyans do and I can't have priests in Madera harassing, bribing and forcing people to become Papists. The Vaidyans have the right to worship their own gods.'

Darnell spoke like Rodrigo, Ynessa thought. Rodrigo had always said that the Church interfered too much and behaved with disgraceful cruelty in its attempts to win souls. 'What if there was no proselytization?' she asked.

Darnell laughed. 'Your priests would never agree.'

'The merchants' council comprises seven members. Only one, Bishop Ephraim, represents the Church. Of the rest, the captain-general represents the military and political interest, and the others are ordinary merchants. So there's a five to two chance your proposal will succeed.'

'And would the council agree to a loan agreement specifying that the Portuguese could never administer the fort?'

'I'm sure they would. They don't want to run your fort. All they want is the opportunity to trade with Vaidya.'

It was a possibility, he thought, staring out of the *tonga*.

In a low voice Ynessa went on, 'To create the fort you want, you need more than just the capital to build it. You need lots of trade. And that means people and investment. And like it or not, your best source of trade and investment is San Thome. Did you know there are over two thousand people here? And many rich merchants, tradesmen and small businessmen, all of whom would jump at the chance of doing business with Vaidya.'

Darnell shook his head.

'Think how quickly your fort would grow if a hundred establishments opened there tomorrow.'

Ynessa spoke sense, Darnell reflected, but again the problem was control. Madera had to remain an English fort. 'We do not want to be swamped by your merchants and traders,' he said.

'You won't be. As Madera becomes more successful, more English will settle there. In any case, as long as you have the *firman* with Prince Seringa, you will always have control.'

That was true. If he could sell the idea to Seringa, Darnell decided he would let her approach the merchants' council. But he'd need cast-iron guarantees. He asked, 'Will the council agree to a limitation on the number of churches and schools? Will they agree that anyone found guilty of proselytization be expelled from the settlement?'

'We can try,' Ynessa said, placing her hand on his. 'Come on, Darnell, let's do it.'

Chapter Fifteen

Three mornings later Darnell sat in the merchants' council chamber, a tall, ceilingless room whose stained-glass windows depicting the council's coat of arms were set high in the panelled walls and cast strands of green, yellow and red on the bare cement floor. The room was something between a church and a meeting room, with heavy, solid, wooden furniture in the centre surrounded by a bare expanse of cement. The captain-general sat in a wooden stall at the head of the room and rows of trestles ran down the sides, flanking a large wooden table on which the councillors rested their documents. Two writers sat at desks below the captain-general's stall recording minutes.

Darnell sat with Ynessa on one of the trestles beside two merchants whom Ynessa had introduced as Roberto de Almeida and Miguel Saldhana. A stout man in bishop's purple sat in solitary splendour at the foot of the table. Darnell hadn't needed to be told that this was Bishop Ephraim, representative of the Holy Roman Catholic Church. Directly opposite them were Joaquim Gonzaga and his cousin Albert Coutinho. Darnell knew that Gonzaga had succeeded to the second largest merchant house in San Thome, and that he was betrothed to Ynessa.

Darnell studied the young man as he lolled on the bench, whispering loudly and sharing private jokes with his cousin. Gonzaga was remarkably handsome, and knew it. His beard was neatly trimmed, his fingernails polished; he wore an expensive, embroidered silk tunic. Ynessa deserved someone better than this dandified pimp, Darnell thought angrily.

Ynessa put forward her case for investing in the English fort, emphasizing all the advantages it would bring. She looked round the room, her dark eyes searching every face. 'My friends, this is an opportunity we cannot afford to let pass. Put everything you can spare into this fort and make it work. This is what the House of da Soares is doing. I urge you all to follow its example.'

Captain-General Rafael Acuna, a burly man in his fifties with thick, greying curls, stood up next. 'As you all know, I am empowered to void this proposition if I believe that the establishment of this fort threatens our military or political interests.' He looked down at his hands. 'The English fort is fifteen miles away. It is expected to be bigger than San Thome or the Dutch fort at Pulicat. It will have twice as many guns as us. It will take trade away from us. It will ruin San Thome . . .'

Acuna was going to oppose the fort, Darnell thought, his heart sinking to his belly.

'. . . unless,' the captain-general was saying, 'we ally ourselves with the English. We have been friends with the English for many years. We have suffered with the English in Java and the Spice Islands. If we had a treaty with the English then I see no reason for us to object to the English fort.'

'Consider such a treaty already signed,' Darnell said, bobbing up from the trestle.

Miguel Saldhana was concerned about the Dutch reaction to the fort and the Portuguese involvement with it. 'By helping the English build this fort we are needlessly provoking the Dutch.'

Darnell was saved from replying by Roberto de Almeida, who jumped to his feet and cried, 'By all means let us provoke the Dutch!' De Almeida fairly bristled with anger, his fiery black eyes flashing. 'The Dutch have consistently refused to make a peace treaty with us. I vote in favour of supporting the English.'

Darnell tried to look impassive as he leaned his back against the hard, wooden bench. With Ynessa, de Almeida and Saldhana in support, his vote was already secure.

Joaquim Gonzaga approached the table, rings flashing in the bands of light from the windows. 'The House of Gonzaga will not support this investment,' he said. 'If council decides we need a fort in Madera, then the Houses of Gonzaga and da Soares will build it.'

Darnell forced himself to be calm. In a low voice he said, 'I am the only person with permission to build a fort in Madera.'

'But you haven't got the money,' Gonzaga sneered.

Darnell struggled to keep from snapping. 'Seringa will not deal with the Portuguese.'

'We will make him, and I tell you this, senhor, Seringa will not refuse the Houses of Gonzaga and da Soares.' He smiled at Ynessa. 'We will build a fort at Madera. It will be a fitting symbol of the union of our two Houses.'

Ynessa sighed with annoyance. 'The English have already started building at Madera,' she said. 'If the fort isn't substantially completed before the monsoon, Prince Seringa will have the fort built by the Dutch.'

De Almeida cried, 'A Portuguese fort at Madera is an impossibility. And between the English and the Dutch, I choose the English.'

Gonzaga said, 'The English are as much our enemies as the Dutch.' He drew a jewelled dagger from his waist and stuck it on the table. 'It would be dishonourable to help the English until their cowardly attack at Swally is avenged and Ormuz is returned.'

Coutinho applauded.

Darnell decided he wouldn't be provoked by Gonzaga's chauvinism. There was too much at stake.

Taking the councillors' silence for approval, Gonzaga turned on Darnell. 'You talk of treaties, senhor, but what are treaties worth if they are not honoured? What use is a treaty if we are deceived as we were at Swally?'

'Well said, Joaquim,' Coutinho called out, lolling slack-jawed against the bench. 'We shouldn't be building an English fort. Damn, we should be attacking it!'

Ignoring Ynessa's muted cry, Darnell strode to the table, locking his eyes on Gonzaga, half-hoping the vain young man would use his fancy dagger. I'd love to mark you with one of my fighting knives, Darnell thought. A knife scar across your cheeks would ruin your looks and your prospective marriage. He said, 'Ormuz was taken by direct attack, and twenty-five years ago at Swally, the Portuguese fleet was out-manoeuvred by five English merchantmen. What's important, however, is that since Swally, our two nations have been at peace.'

Gonzaga started to protest but was interrupted by de Almeida saying, 'Well spoken, sir.'

Contemptuously Darnell turned his back on Gonzaga and addressed the council. 'We are not retired generals meeting to talk about ancient battles. We are traders meeting to decide how best to seize the prosperous future that awaits us, if we build a fort at Madera. As you have already heard, the fort at Madera presents a unique opportunity for our two peoples . . .'

He heard Gonzaga move back to his seat and, moments later, Saldhana cried, 'You needn't go on, senhor. We have read your proposition. It seems a good one. We will take a vote on it now.'

Darnell walked back to his seat and felt Ynessa squeeze his hand in congratulation. He turned and smiled at her.

From the end of the table Bishop Ephraim asked, 'Tell me, senhor, how many churches and schools will you have in your magnificent new fort?' His face was creased with a frown of genuine concern, his mouth set in a narrow line.

Darnell said, 'There will be one church and one school for those Portuguese who choose to live in the fort.'

'One church, one school?' Bishop Ephraim was wide-eyed with surprise. 'Surely, senhor, you understand we have numerous religious orders; if they are to fulfil the work of the Lord, each must have its church and school.'

'I'm afraid your religious orders will have to learn to pray together,' Darnell said. 'If more Portuguese settle than we anticipate, more churches and schools can be built. But for now, one church, one school, no more. Madera is being built to foster trade, not religion. Everyone in Madera will be free to worship in any way they please. Anyone interfering with that religious freedom or attempting to convert others will be expelled from the fort.'

Bishop Ephraim raised his head and stared at Darnell. 'I will not accept that,' he cried in ringing tones as if he were in a pulpit. 'The Lord Jesus himself admonished us to go forth and spread His word. Not to do so would be a sin against the Holy Spirit. Anyone who involves himself in this venture should look to his soul.' He looked sadly at Acuna. 'Unless our freedom to do the work of the Lord is guaranteed, my godson, Joaquim, his friend and I will vote against any Portuguese participation in this fort.'

'As you say, Your Grace,' Acuna said and, taking a quill, made a note in the leatherbound book in front of him. He looked up at Saldhana and de Almeida.

'I – I abstain,' Saldhana said.

De Almeida shrugged. 'The vote is lost then. We will not finance the fort.' He stared straight ahead.

Acuna said, 'It is resolved that the council will not invest in the English fort at Madera.' He shut the book with a snap.

Ynessa couldn't believe it. After forty years they had an opportunity to trade with Vaidya, and the Church had intervened and stopped it, just as they had stopped that first trading mission. She walked to the table filled with an icy anger.

'You're fools and cowards, all of you!' she cried, and

saw all the faces around her pale with shock. 'You won't save a single soul by refusing to finance the English. All you're doing with your refusal is forcing Seringa to replace the English with the Dutch.' She stared down the table at Bishop Ephraim. 'How many souls will you save in a Dutch fort, Your Grace? How many churches will you build? How many schools? And what will you do to prevent the Dutch destroying San Thome?'

'The ways of God are mysterious, my child,' Bishop Ephraim intoned. 'I say that it would be sinful to build a fort in Madera unless we can use it to bring heathens to Christ.'

Ynessa looked down, her fists clenching and unclenching at her sides. 'In that case,' she said softly, 'there is only one thing I can do. The House of da Soares will finance the English fort.'

'You can't!' Bishop Ephraim flushed as if he had been slapped. 'You will be –'

'It will be a greater sin to lose San Thome to the Dutch!'

Joaquim was on his feet, shouting, 'No, no, this will not happen! Ynessa, you can't do this!' He turned to Saldhana and de Almeida. 'As soon as we are married, this financing will be cancelled.'

Ynessa felt the blood pounding in her head. How dare he? How dare he assume ... She bunched her fists and pressed them against her thighs. 'The financing will be completed before our wedding and it will be irrevocable,' she announced, turning to Darnell who was suddenly standing right behind her. 'Come, senhor, let us go. We have much to discuss.' She marched from the council chamber, her head high, forcing herself to look directly at Bishop Ephraim. The anger on his face was terrifying.

Shortly before nine the next morning, formally dressed in French breeches, bombasted doublet with epaulettes and hat, Darnell presented himself at the da Soares warehouse to sign the contract he'd negotiated with Ynessa the previous afternoon.

Two servants showed him into the committee room at the front of the warehouse. The room was large and elegant, with windows opening on to the sea and a long rosewood table in the centre flanked by comfortably curved cane chairs. The walls were pale yellow. A cool sea breeze ruffled lace curtains as it fluttered through the room.

Ynessa sat at the head of the table, wearing a lavender gown with puffed sleeves and a deep, frilled V in front which cradled the gold crucifix lying in the valley of her breasts. There was a pile of papers in front of her and as she looked up at him and smiled, his heart gave a little skip. He was pleased she showed little strain from yesterday's council meeting and their own meeting afterwards.

At first Darnell had been concerned that Ynessa was being impulsive and risking too much on a whim. He had tried to persuade her to finance the fort in partnership with Saldhana and de Almeida, but she had refused. Da Soares could afford the entire cost of the fort if the money was paid in instalments. Then she'd begun to negotiate, demanding – amongst other things – the right to impose a licence fee on any member of the council who wished to trade in Madera, and making everything contingent on the English and Vaidyans helping her to find Rodrigo's killers.

Darnell had objected, arguing that the Vaidyans had no interest in finding her father's killers; that because van Cuyler and Ali Baig knew she was hunting them, returning to Celor was out of the question. But Ynessa had been adamant. If the Vaidyans and the English wouldn't help her, they could sit and watch the Mughal invade Vaidya. So finally Darnell had agreed, and she'd had Figueras prepare formal agreements for their signature, and subsequent ratification by Prince Seringa.

Now Ynessa handed him a copy of the contract. As he read, Figueras and Alvarez came in through a door behind her, both formally dressed as well. 'Manuel and Alfonso will be our witnesses,' she said. She stood up, turned her chair round and sat again.

'Changing your luck?' Darnell asked, taking a quill from the stand and dipping it.

'No. Making sure it stays with me.' She made the sign of the cross and picked up a quill. They both signed the documents, and Ynessa dismissed Alvarez and Figueras before asking, 'When do we meet with Prince Seringa and get his approval to these agreements?'

'He's coming to Madera in two weeks.'

Ynessa placed a sack of money on Darnell's copies of the contracts and pushed them towards him.

Darnell didn't move. He stared at the level set of her brows, the deep, placid pools of her eyes and the rose-petal texture of her small, perfect lips.

Ynessa wondered why he was looking at her like that. She blushed and looked down, acutely aware of his proximity. She felt her hand stop moving the contracts and money towards him; he was speaking to her. 'What did Joaquim Gonzaga mean about changing everything after you were married?'

So that's what he cared about, his confounded contract and his goddamned fort! She stifled her disappointment and pushed the contracts to him. 'You needn't worry about that,' she said, the words tripping out fast and uneven. 'There are enough safeguards in the contract to stop Joaquim doing anything about the loan.'

'I know that. Why are you letting Joaquim take over your business?'

She felt annoyed that Darnell was snapping at her. 'I've no choice. Once I marry Joaquim, everything I own becomes his. That's how it is in Portugal.'

'That's rubbish!' His voice was harsh.

'Rubbish or not, that's what happens. So take your money –'

234

'Do you love him?' Darnell demanded. His scar stretched like a white ribbon along his jaw.

That was none of his business. But she couldn't meet his eyes; and neither could she bring herself to say she loved Joaquim.

'So why marry him?' The words snapped out in the silence in four separate whip cracks.

'I've given him my word and sworn an oath to marry him before Bishop Ephraim, our families and the people of San Thome.'

He slammed the table. Ynessa jumped. The inkwell nearest his hand spilt, sending a stream of black ink over the rosewood. Almost absent-mindedly he dropped a kerchief on the stain. 'You sound like a merchant fulfilling a contract rather than a woman in love,' he said, coldly.

Ynessa watched the ink spread out over the kerchief, a damp, growing stain that matched the colour of Darnell's eyes. What right had he to criticize her? She was honouring an obligation. What did he understand about her situation? 'I've given my word before God and man,' she repeated.

'God!' He was scoffing. 'God did not intend people to live their lives in misery. God wants you to be happy! And if you're worried about the people in San Thome, move to Madera!'

She looked at him, startled. 'What do you mean?' she asked slowly.

'I mean,' said Darnell, his voice barely above a whisper, 'that I want you with me in Madera.'

She couldn't believe he'd said that! Pushing back her chair, she stumbled to the window, her mind a whirl of confusion. He was talking nonsense; there could be no future for them.

She felt him come up behind her, his breath on her neck. His arms pulled her to him, turning her round roughly. His mouth skimmed her forehead, her eyes, her cheeks, her chin. He was saying, 'Ynessa, I love you. I want to take care of you. I won't see you unhappy. I won't let you marry Joaquim.' She smelt the rich male smell of him.

His mouth closed over hers. His lips were warm, passionate, and suddenly she was kissing him the way he'd kissed her, kissing his ears and cheeks, his chin and his scar till she reached his mouth again. Pulling away a little, she framed his head in her hands and looked at him, tracing the outline of his cheeks, running her finger along the smooth ridge of scar below his jaw. She saw the terrible hunger in his eyes and thought – for me! He loves me! Her voice was throaty. 'Oh God, I love you, Darnell. I think I loved you from the moment I saw you in Armagon.'

'And I loved you from the moment you tried to tell me how to defend my fort.'

Their lips moulded together again in a warm moistness. He was pressing her against him with a grip of iron. She was filled with a desire that made her want to melt; a liquid flame blazed through her. Darnell, she thought, I love you. I think I've always loved you.

What was she doing? she thought suddenly. *This is mortal sin!* She tried to prise her head away, and he pulled back, releasing her, his eyes bright with a mixture of passion, anger and concern. 'Ynessa, what's wrong?'

She found herself opening and closing her palms as she looked for the right words. She could feel him still on her face and lips. 'No,' she said, wanting to hold on to something. 'This must never happen again.' She moved quickly back, grabbing the edge of the table in her haste to put distance between them, her hand catching his ink-soaked kerchief.

'Ynessa!'

She jumped back, wiping her hands on her dress. It was irreparably marked now; she thought the stain would always remind her of this moment. 'Stay where you are!'

'Listen to me,' Darnell said sharply. 'I love you, Ynessa, and you love me. We cannot be apart –'

'No,' Ynessa shouted, and repeated, quietly, 'no, no, no.' She saw his mouth twist, his eyes harden in puzzlement and anger. 'It's not possible.' She was shaking her head, refusing to meet his anxious gaze. 'If I married you I'd be damned twice, once for breaking my oath and once for marrying a heretic.'

'No one is damned for love.' Darnell took a step towards her.

She shook her head again. 'Darnell, I can't! I can't marry someone who isn't Catholic!' Abruptly she picked up the bell and rang it. 'We mustn't meet alone again. From now till Seringa comes, I shall leave all the business of the fort to Manuel. We needn't see each –'

'Ynessa, I won't let you go. I won't let you waste yourself on Gonzaga.'

She hung her head. 'Please, help me, Darnell, help me to be strong and do what I have to do.'

'Never,' Darnell said. 'I love you, Ynessa. And you love me. And I won't let you ruin our lives.'

Figueras was at the doorway.

'Senhor Darnell is leaving now, Manuel,' Ynessa said, and turned away.

Figueras picked up the coins and the contracts and held them out to Darnell.

Darnell took them and bowed. 'Goodbye, *menina*. I will see you in two weeks, if not before.'

Ynessa nodded and closed her eyes, so she wouldn't see him go.

Chapter Sixteen

During the next two weeks, Darnell was so busy that, even if Ynessa had let him, he couldn't have seen her. They had to get the factory built as soon as possible. The factory house had to be completed and the perimeter walls erected before the monsoon. Everyone from Armagon was put to work, the men digging and building, the women cooking and mixing mortar. Seringa's workmen too swarmed everywhere.

The centre of the spit was stripped of palms and vegetation, the perimeter of the factory pegged out, and the foundations for the boundary walls dug. In the middle of the enclosure, surrounded by piles of rubble and building materials, the bare walls of the four-storey factory house rose higher every day.

Beyond the knee-high north perimeter wall, the site of the Black Town – the native quarter – became a mélange of men, carts, huts, tents and gaping holes. Under the direction of Meru, Seringa's fresh-faced young architect, a rough pattern of streets emerged along with the skeletal frames of houses and shops. A number of makeshift stalls selling various provisions sent wisps of smoke from open charcoal fires over the site; the smell of currying fish pervaded the air.

Two weeks after Ynessa and Darnell signed the agreements, Seringa arrived with Ghosh and an escort of twenty soldiers. Though the temperature was over a hundred degrees and it was an hour to lunch, work on the site continued at its usual frantic pace. Darnell and Meru showed Seringa round the site. The prince was impressed, especially when Darnell showed him the location of the factory's temple and had him open a street in the Black Town in the name of his grandfather, Ramla Venkat.

They went to lunch in the two-roomed wooden shack of the skeletal factory house, which was serving as the Company's temporary offices. The rooms were normally crammed with trestles, chairs, books, documents and unopened crates. Today, however, Ravi's servants had boxed all the papers, pulled the furniture and crates against the walls and set a small Persian carpet and some cushions on the floor. An array of food stood on a trestle in the centre: metal dishes of *raita*, lentils, curried mushrooms and potato curry, two kinds of fish and tall beakers of the yoghurt drink known as *lassi*.

Darnell waited beside Ravi whilst Seringa and the others were served. The steady thump of a sledgehammer and the scrape of trowels from the factory house filtered through the torn oiled paper that served as window-panes. He found himself thinking of Ynessa. He was as excited as a schoolboy at the prospect of seeing her again and it took an effort to focus on the business he had with Seringa. Through Figueras he'd arranged that Ynessa would come late, so he could first tell Seringa about the Portuguese.

Seringa said, 'You've all done a magnificent job here. I can't tell you how pleased I am.' Seringa paused in his eating, holding the rice and fish suspended in the three fingers of his right hand.

Darnell set his plate down by his feet, his mouth suddenly dry. He drank some *lassi*. 'We've had a problem with money,' he said.

The happiness drained from Seringa's face. His eyes widened and fixed themselves rigidly on Darnell. 'Will you not be able to finish the fort?'

'We'll finish the fort. But we've had to borrow from the Portuguese. It's unfortunate but . . .' He watched Seringa and Ghosh's faces grow rigid. In silence they put down their plates and washed their fingers.

'What exactly does this mean?' Seringa asked.

'It means I've had to give the Portuguese a right to settle here – under English rule.'

Seringa swayed back on his haunches, the red cherry of his mouth collapsing as he pressed his lips close together. He slapped his palm on the carpet. 'There will be no Portuguese in Madera!'

Darnell said, 'The Portuguese will be under our control. A condition of their financing is that they will not attempt to spread their faith –'

'The Portuguese lie!' Ghosh snarled. 'And you, Darnell, also lie. You have broken our trust and are now bringing other *feringhi* to Madera.'

'With safeguards,' Darnell cried. 'We will have the right to expel any Portuguese involved in proselytizing and they are restricted –'

'How can you enforce these sanctions if you are dependent on them for money?' Seringa demanded, getting to his feet.

Darnell's heart sank. Seringa was walking out on him. 'I'll have the Portuguese agree that everyone who settles here must be approved by you,' he said in desperation.

'No, Darnell.' Seringa was adamant. 'I do not want the Portuguese in Madera. I will give you ten days to rearrange your financing. Otherwise –' Followed by Ghosh he strode to the door and swung it open. Ynessa stood there.

Ynessa froze in the doorway at the sight of the stocky white-clad figure charging at her like a water buffalo. Seringa, she thought, catching the glint of the huge jewel in his turban. Why was he leaving? Then she thought: I'd better stop him. She spread her elbows out and steepled her palms in front of her. Seringa could not pass without pushing her. She bowed her head till her nostrils touched her fingertips. 'Greetings, Excellency.'

Seringa stopped, flustered. For a moment he looked as

if he would try to push past. But his natural courtesy prevailed. He stared at her, eyes bright with fury.

'I am Ynessa da Soares,' Ynessa went on. 'The head of the House of da Soares. We have business to discuss.' She placed her hands on her hips and looked directly at him.

Seringa looked as if he would burst. 'We have no business to discuss. I have already explained to Mr Darnell. I do not wish a Portuguese fort.'

Ynessa decided he would have to push her out of the way. 'I am very sorry to hear that. Very sorry because I had hoped this fort would have ended the enmity between our people. Even though what our priests did was inexcusable, forty years is a long time. It is time our two peoples became friends.'

Seringa thought the woman was making him look unreasonable: she was too clever. He looked into her face. Was she really that guileless? From beside him Ghosh said, 'You don't care about our friendship, *menina*. All you want is to make money.'

'We all want something from this fort,' Ynessa said. 'We and the English want money. You want your kingdom protected from Kokinada and the Mughal.'

Seringa said, 'I've told Mr Darnell to make alternate financing arrangements within ten days.'

Ynessa looked past Seringa at Darnell. In the two weeks since she'd seen him he'd grown thinner and burnt darker, as if he'd been working long hours outdoors. She tore her eyes away and looked at Seringa. 'The only reason Mr Darnell agreed to our financing the fort was because no other financing was available. He will not find other financing in ten days.'

Seringa said, 'So be it. We will make arrangements with the Dutch.'

'The Dutch will not fight Kokinada for you,' Darnell said.

Ynessa smiled sweetly. 'The Dutch are as short of money

241

as everyone else is.' She fixed her gaze on Seringa. 'Think, Excellency, how much more quickly Madera will be built if the Portuguese help the English. Think how much more quickly Madera will grow if the Portuguese and English work together.'

Seringa frowned and looked down to hide his confusion. It was true that negotiations with the Dutch could take time, and it was possible they too wouldn't have the money. With Portuguese help, the English would build the fort more quickly. The sensible thing was to agree to Portuguese participation. But of all the *feringhi*, the Portuguese were the most untrustworthy. They would sneak in their priests and force Hindus to accept their crucified God. He turned to Darnell. 'My decision remains unchanged. You have ten days to find alternative finance.' He turned back and glared at Ynessa. 'Now, *menina*, allow us to pass.'

Ynessa didn't move. 'Excellency, may I please say one thing more?'

'You've already said enough, *menina*.'

'But with respect, Excellency, Madera is not being financed by the Portuguese merchants' council, but by the House of da Soares. The House of da Soares has always wanted a good relationship with Vaidya, and has always felt that our priests behaved badly. The Portuguese council should have acted years ago to make proper retribution. Because we believe that, we have agreed there will be no proselytizing, that the Portuguese will be restricted to one school and one church for their own use, that the fort will be administered by the English and defended by English soldiers. In return for our financing, all we have asked for is the right to trade. We come as traders, not soldiers. We will have no power to defy you or the English.'

'Your priests will never allow any Portuguese to make such an agreement.'

Ynessa held her hand out to Figueras, who was standing behind her. She took the documents he handed her and told Seringa, 'These, Excellency, are the agreements we have made with the English, setting out the conditions I have mentioned.' She separated two documents from the pile and held them up. 'These are agreements signed by Senhor Saldhana and Senhor de Almeida, two of our leading merchants. They unequivocally agree to the terms and conditions I have just stated.'

Seringa took the agreements and read, then handed them to Ghosh. The woman spoke the truth. The Portuguese would be no threat to Vaidya. He exchanged glances with Ghosh, then turned to Ynessa with a thin smile. 'All right, *menina*, you have persuaded us.' He turned to Ghosh. 'Let all this be formally inscribed. We will sign the new *firman* before we leave.'

Ynessa felt her shoulders slump in relief. Then before she could stop herself, she said, 'There is one condition, Excellency.'

'Condition?' Seringa asked suspiciously. 'What condition?'

Darnell said, 'Ynessa – *menina* – perhaps this could be discussed –'

'It is in our agreement,' Ynessa said firmly. She looked from Darnell back to Seringa and Ghosh. She had to tell them now; later they wouldn't agree. She told Seringa of Rodrigo's murder, her aborted investigation at Celor, the raid at Armagon and Darnell's finding the pearls in Pulicat. 'I want you to help me find the men who killed my father. I want some of your trusted people to accompany me to Celor and help me investigate what happened there.'

'That's impossible,' Seringa said, 'Ali Baig will kill anyone found in Celor on a mission like that.'

Darnell said, 'You can't go back to Celor. Ali Baig knows you're hunting him. He will kill you and anyone with you.'

Ynessa felt the blood rush to her face. But she wouldn't lose her temper. She took a deep breath and gripped the side of her loose green shift. Speaking softly, she said, 'We

243

could go disguised as priests – there has been no service yet for my father. If we can get to Ali Baig's cousin, Mirza Baig, he will talk.'

Seringa shook his head. 'Even if you are right, *menina*, I cannot let any of my people run such a risk.'

Coolly she said, 'It is a condition of our involvement in your fort, Excellency.'

Silence descended on the room. The men looked at each other, then Ghosh said, 'I will go. It will give me a chance to see what Kokinada is planning.'

'No, Dorai, it's much too dangerous. If Ali Baig got you –'

'No one will get me,' Ghosh laughed. 'I am uncatchable.' He came and stood in front of Ynessa and bowed. 'At your service, *menina* – say, five days from now?'

He couldn't let her go with only Ghosh to protect her, Darnell thought. But how could he stop her? She was even more obsessed with finding her father's killers than putting the Portuguese into Madera. 'Who'll be your priest?' he asked.

Ynessa frowned. She'd originally planned this investigation to include Darnell. But after what had happened between them she couldn't let him come. Darnell made the decision for her. 'Ravi will go,' he said.

A week later Ynessa rode to Madera with Figueras and a bodyguard. All week she'd argued with Bishop Ephraim, Joaquim and Mama; finally she'd convinced all of them it was her duty as Rodrigo's oldest surviving child and the head of the House of da Soares to erect a memorial stone over Rodrigo's grave.

Madera loomed ahead to the right, backlit by the bloodshot sun. In the past week it had grown, and now the shape of the fort was clearly discernible: square with bastions at each corner. The curtain walls were already eighteen inches high and the north-west bastion was the height of a man.

There was a roof on the factory house, and in the Black Town she could see the scaffolding surrounding the temple's *gopuram* and Timana Chitty's mansion.

They were nearing the Land Bridge opposite the Black Town which joined the spit to the mainland. Two heavily swaddled figures rode across the bridge, their heads and faces shielded from the chill morning air by shawls draped over their turbans.

Ynessa turned to Figueras, who was the only one who knew the truth about her journey. 'Go home safely, friend,' she said, hugging him.

'Come home safely, Madonna,' he echoed and rode away with the bodyguard.

Ynessa rode towards the men on the Land Bridge.

'We're all here, *menina*,' Ghosh smiled. 'Shall we go?'

Ynessa turned to thank Ravi for joining them and felt her jaw lock. She'd know those blue-black eyes anywhere. The man riding next to her was Richard Darnell!

'What are you doing here?' she gasped. 'You can't – you mustn't –'

'I make a better priest than Ravi,' Darnell said. 'And right now Madera needs Ravi more than it needs me.'

She forced herself to look away from him, to stare ahead at the sunspeckled trail meandering between the palms. 'Darnell,' she said, her voice strained. 'Please go back. Have Winter travel with me.'

'He's better building Madera, and I'm better doing what will need to be done in Celor.'

'No. No. You must understand. We mustn't be together. I am going to marry Joaquim and it isn't right –'

'So it's all right for you to be with Ravi and not with me?' Darnell laughed. He reached across and took her hand. 'I need to come to Celor too. I have a score to settle with van Cuyler. If I get rid of him, the Dutch will not attack Madera.'

She took her hand away. She wouldn't be persuaded.

'It's better then that Ghosh and I go. We'll bring all the evidence back.'

'The risk is too great. Neither of you know van Cuyler. And if you were discovered and Ghosh killed, what would you do then?'

'All right,' she agreed reluctantly. 'We'll travel together. But this is purely business.'

Darnell raised an eyebrow. 'What else could it be, *menina*?' he asked innocently. 'What else could it be?'

They rode all day, and all day they talked. She told him all about her childhood and being brought up in the warehouse by Rodrigo and Figueras; about how much she loved the business.

He told her about Robina and Crispin, of his sister Caddy and the death of his brother, Roland. How he'd lost his fortune and returned to work for the Company at Armagon.

They stopped before sunset in a clearing away from the road. They cooked, ate and settled down to sleep. But Ynessa couldn't sleep. Two hours later she was still turning restlessly beneath her sleeping roll. She told herself her wakefulness was due to the journey, to being in the open surrounded by the unaccustomed noise of wind and forest and sea. But she knew it was really because she wanted to feel Darnell's arms around her, to feel his mouth searching her face and kissing her lips.

No! she screamed silently, kicking against her bedding. Such thoughts were sinful! Even thinking about kissing a man was a mortal sin, more grievous for her because she was already betrothed. She looked round the clearing. Darnell lay about fifteen feet away, barely illuminated by the light of the dying fire; Ghosh was barely visible at the edge of the clearing. Make me remember who I am, she prayed. Never let me forget I am going to be Joaquim's wife. She shuddered involuntarily. She didn't want to think of

Joaquim embracing her, fondling her, taking her. She closed her eyes.

She was falling down and down. Joaquim was reaching out for her. Bishop Ephraim was crying out with his crucifix raised, 'This man is your lawful wedded husband!' Ynessa was saying, 'I can't get married. Father wouldn't have wanted this.' Then Joaquim was coming towards her, arms outstretched. 'Ynessa, I am your husband!' His words echoed and re-echoed.

'Ynessa! Ynessa!' Someone was calling her and cradling her. Startled, disoriented, she opened her eyes and looked into Darnell's face. She felt his arms around her and struggled to sit up.

'You were shouting in your sleep,' Darnell said. 'And you've been crying.'

True. Her cheeks were wet with tears.

'What's wrong?' Darnell asked gently.

It was difficult to speak but she forced the words out. 'Nothing . . . a bad dream . . . I'm sorry I woke you.' She closed her eyes for a moment. It was so nice to be in his arms. She wanted him to embrace her again, to touch her, to tell her he loved her and that she need never go home again.

'Tell me about your nightmare,' he said.

'It was nothing. I'm all right now.'

He lowered her down and she felt a wave of panic. She took his hand. It was warm and calloused. It was better holding on to something. She did not feel so alone. Or so terrified or vulnerable. I love you, Darnell, she thought. I love you.

Suddenly he was lying beside her, caressing her, his body strong, his arms like bands of iron. Poor, poor darling, she thought, I am not yours. I can never be yours. The thought burned like acid.

His lips were brushing her cheeks and forehead and chin again, tenderly, lovingly, in awe almost. They rested on

247

her mouth, lip against lip. She felt his breath against her face, her own breath beating back from his. Slowly he ran his tongue over her mouth, probing gently, sending little shivers of delight to the base of her spine. She longed for him to force open her mouth.

He did with one swift movement that brought their tongues together. Little spurts of flame licked through her. She wanted him, wanted him now. Then his hands came round, kneading her breasts. She felt her nipples grow erect. He stroked them gently, raising them, the pain of their erection mingling with the heavenly sensation of their locked mouths.

She felt herself dissolving. She could not hold back. She would explode any moment. Then his mouth was withdrawn and she felt cheated. But only for a moment. He was taking her nipples in his mouth, first the left, then the right, running his tongue around them. 'Do it harder,' she gasped, trembling with pleasure.

He was beside her under the blanket and it felt good. She reached her hand under his tunic, feeling the bunched muscles of his back. This is wonderful, she thought, oh darling Darnell, this feels so very good. You must never stop, never. She grasped his head and pulled it hard to her breasts. Don't stop. Don't stop.

He swept his hand over the flat of her stomach. She could hardly breathe for pleasure. His hand kept going down. He was going *there*! For a moment she stiffened with embarrassment. She was wet, and then his hand was there, easing into her, teasing her. She pressed hard against his finger, pulling his head down to her breast, pushing against him, feeling the stubble of his chin press into her skin.

She kissed him hurriedly, bending her head forward, kissing his cheeks, his head, his forehead, anything she could reach. 'I love you Darnell,' she said. 'I love you.'

Drawing his head away from her breasts, he took her

lips again. She kissed him, kissed his lips, the inside of his mouth, took her head away and kissed his chin and cheeks and forehead the way he had kissed her. He took her mouth again and held it in his lips, then opened her lips once more with his tongue. She quivered as her tongue met his, quivered as they explored and touched, while his finger probed and teased till she wanted to scream with pleasure.

She felt his hardness against her legs and thought, no. This has gone far enough. I must stop him. But he was moving over her and his lips were closing on hers and she wanted him, wanted him more than anything in the world.

She lay still as he parted her legs and felt him touch her there with it, felt it press against her.

'Darnell,' she said, 'I have never –'

'I know. I'll not hurt you.' He lay on his elbows, taking his weight off her, probing her with persistent, gentle thrusts, his lips kissing her mouth and face and breasts again and again. She felt herself opening to him, felt him come in to her, then his mouth was on her lips, his tongue pressing on hers and as she quivered in response to his kiss, he thrust hard and deep and she felt her legs fly apart and screamed into his mouth with pain.

The pain was short and sharp and knifing and there was a warm wetness between her legs and he was moving inside her, up and down, and then the pain was engulfed by her pleasure. She felt she was pinioned to the end of his shaft, felt him dig into her over and over and deeper, felt the strong grasp of his thighs, heard him breathing hard.

Wave after wave of delight engulfed her. She felt a gigantic climax approaching. Her mind was reeling. She gave a scream. Then she was crying out in tiny sobs. She went into spasm after spasm and he kept pounding her and pounding her, repeatedly, incessantly, thundering, quivering, one with her.

She felt him tremble in her arms, saw him writhe helplessly above her, caught in the grip of something so powerful that all he could do was throw his head back and cry out. She felt her power over him as she threw herself up and down, matching his movements, taking them, magnifying them, pulling him down to her, holding him, drawing him in and in till in a paroxysm of pleasure he cried out and exploded inside her, quivering and throbbing and flooding her and subsiding, sobbing, on her chest.

They loved each other again in that blissful night and lay together till morning. Ynessa woke in the reddening light of dawn. They'd slept with their arms around each other and Darnell's face was inches away from hers, lean, covered with dark stubble, relaxed. His eyes flickered open. He looked into her face and smiled. 'Morning my love,' he said. 'The first of all our mornings together.'

Ynessa buried her face in his chest, feeling the tears burn behind her lids. Morning meant everything was over. Morning meant nothing had happened.

'We'll be together for always,' Darnell murmured. 'We will go to Celor and find Rodrigo's killers and then we'll get married,' he promised.

She took her head away from his chest and looked at him. 'No,' she said. 'This must never happen again. We must be sensible. I'm going to marry Joaquim and —'

'I'm going to marry you,' he repeated. 'I will never let you marry Joaquim.' He kissed her and she felt the desire stirring in her again, felt him grow hard against her body, and once more she opened her arms to him.

Chapter Seventeen

Van Cuyler lurched down the gangplank of the *Chingleput Rani* and hurried across the San Thome docks, wrinkling his nostrils at the sharp smells of offal and rotting fish. Coolies and carts jostled round him. He walked through the Sea Gate and turned left on to the Rua Magellan.

He'd come to San Thome to recover the pearls and stop the financing of Darnell's fort. He had little doubt that Darnell would use those pearls to hang him. His enquiries had established that the English were not involved in Madera; if Darnell was building a fort it was a private venture.

Which meant someone was financing Darnell. De Groot had agreed with van Cuyler that the merchants of San Thome were Darnell's most likely source: they were rich from the *entrepôt* trade and would have walked on a crucifix to get a trade deal with Vaidya.

Van Cuyler strode past the row of warehouses on the Rua Magellan till he came to the alleyways crowded with small houses and shops occupied by craftsmen and jewellers. He kicked away the half-naked Portuguese beggar lying across the doorway of Gonsalez's shop and went in.

Gonsalez was in the back, squinting over a ledger. He looked up suspiciously, then rushed forward. 'Senhor van Cuyler, what a surprise! Why didn't you tell me you were coming?'

Soon after he'd arrived in India, van Cuyler had visited San Thome and arranged to give Gonsalez access to Dutch stones in exchange for regular information. Now Gonsalez's worth would be put to the test. 'Let's go through to the back,' van Cuyler said tersely.

Gonsalez's cubicle was small and crowded and smelt of mildewed paper and jeweller's paste. Van Cuyler said abruptly, 'I am looking for the pearls of Celor.'

Gonsalez stopped reaching for a tray of sweetmeats and let his hand fall on the desk. He licked his lips and said, 'Those pearls.'

Van Cuyler caught Gonsalez's eyes and held them. 'Have you seen the pearls? Have you seen Darnell?'

Gonsalez sighed dramatically. 'I don't know . . . so many people come into the shop . . . an Englishman, you say?'

'We are paying a reward of five hundred *guilders* to find out where those pearls are,' van Cuyler said. 'You have seen the pearls?'

Gonsalez didn't say anything, so van Cuyler put fifty *guilders* on the table.

Gonsalez said, 'Darnell came here to sell the pearls –'

'You bought them? You've got them?'

'Alas, no.' Gonsalez pressed against the back of his chair. 'He brought me the pearls together with some Dutch stones. I recognized them and asked for a provenance. When he couldn't produce one I sent for the militia.'

'Really?' Van Cuyler did not try to keep the disbelief out of his voice.

'Really,' Gonsalez said. He looked up at van Cuyler. 'I have no wish to involve myself in Don Rodrigo's murder.'

Van Cuyler tried to stop the colour rising to his face but couldn't. He said, 'Rodrigo was murdered by dacoits. The pearls were brought to us by our chief merchant, Abu Murad. We have no idea how he got them.'

'Exactly.' Gonsalez piled the coins van Cuyler had left, and van Cuyler added fifty more *guilders*. 'It is just as well I informed the militia,' he told van Cuyler. 'Darnell was the rightful owner of those pearls. They had been given to him by Don Rodrigo's daughter, Ynessa da Soares.'

Van Cuyler's mouth dropped open. The stabbing pain started again in his head. 'Who has those pearls now?' he asked.

Gonsalez shrugged flabby shoulders. 'I don't know. But if they've been sold anywhere, it isn't in San Thome.'

'Then how is Darnell financing his fort?'

Gonsalez hesitated, then decided that since the information was public knowledge, he couldn't sell it. 'Ynessa da Soares is financing the English fort.'

'Why?'

'Because it's good business.' Gonsalez looked surprised. 'That fort's going to be the most profitable thing that's happened in Coromandel.'

Van Cuyler wondered if Gonsalez's patriotism would outweigh his self-interest. He said, 'It is not in the Dutch interest to have an English fort in Vaidya.'

Gonsalez frowned and lowered his head.

Van Cuyler said, 'We have recently received some first quality diamonds. I can arrange a big discount if you will find a way to stop the fort.'

Gonsalez remained silent, looking down and rubbing his hands together. After what seemed an eternity he said, 'There's one way. But it'll cost you. On his marriage, Joaquim Gonzaga will control the House of da Soares. He will stop the fort – if it is made worth his while . . .'

Two hours later, after numerous exchanges of messages, van Cuyler and Gonsalez went to the Gonzaga warehouse. It stood halfway along the docks near the Flagstaff. Its street façade was crumbling and pitted with broken brickwork, its dusty steps stained with bird droppings, betel spit and daubs of *chunam*. Gonsalez had been right about the Gonzagas needing money, van Cuyler thought as they were taken to a faded room on the second floor, with sea damp seeping through the walls and paint peeling from the window-frames. It was crowded with old, battered furniture, and the windows were so salt-stained that van Cuyler could barely see the docks below.

Twenty minutes after their arrival, Joaquim Gonzaga came in. His walk was swaggering, his glossy black hair and beard carefully combed and trimmed. Van Cuyler noted Gonzaga wore the latest French tights and sheer silk stockings without garters the better to show off his legs. Vain, arrogant and ignorant, van Cuyler concluded. As soon as the introductions were completed he said, 'I am honoured to make your acquaintance, senhor. I have been sent to ask for your intercession by the governor of Pulicat.'

Joaquim visibly preened himself at having a request made of him by a governor. He strutted to a chair at the head of a jakwood table and sat. 'Welcome to the House of Gonzaga,' he murmured throatily. A dazzling smile split the exquisite line of his face. 'How can we assist you and the governor of Pulicat?'

'We are greatly disturbed by the English fort at Madera,' van Cuyler said. 'We would be most grateful if you would prevail upon your family to cease financing it and stop its construction.'

Ynessa would never agree to that, Joaquim knew. She had fought him in public – even argued with Bishop Ephraim over it. 'I do not think that is possible, senhor. The investment has been made by the House of da Soares, not by us.'

Van Cuyler nodded to show he understood. 'It must be difficult,' he said, 'to control a woman who is rich and has her own business.' He smiled. 'I hear she has a vivid temper.'

Joaquim felt himself flush. The Dutchman was laughing at him. The Dutchman was insinuating that he could not control his woman. He looked at Gonsalez, who avoided his glance, too obviously acting as if he wasn't listening. Soon all of San Thome would know he was dominated by Ynessa, Joaquim thought. How could he convince the

Dutchman and Gonsalez otherwise? 'I have no legal control over the House of da Soares,' he said. 'As you may know, I opposed this investment . . .'

Van Cuyler's smile was both understanding and sarcastic. 'But couldn't stop it. I hope that after your marriage you will have greater control over your wife's business affairs. We are sorry to have taken up your time. Perhaps it is best we talk to your fiancée.' He got to his feet.

'Signora da Soares is away,' Gonsalez said.

Van Cuyler looked shocked. 'Away?' He sat and shook his head in despair. 'I am afraid by the time she returns it will be too late.' He leaned on his elbows across the table and looked sincerely into Joaquim's face. 'Senhor Gonzaga, I had hoped you would have been able to stop this construction. But as it appears you cannot, I must tell you that our armies intend to destroy that fort in a matter of weeks. I'm afraid your fiancée's investment will be totally lost!'

The words galloped joyously through Joaquim's brain. He'd been right and Ynessa had been very stupid! That would serve her right. But she would be losing money which the House of Gonzaga–da Soares needed. He saw the Dutchman and Gonsalez rise. He had to stop them leaving. But what could he do?

With Ynessa on her way to Celor, Figueras was in charge of da Soares. He was only a clerk: he *must* listen to him, Ynessa's future husband and the future head of da Soares. 'Wait, senhors!' he cried. 'I *can* stop the financing. Come with me to da Soares.'

Van Cuyler turned to look at him, hardly believing his ears. His stratagem had worked. He struggled to keep the smile from his face.

Van Cuyler paced about the narrow cabin. The *Chingleput Rani* wouldn't sail for another hour and he was worn out with anger and impatience. He had to get to Celor. After a humiliating confrontation with that woman's pig-headed clerk, not only had he failed to get the fort construction stopped, but he'd learned that Ynessa da Soares was still bent on finding her father's murderers. He had to warn Ali Baig. He wondered if Darnell was inciting the da Soares woman. He had to kill them both. Once they had proof, that would be the end of it. The cabin vibrated with the thump of goods being loaded on to the deck above him. For God's sake hurry, he cried silently. *Hurry!*

There was a pounding on his door which for a moment he confused with the noise of the goods being loaded. Then he took the *sjambok* from his belt and swung the door open. Gonsalez sidled into the cabin, sweating heavily. 'I am sorry for disturbing you, Senhor van Cuyler. But if you will please come ashore, Bishop Ephraim, the vicar-general of San Thome, wants to talk with you. He is counsellor to the House of Gonzaga and a much more astute man than Joaquim. He has a plan that will stop the building of the English fort.'

That sounded promising. Perhaps the threat of a Dutch attack had worked after all. But what if the ship –

As if reading his thoughts, Gonsalez said, 'Don't worry. The bishop has made sure the ship won't sail without you.'

Twenty minutes later they were in a book-lined room in the bishop's palace. A huge crucifix hung on one wall. The grey stone hulk of St Thomas's Cathedral loomed outside the window.

Bishop Ephraim glided into the room, a fat, smooth, clean-shaven man wearing a purple soutane, sash and skull-cap, all made of silk. He settled himself comfortably on a throne-like chair against the wall furthest from the street. The light from the window glinted off the huge amethyst on his finger.

'Like you, sir, I am a man of peace,' Bishop Ephraim began. 'I am most anxious to avoid bloodshed over Madera.'

Van Cuyler wondered what the bishop's interest in the

English fort was. What did it matter to him if the English lived or died? He studied the bishop's purple boots. Expensive, he thought, even for a bishop.

'If the cause of this war is the financing of the English fort, that can and will be stopped,' Bishop Ephraim said. 'But I will need your cooperation.'

His bluff was working, van Cuyler thought. The Portuguese were running scared.

The bishop fluttered his hands as if releasing a flock of doves. 'In a few weeks my godson marries Ynessa da Soares. Joaquim will then control the House of da Soares and immediately cancel the financing agreement. That will stop the English fort.'

The bishop leaned forward slightly. 'Of course there will have to be compensation.'

'We have a small surplus of cinnamon,' van Cuyler said.

'We would prefer cash,' the bishop said. 'Six hundred pounds.'

'Impossible,' van Cuyler snapped. 'To attack the fort won't cost us more than a hundred pounds.'

Bishop Ephraim's eyes slid like greased marbles. 'Perhaps so. But for six hundred pounds I will also ensure that the investigation being carried out by Ynessa da Soares in Celor will also be stopped.'

Van Cuyler drummed his fingertips on his thigh. 'And why should I be interested in Ynessa da Soares's investigation?'

Bishop Ephraim threw another quick glance at Gonsalez. 'Because of the pearls, mynheer. Because of the pearls which Darnell obtained from Pulicat and tried to sell to Senhor Gonsalez. Because of the pearls which have taken Ynessa da Soares to Celor to lay a memorial stone on the grave of her murdered father, but in fact, I suspect, to find out who killed Rodrigo da Soares and his companions.'

If he agreed the exorbitant price he would be admitting that he was involved in the murders. On the other hand, to stop Ynessa da Soares's investigation was worth any price. Van Cuyler's head began to throb. 'It's a lot of money,' he muttered.

'Think of it as penance for your salvation,' Bishop Ephraim said softly.

'I – I can't get that amount of money until next month.'

Bishop Ephraim thought about that for a moment. 'We will draw up an agreement now to which we will attach your promissory note.'

Van Cuyler nodded. He was thinking that if he got to Celor and stopped Ynessa da Soares himself, he'd have no need to give the bishop the money after all.

Chapter Eighteen

Four days after having set out, Ghosh, Darnell and Ynessa rode into Celor, both Darnell and Ynessa wearing the black leggings, boots, waist-length tunics and black, flat-topped, wide-brimmed hats of priests.

The village was just stirring from its siesta, its streets filling with merchants and fishermen and women in bright saris shopping for food. The villagers stared at them, their glances curious and unfriendly. If Ali Baig was here and recognized them, Darnell thought, they'd be dead, he and Ghosh no doubt cruelly tortured first, and Ynessa – he didn't want to think what would happen to Ynessa. Darnell slipped one hand under his tunic and gripped his pistol butt.

With its wide streets and brick buildings, Celor looked a prosperous settlement. In the half-walled ante-rooms of shops, merchants and their assistants sat on carpets sorting heaps of pearls. Other men sat on their haunches before blocks of wood riddled with small, semi-circular holes, into which they placed pearls and drilled them by pressing their foreheads against coconut-shell cups that activated needles fixed to reeds topped with iron points. Working from dawn to dusk, each cutter drilled about six hundred pearls a day. A scrawny, bare-bodied man lurched past Darnell with the disjointed gait of one who had dived too deep or come up too quickly.

Darnell followed Ghosh into the centre of the village. The last four days had been both heaven and hell. Being with Ynessa was wonderful. He loved her. He wanted to marry her. The difference in their ages and their nationalities didn't matter. They were one in everything – except for the fact that Ynessa was a Catholic and had sworn to marry Joaquim Gonzaga.

'How will you ever believe me if I break a solemn promise?' she'd argued. 'How can I break a solemn promise and marry a heretic without going to hell?' She was honest, frightened, superstitious and confused. God damn Bishop Ephraim and his Pope, Darnell thought as they rode into a large paved square surrounded by shops.

The people in the square stared in silence. 'We have come from San Thome,' Darnell said, fingering the crucifix at his waist. 'We have come to pray for the souls of our countrymen who were so brutally murdered on their way back from here.'

A voice called out from between the houses bordering the square. 'You cannot stay here. You have no business here. You must go now!'

Darnell turned towards the sound, heart racing.

A plump, light-skinned man clad only in a damp sarong emerged from between the houses, striding ahead of attendants who were making frantic attempts to towel him off and dress him. He had a vast, drooping moustache and light eyes. Mirza Baig, Darnell thought, recognizing him from Ynessa's description. He felt relieved. Ali Baig was not in Celor.

'You cannot stay here,' Mirza Baig repeated. 'We do not allow strangers in Celor.' One of his guards held out a white tunic and Mirza Baig slipped into it.

'We come in the name of the one God,' Darnell said. 'To pray over the graves of our countrymen, for the salvation of their souls.'

'You cannot stay here,' Mirza Baig repeated. 'Celor is closed to strangers.'

The villagers were looking hostile, but Darnell had to try once more. 'We seek your hospitality, in the name of God,' he said quietly.

Mirza Baig struggled into a scarlet jacket of English broadcloth. He was darting suspicious glances at Darnell. Christians too were followers of the one God; Darnell knew Mirza Baig could not refuse a request from a man of God in the name of God. 'You may stay,' Mirza Baig said reluctantly. 'But only for one night.' He spoke to one of his guards, who scurried away into the village.

Darnell dismounted and approached Mirza Baig, palms steepled in front of him, drawing his attention away from Ynessa.

'We are grateful for your hospitality,' he said. Mirza Baig was clearly someone of importance in Celor; he was also Ali Baig's cousin, and Ali Baig had overall control of Celor. 'You must be Mirza Baig,' Darnell went on. 'Don Rodrigo's daughter described you well. She wishes to be remembered to you.'

Mirza Baig's face clouded. 'Do what you have to do and go. We do not want strangers in the village.'

Darnell said, 'The House of da Soares is offering five hundred pounds to anyone who helps discover the men who killed Don Rodrigo and his escort.'

'A huge sum,' Mirza Baig said. His tongue darted out and moistened his lips. 'But we have not yet found the dacoits.'

So Mirza Baig wasn't going to cooperate. Darnell reached into his pocket and beckoned Mirza Baig close, opened his palm and showed him one of the prize pearls of Celor.

Mirza Baig's eyes widened. He breathed in sharply. 'Where did you get this?'

'The House of da Soares has obtained this and all the other pearls from the Dutch. They were taken from a man named van Cuyler.'

Mirza Baig stepped back nervously. 'I know nothing about this. You'd better go. No one here can help you.'

'Don Rodrigo's daughter believes you can. The House of da Soares is even now communicating with the nizam of Kokinada who will want to know how the Dutch got the prize pearls. He will want to know who in Celor helped the Dutch, and who in Celor knows what happened. And he will find out.' Darnell walked to his horse and turned. 'I think it will be best if the nizam did not have to find out.'

Mirza Baig's eyes darted swiftly round the square. 'We will talk after evening prayer,' he said, hoarsely. 'I will come to your house. Now go.'

Van Cuyler rode into the village beside Ali Baig. Blessed by monsoon winds and the *bakshish* he'd given the captain, they'd made splendid time from San Thome, enabling him to be put ashore that afternoon near Sairin, inform Ali Baig what was happening, and bring him to Celor with eight of his men. Ali Baig had been more than eager to come. He was terrified of the consequences and also wanted revenge for what had happened in Armagon.

Mirza Baig was trotting towards them from the north of the village. Instantly, van Cuyler felt suspicious. He watched Mirza Baig come up to them, panting, his tunic stuck to his body with sweat. What had Mirza Baig been doing at this time in the north of the village? Mirza Baig looked more than usually furtive, he thought, as the head-man pressed his fingers to his forehead and bowed deeply three times to Ali Baig. 'Welcome home, cousin,' Mirza Baig said, still panting. 'You too, Dutch.'

'Have any strangers passed through here?' Ali Baig asked. 'Are there any strangers in the village?'

'No.' Mirza Baig was sweating profusely. 'Only the priests who came this evening.'

'Priests? What priests?'

'The priests who've come to pray over the graves of the Portuguese. I've let them stay in the village because it was late and they asked me in God's name –'

Mirza Baig was meandering. 'Where are these priests?' van Cuyler demanded.

'I – I let them use Abdulla's hut.' Mirza Baig pointed over his shoulder.

Ali Baig urged his horse forward and van Cuyler went with him. Followed by their escort, they cantered along the narrow street and stopped near the end of the village. Van Cuyler dismounted and, with Ali Baig beside him, rushed up the steps of the hut.

A coconut-oil lamp still burned in the hut but the place was empty apart from a flat-topped, broad-brimmed black hat and crucifix. Mirza Baig was pushing his way anxiously into the room past Ali Baig's guard. Van Cuyler thought he looked relieved that the place was empty. 'How many were there?' he asked.

'Three. They were priests. They came to pray –'

'You said that. Where are they now?'

Mirza Baig looked round the hut, bewildered. 'They seem to have left.'

'Why did they leave?' Van Cuyler grabbed Mirza Baig by the front of his sarong. He felt the hard, circular outlines of coins dig into his palms, and yanked at the garment. Mirza Baig yelped as it came free and a shower of gold coins scattered on the floor.

Mirza Baig looked round in panic. Van Cuyler held firmly on to his sarong. 'Where did you get this money?' he demanded.

From behind van Cuyler, Ali Baig cried, 'What did you tell them, Mirza? What did you tell them?' and slashed his cousin across the stomach with his knife. A bright red stripe flashed across the front of Mirza Baig's tunic, growing deeper, darker and wetter. Mirza Baig screamed and tried to pull away.

Ali Baig thrust the knife beneath Mirza's eyeball. 'What did you tell them?' he demanded again.

Mirza Baig was whimpering. 'Nothing, cousin. I swear, in the name of God, I told them nothing.'

'Then why did they leave?' van Cuyler asked. 'And why

did they give you money?' He pulled out his *sjambok* and hit Mirza Baig across the face.

Mirza Baig cried out and staggered, but van Cuyler and Ali Baig moved after him, backing him into a corner. Van Cuyler hit him again, across the side of his face, then twice more on his hands as he raised them to protect his face. The blows were solid and Mirza Baig staggered from their force. Great weals stood out on the backs of his hands and his face. Van Cuyler raised the *sjambok* again.

Mirza Baig fell to his knees. 'Please,' he sobbed, 'please leave me alone. They were not priests. They were Don Rodrigo's daughter from San Thome and two men. They had the pearls from Celor, the prize pearls which they had taken from the Dutch.' He raised his eyes and looked at van Cuyler. 'If I didn't tell them what happened, they were going to blow up the pearl banks!'

Van Cuyler's hand froze in horror.

'I wanted them to spare Celor . . . the people of Celor –'

Mirza Baig had told them everything, van Cuyler thought. Rodrigo's daughter knew! Darnell probably knew! Then he had another thought. They had no proof unless Mirza Baig confirmed what he'd told them. 'Kill him!' he ordered Ali Baig. 'We have to shut his mouth.'

Their horses were tired; the occasional snatch of pounding hooves and urgent cries from behind them were becoming louder. Darnell knew it must be Ali Baig's men who were catching them up fast, and there was nothing they could do about it. He thought furiously about some form of ambush, anything to give them an advantage.

The trail curved between a thicket of jungle and palms. Ghosh waved Ynessa ahead, then turned to Darnell. 'Quick. Do as I say!'

Ghosh edged his horse into the thicket, dismounted, took a bag from his saddle and extracted a thin rope. 'Tie this round that palm, there.'

A trip wire would at least catch the first few horses. Darnell picked up one end of the rope and ran across the trail, tying it firmly to the palm at the height of a horse's knee. Running back, he crouched beside Ghosh, feeling the pulse throb in his throat. In the silence, the pounding of hooves was louder than surf. Darnell listened anxiously.

The noise grew louder, a steady drumming accompanied by the shift of leather and tinkle of metal buckles. He could feel the earth vibrate under his feet. Then he saw them, dark shapes streaking through the trees, men crouched low in their saddles, scudding over the earth. They were rounding the corner, heeling with the force of the turn. He saw Ali Baig and van Cuyler in the lead, heads pressed close to their horses' necks.

Too late van Cuyler saw the rope. His horse slewed sideways and was hit from behind, sliding into the rope and flopping over. Van Cuyler cartwheeled through the air; Ali Baig's mount hit the rope without slowing and fell, also throwing its rider. Behind them the others slewed and reared and stumbled over the already fallen horses and men. For a while there was the continuous thud of falling bodies and the frightened whinnying of horses, mingled with the angry, frightened shouts of men.

Then Ghosh reached into his bag and pulled out some *chakrams*: flat, metal quoits with razor-sharp edges. He hurled them into the mêlée, and the cries of pain and anger turned to screams of terror.

'Come Darnell! I have no more *chakrams*!' Ghosh shouted.

Darnell saw van Cuyler lying on his back, stunned. His pistol was levelled at van Cuyler's head. One ball, he thought, and everything is finished. Then he thought, this is no revenge. I want him to know it is I killing him. I want him to die slowly.

He lowered the gun. He ran with Ghosh to the horses.

*   *   *

The sun rose liverishly behind a bank of dark, scudding cloud casting a translucent, shadowless light on the beach. Ynessa listened to the restless gusting of the sea wind and snuggled in the blanket, secure with the feel of Darnell's arms around her. It had been six days since they'd left Celor with Mirza Baig's signed confession; six days during which she'd come to love Darnell more than she'd ever thought possible; six days that had made her realize how impossible it would be to leave him, and how impossible it would be to stay.

She studied his face, drawn from the journey, but relaxed and vulnerable in sleep. I love you so much, she thought, and as if echoing her thoughts, his eyes fluttered open and he smiled. 'I love you,' he said.

She turned away, unable to face those dark eyes. His arm caressing her went still. Suddenly the roar of the sea seemed deafening.

'You have decided,' Darnell spoke tightly. It was not a question.

She still couldn't look at him. 'I'm going back to San Thome. I am going to honour my promise and marry Joaquim Gonzaga.' At last she turned, her eyes filled with tears. 'You know I must, I've given my word –'

Darnell's expression was anguished. 'But that was before *this*! *This* is what is important, not that confounded promise.'

She closed her eyes and raised her hands to her face. It was torture to think of her future without him; his anger now was compounding her agony. 'Don't,' she pleaded with him.

'Don't what?' he demanded, twisting away from her and standing up. He was looking down at her, his face taut and bitter, his dark eyes filled with pain. 'Don't tell you how miserable you will make yourself, how miserable you will make me. Don't point out what empty pointless lives we will live without each other; how you have condemned us both to purgatory.'

She too stood up, reaching desperately out to him. 'My darling, darling Darnell. I'll never love anyone the way I love you. I'll always remember our time together. I'll never stop loving you. But now I must go and do my duty. I must do what I believe to be right.'

For one long moment he stared deep into her eyes, then suddenly his gaze became tense and withdrawn and he turned abruptly. 'Go if you must,' he said as he walked away. 'I wish you all the unhappiness you deserve!'

Chapter Nineteen

'Most Gracious Ruler, I have come to demand vengeance!'
Ali Baig threw himself face down on the marble steps of
the nizam's throne.

Ali Baig was a good actor, van Cuyler thought. They
had come to Kokinada to ask the nizam to attack Darnell's
fort. Van Cuyler would send van Roon and a party of
Dutchmen with the nizam's troops to ensure that Darnell
was killed in the attack. With the fort destroyed and Darnell dead, he did not have to worry about the English taking
over Coromandel, or the investigation. Without credible
witnesses, Ynessa da Soares's story would not stand up.

They were in the *diwan-i-am* or public courtyard of the
nizam's palace, a large paved rectangle bordered by empty
stone galleries. It was divided into sections by wood, silver
and gold railings. Because this was a private meeting, only
the area within the gold railings was occupied, partly filled
with a mixture of courtiers, soldiers and mace-bearers
standing on either side of a central aisle. At the head of
the aisle the nizam sat on a jewelled throne placed on a
platform of red stone.

The nizam was a man in his early fifties, dressed in a
cream tunic whose material was interwoven with gold
thread. He wore an unlined satin coat with a large collar
and embroidered sleeves over the tunic. His legs were
covered with an ankle-length silk *shalwar*; his feet with
silk stockings and velvet shoes decorated with rows of
pearls and diamonds. The aigrette on his turban rose from
an emerald, flanked by a ruby and a diamond. His lined
face was thin and long, with a heavy grey moustache and

sunken eyes that were large and piercing. He watched Ali Baig carefully as he said, 'Speak, cousin, and tell us for what you demand vengeance.'

Ali Baig began to wail and rip his clothes. Tears dampened his scrawny beard. 'I seek vengeance, Your Majesty, for the brutal murder of our cousin, Mirza Baig, who was killed by the unspeakable Hindu Vaidyan dogs.'

The nizam looked surprised. 'I was not aware, cousin, that you loved Mirza Baig so. My recollection is that as boys you were the first to bully him and tease him about his *feringhi* father.'

Ali Baig had overstretched his case, van Cuyler thought.

Ali Baig pressed his forehead to the ground. 'That is true, Your Majesty. But as we worked together these last few years, we became the closest of friends. I respected Mirza Baig. I admired his courage and his clear-sightedness and his constant readiness to help others.'

The nizam was still looking suspiciously at Ali Baig, stroking his long chin with the finger and thumb of his right hand. 'When did this attack take place?' he asked, clearly unable to believe that the Vaidyans would dare attack Celor.

'Six days ago, Your Majesty. It was a band of *goondas*, the same *goondas* who robbed and killed the Portuguese merchants. Mirza Baig and a few of the villagers tried to repulse them. Mirza Baig was killed.'

'What damage did these *goondas* do?'

'They set fire to some huts in the north of the village before they were discovered and frightened off.'

'That seems such a senseless thing to do.'

'The *goondas* were sent to frighten us. We captured one of them, Majesty, and made him talk. He told us they were from Vaidya and had come to probe our defences and intimidate us as a part of a larger plan by Prince Seringa to take Celor with the help of the English.'

The nizam frowned. 'Vaidyan *goondas*,' he muttered,

'Prince Seringa, and now the English.' Raising his voice, he asked, 'Where is this *goonda* you interrogated?'

Ali Baig's shoulders sagged and he turned open his palms helplessly. 'Alas, Majesty, he died.'

The nizam said, 'I cannot believe the English will join Seringa and attack us. They have many forts in Kokinada and depend on good relations with us for their trade.'

Ignoring the glares of the mace-bearers, van Cuyler stepped into the aisle and bowed low. He placed the palm of his right hand against his brow, then slowly lowered it as he came erect in a perfectly executed *kornish*. 'Your Majesty, I bring greetings, from the president of the Dutch Compagnie in Batavia. I am his envoy. What Ali Baig tells you is true. May I be permitted to explain?'

'I wish someone would,' Kokinada said.

'A few weeks ago,' van Cuyler began, 'with Prince Seringa's permission, the English started building a large fort at Madera. The fort is so situated that its guns will effectively prevent any attack on Vaidya. It is our understanding that the English are training Seringa's army in the use of guns, so that they may invade Kokinada.'

'You have evidence of this?'

'The fort exists, Your Majesty, I have seen it, Ali Baig has seen it, and if any of your people cross the Vaidyan border, they will see it.'

'But how do you know the English are training Seringa's army?'

'Because I negotiated with Prince Seringa on behalf of the Compagnie for permission to build a factory at Madera. Prince Seringa gave permission to the English, because they offered to train his army and we wouldn't.'

Ali Baig said, 'As Your Majesty knows, Seringa has never fully accepted the peace treaty agreed between you and Raja Railoo. He has always wanted to retake Celor, which was once part of Vaidya.'

The nizam leaned back on his throne, fingers caressing

his beard. He conferred with his courtiers then asked van Cuyler, 'What is the Dutch interest in this matter?'

'It is twofold, Your Majesty. We do not want Celor to fall to Seringa and his English allies, because that will exclude us from the pearl trade. We also do not wish the English to prosper by settling in Vaidya.'

'Honestly spoken,' the nizam said. 'I'll send some troops back with you to defend Celor.'

Van Cuyler's glow of satisfaction at the compliment subsided. That wasn't what he wanted. He wanted the nizam to destroy Madera.

'That is not enough!' Ali Baig cried. 'We must destroy the English fort at Madera. We must seize the Vaidyan terrorists hiding there and kill them!'

The nizam shook his head. 'You were always too impulsive,' he told Ali Baig. 'The time to attack Vaidya is later. At the right time we will destroy Prince Seringa and take Vaidya.'

That would be far too late, Van Cuyler thought. He said, 'With respect, Your Majesty, if you don't attack Madera now, you will never take Vaidya.'

'Never! How can you be so sure of that, Dutchman?'

'The English fort will be completed before the monsoons, and when it is completed, English guns will cover the only road from Kokinada into Vaidya. No matter how large your army is, it will not get through.'

Again the nizam summoned his courtiers around him, then said, 'I will discuss this matter with Raja Railoo and have him bring Seringa under control.'

Van Cuyler said, 'Raja Railoo cannot stop Seringa. Once Seringa takes Celor, he will be richer and more powerful than Railoo. Then he will turn on Railoo.'

'That must not happen,' the nizam said. 'But I do not think attacking Madera will prevent it. It is not the right season for war, and if my army suffers great losses, I will not be able to implement my plans for the future. I cannot afford a war right now, with both the English and Railoo.'

Van Cuyler's mind raced. 'It needn't come to that, Your Majesty,' he said, and paused to get the nizam's full attention. 'If your attack is directed only at Madera, Railoo will be delighted at your curbing Seringa's power.'

'What about the English?'

'The English are not fully committed to this fort. Their principal agent in Pettahpoli has written to us that this fort is a private venture and that the fort has not yet been adopted by the Company.'

The nizam stared thoughtfully then finally asked, 'How many men will we need?'

Van Cuyler was so relieved that he couldn't speak, and it was Ali Baig who said, 'About a thousand.'

Van Cuyler cleared his throat. 'If Your Majesty permits, I will have a squad of Dutch soldiers join your army on the Vaidyan border.'

Again van Cuyler waited tensely.

'All right.' The nizam nodded.

Van Cuyler bowed to hide his smile.

Chapter Twenty

In the two weeks since she'd returned from Celor, Ynessa had tried everything: throwing herself into her work, spending time with Joaquim, praying. She'd read a life of St Thomas, gone for long, hard, fast rides, organized the planting of an orchard on land Rodrigo had bought shortly before his death, planned the laying of a new ship. But nothing worked.

All she had was her work. She forced herself to concentrate fiercely on the final draft of her report on Rodrigo's murder which she intended submitting to the merchants' council so they could make formal complaints to the Governor of Pulicat and the nizam.

There was a knock on the door, and Figueras came in. He looked anxious.

'What's the matter?' Ynessa asked him, concerned.

Figueras took a deep breath. 'It's you, Madonna. You're tired, and you've got so thin. You don't eat enough, you work too hard and you don't rest enough. If you don't stop, you'll become seriously ill.'

'I'm fine,' Ynessa said briskly. 'There's just been so much work –'

'It's not the work,' Figueras said firmly. 'It's you. You're trying to put forty-eight hours into a day. You're never still. And if there's no work, you make it . . . What's troubling you, Madonna?'

'It's nothing,' she said. 'Nothing!'

There was an awkward pause. Ynessa shuffled papers nervously, not wanting to look into Figueras's eyes.

'Is it Darnell?' Figueras asked, finally.

She jumped in her chair. 'Darnell? Why should it be Darnell?' Her voice had broken. She hoped Figueras hadn't noticed.

'Because he went to Celor with you instead of Winter. Because your face lights up at the mention of his name. Because ever since you've asked me to deal with the English, you've been unhappy.'

Ynessa felt the tears welling. She closed her eyes and nodded and heard Figueras walk up to her, felt his arms go round her. 'And does he love you, Madonna?'

'Yes,' she sobbed. 'Yes. He loves me very much. He wants to marry me. But I can't. He's not a Catholic and I have promised myself to Joaquim.'

Figueras pressed her to him and stroked the back of her head the way he'd done when she was little. 'There, there,' he said.

As her sobs subsided, Figueras walked back round the desk and sat opposite her. She could feel his tension, and she looked up quizzically, her eyes still wet with tears. She waited for him to speak.

He began hesitantly. 'I must tell you something . . .' He coughed and began again. 'When you were away, Madonna, Joaquim came here with Karel van Cuyler.'

Figueras had to be mistaken! Joaquim did not even know van Cuyler. Her mind was whirling, but Figueras was speaking once more.

'Van Cuyler was here on a peace mission, or so he said. He wanted to stop the English building their fort and offered us compensation and some cinnamon if we would cancel the agreement. I insisted he waited till you returned. Then Joaquim ordered me to cancel the English loan agreement. He –'

'*Ordered* you!' Ynessa could not believe her ears.

'Yes, Madonna. He threatened that unless I cancelled the agreement he would dismiss me as soon as he took charge of the House.'

'Joaquim said that? For van Cuyler?' Her blood was boiling. 'Why did you not tell me?'

'It was not my place to question my future master's actions; but after what you have told me –'

She picked up her doublet and slipped it on.

'Madonna, what are you doing? Where are you going?'

Ynessa was furious beyond measure. While she'd been going through hell so she could keep her promise to him, Joaquim had been ready to sell her to the man who'd murdered Rodrigo. She took the emerald engagement ring she'd left in her drawer before leaving for Celor. There was a stiletto beside the ring. She tucked it into her waistband and marched to the door.

Figueras was on his feet. 'I'll come with you.'

'No. I have to do this myself.' She flung open the door and ran down the stairs.

Ynessa ran all the way to the Gonzaga warehouse, clumping up the steps past startled beggars and lounging guards. At the end of the first-floor corridor was Joaquim's office. She flung open the door.

Joaquim was lolling behind his desk, feet up, chair tilted back. 'Ynessa!' He swung his legs off the desk and started to come upright.

Ynessa flung the ring into his face; startled, he raised a hand to it as if it were a wasp-sting. 'What –'

'You rotten, lily-livered, snivelling pimp!'

'Ynessa, what is –'

'Our engagement is over, understand? It's finished! I will not marry you! I never want to see you again!'

Joaquim came round the desk towards her, arms spread out, trying to force a smile. She whipped out the stiletto and held it out in front of her. 'One step closer and I'll slash you from cheek to cheek.'

Joaquim stopped and lowered his hands. 'What's wrong?' he asked, plaintively. 'What have I done?'

Her stomach heaved. Her fury was making her sick. 'What did you do with van Cuyler?' she shouted. 'Does the House of Gonzaga need money so badly that you need to deal with the man who killed my father?'

'Ynessa, listen, I didn't know –'

She slashed the stiletto at his hand and he jumped back. 'Liar!' she shouted.

'Please listen. The Dutch were threatening to attack San Thome and I had –'

Ynessa stepped forward and placed the tip of the stiletto on the bridge of his nose. 'Listen carefully, Gonzaga,' she said. 'I don't want to hear your excuses and I don't want to marry you. And if you come running after me I'll stick this down your throat or put a pistol ball through your head.' She turned and marched out through the door.

Chapter Twenty-One

Three days later Ynessa went alone to Madera. Her explanation for the broken engagement had not been accepted by Mama; her confession of love for Darnell had been greeted with horror. Bishop Ephraim had of course become involved: he had warned her of the penalties for loving a heretic, forbidden her the sacraments and threatened her with excommunication. She hoped Darnell would forgive her; now, he was all she had.

She crossed the Land Bridge and rode through the Black Town, now a noisy, spicy mix of houses, shops, warehouses, eating houses and bars. Towering above it was the sixty-foot *gopuram* of the temple, and the scaffold-shielded walls of the Chitty mansion.

Inside the fort the newly finished factory house gleamed, its wood-work fresh and shiny, a fine coating of builder's dust on its steps. Levelled roads ran from it to each of the gates, St George Street to the south, Choultry Street to the north, the Avenida Rodrigo da Soares to the west and the Sea Road to the east. A coolie squatting by the steps told Ynessa that Darnell was working on the docks warehouse by the sea wall. Leaving her escort at the factory house, she hurried there.

The east of the settlement was a mass of bamboo scaffolding, incomplete buildings, heaving bullocks, rutted tracks and ditches. Dust hung thick and heavy in the air. Labourers jogged with loads of bricks and building materials in panniers, whilst others, with sacks covering the backs of their heads and shoulders, clambered all over the scaffolding. On a platform by the beach, a large warehouse was being built.

Ynessa dismounted and walked to the warehouse. Looking up to the scaffolding above, she suddenly saw him, bare to the waist, clad only in grubby white pantaloons and boots, and felt her heart start to beat uncontrollably fast.

Darnell was shouting orders to a worker down below. For a moment she thought he hadn't seen her, but then he was scrambling down the scaffolding like a monkey, jumping off and landing before her in a puff of dust. His hair was tied behind him with a strand of ribbon, his bare torso covered with dust and sweat. She wanted to feel his sweaty arms around her, wanted him to hug her, to rest her cheek against that splendid breadth of chest and shoulder. Oh God, how she had missed him! How could she have ever thought to leave him? She looked into his face, darker now and wasted, the eyes sunk so deep they were like burning coals.

'Ynessa,' he said, thickly. He hesitated, eyes scanning her face anxiously. 'Why have you come?' he whispered finally.

She moved closer to him, took his hand. 'I came because I want to marry you,' she said, softly.

He pressed her hand to his lips, closed his eyes and breathed so deeply. Then slowly, gently, he kissed each of her knuckles.

She felt a soft stirring in her loins, a warm, gentle excitement. 'Is there somewhere quiet we can talk?' she asked.

He took her hand and led her on to the beach away from the building site. She told him what had happened; he walked beside her, turning from time to time to throw her a piercing glance. Was he accepting? she wondered. Or had she hurt him so much he would send her away? She said, 'And so I came to tell you I will marry you . . . if you still want –'

He swept her into his arms and kissed her, his mouth closing fiercely on hers, the sweat from his face wetting her cheeks, his embrace threatening to crush her ribs. She twisted her head away and framed his face in her hands, then kissed him slowly on his mouth and chin.

'Dar-nell! Dar-nell!'

Ghosh was galloping along the beach, his green and brown tunic fluttering behind him, showers of sand flying from the hooves of his speeding mount. He reined in fiercely and dismounted, his feet skipping on the sand as they touched the ground before the horse stopped. His cheeks and forehead were shiny with sweat, his dark eyes bright with excitement. He cried, 'Our spies have reported that Kokinada is going to attack Madera! The report is from one of our people in the nizam's palace. The nizam is sending an army of a thousand men which has already left his capital.'

Darnell was alarmed. With only twelve soldiers and no cannon yet, he couldn't defend the fort against a thousand men. 'How many men can Seringa spare?' he asked Ghosh.

Ghosh said, 'Seringa has ordered Bharatya here with one hundred men. They're good soldiers.'

Outnumbered ten to one, their quality as soldiers wasn't relevant. 'We need cannon,' Darnell said. 'We cannot save Madera without cannon.' He turned to Ynessa. 'Can the Portuguese lend us three heavy and two light cannon?'

Ynessa thought for a moment. Because of her investment, the council would regard the fort as Portuguese. In addition, some small Portuguese traders had already moved in; now that the fort was being built, the council was in favour of its completion. The loan of the cannon could easily be kept secret and not expose the Portuguese to reprisals. 'I think the council will agree,' she said. 'Let me get back to San Thome at once and call a meeting.'

*　　*　　*

The flare of the torches made the council chamber look even more like a church than ever. The shadowed ceiling seemed higher and, in the evening silence, their voices sounded more hollow. Ynessa felt as if she were speaking from somewhere deep in the earth. She forced herself to concentrate on a spot above de Almeida's head so she wouldn't be distracted.

'Madera is as much a Portuguese fort as an English one,' she said. 'It is financed with Portuguese money. Already Portuguese shopkeepers live in its Black Town and run two of its waterfront taverns. And there will be more Portuguese in Madera shortly. Senhor de Almeida is building a warehouse and Senhor Saldhana is renting offices. In a year, about a third of the merchants in San Thome will be doing business there. So we cannot let Madera be destroyed. Madera is the future of the Portuguese in Coromandel – just as it is the future of the English.'

She paused and looked round the room. Everyone had their eyes on her, Joaquim's narrow and angry, Bishop Ephraim's studied and watchful. Let them vote how they liked, she thought. If she could convince the captain-general there was no military risk, everyone else would vote to help the English.

'So I ask you, gentlemen, to approve the loan of five cannon and appropriate ammunition to the English on the terms I have already set out. The payment is fair. San Thome makes a good return. We risk nothing, and we save a magnificent Portuguese investment.' She bowed to the captain-general and sat.

'Won't providing the English with cannon affect our other factories in Kokinada?' de Almeida asked, his moustache crinkling over his upper lip, his face creased by a worried frown.

'That is unlikely, Senhor de Almeida.' Ynessa flashed him a smile. 'The nizam will assume that guns fired by Englishmen belong to them; this transaction will be kept secret. But if he does find out, we will claim the cannon were part of the original financing agreement and it was only coincidental they were delivered at the time of his attack.'

'I think it will work,' the captain-general agreed. 'As long as we don't have our soldiers fighting for the English.'

Ynessa felt her heart quicken as Bishop Ephraim got to his feet. For a moment he paused and looked round the room before beginning. 'We know that in the eyes of God, in providing guns for the English we are participating in war. The Church has very clear rules about what kind of wars we may fight. The only war we may participate in, my friends, is a just war. And this English war is not just. The fort at Madera is the work of the devil. It is God's wish that this fort be destroyed.' Bishop Ephraim stared hard at each of them. 'Do you think God will forgive those who thwart His will?' he boomed.

There was a hushed silence, and Ynessa looked round the room in alarm. Surely they wouldn't be influenced by Bishop Ephraim's outburst? Surely they would see that he was blustering, that he was frightening them with meaningless threats? Saldhana and de Almeida were looking down, the captain-general suddenly busy with the papers on his desk. Joaquim was staring at her, half smiling in triumph.

Saldhana got up and hurried from the room. 'Excellency,' he called from the door. 'I would prefer not to vote.' De Almeida followed him.

Ynessa watched dumbstruck as the other council members walked out. Only Joaquim, Bishop Ephraim and the captain-general were left. 'I'm sorry, Ynessa,' the captain-general said. 'The council cannot protect your investment.'

Ynessa swallowed. 'It is not just money. There are women and children in Madera. Surely you will not allow them to die?'

Bishop Ephraim spoke from across the chamber. 'They are heretics my child, and must pay the price for their heresy.'

'And the price of heresy is death?'

'It is worse than death, my child. It is eternal damnation. So pray that they will repent. And do not question God's will. Far better concern yourself with saving your own soul. Are you ready to reconcile yourself to God, my daughter? Are you ready to honour your solemn word?'

'With respect, Your Grace, the condition of my soul has nothing to do with the lives of the people in Madera.'

'On the contrary, my child, it has everything to do with it. How can I recommend that the council support an investment made by an apostate? An investment made by a person who breaks her solemn word and forsakes the sacraments? When you refused to honour your word, Ynessa, you left the family of God. If you want our help, you must join the family again and obey its strictures.'

Her lips were dry. She ran her tongue slowly over them. 'You mean, agree to marry Joaquim?'

Bishop Ephraim nodded. 'That would be a start.'

Ynessa clasped her hands together and bowed her head. Without the cannon, Darnell had no way of defending Madera and all within its walls would be slaughtered. But she mustn't give in to Bishop Ephraim's blackmail. She said, 'The House of da Soares will repay your assistance in protecting its investment by paying you a sum equal to that paid for the cannon.'

'My child, the Church cannot be bought. There is no sum of money in the world that can divert me from my duty to God.' In a softer tone Bishop Ephraim added, 'Repent, my child. Keep your oath. Be reconciled with God.' He walked across the chamber, arms outstretched.

She couldn't give up Darnell. But if she didn't he would die fighting. *She* would have killed him.

Bishop Ephraim was standing in front of her. 'Repent

and the cannon will be on its way to Madera tomorrow. Repent and Madera will be saved.' His hands were on her shoulders. 'Kneel, Ynessa. Confess now. And swear on the living God that you will marry Joaquim Gonzaga and no other. Swear that you will not expose yourself to any man other than your betrothed for the rest of your life. Come now, child. Kneel. Repent. Swear.'

A sob racked her body as she knelt. Tears trickled from behind her eyes. 'Bless me father, for I have sinned,' she sobbed.

Chapter Twenty-Two

As Bharatya felt uneasy working in an office, they met below the steps of the factory house, Ghosh and Bharatya squatting opposite Darnell and Ravi, the space between them covered with crude diagrams drawn with sticks in the earth.

Bharatya pointed his stick at one of the drawings. 'This is the Ellora plain,' he said. 'Right here where the plain runs into the foothills of Axoor is the hill stockade of Vellacottai. If we seize Vellacottai, we can ambush Kokinada's army as it passes.'

After long discussion they had decided to take the offensive against Kokinada's army. Without Company support, and with so few cannon and men, Madera was too vulnerable to attack or siege. They have to risk everything and try to seize Vellacottai.

'What if we can't take the stockade?' Darnell asked.

'We will!' Ghosh cried. 'There're never more than thirty soldiers in Vellacottai.'

Darnell said, 'It would be better if we set up ambush here.' He pointed to the forest beyond the foothills.

Bharatya and Ghosh both shook their heads. Bharatya said, 'They are a thousand and we're only a hundred. To survive with those odds we must fight from a distance. If we ambush them on level ground, even in a forest, their sheer numbers will overwhelm us.'

'But the cannon?'

'Will be useless if they've killed the men who fire it.'

Darnell scratched his stick in the earth and thought that, with their experience of guerrilla warfare, Bharatya and

Ghosh were probably right. But he still worried about the plan.

He worried too about Ynessa. Yesterday Figueras had ridden into Madera followed by three teams of bullocks drawing two massive 2,500lb myrmions and a 700lb fawcon. Ynessa hadn't been with him, though, and when Darnell had tried to find out why, Figueras had been evasive, saying she had plenty to do in San Thome.

Darnell had hidden his disappointment, asking Figueras to tell her that they were taking the attack to Kokinada.

'I'll tell her,' Figueras had said, his face as sad as ever. He'd touched the brim of his hat to Darnell and left.

They left in two groups, Bharatya taking the attack force of about seventy soldiers the direct, steeper way, while Ghosh, Darnell, Eckaerts and the rest of the troops followed with the fawcon hidden in a cart and a second cart containing their baggage and ammunition. They travelled along the flat valley that would bring them to the rear of Vellacottai in about five nights' time.

They travelled by dark, avoiding established trails and roads, moving across country like ghosts, guided by scouts who'd been sent out earlier. They laid up during the day in coconut groves, sugar-cane plantations or forests. They took no tents and little food. Each man slept in his baggage roll; they ate off the land and drank only water. Their eyes became raw from lack of sleep and the strain of peering through the dark. Their throats became parched from the limited amounts of water they drank; their stomachs shrivelled from the small amounts of food they ate. They were constantly watchful, knowing they were in hostile country and surrounded by the enemy.

On the fifth night they came to Vellacottai, the ugly black shadow of the hill looming ahead of them, blotting out the star-speckled sky. Darnell rode beside Ghosh at the head of the group, the hooves of their horses muffled.

From time to time Ghosh or one of his men gave a soft, ululating nightbird cry. Suddenly the cry was repeated, from their right, then from their left and in front of them.

Without warning three men appeared on the trail, *khatars* in their right hands, drawn swords in their left. There was a brief exchange of greetings before they were sent up to another checkpoint and eventually into the stockade.

It was a small place, a dozen or so wattle-and-daub huts perched on the hill and fenced in by head-high palings. Bharatya was waiting beyond the palings at the front of the village, surrounded by receptacles of all shapes and sizes containing water and coconut oil. Though the night was warm, a large fire burned, illuminating the shadow round Bharatya's cheeks and making his eyes dance. Bharatya's tunic and pantaloons were stained with mud and sweat; but he looked as sprightly as ever. He greeted them serenely. 'Taking Vellacottai was no problem,' he said. 'There were only three soldiers here.'

'Where are they? And the villagers?'

Bharatya waved a nonchalant arm. 'We disarmed them and sent them away.'

Darnell was furious. The soldiers and villagers would have run to Kokinada's army; all surprise would be lost. Before he could say anything, Bharatya pointed into the valley and said, 'There is our enemy. He is about to attack us.'

The valley below was covered with tiny lights. Over the crackle of the fire Darnell could hear the clank of metal and the crush of movement. Taking the stockade had given them distance, but now they were trapped. 'We'll set up the cannon here,' he said. 'Some shot is sure to frighten them.' He'd been right all along. They should have stayed in Madera, or ambushed Kokinada in the forest.

Bharatya pointed to his left. 'Over there will be better.

Have your men angle it so your shot will fall into the middle of the encampment.'

'But they're already advancing!' Darnell could make out clumps of men moving in the starlight. 'We should aim down the hill.'

Ghosh grabbed his sleeve. 'Do as Bharatya wants. Otherwise we'll all die.'

Darnell looked down the hill. They were in a trap, surrounded, and the only way out was to fight Kokinada's army. Even with a cannon that was going to be virtually impossible: they were hopelessly outnumbered, and the conflict Bharatya had so feared would come about as soon as Kokinada's troops climbed the hill.

Bharatya told Ghosh he wanted him to take his men to a defile down the hill. Seeing Darnell's expression, Ghosh turned away from Bharatya and took Darnell's arm. 'Darnell, please do as Bharatya wants. It may not look like it, but he knows what he's doing.'

'We're trapped,' Darnell protested. 'We must frighten them away with our cannon.'

'I've been with Bharatya in situations like this before, and we've always come out victorious. It'll happen again. You'll see.' Ghosh squeezed Darnell's arm and went back into the village.

Darnell saw Bharatya looking at him and turned away. The sounds of tramping feet and voices carried from the foot of the hill. The congealing mass of men were beginning their climb. A cannonball or two and they would flee. He decided to trust Ghosh's judgement and he turned to Bharatya. 'Where exactly would you like the cannon placed?' he asked.

Bharatya showed him, and Darnell had Eckaerts and the gunners unhitch the cart and face the cannon towards the enemy. Kokinada's men were about a third of the way up the hill, their passage clearly audible by the clink of metal and the clatter of dislodged rock. Bharatya's soldiers stoked the fire, bringing out more water and oil from the village. Darnell watched, hoping he'd been right, that whatever Bharatya was planning would work.

Kokinada's army was coming up the hill in a solid phalanx. Some of the men wore metal helmets, others carried circular shields of watered steel or hide. They carried battle-axes and *shamshirs*, *khanjars* and lances. They were a formidable force, well trained and well armed. Even if they were equal in numbers Darnell would have been concerned about the outcome. He looked sideways at Bharatya, who stood watching the approaching troops with dispassionate calmness.

Kokinada's troops were more than halfway up the hill, walking with a careless self-confidence and making little effort to keep silent or to hide their approach. Some of them smoked as they walked, and the sickly sweet smell of hashish drifted upwards, over the smell of burning wood.

An officer raised a lance aloft, screaming out the ancient battle-cry, '*Allah Akbar!*' The cry was taken up by others and seemed to reverberate around the valley. '*Allah Akbarrrrrrr!*' The men came pounding up. Bharatya stood stock-still.

For heaven's sake do something! Darnell thought. Then he realized that Bharatya's men had disappeared, that he and Bharatya were alone beside the fire. He looked to his left, sensing the unease of Eckaerts and his soldiers. Should he order them to fire? Slowly he raised his hand.

At that moment Bharatya moved. He pulled a flaming rush from the fire, waved it in a slow circle above his head, and hurled it down the hill. The brief light illuminated men moving behind Kokinada's army. Suddenly the grass behind the advancing troops erupted in flame. Darnell saw the white-clad figures bearing rushes dart into the fire and run along the line of flame, igniting more grass. At last Kokinada's men had realized what was happening and were rushing upward. Almost immediately a line of Bharatya's men grabbed flaming rushes and ran towards them. Darnell heard the hiss of arrows and saw men felled by lances. Then a ragged line of fire erupted before the oncoming army, and their shouts of anger turned to screams of pain and terror.

The flames leaped skyward as Bharatya's men, their heads and bodies swathed in cloths soaked in water, raced up the hill, fire sparking off their bodies. The men twisted and turned, darting away from the growing wall of flame, hurling themselves on to the ground and rolling over and over as soon as they reached the top.

More of Bharatya's men rushed out of the stockade and stood with containers of water to fight the fire if the flames should spread towards the village. In front of them the flames roared, flaring up to the sky, their sharp, rushing crackle mingling with terror-filled screams.

Darnell watched fascinated as one after another Kokinada's army turned into human torches. Men leapt up and down as the ground became a furnace. Some fell to the grass, choking on smoke. Others turned to run downhill, bumped into men trying to get away from the fire below and were locked in agonized, terrified immobility as the flames devoured them. Hundreds of men were choking and burning to death, and those who managed to escape the conflagration were being butchered by Bharatya's troops hidden at the foot of the hill.

Darnell saw a gap where the fire had not caught; survivors were filling the gap and massing to move upwards. He looked to his right. Bharatya and his men were gone, stoking the flames or putting them out. He saw the shadowy figures move up the hill.

'Cover me!' he yelled to Eckaerts, taking a torch from the cauldron, picking up a pot of oil and running, the oil spilling on to his boots. He ran downhill towards the flames, the smoke choking him. Trying not to breathe, he turned and ran along the hill, dripping oil behind him.

Kokinada's men saw what was happening. There were shouts and an arrow hissed in front of his face. A lance quivered into the ground in front of him. Tripping, he fell.

His torch hit the grass and the rest of the oil spilt. A wall of fire gushed upwards, its heat flaking his skin, blinding him. He couldn't breathe for smoke. He was coughing, his eyes watering. He saw his boot was burning and beat it on the ground as he stood up. He could barely see. He staggered forward but his mind shrieked a warning.

Uphill, not down. Uphill! He forced his body round. The flames singed his eyebrows. He couldn't see the hill, couldn't see the village, Eckaerts or the cannon. He had to move up and forward. Kokinada's men were behind him. His lungs seared. He closed his eyes against the flame and the heat. And lunged upwards.

The heat was overpowering. The flames roared. He choked and coughed and covered his face with his hands. His arms and hair were burning. He felt his clothes come alight and then he was through and something cold and wet hit him and he heard his body sizzle and he fell. Someone was dragging him uphill, someone else beating at his body, another bathing it with more water. Above the crackle of the flames he heard the fawcon roar.

When he could breathe, when he could move, Darnell realized he was lying behind the palings, that Bharatya and two of his men were standing over him, that someone had applied poultices of wet leaves to his face and hands.

'If not for you, we'd have lost the stockade,' Bharatya said.

Darnell tried to talk. But there was no air in his chest and he choked.

They helped him up and took him to the front of the stockade. In the soft, pre-dawn light he could see the battle was over. The hillside was a blackened mass of soil, ashes and horribly contorted bodies, charred beyond recognition, their limbs twisted into hideous, blackened rigidity. At the foot of the hill were more bodies, men slain as they retreated. And the camp itself was a mess of burnt-out tents, capsized carts and crumpled bodies.

Few of Kokinada's men had escaped the carnage. It was a total, overwhelming victory. Darnell breathed cool morning air that reeked of smoke and burnt flesh.

Chapter Twenty-Three

Darnell rode past the high walled warehouses on the Rua Magellan, his heart beating faster with excitement at each step. He was going to see Ynessa again. He stopped before the large, yellow hulk of the da Soares warehouse, threw the reins to an urchin and ran past the beggars on the steps into the warehouse. He was so excited he did not notice one of the beggars eye him carefully, then limp hurriedly down the steps to the centre of the town and the ponderous Cathedral of San Thome.

Figueras conducted Darnell to the committee room. In the dock below, a da Soares coaster was being unloaded, men scurrying over its decks and along its skeletal masts.

A door opened behind him and he whirled. Ynessa stood halfway between the small door at the back of the room and the long rosewood table. Darnell's heart leapt at the sight of her. Then, full of concern, he rushed forward, arms outstretched. 'Ynessa, darling, what's happened?

It was the moment she had dreaded and dreamt about. She'd sworn a solemn oath never to see Darnell alone again, yet the news of his arrival had made her shiver with excitement. She'd told herself she mustn't see him, but she knew that she had a duty to tell him that their relationship was over.

Darnell looked lean and strong and confident, and she nearly choked with the excitement of being so close to him. He was coming to her with his arms outstretched, and she longed to feel them round her, to rest her head against his chest. But she must not let him touch her! She moved away from him and walked to the head of the table and sat, her legs quivering.

Darnell let his arms drop. She was wasted. The gown she wore could not hide her thinness; her complexion was pasty, her eyes huge in her drawn face. 'Ynessa, what's wrong? Have you been ill?'

'I'm fine.' Oh God, she couldn't bear to be so close to him and not touch him. She looked past him out of the window and asked, 'What happened in Kokinada?'

'What's happened to you?' he asked again.

She couldn't tell him; it would only make things worse. 'Tell me first about Kokinada,' she said.

She heard little of it, sitting as if she were asleep, listening without hearing and staring out of the window with dead eyes. Darnell took her hand. 'What the devil's wrong, Ynessa? What's happened to you? Why won't you let me touch you?'

She stared out of the window, as if she hadn't heard him.

'There's something –'

The door behind her opened. Bishop Ephraim hurried in, his face flushed, his brown eyes scudding over her and Darnell. She snatched her hand away from Darnell as Bishop Ephraim moved briskly up to her with a rustle of silk robes. 'Ah, there you are, my dear,' he said. He touched her immobile shoulder and sat. 'You must be Senhor Darnell,' he said smoothly. 'I am very pleased to meet you.' His voice was warm and friendly. 'May I congratulate you on your victory?'

The bloody priest was behind it all, Darnell thought, with his threats of hell and damnation. That's why Ynessa looked so ill. That's why she'd been avoiding him. 'What the devil have you done to her?' he demanded. 'What damned Papist lies have you told her?'

'I speak for the Church,' Bishop Ephraim said, 'and I speak the truth. I have known Ynessa since she was a little girl. I am her confessor. Ynessa has told me about your relationship. I am sorry, Senhor Darnell, but for the sake of her immortal soul I have forbidden her to marry you.'

'Who gave you the right to forbid her anything?' Darnell was leaning towards the priest, his voice a low hiss.

'Ask her. It was her decision. Ynessa has sworn to do what God wants. As I am sure you know, senhor, it is the law of our Holy Mother the Church that a Catholic may not marry a non-Catholic.'

'I'll become a Catholic,' Darnell shouted. 'She *must* marry me.' He turned to Ynessa and grabbed her hands. 'Go on, Ynessa. Tell him you don't love Joaquim. Tell him you love me! Tell him we're going to be married!'

Ynessa looked into his eyes. *I love you more than life*, she thought, *but I promised*. She spoke in a voice that came from the grave. 'I can't marry you whatever you do,' she said. 'I am betrothed – to Joaquim.' She took her hands away. 'Now leave me. Please go.'

'Not until you tell me why you've changed.'

Ynessa reached out and rang the bell at the head of the table. There was the sound of hurrying footsteps. 'Go, Richard,' she said. 'Please go. And – and don't come back.' She got to her feet and stood away from him. 'Please go now . . . Believe me, it is for the best.'

Figueras was almost brushed aside at the door as she hurried from the room followed by Bishop Ephraim. Darnell stood staring blindly after her.

Figueras took his sleeve. 'Come, senhor,' he said softly, 'there is nothing you can do. She believes that by marrying Gonzaga she is saving her soul. There is nothing you can do, at present, to change that.'

'But damnit, I love her.'

'Be patient, senhor. As the date of the wedding draws nearer she will realize the folly of what she is doing.'

'When is the wedding?' Darnell asked, his heart sinking with despair.

'The date has not been set. Please return to Madera, senhor. You can't do anything here and I will bring you news of her when I deliver the weekly loan instalments.'

Darnell stared at Figueras. 'I cannot lose her,' he said hoarsely.

Figueras took Darnell's shoulder. 'Be patient,' he whispered. 'Be patient. Something good will happen.'

Van Cuyler rode with de Groot along the rugged plain west of Pulicat. It was the last day of the week de Groot had granted him to write his defence of the charge that he and Ali Baig had murdered Don Rodrigo da Soares. De Groot had received a report from the captain-general in San Thome, no doubt prompted by Darnell and that meddling woman. Van Cuyler knew what had to be done, and that there could be no half-measures. He had invited de Groot to ride outside the fort with him and watch the sun rise from the steps of an ancient temple to Shiva.

The countryside through which they rode was rocky and gently undulating, covered with thick dust that muffled the hooves of their horses. Scrawny scrub clung fiercely through the dust to land as hard as iron, and this part of the plain was criss-crossed by *nullahs*, scoured deep by the rain of many monsoons, filled with stones and boulders and barely visible in the shadowless early-morning light.

Van Cuyler stopped and stretched in the saddle; out of the corner of his eye he watched de Groot do likewise. As they moved forward together, van Cuyler wondered if Ali Baig had done what he should.

'I will not move against a Dutch governor,' Ali Baig had said, huddled in the room at the side of his house, drinking geneva and smoking hashish.

'It is the only way to stop him finding out,' van Cuyler had urged. 'If I become governor, any investigation instigated by the nizam will have to stop.'

'Of you, maybe, but not me. So you do it.'

'I can't,' van Cuyler had said. 'You're the one with the contacts.' He'd paused and added, 'I can always escape to Batavia. But where can you run?'

And Ali Baig had glowered at him and drunk more geneva and had come to Pulicat the next day. But had he done it, van Cuyler wondered?

De Groot's cheeks were red from the exercise and the briskness of the morning air. His blue eyes glinted sharply. It had to take place before they reached the defile. Van Cuyler said, 'We should bring weavers from Vaidya to Pulicat. That will help reduce the English advantage with Madera.'

'Excellent idea. Excellent idea.' De Groot peered ahead. 'I wish the sun would come up. It's so difficult to see these damned *nullahs*.'

'It'll be worth it when we get to the temple,' van Cuyler said. Then to divert de Groot's attention, 'We can send *gomastahs* to the border villages with offers of high pay and permanent service.'

'Muslim *gomastahs* canvassing in Hindu territory?'

He'd succeeded in diverting de Groot. 'Perhaps not. Perhaps we'll go ourselves.' And he thought, if they rode back slowly, de Groot would be safe. But then he thought, if he didn't stop de Groot, he would be finished, together with Holland and the Empire. 'Muck sticks,' he said. 'Perhaps it would be best if you and I were to deal with the Portuguese allegations over the pearls.'

De Groot flashed him a sideways glance. 'No,' he said. 'That must be dealt with by Batavia. And please don't try to change my mind. It is quite made up.'

There was no alternative. The governor of Batavia was no friend of the Coordinator's Office and would not hesitate to summon him back for trial. He *had* to do it, for Holland and the Empire. Van Cuyler pulled his horse to a stop as a flock of teal, disturbed by their approach, took wing from the grass beneath the rocky outcrop. He pointed. 'See that!'

De Groot stopped beside him. 'Marvellous!'

Van Cuyler stretched himself and yawned, then quickly drew his pistol and fired before de Groot realized what was happening, the shot echoing and re-echoing against the rock. He held tightly to the reins as his mount reared; de Groot's horse streaked forward, totally out of control and completely terrified. De Groot hung on for his life, cheek pressed to the horse's mane, too frightened to jump.

Then de Groot's saddle slipped to the right. The panicking horse bounded forward again. De Groot should have been thrown, but instead he freed his right foot and stood in the left stirrup, then jumped forward and clung to the horse's neck. The horse careered forward again as the saddle slid out from underneath de Groot and crashed to the ground. De Groot screamed once as the horse swooped blindly over the edge of a steep-sided *nullah* and crashed helplessly to the bottom.

Van Cuyler dismounted by the abandoned saddle and took out the hard thorn embedded in the padding. He looked carefully at the girth. Ali Baig's man had cut it so carefully, no one could ever know it had been deliberate. He threw down the saddle and walked to the edge of the *nullah*.

De Groot lay beneath the horse. Even from thirty feet above, van Cuyler could see that his body was badly crushed and his skull smashed. The horse thrashed feebly, then its head drooped. Van Cuyler turned and walked back. Now he had nothing to fear from the nizam. Now he could do what needed to be done finally to destroy Darnell and the English fort in Madera.

Chapter Twenty-Four

Three days after he'd returned from San Thome, Darnell sat with Ravi in his office at Madera. Ravi had never seen him so despairing or helpless. 'I just can't understand it,' Darnell repeated for the hundredth time. 'She came here before we went to Vellacottai, wanting to get married, wanting to move here.'

'If them priests have convinced 'er not to marry you, there's little you can do about it,' Ravi said. The room was hot and he narrowed his eyes at the early evening sun angling through the open window. Street noises filtered through the dusty air. 'She's got to fight those priests herself and come to you.'

'Maybe she needs help.'

'Then Figueras'll tell you.'

'A ship! A ship!' The cry was taken up, there was a rush of feet beneath the window, and Darnell and Ravi rushed downstairs to join the throngs hurrying to the Sea Gate.

'It's a Company coaster,' Ravi cried as they neared the boat. 'The *Unity* – that's Cogan in the longboat!'

Darnell could see dozens of people crowding the deck of the *Unity*. Had there been some disaster at Pettahpoli? Were Caddy and Crispin all right? Pacing impatiently, he waited for the longboat to draw into the shallows.

'You've made a right mess!' Cogan shouted without preamble as he stomped on to the beach, water draining from his boots. 'You've bloody ruined us!'

'What's happened?' Darnell asked, his whole body tight with tension.

'Because of your private war with Kokinada, we've been forced out of Pettahpoli.'

'Where's Caddy, Davey and the children?'

'They're on board. There was no fighting. We simply had an ultimatum from the nizam. Leave Pettahpoli or fight.'

And sensibly Cogan had chosen not to fight. 'What about the other factories in Kokinada?'

'They're all right as far as I know. But you'll pay for this, Richard. You'll pay for all the trade we've lost. You'll pay for Pettahpoli.'

'Why did you come here?' Darnell asked.

'We were forbidden to stay in Kokinada.'

The arrival of the English was a disguised blessing, Darnell thought. With all the trading capital from Pettahpoli now being spent in Madera, business would be five or ten times greater than it would otherwise have been.

'You had no right to build this place, no right to make war on Kokinada,' Cogan grumbled.

'We can argue that later. For now we'd better concentrate on finding food and accommodation for you lot.' Darnell thought rapidly. There would be about a hundred and fifty men, women and children on board the *Unity*, and it would be impossible to find accommodation for all of them ashore. He said, 'For tonight, everyone except you and Caddy's family will stay on board. First thing tomorrow we'll appoint a council and see what needs to be done to get everyone ashore as fast as possible.'

Darnell turned to Cogan. 'Now send the longboat back. I want Caddy and her family ashore.'

The evening with Crispin and Caddy and her family lifted Darnell's spirits hugely. Early the next morning he met with Ravi and Cogan in the factory house.

'With all due respect for what you've done here, Richard,' Cogan began, 'I must now be agent at Madera.

I am principal agent of Coromandel, after all . . .' He paused and smiled at everyone. 'You must admit it's logical. You will be my second.'

Clever move, Darnell thought. With the construction nearly complete, founding Madera was hardly a risk any more. The Company would adopt Madera, and whoever was agent at the time would be confirmed in the post with all the power, prestige and opportunities for wealth that went with it. But a head-to-head confrontation with Cogan at this stage would only result in a division: he had to sidestep Cogan's challenge and make him voluntarily withdraw it. He said, 'Madera is not yet Company property, Andrew.'

'I know that. But what difference does it make? We're all Company people here.'

'Quite right. But if you're going to be agent, you'll take personal responsibility for everything that's happened at Madera, and assume personal responsibility for over a thousand pounds' worth of loans.'

'Personal! What the devil d'you mean?'

'The Company's not adopted the fort, so the agent's got to be responsible. That's how it is, Andrew. No power without responsibility.'

Cogan turned a deep red. Becoming personally liable for a thousand pounds was crazy! If the Company didn't approve the fort, he'd be broken. He looked round the room.

Darnell saw Cogan wanted a way out and said, 'You will also have to be accepted by the House of da Soares and Prince Seringa. I'm not sure we have the time for that.'

Cogan nodded gratefully. 'You're right. That could take months. You must be agent,' he said to Darnell. 'I'll be your second. And carry on as principal agent from here.'

They appointed a council which decreed that all building

supplies and labour be immediately diverted to construction of accommodation for the evacuees, and until that
was complete, no other work would be done.

Darnell threw himself into the construction, the difficulties
of organization and constant physical activity – together
with the presence of Crispin and Caddy – anaesthetizing
his pain over Ynessa. He allocated one of the first houses
to Davey and Caddy and moved in with them, giving his
apartment in the factory house to Rawlins and three other
writers who had come from Pettahpoli.

The monsoon burst. Every day it rained: thick, hard,
driving showers that drenched everything. Ditches flooded.
Roofs collapsed. Outside the factory there were mudslides.
Between showers the roadways steamed and the air grew
fetid and still. Movement became difficult and a sickly,
sticky languor descended.

Being with his family made the wait for Ynessa to come
to her senses tolerable. After a period of initial shyness
Crispin allowed himself to get friendly with Darnell.

Figueras came regularly with money and news. Ynessa
hadn't got any thinner, but she was still unhappy. And still
determined to marry Joaquim Gonzaga. She was working
maniacally, and, no, the time was not right for Darnell to
see her.

Portuguese began to move from San Thome. With the
fort already crowded, many of them settled north of the
Black Town. They brought their own craftsmen, carpenters
and building materials, and built houses of brick plastered
with *chunam*. Because of its eye-aching brightness, and
because it was settled mainly by Europeans, the area
became known as the White Town.

Six weeks passed. The accommodation was completed
and all the evacuees from Pettahpoli moved into houses.
Saldhana transferred his offices to Madera. The rains eased.
The days remained still and very hot. There was news from

Seringa that Kokinada had refused to join the Mughal and that the Mughal forces had not left their forts in the Deccan.

Darnell loaned the fishing village money to build *masoola* boats for the transfer of freight and passengers between ships and shore. With five boats the village would have a regular income and be less dependent on the vagaries of fishing.

Country ships plying the coastal trade started to call. Merchants began to buy and sell cloth and other local goods. The temple, the eastern warehouse and the Chitty mansion were finished. The fort's bastions were finished and its walls made twelve feet wide. South of the factory house, the Portuguese and English built churches opposite each other. Twelve weeks after they had moved from Armagon, the fort at Madera was complete.

Darnell decided to mark the occasion with a party. The captain-general and the merchants from San Thome were invited together with all the leading Indian merchants and their families: Meru, the architect, and his builders; and, of course, all the English who'd come from Armagon and Pettahpoli. The main floor of the north-east bastion was hung with torches and strung with lanterns. A rectangular wooden bar was erected against the west wall and the large area directly in front of it covered with benches, trestles and forms. In the space beyond, a circular dance-floor and a bandstand were built, and massive open spits were erected along the wall furthest from the entrance.

Ten pipes of madeira were laid in, together with four hogsheads of claret, six of rhenish and ten barrels of beer. There were also thirty tureens of arrack punch and three barrels each of port and sherry. There would be dancing all night to two bands, and a dinner of suckling pig and beef. There would be fresh salads, pilau, fish kebabs and dumpoked fowl, mango *achar* and sony sauce. Dessert would be a lavish confection of pastries and sweetmeats, and the meal would be followed by an extravagant display of fireworks from the deck of the *Unity*.

Darnell stood with Caddy by the narrow doorway at the head of the stairs greeting the guests. Torches, set in sconces high against the walls, gave off a warm yellow-orange glow. A refreshing breeze blew in from the balustrade outside, where from time to time the regularly striding legs of a Company soldier could be seen.

Everyone was there: all the English and all the important Portuguese, some Indians and a party of Danes who'd arrived that afternoon from Tranquebar, looking to buy sugar and cloth. Darnell signalled to the soldier standing by the doorway leading to the battlements, who in turn made a signal to someone in the landing outside. Moments later, the cannon of Madera – one rescued from Armagon, three loaned from the Portuguese, four brought from Pettahpoli, and some commandeered from visiting ships – boomed.

The sound was deafening. The whole bastion shook. A shower of plaster loosened and floated on to the dance-floor. Ladies shrieked and stuffed fingers into their ears. As everyone applauded, Darnell fired a pistol into the air. 'I name this fort, Fort St George!' he cried.

In San Thome, the cannon of Madera were a dull distant boom and a flash in the sky like a receding thunderstorm. Ynessa sat in the parlour, trying to read, trying not to think who Darnell was with on this, the biggest night of his life.

She wanted to be there with him. The fort was as much hers as his. It should have been her night of triumph as well. But of course she couldn't go to Madera. Figueras, who had gone, would tell her about the celebrations tomorrow. That, she thought, would be like vinegar on an open wound.

The book slipped from her hands as she nodded sharply. She was exhausted. She hadn't let up on her twelve-hours-a-day schedule, not only because the work made her forget the pain of losing Darnell. With Figueras's help she was busy siphoning cash and assets out of da Soares which Figueras would administer in trust for Mama and the children. It was the only thing she could do to save them from Joaquim's depredations. More than once Figueras had asked her why she didn't save herself. She had sighed and said that it was God's will.

She started as she heard voices outside the room. With a gentle knock on the door, Mama came in. 'Ynessa,' she said, 'Bishop Ephraim is here. He would like to see you.'

What did the priest want at this time?

'I'll see him on the veranda,' she said reluctantly.

She waited ten minutes before going on to the veranda. Bishop Ephraim and Mama sat facing the street, sipping sherbet. The night was warm and Bishop Ephraim had undone the top two buttons of his cassock. Fireflies flickered in the garden below and along the slope of the front steps. The street beyond the boundary wall was empty, its potholes dimly illumined by the lanterns at the gate.

Mama cried, 'Look. The English fort!'

The sky to their left blazed a fiery orange yellow. Then a scarlet flame shot across the night sky and died. A shower of golden sparks arched up, followed by a darting, diving, dipping wheel.

Ynessa felt a great emptiness. She imagined what it would be like standing on the battlements of Madera with Darnell. She could feel his hands in hers, feel the hard ridge of calluses across the base of his fingers, and the rough flesh on the inside of his right thumb. Oh Darnell, Darnell! Her whole being ached for him.

Bishop Ephraim was saying, 'Ynessa, you promised to give me a date for the wedding as soon as the English fort was finished.'

That was true. That had been her last gift to Darnell,

delaying the wedding until the fort was completed so that Joaquim couldn't stop it. Now it was all over.

'Ynessa, Bishop Ephraim's waiting.'

Yes, of course. She had to marry Joaquim. That was what she had sworn to do before God. And there was no reason for delay. Madera was built. She'd siphoned off as much money as she reasonably could. Delay was only postponing the inevitable. Ynessa squared her shoulders and asked, 'Will next week do?' She heard Bishop Ephraim stir with surprise.

'Next Wednesday?'

Eight days from now. Days, hours, what difference did it make? 'Yes,' she said and walked away before Mama could kiss her.

Chapter Twenty-Five

Darnell looked up in surprise as Rawlins showed Figueras into his office. Two nights ago at the party the Portuguese had said that, with the last loan instalment paid and the first payment of interest not due for three months, he would keep in touch by peon. Now he stood there, eyes red-rimmed and brooding, his pepper-and-salt beard flecked with dust, his shoulders heavy with disappointment.

'What's happened?' Darnell cried, getting to his feet and waving Rawlins away. He took Figueras's hat and hung it on a peg behind the door.

'The wedding's next Wednesday,' Figueras said, sitting on the hard, upright visitor's chair beside Darnell's desk.

Darnell stared at Figueras. Even though he'd been expecting it, the announcement chilled him. Marriage meant everything was over. He strode round his desk and flung himself into his chair. 'Goddamnit, I knew we should have done something. We shouldn't have just sat here and –'

'What could you have done, senhor?' Figueras asked. 'I talked to her till I was hoarse but it didn't do any good.'

Figueras took out a sheaf of paper from the satchel he'd brought with him and pushed it across the desk.

Darnell read. It was an assignment of his loan to the House of Gonzaga. He read it again. 'What's the point of this? Doesn't Gonzaga get control of all da Soares owns simply by marrying Ynessa?'

'More or less.' Figueras shrugged. 'But Joaquim needs

to discount your loan as soon as possible, and to do that quickly he needs the loan assigned to the House of Gonzaga.' Figueras paused for a moment and added, 'Joaquim is in serious financial trouble. Since the wedding date was settled, Joaquim is having all the da Soares debtors assigned to Gonzaga.'

Darnell leaned back in his chair and rubbed his fingers together. There was something he could use here to get at Gonzaga and stop the marriage. He looked intently at Figueras, waiting for him to reveal why Joaquim was assigning all the da Soares debts.

'A few months ago, Joaquim gambled all the assets of the House of Gonzaga and everything he could borrow on cornering the market in indigo.' Figueras smiled ruefully. 'He cornered the market, all right. But as Ynessa had warned him, there was an over-supply of indigo and the price went right down. Now, unless Joaquim marries Ynessa, the House of Gonzaga is bankrupt.' Figueras looked up at Darnell and added, 'Gonzaga has promised to pay off his creditors a week after the marriage. Which is why he wants all the da Soares loans transferred to the House of Gonzaga now.'

Darnell felt a gush of light-heartedness bubble through him. 'Manuel, this is wonderful news,' he laughed. 'First of all I won't assign my loan to Gonzaga. Then we tell Ynessa what is happening.'

Figueras looked down, gloomily. 'I've already told Ynessa, senhor. She simply repeats that it is the will of God, that she is bound by the oath she swore before Bishop Ephraim, her family and the Gonzagas.'

'But she'll be ruined, goddamnit! And the House of da Soares! And her family!'

'She has taken certain steps to protect the family. But she is determined to fulfil her promises.' Figueras swallowed. 'I'm sorry, senhor. I don't think there is anything we can do to save her.'

There had to be, Darnell thought. He pulled the loan agreement and read it again. 'I'm not going to assign this loan,' he said.

'But senhor, you have a notarized instruction from Ynessa demanding that you do that.'

'That isn't something Ynessa can demand.' Darnell explained that the loan agreement was secured on his share of the pearls and contained certain mutual obligations that were personal. 'Where personal obligations are concerned,' he told Figueras, 'the parties can only be released by expiry of the agreement or mutual consent. I do not want Gonzaga replacing Ynessa on this contract. So I will not agree to the assignment and there is nothing anyone can do about it.'

'With respect, senhor, that will not stop the marriage. It will only delay –'

'Manuel, go back to San Thome and arrange for me to meet with Ynessa tomorrow. Unless she meets with me, that agreement will not be assigned. More importantly, I want you to find out how much Gonzaga owes, whom he owes it to and when the monies are due. Then I want you to buy two or three of the overdue loans for me.' He stretched out in his chair and smiled. 'When I see Ynessa I will tell her that, unless she gives up Gonzaga, I will call in my debts. Which means that on his wedding day, Joaquim will be in jail.'

Darnell presented himself at the da Soares warehouse punctually at eleven the next morning. Once again he was formally dressed, wearing knee-breeches, a high-collared tunic, and a close-fitting doublet.

Figueras met him inside the warehouse and pressed a sheet of paper into his hand. 'The list you wanted,' he said softly, and preceded Darnell up the stairs.

Darnell looked at the list quickly. Gonzaga owed around forty thousand *escudos*, nearly eight thousand pounds.

'On top of that there's the cash he's invested and the assets he sold,' Figueras murmured.

Darnell exhaled with relief. Gonzaga was in very deep and could easily be buried. 'What debts have you bought?' he asked.

'Alas, senhor, none.'

'None! What the devil –'

'Not so loud!' Lowering his voice, Figueras told Darnell that Gonzaga had promised his creditors they'd be paid immediately after the wedding. To prevent any one of them putting premature pressure on Gonzaga, the creditors had agreed among themselves not to seek preferential payment. Anyone buying the debts had to comply with that agreement and wait till after Gonzaga's marriage.

God's blood! He couldn't use the debts to threaten Joaquim after all! Darnell felt the colour drain from his face.

'I'm sorry, senhor.'

Darnell put his hand on Figueras's shoulder. He had to think of something else quickly.

Figueras threw open the door of the committee room and waved Darnell in. Ynessa sat at the head of the table and, beside her, looking for all the world like a purple toad, was Bishop Ephraim.

Darnell heard the door close behind him as he walked towards them, his boots setting off a hollow drumbeat on the boarded floor. A death march, Darnell thought, the roll of drums that preceded a hanging.

Ynessa was staring at him as if he were a stranger, her eyes vague and distant. Bishop Ephraim looked more wary. He licked his lips at Darnell's approach, reminding Darnell of a bloodsucker waiting to strike.

'What's he doing here?' Darnell demanded as he walked to the far end of the table and sat. 'I came here to talk business, not religion.'

It was the priest who answered. 'It is essential that no

temptation be allowed to come between Ynessa and her God-given resolve. That is why I am here. To protect her soul.'

'You wish to discuss the assignment of your loan?' Ynessa's voice was toneless, without inflection, the voice of a dead woman.

'That's right. I do not wish to deal with Joaquim Gonzaga.'

'Senhor Darnell, with the greatest of respect, you are being foolish.' Bishop Ephraim had folded his hands on the table and was leaning forward on them. 'Compelling Ynessa to comply with her obligations under this agreement will not enable you to continue your association with her. Assign the loan and return to your work in Madera.'

Darnell got to his feet and walked to the window. There was a ship in the docks preparing to sail, its hatches closed and its decks covered with scurrying sailors. He turned to face Ynessa and Bishop Ephraim. 'My objection to dealing with Joaquim Gonzaga has nothing to do with my past association with Ynessa. I refuse to deal with Joaquim Gonzaga because he is a rotten businessman and will soon be bankrupt.'

'Senhor, that is a most scandalous thing to say! The House of Gonzaga is the most prestigious merchant house in San Thome after –'

'The House of Gonzaga currently has debts of forty thousand *escudos* which it cannot meet without Joaquim Gonzaga marrying Ynessa and taking control of the House of da Soares.' Darnell eased away from the wall and walked to the table. 'Isn't that the truth, priest? Isn't that why Gonzaga needs this assignment? Isn't that why Gonzaga is marrying Ynessa?'

The blood flowed from Bishop Ephraim's face, then flooded back. 'You are wrong, senhor. You do not understand business. The Hou –'

'Enough lies, priest! Hold your tongue!' He went and

stood right in front of Ynessa. 'Ynessa, look at me.'

Slowly she raised her head, her expression still blank.

'What I tell you is true. Joaquim is heavily in debt. The House of Gonzaga is ruined. Joaquim is marrying you to take control of the House of da Soares and save himself and the House of Gonzaga.'

Ynessa looked down at the table. The grains on the wood were like the veins on the back of Darnell's hand. She couldn't bear to look up at him. 'I thank you for your concern, Senhor Darnell,' she said, softly.

Darnell strained to hear her words.

'But my decision to marry Joaquim Gonzaga is final. You must do what you must with the assignment. Please convey your decision to Senhor Figueras.' She bowed her head. 'Now, please leave us.'

'Ynessa! You can't mean that! You can't ruin yourself and ruin the House of da Soares because of this priest!'

'I do it for God and my immortal soul,' Ynessa said softly. Then cried out, 'Now for God's sake go!'

Darnell backed away from the table, stung by her words. He saw Bishop Ephraim looking at him with an expression of gloating triumph. The priest! he thought. He had an overpowering sensation of having missed something very important.

Darnell paced along the Rua Magellan. It was lunchtime and coolies and carters squatted by the roadside or huddled in the shade of carts, eating. The taverns were full. He shouldered his way into a punch house, ate rice and vegetables baked in a banana leaf and drank a salted *lassi*.

What had been so significant about the priest? The thought had come and gone as quickly as a lightning flash on a sunny day. What?

He thought back to his last moments with Ynessa. She'd been leaning forward, her eyes cast down on the table. '*I do it for God and my immortal soul. Now for God's sake go!'*

The priest had turned and looked over his shoulder. Darnell had seen the lips pull back from large, yellow teeth, the expression of gloating triumph wash down over the face from eyes like dissolving mud. But just before that – something else. He went over the scene again. Bishop Ephraim was gloating. Triumphant. Then Darnell saw it.

The bishop was relieved!

Why? Because Ynessa had chosen his way instead of Darnell's? Because he was seeing the last of Darnell?

Darnell had an idea. He finished his lunch and walked across the street to the Saldhana warehouse. It was an old, dark, tall building, rich in odours. In the afternoons, clerks on the east side of the building had to work with lamps. Unlike that of da Soares, the storage area was separate from the offices. Darnell was led up six flights of narrow, wooden stairs to the topmost floor. There Saldhana sat in a room hardly bigger than a garret. It was crowded with ledgers and piles of paper that spilled out of bookshelves on to a faded Turkish carpet. Saldhana himself, dark and serious-eyed, wandered round the room dressed in a long brown merchant's robe and a flat, four-cornered cap. Lifting some ledgers off a chair, Saldhana placed them beneath a dusty globe. He wiped the seat of the chair with his sleeve and asked Darnell to sit.

'Well, what can I do for you?' Saldhana's tone was neutral, his eyes suspicious and watchful.

'I come in confidence,' Darnell said carefully.

Saldhana's expression did not change. 'Yes.'

'We have been asked by the House of da Soares to assign our loan to the House of Gonzaga.' He paused and frowned. 'We are concerned about the financial stability of Gonzaga. We've heard rumours . . .'

Saldhana blinked quickly. 'There are always rumours. The financial stability of Gonzaga need not concern you, surely. You've received the full amount of your loan, have you not?'

Darnell nodded.

'So what is your problem?'

'We are concerned about dealing with Joaquim Gonzaga. We have observed that his spiritual adviser exerts a great deal of influence over him. We are concerned that this influence may lead to difficulties over the number of Portuguese churches and schools in Madera, which in turn will lead to problems with Prince Seringa.'

'I doubt Bishop Ephraim will do anything to endanger the da Soares investment in Madera.'

'Why do you say that, senhor? At the council meeting Bishop Ephraim impressed me as a man who would do whatever he thought God wanted him to – regardless of consequences.'

Saldhana swayed back and forth slowly in his chair. 'That council meeting was many months ago. The situation is different now. There is now a substantial Portuguese investment in Madera, quite apart from that of da Soares. Bishop Ephraim will not endanger that.'

Darnell steepled his hands in front of him and studied them. 'I wish I could be convinced, senhor. I still feel Bishop Ephraim is a driven man, unfamiliar with the needs of business.'

'That is not true. Bishop Ephraim is an administrator of the Church and the treasurer of his order.'

Darnell could feel his heart quickening. 'Are you telling me that Bishop Ephraim invests? That the Church trades?'

'Oh yes!' Saldhana said. 'What do you think the Church does with its money? The Church is the biggest single investor in San Thome. We merchants frequently borrow from the Church to tide us over difficult periods.'

'And Bishop Ephraim invests money on behalf of his order?'

'Yes, senhor.'

'And personally?'

'That too,' Saldhana said. 'After all, senhor, why else do people come to India except to make money?' He walked Darnell to the door. 'When you have been in Coromandel longer, you will find that everyone trades, even priests.'

And invests in indigo? Darnell wondered.

Darnell hurried down the street to the de Almeida warehouse. Half an hour later de Almeida saw him in a bright office overlooking the docks.

'I apologize for keeping you waiting, Senhor Darnell. There was something I had to finish –'

'It's my fault entirely,' Darnell said. 'I should have let you know I was coming.' De Almeida was impeccably groomed and richly dressed. He smelt agreeably of orange-flower water. Over *cha* served in delicate china cups, Darnell told him of his reservations about Bishop Ephraim.

'You have nothing to worry about,' de Almeida assured him, his eyes sparkling as brightly as his rings. 'Underneath those purple robes, Bishop Ephraim is a businessman like any of us.'

Darnell frowned. 'But what kind of a man is he? That is what worries me. Who is Bishop Ephraim?'

'A man like you and me,' de Almeida repeated, smiling. 'There are two stories concerning the bishop's origins. He is either the oldest son of an apothecary in Lisbon, or a Church foundling. We do know that, as a young priest, he came to Goa, and was then sent here to expand the work of his order. He came to the attention of Donna Gonzaga, who made him her confessor and chaplain to her family. He was treated as a member of the family, and his association with the Gonzagas undoubtedly helped him in his rise through the Church hierarchy. He is now head of his order and still chaplain to the Gonzagas.'

Darnell asked, 'As chaplain to the Gonzagas would

Bishop Ephraim have participated in important financial decisions?'

'Knowing Don Luigi Gonzaga, I wouldn't have thought that likely. Luigi Gonzaga kept everything to himself. If he wanted to share financial secrets, it wouldn't have been with a priest.'

'But the bishop has a strong influence over Joaquim?'

'Yes. He practically brought the boy up.'

'Did Bishop Ephraim invest his own or the Church funds in Joaquim's speculation on indigo?'

De Almeida shook his head. 'I don't know.'

'Would you know if the Bishop has invested on margin, or borrowed money for investment?'

'If he has, it is not from this house, senhor.' He leaned forward. 'What is the point of these questions? I had assumed you were interested in Joaquim Gonzaga, not the bishop.'

'That is correct. My interest in the bishop is limited to the influence he has over Joaquim.' Darnell stood up. 'I have burdened you too much, senhor. Thank you for your time. I look forward to seeing you in Madera soon.'

'That you will. That you will.' De Almeida clapped him on the shoulder and walked him to the door.

Walking in the street outside, Darnell was thinking hard. He had discovered Bishop Ephraim invested personally and on behalf of his order, but he needed to know whether he'd invested in Joaquim's indigo scheme. Had he borrowed money? Was he too under pressure from creditors?

Two hours later, having visited several of the merchants who had financed da Soares, Darnell was beginning to think Bishop Ephraim was clean. The bishop was simply a businessman and a man of God. No one knew anything about his investments. And no one admitted to lending the Bishop a *fanam*.

Darnell paced the streets. The sun was setting. The warehouses and offices were closing. Maybe this was all nonsense. Perhaps he should talk it over with Figueras and go home.

He stopped, his attention caught by a crucifix over the door of a dingy shop. With a shock he realized he'd walked inland to St Paul's bastion and was outside a shop where he'd tried to sell the pearls first before taking them to Gonsalez.

He pushed open the door and went in. The shop was dark, its jumble of furniture and dusty show-cases deep in shadow. Paiva, the owner, moved from the rear, a ghostly figure in long gaberdine robe and skullcap. He peered forward, thrusting out his head. 'Senhor Darnell, isn't it?' he asked hesitantly.

'Yes.'

Paiva lit a lamp and placed it on the counter between them. 'How can I help you today, senhor?'

'Do you lend money?' Darnell asked.

Paiva's eyes flickered. 'Yes, senhor. We are permitted to lend money. How much would you like to borrow and for what purpose?'

'Have you ever lent money to Bishop Ephraim?' It might have been the flickering of the lamp, but Darnell saw Paiva's expression change. 'I – I don't believe that is any of your business, senhor,' he said warily.

So he *had* lent Bishop Ephraim money. 'How much?' Darnell demanded. 'Has it been repaid?'

'Senhor, that is none of your business,' Paiva repeated, more firmly this time.

Grabbing him by the front of his robe, Darnell dragged him across the counter. He whipped out his knife and pressed it to the merchant's throat. 'Tell me, goddamnit! Have you lent money to Bishop Ephraim?'

Paiva choked. He looked into Darnell's face, his eyes full of fear and something else. 'Leave me alone,' he pleaded. 'I can tell you nothing.'

Darnell pressed the knife against the tautened skin of Paiva's throat. A pimple of blood appeared below the knife. 'I have to know. Tell me.'

'I can't.' Paiva did not move in his grip. For fear of being cut, Darnell thought, then saw the resentment and the hatred in the Jewish merchant's eyes. Paiva was a Jew, used to abuse and threats; he only had his own integrity to hold on to and would not give that up easily.

Shamed, Darnell released Paiva and put away the knife. 'I'm sorry,' he said. 'Bishop Ephraim is trying to destroy me and I have to stop him, but this is not the way.'

Paiva brushed his throat and looked down at the blood on the tips of his fingers. 'I'm sorry senhor. I cannot help you.'

As Darnell turned and walked to the door, he looked up and saw the crucifix again. He turned to Paiva. 'Are you a Christian or a Jew?'

Paiva stared at him. 'I am a New Christian.'

Darnell spoke quickly, urgently. 'How would like to live where no one will force you to kiss that cross or place it in the doorway of your shop? How would you like to live where you could practise your religion without interference, threats or intimidation?'

Paiva's lips moved. 'I – I don't understand.'

'If I guarantee your religious freedom, will you and all your people move to Madera?'

'You will let us worship as we wish? Do business as we wish?' He looked suspiciously at Darnell. 'Have our own synagogue?'

'Yes,' Darnell said. 'I will give you a paper now. But first, how much did you lend Bishop Ephraim, on what security, when and why?'

Paiva buried his face in his hands. 'I cannot answer now – I need time to think – to talk with my people.'

'I must know now.'

Paiva walked to the back of the shop. There was a long

silence and then he said, 'Bishop Ephraim forced me to discount a promissory note for three thousand *escudos* – six hundred pounds.'

'Why?' Darnell asked, his excitement and relief so vast he could hardly speak.

'He had invested his own funds and the funds of his order in indigo, and lost. There was to be an audit. He needed the money to cover his borrowings.'

'Why did he come to you instead of the other merchants?'

'He could not show his security to them.' Pava emerged into the pool of light holding a document.

Darnell read it. And couldn't believe it. Attached to Bishop Ephraim's acknowledgement of the loan were a promissory note and a contract undertaking to stop the English fort and Ynessa's investigation into the death of her father. Both documents were signed by Bishop Ephraim, Joaquim Gonzaga and Karel van Cuyler!

'I'll keep these documents,' Darnell cried.

'But senhor, that is my security!'

'I'll give you a paper. And one concerning our agreement about Madera.' He wrote standing up, the words flying across the paper. Then, putting Paiva's documents safely into his doublet, set off at a run to the da Soares warehouse.

Both Ynessa and Figueras had left. He turned and ran back to the Praca das Flores, to the da Soares mansion. The gates were open and a stream of men were climbing the steep steps to the mansion, manoeuvring chairs and tables. The guards smiled as Darnell entered.

He went up the steps, sidling round the straining men. In the garden below and along the side of the steps, men were fixing lanterns to trees. As he approached the house, smells of cooking wafted out.

The veranda was a confusion of people, moving chairs and arranging more lanterns. A woman scurried by carrying a giant basket of washed rice. He tapped her arm. 'Signora Ynessa?'

'No here, no here.' The woman rushed indoors and Darnell followed her.

A woman came into the room. Ynessa, Darnell thought, his heart leaping. Then he saw she was smaller, older, fairer, but with the same bustling energy. She looked straight at Darnell. Darnell recognized Ynessa's dark eyes, but without the brightness and the depth. Ynessa's mother, he realized as she walked up to him and said, 'Senhor?'

Darnell bowed. 'I wish to see Ynessa. I am a friend.'

'She isn't here. We are preparing for her wedding –' She stopped. 'Who are you, senhor?'

Darnell's first thought was to lie. But that would be both wrong and foolish. He said, 'My name is Richard Darnell. I am a friend of Ynessa's.'

'I thought so,' she said, expelling the words and drawing herself up. 'You must not see her. It is not proper, and nothing can come of it.'

'But I have something important to show her. Something she must see.'

Donna da Soares held out her hand. 'Give it to me. I will see that she gets it.'

Darnell shook his head and smiled. 'Unfortunately, *signora*, it is something I must deliver personally. It is do with our business.'

'You can give it to her after the wedding. Or to her husband.'

'It is very important that she sees this before the wedding.'

'You will wait till after the wedding, senhor, and then you will see Ynessa, if her husband permits. Now, please go. Otherwise I shall have to send for Sergeant Ruiz and have him take you to jail for disturbing us.' She looked past him at the guards. 'Escort Senhor Darnell off the premises, and ensure he does not return.'

319

Chapter Twenty-Six

Her bridal train spread out around her, Ynessa sat in the carriage beside Captain-General Rafael Acuna and willed her legs to move. Through the window of the carriage she could see the faces lining the steps of St Dominic's Church, the men wearing ruffs, the women in long gowns, head-dresses and tiaras. She was being married in St Dominic's instead of St Thomas's Cathedral, because Mama had thought a week's notice wasn't enough to fill the cathedral. But the crowds were there, a sea of gaping faces. Ynessa shivered and felt the carriage lurch as Captain-General Acuna, who had so kindly agreed to substitute for Rodrigo, climbed out and held his hand out to help her down.

She had to get out of the carriage! She pressed down with clenched fists on the seat and forced herself up, hearing a sustained 'Aaaah' from the people gathered on the steps as she emerged. Acuna's arm took hers and held it firmly. Leaning on it, she walked towards the church. Eight little bridesmaids fell into place behind her, holding her train.

The organ's notes filled the coolness inside. Despite Mama's fears, the church was full; army officers in the rear pews wearing red and green uniforms, craftsmen and jewellers and small shopkeepers in front of them, then merchants and their wives glittering with gems. At the foot of the altar stood Bishop Ephraim, a gold embroidered, white silk chasuble gleaming over the dark sheen of his purple robes. He carried a large missal in his hand.

This is it, Ynessa told herself. Now it ends. From now, there is nothing to remember. She looked at the light slanting through the stained-glass windows, adding to the brilliance of the ladies' gowns. Ahead of her Joaquim knelt at the altar rails, dressed in white velvet and cream silk, the back of his head gleaming like a raven's wing. Stay with me, Lord, Ynessa prayed. Give me the strength to forget and to live.

Acuna released her hand. She walked the last few steps to the altar rail and knelt before Bishop Ephraim. Joaquim looked at her, smirking and quietly confident. Ynessa shuddered at the thought of his hands on her, of his mouth closing over hers . . . She forced the thought from her mind. She bowed her head as Bishop Ephraim began the homily.

'We are gathered here today . . .'

Goodbye, Richard, my love. Ynessa willed herself to hold back the tears. She bowed her head and her throat ached with the effort of not crying.

Bishop Ephraim had reached the end of his homily and was saying, 'If there be anyone among you who knows of any reason why Ynessa and Joaquim should not be joined together in holy matrimony, let him step forward now or for ever hold his peace.'

'*Stop this marriage!*'

Ynessa jumped. Darnell's voice! She must be imagining it! There was a rustling through the congregation like a wind swirling leaves. She heard gasps of horror and the sound of footsteps crunching down the aisle.

Ynessa turned. Darnell was striding down the aisle, wearing a mottled green and brown uniform and a white turban and carrying a pistol in his hand. Darnell was mad! He couldn't . . . She gasped as Ravi Winter appeared behind Bishop Ephraim, dressed in the same mottled uniform and turban as Darnell and carrying two pistols levelled at Joaquim and Bishop Ephraim. Along the side aisles, native spectators had thrown off their tunics and *dhotis* to reveal the same mottled uniforms, drawn sabres and daggers.

This was madness! Had they come to kidnap her? Oh God, how could Darnell be so foolish?

'Stop this sacrilege at once,' Bishop Ephraim cried. 'Put away your weapons! You are all in the house of God!'

Darnell roared, 'Silence, priest! Don't *you* talk to me of sacrilege!'

The congregation was murmuring angrily; Darnell brushed past Ynessa and turned to face them. 'This marriage will not take place,' he cried, 'because this woman,' he pointed at her, 'is being forced to marry this man,' he pointed at Joaquim, 'because this man and this priest have together gambled and lost their fortunes. The only purpose of this marriage is that Joaquim Gonzaga and this priest can seize the da Soares fortune.'

'You lie, Englishman!' Bishop Ephraim roared. 'You lie because you want to marry Ynessa da Soares yourself!'

'If I lie, what are these documents, priest?' Darnell waved a sheaf of papers before the bishop's face. 'A promissory note to Jacob Paiva for three thousand *escudos*. A guarantee to repay him from the da Soares dowry or from the money paid to you by the Dutch.'

The babble from the crowd was stilled.

Darnell thrust another paper at him. 'And do you deny that this is your signature to an agreement to stop the building of Madera? Do you deny this is your signature agreeing to suppress the results of Ynessa's investigation into the murder of Rodrigo da Soares? Do you deny that you and Joaquim Gonzaga made this agreement in consideration of six hundred pounds? That you made this agreement with Karel van Cuyler, the Dutchman who murdered Rodrigo da Soares?'

There was an excited buzzing in the congregation. Darnell strode down the aisle and handed the documents to Captain-General Acuna. 'Read. Examine. See if I lie!'

Ynessa was coming to her senses. Getting to her feet she walked up to Acuna, who handed the documents to her.

It was true. Bishop Ephraim and Joaquim had lied to her, had manipulated her in the name of God so that they could steal the da Soares money. Rage flared through her. She tore away her veil and marched up to Bishop Ephraim. 'You swore to me that you had no dealings with van Cuyler. You swore to me that all Joaquim did was pretend!' She flung her headdress away. 'How dare you talk to me of sacred oaths!'

For once Bishop Ephraim seemed at a loss for words, and Joaquim was staring helplessly at her. 'Ynessa I – I only did what he told me to.'

'Then you are a weak and foolish man, Joaquim,' she said quietly. She turned round to face her guests. 'Ladies and gentlemen, I will not marry the man who tried to cheat me. Or be married by the priest who conspired with my father's murderers. I apologize to all of you. This wedding will not take place.' She held out her hand and felt Darnell take it.

After a moment Acuna got to his feet. Then holding out his arm to his wife he strode out of the church. One by one, with scandalized looks over their shoulders at the altar, the congregation followed, till only the Gonzagas and Mama and the children were left.

For a long while Donna Gonzaga stared at Ynessa. Then she got to her feet. 'Come Joaquim,' she snapped and led her family down the aisle.

Mama came up leading the twins with one hand and Katerina with the other. 'Go home,' Ynessa said to her. 'I will come later.' She waited while Mama and the children walked down the aisle, small figures getting smaller as they drew away.

Then taking Darnell's hand she followed. Ravi and Ghosh's soldiers fell into step behind them. 'Darnell,' she said, 'if I'm never this stupid again, will you marry me?'

Chapter Twenty-Seven

Karel van Cuyler sat on his haunches before Raja Railoo's throne and tried not to wince as the raja played the music box for the hundredth time. Of all the presents he'd brought, Raja Railoo had liked the music box best. He was fascinated by it as a child would be, laughing delightedly and clapping his hands each time it started to play, encouraging his councillors to join in the applause. *'Twinkle, twinkle little star, How I wonder what you are...'*

Van Cuyler swore under his breath. He had come to Vaidyapur to talk Railoo into allowing the Dutch to trade in Vaidya and drive the English from Madera. That combination of events would give the Dutch supremacy in Coromandel and provide them with an alternative to Kokinada, a fact which would make the nizam somewhat less zealous in investigating the murders of Mirza Baig and Rodrigo, or listening to the complaints of Darnell and the da Soares woman. Van Cuyler had come with presents of fine claret, some satins and velvets, some excellent ivory and sword-blades. But all Railoo cared about was that damned musical box. Van Cuyler heard the mechanism start up again and suppressed a shudder.

He was seated cross-legged on cushions before the throne, Railoo's councillors seated in two rows, flanking the area between him and the dais and looking like giant mushrooms beneath their pale cream turbans. Railoo's council chamber was a gloomy place, dark and narrow, with unyielding stone floors whose chill seeped through the cushions. Torches burned smokily high in the walls, staining the fading frescos above the throne and the brooding statue of Shiva beside it.

In the momentary silence after the music box wound down, van Cuyler said, 'Your Majesty, about Kokinada.'

'What about Kokinada?' Railoo said, as if he hadn't heard of the place or van Cuyler hadn't broached the subject three times in the past hour.

'The nizam is most incensed that you allowed an unprovoked attack on his army. Even now, the nizam is planning revenge.'

'An unprovoked attack? Who? When?'

Bowing to van Cuyler and the raja, Bhagwan Dayal rose and, climbing the platform, pressed his moustaches to the raja's ear. Like a stern father he moved the musical box away and sat on a low stool by the throne. 'Six weeks ago Seringa and the English launched a devastating and unprovoked attack on the nizam's forces, killing a large number of his men,' he told the raja.

'My cousin Seringa was always a good fighter,' Railoo laughed. 'He's never liked the peace treaty I negotiated with Kokinada.' Railoo shook his head in admiration. 'Seringa was always a fighter, even when we were children, isn't that so, Bhagwan?'

'Yes, Your Majesty. Yes, yes. But this attack could have serious implications.'

Van Cuyler sighed with relief and said quickly, 'That is true, Your Majesty. The nizam believes that the attack is part of a plan to seize Celor.'

Railoo squinted at him, his long jaws moving beneath the straggle of beard. He pursed his lips and spat out a stream of betel juice. 'Is cousin Seringa going to seize Celor? My, that would be something to feast about, if we get Celor back again.'

Bhagwan Dayal said, 'If the nizam fears that, he will attack Vaidya.'

'But Seringa first, right? Seringa first?'

'Seringa first,' Bhagwan Dayal agreed. 'But if Seringa is defeated, we wouldn't have much of a chance.'

'Nonsense, Bhagwan. We have a larger army than Seringa's. If it came to it, we could defeat the nizam with or without Seringa.' He looked right and left at his council. 'Isn't that so?'

'Yes, yes, Your Majesty,' the councillors chimed in ragged chorus.

'Your Majesty,' Dayal said firmly, 'the Dutch are here to discuss trade terms with us.'

'Yes, yes.' He frowned. 'You discuss the terms, Dayal. You're good at that sort of thing.' He paused and added, 'And report to us on your discussions.' He turned to van Cuyler. 'Don't worry, mynheer. You will have a *firman* very soon.'

The raja had the attention span of a bird, van Cuyler thought. Any moment now, if his attention wasn't seized, he'd take the music box and go to his quarters or wander away to feed his hawks. But to speak when not spoken to, to raise a topic Railoo had not raised, could result in arbitrary dismissal and a total loss of goodwill. He wiped his sweaty palms on his breeches. He'd have to take the plunge. He said, 'Your Majesty, in a few weeks that *firman* will be worthless.'

Railoo turned, his face small, his eyes bright with anger. 'What do you mean worthless? How can a *firman* signed by the raja of Vaidya and his council be worthless?' He chewed furiously and spat out another stream of betel juice.

'A *firman* that cannot be made effective is worthless,' van Cuyler said. 'Your Majesty, I do not think that Prince Seringa, who with English help will soon be the most powerful ruler in Coromandel, will allow his power to be challenged by a Dutch factory in Vaidya.'

Railoo was confused. 'I don't follow you. Dayal, what is he saying?'

Before Dayal could intervene, van Cuyler continued,

fighting to keep his voice steady. 'Your Majesty, with English help, Seringa destroyed a thousand of Kokinada's men. With English help, Seringa is now planning to take Celor. What do you think Seringa will do with the wealth of Celor and the wealth he is now accumulating from English trade? What will he do with all that power?'

Railoo looked uncertainly at Dayal, then defiantly at van Cuyler. 'Seringa is my cousin,' he said. 'He has sworn an oath of loyalty to me.'

'So he will share the wealth of Celor and the profits of his English trade with you? He will acknowledge you as ruler when he is the most powerful prince in Coromandel?'

Railoo looked at Dayal and frowned.

He'd got Railoo rattled, van Cuyler thought with satisfaction. He had to press home his advantage. 'What is Seringa's oath worth against the riches of Vaidya? What is it worth when he could be raja of Vaidya?'

'Seringa respects me,' Railoo said. 'We are like brothers.'

'If Your Majesty is certain of that,' van Cuyler said, 'then by all means let us discuss a *firman*. But if I were in your place, I would think first of all on how to break Seringa's English alliance. It is that alliance which is providing him with men and guns and is the source of his power. If I were to advise Your Majesty, I would say, take away the source of Seringa's power by driving out the English, and then consolidate your own power by entering into an alliance with us.'

Railoo stared at him amazed. Then looked around as if missing the music box. Finally, he slapped his thigh and said, 'Isn't that a wonderful idea. Dayal? Councillors?'

In another ragged chorus, the councillors cried, 'Yes, Your Majesty. Yes.'

And van Cuyler's heart sang.

Darnell saw Seringa's burly figure at the end of the plain and turned his horse; Ghosh wheeled his horse in a wide echelon and followed. They raced towards the white-clad figure who was scudding over the plain on puffs of brown dust. Ynessa and the children were racing each other behind them, whooping with delighted laughter.

Twelve days ago, at a small ceremony in Madera attended only by Mama and the children, Crispin, Caddy and her family, Ravi Winter and Ghosh, Darnell and Ynessa had been married by the chaplain of the *Golden Hind*. At Ghosh's insistence they had come to Venkatapur afterwards as guests of Prince Seringa and his wife, Princess Sita, and had spent a wonderful time there. Crispin and Ynessa had become friends from the first and, a little to Darnell's chagrin, he'd begun to treat her more like an elder sister than a step-mother. Crispin had also been thrilled to discover that Prince Seringa had two sons; Tikka, who was about his own age, and Arjuna had both proved delightful playmates. The three boys hadn't found the slightest difficulty in converting the palace's many rooms, courtyards and corridors into a vast playground.

Ynessa and Darnell revelled in their rediscovered happiness, scarcely able to believe that they were together at last and for always. Every day brought new discoveries about each other, and new pleasures; Darnell knew he could never tire of being with her.

Seringa was riding without an escort and, as he frequently liked to, without a saddle. He spotted Ghosh and Darnell and turned towards them, his long black hair streaming behind him as he rode crouched behind the horse's mane, urging it forward furiously with hands and heels.

Seringa reached them, arms rippling as he pulled the horse to a stop. His sleeveless vest was marked with perspiration and his white pantaloons and riding boots were powdered with dust. 'I've just received a message from Railoo ordering me to close down the English fort,' he said. 'Railoo is making arrangements with the Dutch.' Seringa's sweat-damp hair clung to his cheeks and neck, his dark eyes were flat and serious.

Ghosh said, 'I thought you had a deal with Railoo to share the revenues from foreign trade – and no deals with the Dutch.'

Seringa shrugged. 'That's right, but who knows with Railoo? He's like a child. One moment he wants one thing, the next something else.'

'Children should not be allowed to run men's affairs,' Ghosh said, severely. 'What are you going to do, Serai? Obey Railoo and close the English fort?'

Seringa shook his head. 'No. The time has come to overthrow Railoo.'

Darnell felt the tension flow out of him. 'We will help you with guns and troops,' he said.

Seringa stared at him thoughtfully for a long while. Then he said, 'No, Darnell. We must do this ourselves.'

'Don't be silly, Serai,' Ghosh cried. 'Railoo's troops are no match for us. But the English guns will make our victory certain.'

'We may not shed any blood at all,' Darnell pointed out. 'Just knowing that our cannon are in reserve might make Railoo surrender.'

'And what if Railoo calls on Dutch cannon to make us surrender?' Seringa shook his head. 'Vaidya will be torn apart by civil war. Kokinada and the Mughal will move in and make deals with whatever *feringhi* they please.' He reached across and patted Darnell's shoulder. 'Thank you Darnell, but we must fight this battle on our own.'

Darnell asked, 'What do you mean to do? Railoo's army is twice as large as yours.'

Seringa laughed. 'Railoo's numbers won't matter. Our men are better trained and more experienced fighters. One confrontation and –' Seringa made a scything motion with his hand. 'It'll be over.'

As they turned to rejoin Ynessa and the children, Darnell

said, 'I accept your decision, but I promise you this. I will give you any help you need. If there is anything at all you want, just ask.'

Seringa grasped him above the elbow. 'I thank you, my friend. Now you must take your wife and son back to Madera, while Dorai and I work out our plan to attack Railoo.'

Chapter Twenty-Eight

A week after he'd returned from Venkatapur, Darnell presided over the council's finance meeting. Cogan and Ravi flanked him; William Johnson and Edward Whiting – third and fourth councillors – were seated further along. Johnson, squinting behind large spectacles, read the monthly trading report. Since their arrival from Pettahpoli, business at Madera had increased thirty-fold, and already Madera was the second most profitable factory in Coromandel.

Squinting a little himself, Darnell read out a letter from Ovington. The president and council in Surat had decided to provisionally adopt the fort, and Ovington was on his way to Madera with the necessary documentation and an advance of five hundred pounds towards the financing.

'Wonderful, wonderful news!' Whiting cried from his place at the end of the table. 'Soon Madera will be the new presidency – and you, Richard, will be the new president!'

Cogan gave Whiting a bilious look. 'There's many a slip –' he began sourly.

Suddenly there were shouts and the sound of pounding hooves. They rushed to the window. Three carts were drawn up in the square, their wheels and wooden frames stained with dried mud and crushed leaves, their thatched roofs covered with dust. Around the carts were twenty native soldiers, dressed in the mottled green and brown of Seringa's army. Eckaerts and an escort of Company troops in red tunics, blue denims and black hats milled in an outer circle around them.

As they watched, Darnell saw Seringa climb from one of the carts and wave away the soldiers who'd moved to help him. He was bareheaded and his hair streamed in an untidy mass on to his shoulders. His face was drawn and haggard, his frame shrunken. He wore a dirty, sweat-stained, mottled green and brown uniform.

Darnell raced from the room, ran across the square and greeted Seringa cursorily before asking, 'What's happened? Has Railoo won?' The words stuck in his throat.

Seringa's lips moved but no words came. He folded his fingers till the knuckles whitened, then nodded.

Darnell put his arm around Seringa and drew him aside. 'Tell me,' he said softly, 'tell me. Take your time.'

Seringa stood for a while staring at the ground, then slowly, in a low, hoarse voice, he told Darnell that they had been informed of Railoo's route and had taken a short-cut through the Ruisili Gorge to cut him off. But the infor-mation had been false and Railoo's army had been waiting for them. Hemmed in by the sides of the gorge, with both entrance and exits blocked off by Railoo's troops, they had been out-numbered and massacred. What little was left of his army had fled. Ghosh had been taken prisoner. Seringa had raced ahead of Railoo's army to Venkatapur, loaded his family into carts and rushed to Madera.

'I'm sorry to bring this trouble on you,' he said. 'I had to save Sita and the boys and there was nowhere else to go.' He reached out and took Darnell's shoulder. 'You will protect us, won't you, Darnell? You won't hand us over to Railoo?'

'Where's Railoo's army?' Darnell asked.

'Not far behind. They'll be here soon to demand you surrender us.'

Seringa's defeat altered the whole political equation. It made Railoo the only important figure in Vaidya; now the English would have to reach an understanding with him. If Darnell did not surrender Seringa and placate Railoo, Madera would be finished. Could he risk the future of Madera because of his loyalty to Seringa? What about his loyalty to the Company, to those who had followed him from Armagon? What about his loyalty to Ynessa and to the Portuguese?

'You will use your cannon, won't you, Darnell?' Seringa asked again.

Firing on Railoo would only bring temporary respite, Darnell knew. Railoo was the sole ruler of Vaidya; he would cancel their *firman* and bring in the Dutch. Then they would lose Madera and have to surrender Seringa anyway.

Darnell saw Ynessa push her way through the soldiers, her hat stuck on the back of her head, her eyes dark circles of alarm and curiosity. She'd come from the site of the new da Soares warehouse and her tunic and breeches were covered with brick dust. 'Darnell –' she cried, then realizing what had happened rushed over to Princess Sita and embraced her. She squatted and hugged Arjuna and Tikka.

Cogan took Darnell aside and whispered, 'Seringa's finished. The only way we can keep Madera is by showing Railoo we support him, which means surrendering Seringa.'

Ynessa heard and turned. 'What is this talk of surrender?' she cried. 'Seringa is our friend. If not for him, none of us would be here. We cannot hand him and his family over to Railoo.'

'What do you suggest we do, Mrs Darnell?' Cogan asked.

'We must find a way to keep Seringa and Madera.'

'How do we do that?'

'I don't know, Mr Cogan.' Ynessa's eyes blazed. 'All I do know is that we will not betray our friends.'

The warning bells above the gate towers pealed out. Soldiers raced from the barracks to their positions along the walls. The Company troops who'd escorted Seringa galloped to the west wall. There was a clanging of locks and the scrape of wood on cement as, one after another, each of the fort's gates was swung shut. The streets were filled with men hurrying to and from the walls.

'Mr Eckaerts,' Darnell called as he went past, 'arrange accommodation in the barracks for Seringa's escort, and make the guest house ready for Prince Seringa and his family.'

'Yes, sir.' Eckaerts saluted and hurried away.

'You've no right,' Cogan ground out. 'You must discuss this with the council first. You've no right to endanger all of us.'

'We'll talk later,' Darnell cried, running to the west wall.

Darnell looked down from the top of the north-west bastion on the scene below. Railoo's army was streaming in from the west, some of the men and horses keeping to the trail, others trampling through the bright yellow fields of rape and mustard and smashing through groves of mango and palmyra. There were nearly two thousand of them spread out in a wide swathe of men, carts and horses. Some of the troops wore marigold and crimson palace uniforms, others tunics and *dhotis*. Some wore pieces of chainmail and metal helmets, others carried shields. Some rode, some walked and some clung to carts. Everyone was armed with a sword, battle-axe, pike or *lathi*. It was a large, disorganized army, effective simply through sheer weight of numbers.

'Look at that army!' William Johnson cried, nervously. He'd been besieged before on the west coast.

Ravi whistled through his teeth and said, 'Bleedin' hell, they're all over the flippin' place.'

Captain Martin came and saluted Darnell. 'We've got six cannon covering the island and the gardens, Mr Darnell, and four cannon covering the bridges. The men have orders to take out the bridges if they attempt a charge.'

'It doesn't look as if they're planning anything tonight.' Darnell pointed to the front of the island, where men were setting up tents and lighting cooking fires.

334

'Why aren't we firing at them?' Edward Whiting demanded. 'Once we let 'em settle down, we've had it.'

'If we fire at them now, sir,' Captain Martin replied, 'we'll only drive them back temporarily and we'll have less shot to defend ourselves.'

'You mean to say we can't drive them out of here?'

'Not without a break-out. We've got good men sir, but it'll be a massacre if they were sent against that lot. There's nearly two thousand of them and only sixty of us.'

So much for breaking out of the fort and driving Railoo back, Darnell thought.

Captain Martin said, 'If you gentlemen agree, we're best off conserving our ammunition till they attack the walls, or we're ready to break out. Our best bet is to hold firm and sweat them out. It'll take a while and we must reconcile ourselves to that.'

Cogan watched the captain salute and go, his face crumpled in gloom. In funereal tones he said, 'I'm afraid there is no alternative to surrendering Seringa. By giving him refuge here, we're only upsetting Railoo. It's Railoo we must be friends with now, not Seringa.'

'Quite right, Mr Cogan,' Johnson said. 'The question we must ask ourselves is: what alternatives do we have?'

Darnell said, 'Giving up Seringa doesn't mean that rabble will be dispersed or that we'll get a *firman* from Railoo. The reason Seringa attacked Railoo is because Railoo has made an agreement with the Dutch. Railoo may keep on with the siege until we've given him Seringa *and* Madera.'

Cogan said, 'Our only solution is to surrender Seringa on condition the siege is raised. Then we'll use our treaty to make an Anglo-Dutch deal over Vaidya with Railoo.'

'Pie in the sky!' Darnell snorted. 'I don't trust Railoo or the Dutch. Once we surrender to Railoo, we're out of Vaidya.'

335

'One moment, Richard,' Ravi said. ''Ow does our suf-ferin' the siege 'elp Seringa? At the end of it 'e'd still 'ave no place to go and we'll 'ave to give 'im to bleedin' Railoo. I think you should talk with Railoo and Seringa and agree terms of surrender,' he concluded.

The next morning messengers arrived from Railoo sug-gesting a meeting at ten. Darnell agreed to meet in the open area between the fort and the Island Bridge; shortly before ten, he rode out of the West Gate with Cogan and an honour guard of five soldiers. He and Seringa had discussed the situation at length and concluded that his surrender was inevitable: Bharatya and his troops were too far away to be of help. But there were to be certain terms attached to that surrender . . .

Railoo was accompanied by Bhagwan Dayal and an untidy squad of cavalry escort. Railoo wore an embroid-ered silk tunic and linen breeches and chewed *pan* con-tinuously. He spat out a thick red stream of saliva as he stopped. 'When will you release that criminal dog, Seringa?' he shouted.

'Prince Seringa will only be surrendered after satisfactory terms have been agreed.' Darnell noted Railoo's surprise at being addressed in fluent Tamil and by him instead of Cogan. He moved his horse between Railoo and the guards. 'I am Richard Darnell, the agent of this fort.'

Railoo said, 'I was told we were invited here to take custody of Seringa. That is the only reason I came.'

Darnell said, 'There are certain pre-conditions that must be met before we will surrender Prince Seringa.'

Railoo's mouth quivered, his eyes blazed with a hot flash of anger. 'You cannot make any conditions. If you do not surrender Seringa and all his people you will starve and lose all your business.'

'And you will lose your army.' Darnell locked his gaze on Railoo's and held it.

Bhagwan Dayal asked, 'What do you want for Seringa? Money? Land? Some villages?'

Darnell let his breath out with a soft hiss. He said, 'We want you to honour the *firman* we have with Prince Seringa.'

Railoo spat out a stream of betel. 'Prince Seringa had no power to grant that *firman*. Granting *firmans* is my privilege.'

'But Prince Seringa told you about it and you approved it. We will require that *firman* to be reissued by you.' Darnell reached into his saddle-bag and handed Dayal a copy.

'No need,' Railoo snapped. 'Seringa's *firman* is hereby renewed. Now give me Seringa.'

Darnell said, 'There are other conditions. We want the release of Dorai Ghosh and any other of Seringa's soldiers you are holding prisoner. We want a safe conduct for the members of Prince Seringa's family to travel to wherever Bharatya is. We want guarantees that Prince Seringa will be treated humanely, that we will be granted the right to visit him and examine the conditions under which you are holding him.'

'Never! We will not let traitors go unpunished!'

'In exchange,' Darnell said evenly, 'we will have Seringa formally cede you his lands and everything he owns in Venkatapur, including his rights of inheritance.'

Railoo stopped chewing and looked thoughtfully at Darnell.

'Unsettled heirs can create a lot of trouble,' Darnell pointed out, 'especially if they find others to support their claim.'

Railoo squinted. 'What are you saying? That Seringa's sons will conspire against me?'

'They can't if they have ceded everything to you.'

Railoo said, 'I agree to all your terms. Now produce the traitor, Seringa.'

'First, we must have a signed agreement.'

Bhagwan Dayal said, 'This is a great insult. You must accept the raja's word.'

'I must accept only what I will accept. If the raja wants Seringa, we must have a written agreement.'

Railoo wheeled his horse round. 'I will meet with my council and give you a written agreement,' he said to Darnell. 'In three days.' Raking his spurs viciously, he galloped furiously across the bridge.

For the next three days, nothing came into or left the fort. Supplies of fruit and vegetables ran out and stocks of rice, flour, chilli powder and sugar dwindled.

On the afternoon of the third day, they got Railoo's answer.

Shortly after four o'clock the drums began, a steady, repetitious throbbing like a thousand urgent heartbeats, carrying across the water, rousing both the camp and the fort with their insistent beat. Darnell and Ynessa hurried to the north-west bastion. From there they could see Railoo's soldiers standing on the island shore, facing the fort in a large semi-circle. Midway round the half circle, a throne and footstool had been set up, together with a row of chairs of lesser height. As they watched, a lone horseman galloped across the bridge and shouted that the raja had an answer for Darnell and wanted Seringa brought to hear it.

Darnell sent soldiers to fetch Seringa. Dayal and Railoo's ministers came and took their seats on the chairs beside the throne. The soldiers returned with Seringa. As soon as Seringa was seen, Railoo's soldiers flung their spears into the air and broke formation, darting across the beach, shouting and making obscene gestures. Insults floated across the river. Then there was the wail of a conch and the noise died. The beating of the drums stopped. The silence became expectant, like that of a theatre audience

338

watching the curtain rise. There followed a steady, repeated creaking.

The sound came from behind the trees at the furthest corner of the circle. Moments later Ghosh's gaunt figure appeared clad only in a loincloth. His arms were tied to the shafts of a cart and thick ropes extended from the framework of the cart to hooks embedded in the flesh of his back. Blood ribboned down his back as he pulled the cart on to the beach; riding in the cart, smiling triumphantly and waving to the spectators was Raja Railoo.

Darnell felt anger blaze through him. He heard Ynessa gasp. Her face was pale as death. Seringa was staring at the spectacle in horror.

'Bloody muck-fickin' 'ell!' Ravi swore. 'We've got to stop this!'

Enormous welts stood out on Ghosh's body. One eye had been gouged out and his jaws were fastened shut by two large nails. There were huge blisters on his rump and waist where he had been prodded with firebrands. As they neared the throne, Railoo pulled brutally on the ropes. A hook tore out of the flesh and dangled free. Kept upright by a fierce effort of will, Ghosh drew the cart in a horrifying bloody circle around the screaming mob, blood streaming from his back and from the nails through his cheeks.

Darnell couldn't let this savagery continue. Ghosh was his friend. Ghosh had supported the fort, helped him investigate van Cuyler, helped rescue Ynessa from Bishop Ephraim. He would make Railoo pay for this and the devil with what Railoo was planning. As Ghosh wrenched to an agonizing stop facing the fort, Darnell grabbed a loaded musket from a soldier.

A man clad in white, carrying a crude speaking-trumpet, advanced to stand beside Ghosh. 'This is Raja Railoo's answer to those who insult him,' the man called. 'This is his answer to those who shield his enemies. This is how he will treat them and all traitors.'

Darnell took careful aim. The ball caught Ghosh full in the chest. Ghosh's body twitched against the shafts. His legs folded under him. A hook tore out of his dead flesh and he sagged forward, held by the ropes. Railoo scrambled out of the cart and ran behind a screen of soldiers.

Railoo and his ministers were already fleeing from the beach. 'We will not surrender Prince Seringa or any of his people,' Darnell shouted. 'You have twenty-four hours to remove yourselves from the island and our gardens. If you do not we will blast you out of here with our cannon.'

He stared helplessly at Railoo's soldiers running from the beach, at the empty chairs and throne, at Ghosh's body lying beside the cart. The anger still flamed through him and tears stung his eyes.

From behind him, Seringa said, 'Ghosh would thank you for what you did. Now he is at peace, and beyond Railoo.'

From behind Seringa, Cogan said, 'God rot it, Richard! You've started a bloody war!'

Chapter Twenty-Nine

At the council meeting that evening they had finally agreed to a temporary prolongation of the siege. Putting the best face on things, Darnell argued that the siege couldn't last long: feeding Railoo's army was ravaging the countryside; soon Railoo and his men would start to go hungry. Ynessa pointed out the fort could be supplied by sea; she had sent word through a fishing boat to Figueras asking him to load a ship with supplies and send it to Madera. 'We only need to plan for a few days,' she said optimistically.

Darnell instituted a system of rationing. With Seringa's authority and the help of Meru and the leading native merchants, all the food stocks in the Black Town were brought to the factory house where they were sorted and measured and it was decided how much could be allocated, while notes with the Company seal were prepared which could be exchanged for provisions.

The next day lines spread from the factory house to the north wall as men and women queued for rice, lentils and such other food as was available. A kind of ennui settled over the fort. There was little work to be done, and everyone sat in the oppressive heat and sweated. The milk from the local dairy began to go sour as the cattle weren't able to get out of the settlement to graze.

On the fifth day, the fever began at the home of a carpenter in the Black Town. Its symptoms were abdominal cramps, diarrhoea, muscle aches and fever. The first victim was the carpenter's son who became dehydrated and died. The next day his two brothers and mother were afflicted;

by nightfall all three of them were dead and their father unconscious.

The following day the first Englishman died. It was John Rawlins, who had taken to his bed the previous evening complaining of fever, pains in his calves and diarrhoea. The shock of his passing affected the whole English community.

When after that evening's council meeting Darnell returned to the three-roomed bungalow in St George Street that he'd taken over after their marriage, he found Ynessa had brought Crispin to their bed and was mopping the boy's forehead with cold water. The boy had developed a high fever and had severe diarrhoea. As Darnell watched, Crispin coughed and spat, his ribcage fluttering like a bird's.

Oh God, not my son, Darnell thought. The boy's eyes burned brightly, the bones in his thin face almost glowing. Ynessa had already sent for the doctor, so there was nothing to do but bathe the boy's forehead and wait.

'Dr Littleton didn't save Rawlins,' Darnell snapped, irritable at his helplessness.

Fuelled by his anger and fear, Darnell ran all the way back to the factory house and found Ravi. 'Crispin's got the fever,' he panted. 'I don't trust Littleton. Isn't there anyone else? There must be some native doctors in the Black Town.'

Ravi bit his lower lip. 'There's an *ayurveda*.' With sudden decision he said, 'I know. You go back home and wait for Littleton. I'll run into the Black Town and fetch the *ayurveda*. That way you'll get the best of everything.'

When Darnell returned home, Crispin lay kicking restlessly at a sheet, his eyes screwed shut. Darnell took the damp cloth from Ynessa and cooled his forehead.

Dr Littleton arrived at last, flustered and red-faced. The fever was spreading; he had more patients than he could cope with. He prescribed boiled ipecacuanha bark every hour and told them to keep using the damp cloths to cool the fever. 'If he isn't any better tomorrow, I'll have to touch him to the quick by applying a red hot iron to his heel.'

Darnell asked Ynessa not to administer the bark until Ravi came with the *ayurveda*.

'What d'you want an *ayurveda* for?'

'Rawlins died.'

Ten minutes later, Ravi came in, alone. 'All that bloody *ayurveda* talks about is devils and evil spirits,' he cried in disgust. 'Says spirits 'ave caused Railoo's fallin' out with Seringa and spirits are ventin' their anger on us.'

Ravi went over to the bed and pulled back Crispin's eyelid with his thumb, looked inside the boy's mouth and ear. 'You've got to keep 'is fever down,' he said. 'And better give 'im the bark what Littleton prescribed.'

For the rest of that evening, Darnell and Ynessa sat with Crispin, bathing his forehead and helping him to the toilet. The little mite seemed to be shrivelling right before them. His eyes stuck out like lanterns, and there were hollows in his cheeks. His legs under the thin bedspread were like twigs. He had developed a cough, and his tiny body was now racked by constant hacking that blocked his throat. He was too weak to cry out and merely sighed and sobbed. Darnell helped him sit up and spit. The last time, there was blood in his sputum. By dawn, Crispin was barely able to move and the only sound in the room was that of his harsh breathing.

Seringa came, bringing Sita with him. 'Tikka told us Crispin has the fever,' he said, and looked into the child's shadowed eye-sockets. He pulled Sita forward. 'Her father was the best-known *ayurveda* in Tanjore. She will stop the fever.'

Darnell and Ynessa exchanged glances. Sita's father may have been the best-known *ayurveda* in Tanjore, but that didn't mean she knew anything about medicine.

'He trained her,' Seringa said. 'He trained the whole

family. These are local fevers. Sita knows them better than your *feringhi* doctor.'

That was possibly true, Darnell thought, but how had Sita been trained? She'd been married at sixteen, for God's sake, so what could she have learnt from her father?

Darnell's brain churned wearily. He looked at Sita. 'Will you look at my son?' he asked.

Sita examined Crispin, then turned to Darnell and said, 'He must have more water. Lots more water, boiled, with this.' She took some seeds from a pouch. 'I give this to Tikka and Arjuna three times a day so they won't catch the fever.'

She went with Ynessa to the kitchen and made her gruel, came back and helped Ynessa feed it to Crispin. 'Stay with him,' she said. 'He will sleep a lot. Feed him each time he wakes.' She handed more seeds and powders to Ynessa.

For the first time, Crispin slept. Admittedly not for more than an hour and a half, but when he woke there was colour in his cheeks. Ynessa fed him more of Sita's gruel and he slept again.

Darnell and Ynessa sat by him, nodding off from time to time. After he'd slept and woken the second time, Darnell touched Crispin's throat. It *felt* cooler, but was it? Religiously, he bathed the boy's forehead. Crispin's breathing sounded easier and he'd stopped coughing. Darnell prayed, his prayers mingling with sleep. Once he swayed awake and found Crispin lying absolutely still.

Ynessa sat opposite, her head on her chest, napping. He leaned forward slowly. Crispin's face was pale as the sheet that covered him, his skin covered with perspiration. Slowly Darnell lowered his ear to the boy's face. A faint breath tickled his ears. He looked down. Crispin was in a deep sleep, breathing slowly and easily and the heat from his skin was gone.

Chapter Thirty

'It's time to send for Bharatya.' Seringa looked steadily at Darnell. 'I want you to go and fetch him.'

They were sitting on the veranda, sipping *cha*. Darnell stared at him aghast. 'Me? I've got to look after Madera.'

'I want you to take my son, Arjuna, with you to Bharatya.'

'That's crazy! Arjuna's a child. It's a long and difficult journey; whoever goes to summon Bharatya must be able to travel freely and quickly.'

'Arjuna must go,' Seringa said and Darnell heard the obstinacy in his voice. 'Arjuna is the future, Darnell. If he is safe and with Bharatya, then Ghosh's death and all the deaths that are to come won't be in vain. Arjuna will ensure that Vaidya continues, that Railoo and his children don't abandon or destroy it. If Arjuna is safe, whatever happens to me is not important.'

'But it's impossible.'

'For most people, yes. But for you, Darnell, no. You are a *devrika*.'

Darnell frowned. A *devrika* was someone chosen or loved by the gods. It was also a god in human form.

'You can do it, Darnell.' Seringa's eyes were large, pleading. 'Arjuna has been well trained. He is strong and disciplined and will not be a problem to you. He knows what he has to do and will do it.' Seringa took Darnell's hand in his. 'Arjuna will also be good cover for you. No one will imagine a messenger to Bharatya would travel with a child.'

Seringa had a point there, Darnell thought, but he

couldn't do it. Whatever exaggerated ideas Seringa had of his ability, his place was here in Madera, overseeing strategy and making sure Cogan didn't step out of line. His place was here with Ynessa and Crispin. 'I can't go,' he said, and had another idea. 'Why don't you take Arjuna?'

'The risk is too great. If we are found, both of us will be killed, and everything lost.'

'Why can't you send Arjuna with one of your men?'

'I cannot be certain of their loyalty. No, Darnell, you are the only one who can do it.'

'I don't believe in Shiva,' Darnell said, softly. 'I wasn't trained by Bharatya. Why trust me?'

'Because I know you are my brother,' Seringa said simply.

The next evening Seringa and Arjuna were waiting on the beach outside the South Gate, the boy dressed in cheap travelling cottons and carrying a small bundle. Darnell and Seringa had agreed that the safest way out of Madera was by fishing boat, and that Naidu should drop them off on a beach a few miles to the north. Seringa handed Darnell a money-belt full of gold *mohurs* which he fastened beneath his pantaloons. 'Use what you need. Buy horses if you need to and travel as quickly as you can.'

Darnell stuck the pistol in his waistband beneath his tunic and checked the knife was in his boot.

Seringa put his hand behind Arjuna's head and propelled the boy towards Darnell. 'Now remember everything I told you,' Seringa admonished. 'And obey Mr Darnell as if he were me.'

Obediently, the boy said, 'Yes, *thathi*.'

'And in the presence of other people address him as if he were me.'

The boy stared in front of him. 'Yes, *thathi*.'

Naidu emerged from the shadows and Seringa looked across at Darnell. 'Take him,' he said, his voice strangled.

*   *   *

They reached the village about two hours later, discerning the faint shadows of houses against the back light of the sea. The houses were in darkness. Spread out far across the sea were the tiny lights of fishing boats. Darnell helped Arjuna along the uneven path to the village.

A dog barked. Suddenly a bare-bodied man appeared out of the shadows. He kept his distance, and carried a fish-gutting knife in his hand. 'Who are you?' he asked in a harsh whisper. 'What do you want?'

'I am a merchant travelling with my son to San Thome. We got as far as Madera and had to turn back. There are soldiers everywhere and fighting.'

'Fighting?'

'Yes. There are big guns being fired, making a lot of noise and killing a lot of people.'

'It is war,' the man said with suppressed excitement.

Darnell asked, 'Is there anywhere we can stay the night? We were hoping to stay at Madera, but now we'll have to go back to Mintoor.'

The man put away his knife and walked with them towards the village. 'I am the watchman,' he said. 'You can stay with me if you like.'

'Would you have any food?' Darnell asked. 'And *cha*. The boy is hungry. The soldiers took our horses and we have been walking from Madera.'

'I'll see what can be done.'

He showed them to a small hut outside the village, perched on a rise between the road and the sea. It was a single, insanitary room, smelling of fish and smoke, the day's heat still trapped in it. 'I'll be back soon,' he promised.

About twenty minutes later he returned with bowls of cold rice and some fish. 'This is all I could get. It is late.'

'Never mind.'

He sat and watched them while they ate, then asked from where they had come.

From Pulicat, Darnell said. He was teaching the boy his business.

'What business is that?' the man asked.

Darnell hesitated before he said, 'We buy and sell cloth and foodstuffs and general goods.'

'Why were you going to San Thome?'

'To buy Portuguese copper.'

The man watched them curiously, then pointed to two mats he had spread out at the back of the room. 'You can sleep here,' he said. 'Tomorrow morning I will take you to the village headman. He may hire you a boat to take you to San Thome.'

The man left them to watch for intruders. Arjuna stretched out on one of the mats and was asleep within seconds. Darnell lay awake a little longer. The floor was uneven and hard and there was something about the watchman that made him uneasy. Darnell moved his mat nearer the door and lay listening to Arjuna's regular breathing and thinking of Crispin and Ynessa. He drifted in and out of sleep. Once he thought the watchman had come back into the room but it was only the wind and the hiss of the breakers.

He was woken by a kick in the ribs and a muffled curse. Someone lurched over him. Something moved rapidly through the air; Darnell glimpsed a flash of steel as the watchman slashed wildly at him with the gutting knife. Quickly Darnell rolled over and over. The knife sliced into the mud floor. Kicking out at the watchman, Darnell tried to get to his feet. The watchman staggered, picked up his knife and turned again on Darnell.

Out of the corner of his eye, Darnell glimpsed Arjuna sitting up, wide-eyed and frightened. Hauling the pistol out of his belt, he threw it at the watchman. It caught him full in the face. Blood spurted and the man gave an involuntary cry of pain. Struggling into a half-crouch Darnell flung himself at his boots. The watchman, surprised at this change of tactics, turned to come after him. Pulling the knife out of his boot, Darnell jumped up, knife held in front of him. The watchman feinted. Darnell remained still. The watchman feinted again. Darnell swayed, thrusting the knife into the man's side and feeling it shudder as it hit flesh and muscle.

The man twisted away, the knife suddenly free. Blood welled from the wound at his side. His eyes widened in surprise and fear. Darnell moved at him, dagger extended. 'Come on, you muck-fickin' gillie, come on and fight.' But, crying out in pain and fear, the watchman dropped the fish-gutting knife and ran out of the hut.

A silvery-grey light filtered through the open door. Darnell picked up the pistol and loaded it. Carrying both knife and pistol he followed the trail of blood outside the hut. The man had collapsed by the first of the village huts and lay surrounded by a number of bare-bodied men just back from the night's fishing. Arjuna came and stood by Darnell. Darnell squeezed Arjuna's hand with a reassurance he did not feel.

The fishermen came up the path at a run. Darnell levelled the pistol and fired at a crow above their heads. The bird plopped down in front of the running men, who stopped and looked incredulously at its bloodied feathers and shattered body. They looked up fearfully from the bird to Darnell, made to move forward again and stopped as Darnell pointed the gun at them. 'Stay where you are!' he cried. 'Only one of you approach.'

The men stopped, confused and staring belligerently. After a few moments an older man pushed through the crowd. 'You have abused our hospitality,' he said from the front of the crowd. 'You have attacked our watch –'

'He is someone who disgraces your village,' Darnell cried. 'I am a merchant escaping with my son from the war at Madera. I did your watchman no harm and would have paid for our lodging and any help he gave us. But your watchman gave us shelter only so he could rob us.'

The headman looked back at the watchman, then at Darnell. 'That is not what he says. He says you tried to rob him.'

'Of what?' Darnell laughed. 'What does he have that I want? Or could not afford?' He took a gold coin from the folds of his tunic and held it up. 'That is what I would have given him for his hospitality. I have important dealings with the English in Madera and with the Portuguese in San Thome. I carry money and messages to them from the Dutch and the nizam of Kokinada. If your watchman had succeeded in killing me, your village would have been ravaged by at least two armies. The messages I take are that important.' He waved the gun. 'That is why they have armed me with such a powerful weapon and taught me how to use it.'

The headman came closer, staring respectfully at the gun. 'It is difficult to learn how to use this? Can you show –'

'For anyone but a foreigner to possess such a weapon, special permission is needed. Anyone found in possession of such a weapon without that authority is executed.'

'Truly?'

'That is a fact.' Darnell put down the gun and gave the headman the gold piece. 'I give this to you in compensation for the loss of your watchman, and to provide a cart to take me and my son to Mintoor.'

The headman nodded sagely and shouted to the fishermen to arrange for a cart. 'What is this about war?'

Darnell told him that native troops were camped around the English fort at Madera and the English were firing huge guns. When he'd finished, the headman nodded and said, 'I offer you the hospitality of my house until your arrangements have been finalized.'

Ynessa woke the next morning to the rush of feet and the welcome cry of 'A ship! A ship!' She carried Crispin to the veranda to show him a da Soares coaster mooring in the roads. Ynessa felt happiness bubble through her. For the present at least the siege was over.

Three days after Darnell left Madera, Railoo's soldiers found a man hiding in the forest near the Company Gardens. They bound his hands behind him and stripped him to his loincloth. Then, with kicks and prods, they hurried him across the Great Bridge to Bhagwan Dayal's tent in the centre of the island. The man rushed in and prostrated himself at Dayal's feet.

Dayal looked from the soldiers to the man quivering helplessly before him. The man was obviously a fisherman from Madera. 'Why were you spying on us?' Dayal asked and kicked the man upright.

'I wasn't spying!'

Dayal kicked the man sideways. 'We know who you are, dog! You're one of Seringa's relatives from the fishing village! What did Seringa send you to look for?'

'No! No!' the man wailed. 'I'm not from the village! I am from Tiruvil!'

'Liar!' Dayal grabbed a stave from one of the soldiers and beat the man across his curled-up body.

'I speak the truth,' the man gasped, twisting around the floor like a dog with a broken back. 'Why should I lie? I am the headman of Tiruvil. If you take me there or send someone to ask for me you will know I am telling the truth.'

Dayal stopped beating the man. Perhaps he *was* telling the truth. 'What are you doing here?' he panted. The exercise had made him sweat.

'I came,' the headman said hesitantly, 'to see what was happening. We heard there was a war, that the English had fired their cannon, that there was a great shortage of food. When I saw your soldiers, I hid. I did not know what they would do if they found me. I believed they would not let me pass. And I had not come all the way from Tiruvil to go away disappointed.'

'Why *did* you come from Tiruvil?'

'To see if we could sell fish here. And other food.'

Dayal gestured to one of the soldiers to free the man's hands. 'How did you know what was happening here?'

'The merchant told us. The one travelling with messages from the nizam to the Portuguese and Raja Railoo.'

Dayal leapt on the man again, seized him by the hair and punched him in the face. 'Do you think I'm stupid? Do you think you're talking to your father?'

The man swivelled to avoid the blows, taking care not to provoke more violence. 'I am telling the truth,' he sobbed. 'By Shiva, I swear it! The merchant had many gold coins. He said he was from Pulicat and couldn't pass here because of the guns. He had his son with him, a boy of about eight. And he had a gun about this big –' The head-man spread his hands out to show the size of the pistol.

The rain of blows stopped. The headman wiped blood away from his mouth. 'Though the man spoke Tamil, he was not one of us. He looked as if he came from the north.'

'Describe the boy,' Dayal cried excitedly. 'Describe the boy.'

'An ordinary boy,' the headman said. 'About eight or nine. Black hair, black skin, darker than his father.'

'What was he wearing?'

'A cotton *dhoti* and turban.'

'Did you notice anything else, fool? Did he wear rings? Or chains? Were there jewels in his turban?'

'No.'

Dayal slumped thoughtfully on his couch. It couldn't be. But it was a possibility. 'Tell me again about this merchant and his son,' he demanded.

The headman described them again. Gold, Dayal thought, guns, a man who looked like Darnell, a boy the same age and build as Arjuna. It was too much of a coincidence. If Seringa had sent Arjuna from Madera it would have been to Hosur, where Bharatya and his men were.

He jumped to his feet and, ordering the soldiers to follow with the headman, hurried to Railoo's tent. They would send carrier pigeons to Vaidyapur ordering soldiers to occupy the lower reaches of Hosur and seize Darnell and Arjuna.

Darnell and Arjuna had been travelling for three days, at first in the bullock cart provided by the headman of Tiruvil, then on the horses they bought in Mintoor. Darnell was amazed at Arjuna's endurance and stoicism. Though saddle-sore and weary, the boy never admitted to being tired; he ate only when Darnell ate and drank only when Darnell did. Once or twice Darnell had had to catch him before he fell off the saddle asleep. On those occasions Darnell had stopped immediately and insisted that the boy rested. Now he recognized the signs of exhaustion that the boy tried to hide, and stopped at the first indication.

Their journey since Tiruvil had been uneventful. After their experience with the night-watchman, they'd slept outside villages, tethering their horses in a field and sleeping under saddle-blankets. They ate frugally, stopping in native cafés if they passed a town, or buying food from the villages they passed. They attracted no attention. Darnell's Tamil was fluent and Arjuna behaved impeccably, calling Darnell 'thathi' whenever anyone else was present.

Chapter Thirty-One

By the time Ynessa got to the north-west bastion, Cogan and the rest of the council were there, standing with their backs to her, looking into Railoo's camp. It was not yet eight o'clock in the morning, but the day had lost its coolness. Already the sun was glowing silvery-white against a feathered bank of cloud.

Cogan turned as she approached, his greying curls pasted to his neck with sweat. His eyes were reddened and there were flecks of sleep in their corners. He said, 'Now you're here, Mrs Darnell, we can begin.' His tone was noncommittal.

Ynessa walked over to the wall and looked. Fair-skinned, blonde-bearded men in doublets, breeches and plumed hats strode between new green tents in the island and garden camps. The Dutch, Ynessa realized, and suppressed a shudder. She looked at their pistols, swords and muskets, and at the ugly snouts of cannon gleaming from both camps. She knew Darnell wouldn't be back with Bharatya's army for at least a week and thought: *We're done for. Only a miracle can save us now.* 'Will they take us?' she asked Cogan, glad that her voice came out even.

'That's something we must ask Captain Martin and Commander Eckaerts,' Cogan said. He turned round and leant against the wall and waved to everyone to form a circle around him. 'I called this meeting here,' he began, 'so that you could all see the danger of our situation.' He glared at Ynessa and then nodded to Captain Martin and Eckaerts. 'Now gentlemen, tell us, can the Dutch take us?'

'No,' Captain Martin said. 'We have much more cannon

than they have and the advantage of a fort and the high ground.'

'But they could harass us,' Eckaerts said. 'With two cannon covering the Island Bridge and one covering the Land Bridge, they will certainly stop us breaking out.'

'Or make it more difficult,' Captain Martin said. He walked past Cogan to the wall. 'What worries me are those two rascals.' He pointed to cannons at the southernmost edge of the island and the northernmost part of the gardens. 'Those cannons aren't covering the fort, they're covering the beach. As long as they remain there, it's going to be difficult for us to be resupplied from the harbour.'

'Why?' Ynessa asked.

'They're aimed to lob cannonballs on to the beach and stop anything being unloaded. Given the right elevation and some luck, they could even hit a ship moored in the roads.'

Ynessa thought of the da Soares coaster which would return with fresh supplies. If they couldn't land them, they'd starve. Come quickly, Darnell, she prayed silently, relieved she'd been able to send most of the women and children away on the coaster, including, after considerable argument, Crispin, Caddy and her boys.

'How do we eliminate the Dutch?' Cogan asked.

Both Eckaerts and Captain Martin frowned. Captain Martin said, 'The only way of doing that is by breaking out. And we don't have the men for that.'

'It was bad enough before,' Eckaerts added. 'With the additional Dutch troops, it's hopeless.'

'So we're besieged and will starve as soon as our food runs out,' Cogan said. 'And without trade we will soon be bankrupt.' He looked to Whiting and Johnson for approval and continued. 'Gentlemen, Mrs Darnell, it's time to do something to end this crisis. I propose we open negotiations with the Dutch. Without Dutch support, Railoo must withdraw.'

'No,' Ynessa snapped. She couldn't let Cogan surrender Seringa and his family. In a week Darnell would be back with Bharatya's troops and the English would be able to break out of Madera. She looked directly at Cogan and said, 'By rushing to negotiate at the first glimpse of their cannon, we will let the Dutch know we are cowards.'

Cogan flushed. 'Madam, how dare –'

'We will get better terms if we let the Dutch experience the hardships and difficulties of a siege for a while.'

'Right, Mrs Darnell,' Ravi said. 'Let's show 'em we're not the kind of English who run at the first whiff of powder.'

'Besides,' Saldhana said, 'won't Mr Darnell be back in a week with more English soldiers?'

'Or Portuguese,' Ynessa said. Darnell had not wanted Cogan or the council to know the details of his mission. Apart from Ravi, everyone believed he was raising mercenaries in San Thome and finding whatever soldiers he could from the English factories in Kokinada.

'Darnell won't be back in a week,' Cogan scoffed. 'And as few of our factories have troops to spare, he won't bring many English soldiers with him.'

'Why don't we see what he returns with?' Ravi asked.

'There's no point in delaying, Mr Winter. The sooner we get a settlement, the sooner we can return to business and start recovering the profits we have lost. After all, that's why we're here, isn't it? To make profits for ourselves and the Company.'

'Hear, hear,' Johnson and Whiting said.

'I think we should wait,' Ynessa said. 'We aren't going to lose much in a week, and you will only increase your losses if you negotiate from a position of weakness.'

'We could at least commence the negotiations,' Johnson said. His brow was reddening from the sun and he dabbed at it with a kerchief. 'Then if Mr Darnell's return changes things, we can alter our negotiating position.'

Ynessa knew that once they began negotiating, the opportunity to drive the Dutch from Vaidya would be lost. 'No negotiations yet,' she said.

Cogan looked at Whiting and Johnson and said, 'Let's vote. Who supports immediate negotiations?' Johnson and Whiting raised their hands. 'That makes three of us.'

Ynessa saw Ravi raise his hand against and said, 'And three of us. I hold my husband's proxy.'

Cogan glowered and started to say something, then turned to Saldhana. 'I suppose it all depends on you,' he said. 'Think carefully, senhor, because what you decide could make the difference between life and death for all of us.'

Saldhana frowned and pressed his eyebrows together. A scrap of breeze teased his grey locks. He licked his lips and looked from Cogan to Ynessa and back again.

Ynessa found his nervousness contagious and felt a tightening in her throat. Come on, she thought, make up your mind. Remember Cogan's talking about a deal with the Dutch. You know as well as I do, if he makes such a deal we're finished.

Saldhana cleared his throat. 'When will the siege be over?' he asked. He looked at Ynessa and shrugged. 'I must know. My business here is all stopped. Each day I am losing money.'

'So are we all, senhor,' Ynessa said, tersely.

'I think we should stop losing money and get on with our businesses,' Saldhana said.

'You should remember you are Portuguese, senhor,' Ynessa snapped. 'You should not be approving negotiations with those who took Malacca.' She shrugged. 'Of course, if money is worth more than patriotism –'

Cogan cried, 'Mrs Darnell, this is unfair!'

'No,' Saldhana said, and smiled. 'Donna Darnell is quite right. We will not negotiate with the Dutch. I vote against.'

Cogan's face darkened. 'You'll be sorry,' he ground out. 'All of you will be sorry when the food runs out and the fever runs its course.'

Chapter Thirty-Two

Darnell and Arjuna looked up the steep, stony trail and reined in their mounts. The horses' flanks were heaving. The air was thinner here, which made the horses tire more easily, and they were high enough for the winds to make the short, hot, searing rays of the sun feel deceptively cool. On the small plateau ahead of them was the village of Axoor, a collection of wattle-and-daub huts and white brick houses petrified by the afternoon heat.

Beyond the village, to the right, and separated from it by a narrow trail and paddy-fields was a muddy, white-walled enclosure which rose out of a platform of rock just below the summit: the ancient hill fort of Hosur. Dome-shaped, patched together in its lower reaches by trees, shrubs and bare earth, it was topped by a cap of solid rock. Winding up its side were narrow ribbons of brick wall, punctuated with guard-houses, bastions and block-houses. Some of the wall screened a mixture of uneven steps and narrow, stony paths that led to the summit.

Darnell swayed wearily in the saddle; beside him, little Arjuna clung tightly on to his pommel. Their journey was nearly over. Darnell looked at the fort and allowed his eye to run along the walls, scaling the hill. At the bottom was a block-house standing across a pathway that was the only means of access to the fort. As he looked he saw two men in the crimson and marigold uniforms of Railoo's army walk quickly across the trail between the buildings.

His heart skipped a beat. What was Railoo's army doing here? Were they a routine patrol, or had they been sent to apprehend him and Arjuna? In any case, how could he get past them? He kept staring at the block-house, and when after five minutes nothing moved, turned his attention to the village.

It was mid-afternoon, and the village drowsed in the heat. It stood on one of a series of little plateaux that characterized the mountain, a cluster of brick-built houses with thatched roofs set well apart from each other. It would attract too much attention to ride in; perhaps he should walk in and see if Railoo's army was in occupation of the village, find out what they were doing in Hosur. It would be better if he went alone, Darnell decided. But he couldn't leave Arjuna on his own, so they tethered their horses in the forest and walked together to the village, keeping to the edge of the trail.

The village was small, a few shops and dwelling-houses, a blacksmith's and a provision store with a thatched awning outside its front door. Each building was set well apart from its neighbour along a dusty stripe of earth which through usage had become a street. At the far end of the village was a small temple, its thin *gopuram* clearly visible over the low buildings.

The street was empty, the houses and shops shuttered. A dog followed them hopefully, then wandered into the shade of a veranda. A man was seated in the half-dark of the provision store. Darnell led Arjuna in. The store was crowded. Sacks of grain and flour were piled high against the walls mixed with open boxes of rice and condiments and jars of pickle. The place smelled strongly of dried fish, coriander and turmeric. The man eyed them suspiciously. He was bare-bodied, about Darnell's age, with shoulder-length, curly hair and a heavy moustache. 'Who are you and what do you want?' he asked, belligerently.

'We're travellers,' Darnell said. 'We'd like to buy some food and *cha*.'

The man rose and came round the counter to them. As he rose, Darnell saw that his right arm had been cut off below the elbow. He looked carefully at Arjuna and then at Darnell. 'The boy is your son?'

Darnell felt a tremor of uncertainty. There was something threatening about the man. 'Yes.'

'And you're coming from?'

It was best to leave the store and find someone else to ask about Railoo's soldiers. 'Otucotah,' Darnell said, taking a step back as the man moved up to him.

'Where are you going?'

'To Kandecheri, across the mountain. I'm going to leave the child with his mother's people. My wife died two months ago, and there's no one to bring him up.'

'How did your wife die?' The man moved away, looking speculatively at the sacks behind Darnell. He reached behind the counter and picked up a large knife, as if to open one of the sacks.

'A fever,' Darnell said. 'She was ill for three days and –'

Suddenly the man's stump hit Darnell in the throat. His shoulder cannoned into Darnell and threw him against the sacks. Pinning Darnell to the sacks with the weight of his body, he pressed the cutting edge of the knife against Darnell's throat.

Darnell couldn't reach the knife in his boot. Choking, he said, 'If it's money you want –'

'Is the boy your son?' the man hissed.

'Yes.'

Arjuna had rushed up to them; he was shouting and trying to grab the man about the waist. The man shoved the boy away with a twist of the hips. 'Quickly! Is he your son?' he asked again.

'What's it to do with you?' Then Darnell saw the amulet tied with a sacred thread on the man's upper arm, a replica of the amulets both Seringa and Arjuna wore. 'Why do you wear the same amulet?' he asked quietly.

The man stepped back, holding the knife in front of him, moving on the balls of his feet, ready to spring. 'Who are you?' he asked. 'What are you doing with this boy?' Turning quickly he asked, 'Son, in the name of Shiva, is this your real father?'

Arjuna paused. He looked confusedly from the man to Darnell and back again. Then, in a clear, piping voice he said, 'No.'

The man whirled on Darnell, his eyes reddened and blazing. Darnell dropped a hand to his boot.

'This man is my father's best friend,' Arjuna said quickly. 'My father entrusted me to him. He is my best friend also.'

Slowly the man lowered his knife, frowning in puzzlement, head swivelling from Arjuna to Darnell.

'Why do you wear the same amulet as Arjuna?' Darnell asked once more.

'Because we are both disciples of Shiva,' Arjuna said. 'Because we are both loyal to Bharatya.'

'You are a disciple of Bharatya's?'

'I trained with him. And fought for him.' The man held up his stump. 'I left the rest of this in the Deccan four years ago.' He looked again at both of them. 'My name is Muttiah. Who are you?'

'Is Bharatya at Hosur?'

'Yes. Who are you?'

'My name is Richard Darnell. I am a friend of this boy's father, Prince Seringa. This is Prince Arjuna.'

Muttiah flung away his knife and went down on his knees before Arjuna. 'Your Highness, I ask forgiveness for thrusting you away. I was seeking to protect you . . .' He stooped forward until his forehead touched the floor.

With surprising assurance, Arjuna moved forward and touched the man on the back of his head. 'Will you take us to Bharatya?' he asked. 'That is why my father sent me with Darnell.'

Muttiah sat up on his haunches and looked from Arjuna to Darnell. 'You are not one of us.'

'He is my father's brother,' Arjuna said sharply. 'And my second father.'

Muttiah touched his forehead to the floor in self-reproach. 'Beg pardon, Highness.'

'Prince Seringa is besieged in our fort in Madera,' Darnell said. 'He's entrusted me with delivering his son to Bharatya.'

Muttiah shook his head. 'Getting to Bharatya is almost impossible. Two days ago, soldiers came from Vaidyapur and took charge of the block-house. They told us they were looking for a man and a boy travelling together and would pay a gold *mohur* to anyone who found them.'

Somehow Railoo had discovered they had escaped, Darnell realized. But it was too late to do anything about it now.

'When you came into my shop, I thought you were the people the soldiers were looking for. Then I saw the boy had an amulet and you hadn't and thought you'd kidnapped the boy and were taking him to the soldiers.' Muttiah got to his feet. 'Forgive me, I forget myself. Both of you must be hungry and very tired. Let me get you some food and *cha*. Then we can talk –'

He stared out of the doorway and beat his forehead. 'By all the Gods!'

They followed his glance. Standing in the middle of the deserted street was Arjuna's pony.

Arjuna darted to the door. Muttiah grabbed him by his tunic. 'No! Highness.' Gesturing to them to remain still he walked to the door and squinted up to the fort.

'You must hide,' he cried, hurrying them to the back of the shop. 'The soldiers have seen the horse and are coming down from the fort.'

Muttiah opened a door at the back of the shop and led them into a room piled high with sacks of grain and condiments. 'Help me,' he said, and started to hump the sacks away from the back wall. Briefly he left them to return with a youth. 'My son, Puran,' he grunted. Quickly the four of them created a space at the back of the sacks in which Darnell could crouch and Arjuna could just about stretch out. 'Get in there,' Muttiah cried, pointing to the opening. 'Puran and I will build a wall of sacks in front of you. Whatever happens, keep still. And for all our sakes, keep silent.'

Darnell and Arjuna crowded into the space and Muttiah and Puran started to pile the sacks back. The space in front of Darnell and Arjuna was growing smaller and narrower and darker with every heave. After a while the sacks obscured everything. The sounds of heaving and Muttiah's muttering stopped. The door to the storeroom was shut and locked. Darnell and Arjuna waited. It was hot and clammy. The rough surface of the sacks itched. Dust irritated their nostrils. There was barely room to move and Darnell found himself getting stiff. Arjuna, exercising great self-discipline, managed to remain virtually motionless. Powerless behind the mounds of sacks, Darnell felt a moment of panic. Had Muttiah put them there to die? Was he going to keep them prisoner and hand them over to Railoo's soldiers? He pushed the thoughts from his mind. Muttiah was a brother and totally devoted to Bharatya and Arjuna.

The hot air and dust seared his chest. He tried to take a deep breath and almost choked. He heard the room door open and the sound of raised voices. Starting upright, he bit back a cry of pain as he hit his head on a sack. He reached cautiously for his knife. He was drenched in sweat. He glimpsed Arjuna's eyes in the half-darkness, wide and unblinking like those of some small animal. He took the boy's hand. It was dry.

'I tell you there's nothing here except grain!' Muttiah's voice was loud and wheedling. 'Why should I hide strangers? What loyalty do I owe to strangers?'

There was the sound of a slap.

Darnell tensed. He drew his knife.

Another voice said, 'Move the sacks,' and there was the sound of another blow followed by Muttiah's piteous wail, 'Don't hit me sir, please don't hit me. Can't you see I have only one hand?'

Darnell and Arjuna pressed themselves back as there was a frantic prodding at the sacks.

'Sir, sir, please,' Muttiah's voice came again. 'You're spilling our grain. We're poor people, sir. It's all we have.'

There was the sound of another slap, followed by more prodding, and finally the tread of feet going away from their hiding place. A voice growled, 'If we find you've been hiding anyone, we'll flay you and your family alive.'

'Yes, sir. No, sir. I wouldn't hide anyone. I promise.'

'We'll be back later with men to move those sacks. And we'd better not find anyone there.'

'You won't, sir. You won't.'

The door shut with a thump. In the ensuing silence, Darnell released a long sigh.

Muttiah returned twenty minutes later with Puran. Quickly, they moved the sacks. As soon as there was a space large enough, Darnell crawled out followed by Arjuna. Darnell was soaked in sweat, his body covered with dust.

'Filthy, arrogant lumps of cow-shit,' Muttiah muttered. 'If I'd had both my hands I could have taken them all.'

'Don't think about it,' Darnell said.

'Gutless sons of whores,' Muttiah grumbled. 'I could still take any two of them with one hand.'

'Where are the soldiers?' Darnell asked. 'Are they coming back?'

'We'll know if they do. But right now, I think they're concentrating on strengthening the guard at the block-house. They found your horse and know you're around here somewhere. They expect you will attempt to climb

Hosur tonight. If they don't find you tonight, they'll search the village more carefully tomorrow.'

'So we must get to Bharatya tonight,' Darnell said.

'That's impossible,' Muttiah said. 'Especially with the boy.'

Darnell stared at Muttiah. 'What do you mean it's impossible?'

'Let me show you.' He took them into the shop. It was the short half-hour of twilight and everything was bathed in grey, translucent light. They stood just inside the doorway and looked at the fort. The blockhouse at the bottom of the hill was full of soldiers. Darnell counted twenty of them.

'They usually have a guard of five,' Muttiah said. 'Tonight they've got everyone guarding that trail. Not even an insect can get through.'

Darnell stared at the block-house. Behind it the wall climbed upwards, screening the pathway of steps up the mountain. Halfway up was a bastion and beside the bastion a series of buildings spread sideways to the right, while the wall wound upwards to the left before disappearing past a series of guard-houses round the side of the hill, and then reappearing higher up and rising straight up to Bharatya's fort. 'There must be another way,' he said slowly. 'You've lived here all your life. You must know some route . . .'

Muttiah stared into the rapidly falling dark. 'As children,' he said, 'we often used to get to the path behind the block-house by climbing the wall.' He pointed to a spot about halfway between the block-house and the bastion, where the wall passed below two overhanging rocks. 'We used to climb over just there. It's easy with a strong rope. There is a spur of rock just outside the wall. You loop your rope over that, haul yourself over and step on to the wall.' He pointed to the area below the rocks, a steep slope covered with jungle at the foot, then scrub, then bare rock. 'We could get up there easily in the dark.'

*   *   *

This time the Madera council met in the committee room and Ynessa kept staring at the chairs, as if she expected Darnell to appear and fill one of them. She missed him terribly, more so since Caddy, Crispin and the children had gone. The house was so empty and, with little to do because of the siege, she had plenty of time to worry. She wondered if Darnell's disguise had been good enough, if little Arjuna hadn't given their deception away, if they had been robbed, if Railoo's troops had somehow found them. It was four days before she could send Naidu to the rendezvous on the beach between Madera and San Thome. She wished with all her heart it was today, and dabbed angrily at her eyes as Cogan took Darnell's place at the head of the table.

There was an atmosphere of weary irritability in the room. The siege had gone on for another week, and because food had continued to be rationed – at the last meeting Eckaerts and Captain Martin had insisted she did not risk sailors or ships with another load of supplies – everyone lacked vitality. The fever had continued to kill . . .

Cogan said, 'We must resolve this situation. We've waited a week, and all that's happened is that we've got weaker, poorer and fewer.'

'Give Darnell a few more days,' Ynessa begged. 'He'll be back and this'll be over.'

'We've already given him a few more days,' Cogan said. 'By the time he comes we'll all be dead of hunger or the fever.' He threw a wry smile at Whiting and Johnson. 'And we'll certainly be bankrupt.'

'I still think we should wait,' Ynessa repeated. She knew she was being obstinate, that the reasonable thing to do was explore a way to end the siege. But negotiating with the Dutch meant accepting the possibility that Darnell might never come back. Negotiating with the Dutch meant defeat. Negotiating with the Dutch meant victory for van Cuyler, the man who had killed her father. She could never agree to that. Never!

Cogan said, 'It would be irresponsible to continue to do nothing. In the past week seven people have died from the fever, and lots of women and children in the Black Town are suffering from an insufficiency of food. We must end this siege. And as we cannot drive Railoo and the Dutch from Madera, we must treat with them.'

'Hear, hear,' Johnson said. 'Well spoken, sir.'

Ynessa stared at the table. Yesterday, Saldhana had died from the fever. Was she responsible for that death? And the deaths of all those others? If she persisted in her obstinacy wouldn't she be responsible for the deaths that would surely follow? Was it realistic to expect everyone to wait and risk their lives in the hope Darnell would return and drive the enemy from Madera? Wasn't that some kind of self-glorification, some kind of pride? But if they negotiated, what would happen to Seringa and Sita and little Tikka? And to the soldiers who had accompanied Seringa to Madera?

'I insist on a vote now,' Cogan was saying. 'We must open negotiations with the Dutch.'

'Agreed,' both Johnson and Whiting said.

They all turned to her. She had to decide now. She had to face reality. She looked down. 'I agree,' she said. 'Subject to the negotiations being approved by council.'

Cogan glared at her before he said, 'I will arrange to talk to the Dutch as soon as possible.'

They left after a supper of unleavened bread and vegetables in the back room of the shop where no one would see any light. Darnell carried a coil of rope attached to a metal hook, and a *shamshir* Muttiah had given him; Muttiah had a rope ladder and an unusual steel *tabar* with a crescent-shaped blade opposite a sharp pick, and the sixteen-year-old Puran carried brushwood for the signal fire he would light to attract Bharatya's attention. They followed each other in single file in the darkness, along

367

the road Darnell and Arjuna had come that afternoon.

After a short distance, Muttiah led them into the scrub. The scrub soon thickened into forest, and Muttiah passed a hank of rope over his shoulder, so they could keep together. The foliage was thick, and Muttiah hacked at it noisily with his battle-axe. Branches and twigs scraped at them. Creepers twined themselves around their ankles and calves. The darkness was like a heavy curtain and Darnell felt completely lost. The forest was filled with mysterious rustles and surreptitious scurryings. Night birds hooted. Once something, a rabbit or a snake, slipped out from underneath his foot and rushed into the darkness. Darnell thought how much more frightening this must be for Arjuna and stroked the boy's head.

Covered with tiny scratches, and irritated from countless stings, they came out of the jungle and into scrub again, where they could walk more easily. The path climbed sharply. Below them to the left they could see tiny rectangles of light from the block-house. The village was a shadow bordered by rice paddies glistening meagrely in the light of a faint moon. They spread out sideways in a line as they came to the rock, the faint light making it easier to see their footing, but also making them more visible to the soldiers in the block-house.

The climb grew steeper. Each of them slipped in turn. Arjuna bruised his shin but refused to cry. They walked more slowly and more cautiously as they neared the wall. Then the wall was shimmering in front of them and they hurried into the darkness beneath the overhanging rocks.

'Now!' Muttiah whispered, pointing upwards at the spur of rock.

Darnell coiled the rope and threw it. The hook clinked, dragged and caught. Darnell pulled. The rope held. Muttiah grinned at him in the darkness.

He and Puran helped coil the ladder around Darnell.

Darnell tested the rope again, then shinned up it. The scimitar tied to his waist and the pistol beneath his tunic were unbalancing him, but at last he dragged himself over the top of the spur and crouched down. The top of the rock sloped down to within two feet of the wall, and beneath the wall, the path snaked in a series of steps, dark and hidden in shadow. As Muttiah had said, you could step on to the wall from the rock and jump down on to the path.

Releasing the hook, he allowed the rope to fall. He fixed the ladder around the spur and whistled softly, felt a tug on the ladder, then a repeated pulling and swaying as Arjuna came up. Darnell crouched on the spur of rock and kept hold of the ladder, steadying it. Then, as Arjuna's head appeared over the edge, he stood up and stepped off the rock on to the top of the wall.

Arjuna pulled himself up and crouched. The boy was frightened, whether it was of heights, darkness or both, Darnell had no idea. He whistled softly and saw the boy's head turn stiffly.

'Turn round slowly,' Darnell called softly. 'On your hands and knees.' Arjuna hesitated.

Don't go rigid, Darnell urged silently, whatever you do, don't turn into a statue.

'Here,' he whispered. 'I am here. Come.' He held out his hands.

Slowly, agonizingly, Arjuna turned, moving one hand sideways, then one foot, then the other hand, then the other foot, repeating the process until he was crouched facing Darnell.

'Come on now, come down to me. That's it. Easy, one step at a time.'

Arjuna was crouching at the edge of the rock, his face contorted in fear. Tears rolled down his cheeks.

'Stand up, Arjuna. Stand up.' Darnell fought to keep the urgency out of his voice; the longer Arjuna dallied, the greater the chance they would be discovered. Darnell leaned forward to encourage him by touch, but the gap was too wide. Then he saw Muttiah's head rise above the edge of the rock. Unless Arjuna moved they were stuck, unable to go forward or back.

'Arjuna, don't let your father down! The raja of the Vaidyas cannot be afraid of the dark or of heights. Please, now! Stand!'

Arjuna's back arched. With agonizing slowness, his hands touched his knees, and he got on to one knee. He crouched forward, and gradually his legs straightened. He stood teetering on the sloping edge of rock.

'Now step forward, quickly. Hurry.' He couldn't allow Arjuna time to think or time to look at the gap between the rock and the wall. 'Hurry. Muttiah is behind you. Come, step, jump, don't worry, I'll catch you!'

Arjuna took two teetering steps, then with a little cry, jumped.

The strength and length of his leap took Darnell by surprise. He caught the boy, but was nearly knocked over backwards, and struggled momentarily for balance. Then, holding Arjuna tightly to him, he recovered and stood erect, spreading his feet. 'There, you see, it wasn't difficult at all.' He helped Arjuna sit on the wall, his legs dangling over the path. Muttiah appeared, balancing on the edge of rock.

Somewhere below them, a conch blew. A voice shouted, 'I see them! By the rock!' Feet raced up stone steps. Fifteen yards below, Darnell saw five men running between the walls, their swords glinting in the dim light.

To go or not to go? Darnell remembered Arjuna, and knew they'd never make it back to the rock. Grabbing Arjuna with one hand, and the sword with the other, he allowed himself to drop, lifting Arjuna slightly as his feet hit the stone.

'You all right?' he asked the boy.

'Yes.'

Darnell turned Arjuna round. 'Run,' he said. 'Run as hard as you can and tell Bharatya we're here.' He drew the scimitar and saw Muttiah appear on top of the wall. With a savage cry of triumph, Muttiah ran along the wall and launched himself at the onrushing guards.

Muttiah's violent launch had brought the men down in a huddle, his flailing axe striking solidly as he fell. Darnell rushed down the steps, scimitar in his right hand, dagger in his left. The scimitar felt light and nicely balanced. He slashed at one man and drew blood.

Muttiah jumped up, his axe chopping savagely at one of the men, the rising, pointed reverse-end catching another as he lunged. Muttiah broke free of the men and ran. 'Back!' he shouted. 'Up!'

Darnell turned and sprinted up the steps, running as hard as he could for the summit. On the further side of the wall, Puran's signal fire flared. Muttiah caught up with Darnell. 'Those bastards can't fight!' he panted, laughing. 'I got two of them, first time!' Darnell looked over his shoulder. Two soldiers were coming after them, one of them blowing frantically on his conch.

Darnell's legs began to ache and Muttiah's breathing became ragged. The steps had levelled out on to an unmade path not protected by the walls. Darnell stopped and wheeled round. 'Let's take them!' he shouted. Beside him Muttiah crouched, ready to spring.

The soldiers stopped. Muttiah went for the nearest, the one with the conch. The axe chopped into the soldier's arm before he could get his sword up.

The other lunged at Darnell with his *tulwar*. Darnell parried with his dagger and thrust with the scimitar. It caught the soldier in the chest and he gasped and staggered backwards.

Muttiah swung the axe again. The reverse-end embedded itself under the soldier's chin and ripped his jaw off. He leapt after the reeling soldier. Two more savage blows and the man was down.

Darnell closed with his opponent. The dagger darted twice. The soldier's gasps sounded thick and frothy. He fell. Darnell withdrew the dagger. Below them a gaggle of soldiers were stumping determinedly up the steps. Darnell and Muttiah turned and ran for the summit.

They heard the cries of anger as their pursuers reached their fallen comrades. Then they were back within the walls, pounding up the uneven steps, their bodies covered in sweat, their chests heaving. Where was Arjuna, Darnell wondered. They should have caught up with him by now. The sword and the pistol were weighing him down. His legs were heavy and his breathing ragged. Liquid squirts of fire flamed the bottoms of his calves and the fronts of his thighs. He looked up and saw the bastion. They'd only reached halfway.

Arjuna couldn't have travelled any quicker than this, surely? He was only eight and had had a long and wearing day. Darnell waved to Muttiah to stop.

Muttiah doubled over, panting. Over the harsh rasp of their breathing came the sound of their pursuers, a steady, dogged chipping of boots on stone.

'Arjuna,' Darnell gasped. 'We should have caught up with him by now.'

Beside him, Muttiah nodded.

Darnell pointed to the battlements to the right. 'I'll . . . look for . . . him . . . there. You go –' he pointed to the path that curved up the mountain to the left.

Muttiah shook his head. 'Together . . . we go . . . together.'

There was no time for argument. Darnell turned and jogged on to the battlements, surprised at how easily his legs moved over the flat. 'Arjuna!' he shouted. 'Arjuna!'

Muttiah grabbed his arm. They stopped and waited. The

only sound was the steady tramp of their pursuers below.

They ran further along the battlements. Below them Puran's signal fire burned brightly, illuminating the rock by which they had crossed.

'Arjuna!' Muttiah shouted, then to Darnell, 'Perhaps he has gone on up.'

'Impossible! Arjuna! It's Darnell!'

'Darnell!'

The two men looked at each other. It wasn't an echo. The voice came from further along the battlements.

'Stay where you are!' They ran along the battlements and spied a small figure crouching behind a short flight of steps beside one of the boundary walls. 'Come along! This way!'

Taking the boy's hand they ran quickly back, almost lifting him off the ground. The tramp of the soldiers' feet was much louder. They ran back to the spot where the wall divided. Darnell's heart sank at the thought of the long, curving uphill path around the mountain and then straight up to the summit.

'Come with me!' Muttiah dragged Arjuna and ran up the hill. A few yards on he stopped. There was a gate embedded in the wall. He smashed the lock with two blows of his axe and dragged the gate open.

'There,' he said, pointing to the steep flight of steps that ran directly to the summit. 'Go straight up those steps. Don't turn round. Don't stop. Go straight up and tell Bharatya we need him.'

Arjuna paused a moment, looking for Darnell's approval.

'Go,' Darnell said and ruffled his hair. The boy set off at a run.

From almost behind Darnell's shoulder a man's voice cried, 'There they are!'

Darnell turned. There were ten of them, sweating heavily, breathing harshly, swords drawn. Muttiah fell in beside him. There may have been ten soldiers, but the passage was only wide enough for three.

The first three rushed at them, swords extended. Muttiah's axe crashed down on a sword, the vicious reverse-end slicing through cheek and nose.

Darnell parried with his scimitar, pressed his opponent's weapon against the wall. He lunged with the dagger. The dagger went home and the pressure against his weapon stopped. The man fell away, the sword dropping from his lifeless hand.

There were three more of them now, darting, thrusting, hacking. Darnell felt a blade slice through his sleeve. He stepped back and dropped the scimitar, pulling out the pistol. Two men closed on him. Hands grasped his shoulders. A blade sliced his ribs.

He fired.

The first man flopped over backwards. Darnell ground the useless pistol into the face of the second. Picked up the scimitar. Lunged. Three more men. Muttiah swung the axe. It hacked into a shoulder. A man screamed. A sword dropped. The reverse thrust hissed emptily through the air. Darnell had two men confronting him. Thrust, parry, block. He moved backwards, his feet sliding on blood. The men came with him. Muttiah appeared behind one of the men, axe raised. The crescent-shaped blade smashed through sinews and small bones. Blood spattered. Eyes still fluttering, a man fell, his head angled crazily.

Darnell thrust at his distracted opponent. The blade sliced through bone gristle. He closed in with the dagger, once to the throat, once to the chest, knife moving in and out quickly before he stepped back, arms and wrists sticky with sweat and blood.

There were two more men in front of him. He raised his sword. Thrust, parry, sidestep, step back. He wondered about running back, saw a figure loom on top of the wall, turned too late to see it drop down on Muttiah and Muttiah

374

go down. Then he was pinned against the wall by two flashing swords. Out of the corner of his eyes he glimpsed daggers rise and fall, saw Muttiah's axe flail feebly. He must concentrate. Darnell speared one man above the hip, but another filled the gap and thrust at him. The sword went home, high against the left side of his chest. Blood spurted; Darnell felt his arm go heavy. He couldn't thrust the dagger properly. The point of a sword caught him beneath the armpit and he let the dagger go.

He swung a desperate swathe with the scimitar. The men danced back. Then they were at him again, their swords dancing pinpoints of light.

The men were getting murky; even the swords were getting dull. But he couldn't let himself fall. He mustn't go down. A fist slammed into his face. He bounced into the wall. A dagger came at him and he rolled along the wall. He couldn't get his arm up. *He couldn't get his arm up*! The darkness loomed, his legs wavered. He began to slide down the wall.

The swords were coming at him. And men were shouting. And more swords were clashing. Bodies leapt from the top of the wall. Darnell slumped on the steps. The darkness grew heavier. Over the noise and the clashing of swords he heard a voice, 'Dar-nell! Dar-nell!'

Bharatya!

He slumped sideways. He had delivered the boy. He had kept his promise . . . but he wouldn't be going back. Couldn't. He wondered if Crispin would understand . . . and what would happen to Ynessa? Ynessa – Ynessa, I love you . . .

Blackness.

Chapter Thirty-Three

Van Cuyler sat sweltering in Railoo's tent, choked by the fear and anger that rose from his belly. The tent stood in the centre of the island. It was a massive affair comprising audience chamber, workroom and bedroom, each section separated from the other by guards and chintz curtains. Outside, flags fluttered from a central pole; the tent's ropes were decorated with gaily fluttering silk streamers. Inside, the filtered sunlight gave everything a greenish tinge.

At the back of the audience chamber, a makeshift throne had been erected on a raised platform covered with Oriental carpets. Bhagwan Dayal sat on a chair at its foot, flanked by the six empty stools of Railoo's councillors who had returned to the capital. Railoo sat imperiously above Dayal, shimmering in pale grey, the marigold and crimson umbrella of state open over his head. Two bearers stood behind Railoo, patiently waving fans. Railoo was the only person who had bearers with fans. Everyone else sweated.

Van Cuyler watched the great beads of sweat roll down Andrew Cogan's temples and cheeks as, with shoulders stooped and voice quavering, he asked Railoo to agree to a withdrawal. 'This pointless struggle has gone on long enough,' he brayed. 'The time for peace is now!'

Goddamn, *scheithaus*, craven imbecile. If Cogan agreed a surrender, he was done for. He'd risked censure from Batavia and come here with eighty men and five cannon to secure Madera and Dutch trading rights in Vaidya *and* to seize and destroy Mirza Baig's confession. That confession was a sword over his head. At any time, Darnell and his wife could use it to destroy him – as Ali Baig had

376

been destroyed. As soon as they learned of de Groot's death and realized their complaint had not reached Batavia, they would send the confession direct, inciting Batavia to investigate van Cuyler's activities in Coromandel and the deaths of Rodrigo and de Groot. Van Cuyler felt the sweat stream off his face as he realized what such an investigation would uncover. There was no way van Speult or Uncle Hendrijk could save him then.

He dragged his mind back to Cogan. Somehow he had to stop the Englishman. Cogan was saying, 'As Your Majesty insists, we will hand over Seringa's family and retainers without pre-conditions of any kind.'

By the Cross, he was ruined! He only needed to look at Railoo's ecstatic smile to know that Railoo would agree to Cogan's proposals. He had to stop them, somehow. He looked from Railoo to Dayal and back again. Railoo was eager to get home; the fear and hatred of Seringa which had made him sit outside Madera was diminishing with every passing day.

Dayal was climbing on to the dais to stand beside Railoo. Railoo said, 'We have no quarrel with you English. What you've said is acceptable. Seringa is what we came for.'

Damn, damn, damn! He had to do something, say something. But to interrupt Railoo at any time was dangerous; to raise objections to the ending of the siege suicidal. Van Cuyler shifted in his chair, hoping the movement would catch Railoo's eye.

Cogan said, 'We will enter into a formal undertaking not to interfere with the construction or trade of any Dutch fort anywhere in Vaidya. In return we ask that Your Highness permits us to remain in Madera and ratifies the *firman* granted by Seringa.'

Railoo would surely balk at that. Van Cuyler saw Railoo frown and Dayal bend forward. Van Cuyler watched the two men confer, turbans close together like giant turnips. Railoo turned away from Dayal and said, 'We agree.'

Cogan smirked with satisfaction. 'If Your Highness has no objection, we will sign a memorandum setting out details of the exchange and the timing of the withdrawal.'

'Your Excellency!' Van Cuyler had jumped to his feet. He hadn't meant to shout. There was a pale, angry line round Railoo's lips.

'What is it, Dutchman? We have secured peace!'

Van Cuyler wished his breathing would slow, that he had time to bring his voice under control. 'Your Excellency, there is one import –'

'We have decided.' Dayal moved protectively to the front of the dais, and stood looking down, plump feet spread wide apart.

'What about Darnell, Excellency?' van Cuyler cried. 'Without Darnell's approval, any agreement you make with the English is worthless.'

'Enough speech,' Dayal cried, but Raja Railoo was frowning.

'What has Darnell got to do with this?' he demanded, his narrow face lined with suspicion.

Quickly van Cuyler said, 'Your Highness, Darnell built this fort against the orders of Mr Cogan here and his Company. He will treat any agreement he doesn't approve of in the same way. Unless he agrees to the peace, he will attack you as you leave and stop any factories we may try to build in Vaidya.'

His voice still quavering, Cogan said, 'I assure you, Excellency, Darnell will be bound by this agreement. I am here with the full authority of our council –'

'Does Darnell know and approve of all this?' van Cuyler cried, determined not to give Cogan any opportunity of convincing Railoo.

'He doesn't, but I am –'

'So if Darnell returns between now and our departure, he can overrule you and abrogate the agreement?'

'It will be too late for him to do that. Besides, I am

perfectly within my sphere of authority in making this agreement.'

'The question is not whether you are acting properly, but whether you can control Darnell.' Van Cuyler turned back to Railoo. 'With the greatest respect, Your Highness, if we are going to enter into an agreement with the English, then it must be with Darnell. Darnell is the agent of this fort, not Cogan.'

'But I am acting with proper authority.' Cogan was red-faced now and flustered. 'In any case, Darnell's approval doesn't matter. Darnell isn't here, and if we have the papers settled by this evening, we can deliver Seringa and his people by dawn tomorrow.'

'A very practical solution,' Dayal said.

Fool, van Cuyler shrieked silently as Railoo smiled and nodded. Through stupidity and *karma*, Cogan had won. There was, however – he turned to Cogan, heart fluttering. 'Where is Darnell?' he asked, trying to keep his voice steady.

'Darnell – well –'

'Surely you must know?'

'Well, yes, Darnell is currently in Kokinada, trying to raise English troops to relieve Madera.'

Excitement surged through van Cuyler. Cogan didn't know where Darnell was! 'Darnell is not in Kokinada,' van Cuyler announced solemnly. He turned to Railoo and bowed. 'As His Excellency and all of us here know, Darnell is somewhere between here and Hosur, delivering Prince Seringa's eldest son to Bharatya.'

'What do you mean . . . ?' Cogan paled at the authority in van Cuyler's voice and the knowing looks in the faces of Railoo and his courtiers. Now that he thought of it, he hadn't seen Seringa's eldest boy for a while. But Ravi Winter and Ynessa had said . . . *Lying bitch!* he thought, and licked lips which had gone suddenly dry.

'And who knows if Darnell is coming back alone?' van

Cuyler asked. 'Who knows if he isn't returning with Bharatya's whole army? Who knows if you, Mr Cogan, aren't part of an elaborate scheme to make us drop our defences and enable Darnell and Bharatya to defeat us?'

Railoo's face darkened in anger.

'No – no. I swear I'm telling you the truth. Darnell left to raise – at least that's what I was told by his wife.'

'By his wife!' He shook his head in amazement. 'Don't you realize Darnell's wife is a party to whatever Darnell is doing? We know you mean well, Mr Cogan, but if Darnell returns with Bharatya's army, do you think he'll give a tinker's curse for what you have agreed? I'll tell you what Darnell will do. He will use your cannon and Bharatya's troops to destroy Raja Railoo's army. Then he will hang you for treason.' His heart surged as Dayal backed to the throne and whispered urgently to Railoo. Raising his voice so it carried to the back of the chamber, van Cuyler said, 'Now do you see why I say that, unless you have Darnell's approval, anything you agree here is meaningless?'

Cogan looked about him wildly. It was true he had no control over Darnell and could do nothing to prevent him attacking Railoo and the Dutch. 'No,' he said, 'no. Darnell must be bound by our agreement – that's the law – the Company –' He saw Railoo glaring at him malevolently. He had to placate Railoo, he had to make his peace with van Cuyler. He lowered his head. 'I – I suppose you're right, mynheer.' Head still lowered, he mumbled, 'Your Highness, I apologize. It seems I was misled.'

Railoo stared at him for a long while. Then he spat. 'There will be no peace,' he said, and stalked from the throne. Dayal followed him.

Van Cuyler watched them go, relief burning his chest. Cogan waited beside him with lowered head, hands dangling by his sides. 'Don't blame yourself, mynheer,' van Cuyler said softly. 'It wasn't your fault. You couldn't be expected to know what Darnell and his wife were planning.' He put an arm around Cogan's shoulder and led him back to his stool.

'No,' Cogan said. He shook his head in despair. 'What a shame. We could have had this settled by tonight.'

'You will never settle anything as long as Darnell is in charge,' van Cuyler said. 'Darnell will not surrender. Neither he nor his wife will give up their friend, Seringa. It is a shame, mynheer, that so many of us must die because of one man's ambition, greed and obduracy. That one man should make us all lose everything.'

Cogan looked up into van Cuyler's face. 'What exactly do you mean?'

'I mean that as long as Darnell is agent of Madera, there cannot be peace. Not now and not in the future, not between us and the English, or between the English and Railoo. Whatever you and your council decide, Darnell will fight to put Seringa on the throne of Vaidya. That is the only way he can become ruler of Vaidya himself. That is the only way he can become a true lord!'

Cogan gasped. He hadn't thought of that. He'd known Darnell's ambition was vast, but ruling Vaidya . . . In Java Darnell had merely been rich; as effective ruler of Vaidya he would have power too. Even the Company would be subject to him. If Darnell put Seringa on the throne, he would be the most powerful Englishman in all of India! 'What are you suggesting?' Cogan asked again. 'That we get rid of Darnell?' He paused, eyes desperately searching van Cuyler's face.

'I am telling you, mynheer, that if you want a lasting peace with Raja Railoo and the Dutch, that if you want to be agent of Madera, you must neutralize Darnell and his wife.'

'Neutralize?' Cogan asked, his shoulders straightening. 'How?'

Van Cuyler drew a stool up to Cogan and told him.

Chapter Thirty-Four

Ynessa paused on the steps of the factory house to allow her eyes to adjust to the darkness. After the brightness of the council offices she felt blind. Cogan had called a surprisingly late meeting of council and, as she walked carefully to the gate, she wondered why. True, Cogan had spent most of the day with Railoo and the Dutch, but he'd returned at dusk and could have called the meeting then. In any case, what he'd had to report could have waited till the next day. It was just Cogan being self-important, she thought, acknowledging the guard's salute with a wave.

'Are you all right to walk home, ma'am?'

'Yes, I'm fine.' Ravi too had wanted to walk her home, but home was only two hundred yards away, and who would dare to harm or rob her in a besieged fort? She walked round the dim gleam of a puddle on to the street. Her eyes were used to the dark now. She was seeing like a cat and would enjoy the walk. It was the coolest time of the day, and the quietest.

She hurried down the middle of the street, thinking about what Cogan had reported. The negotiations with Railoo and the Dutch had gone well and everything had been agreed, except the handover of Seringa and his party. Railoo still wanted everyone; Cogan and the Dutch were trying to persuade him that Seringa was enough.

'We cannot deliver Seringa to be treated the way Ghosh was,' Ynessa had said, and had suggested that instead Seringa should cede everything he owned and agree to remain on English territory for the rest of his life. To her surprise, Cogan had accepted that without argument, promising to

382

place it before Railoo and the Dutch the next day.

Her thoughts turned to Darnell. He was a week late and, two days ago, Naidu had stopped visiting the rendezvous. She must persuade Naidu to go again tomorrow night, she decided. She hoped Darnell wasn't hurt, wasn't ill . . .

The fort was quiet, all the houses shut fast against the night. Somewhere cats yowled. As she turned down St George Street, a cart emerged from the square and followed her down the street. She was glad of its friendly creaking and the rhythmic jingle of its bells.

The cart drew alongside. It was one of the larger type of vehicle, drawn by two heavy-shouldered bullocks. It had a curved roof made of a dense thatch with pointed overhangs at the front and rear. She wondered where it was going at this time of the night, and saw that its driver was fair enough to be a European. It drew past, forcing her to the side of the road against the wall of a compound; she noticed one of its lanterns was out. She was about to call to the carter when she heard a sound behind her and turned.

Two men were standing behind her, hands outstretched. She turned quickly back, confused and suddenly scared, but two more men blocked her exit in front of the cart.

She couldn't run forward or back. She cursed herself for not bringing the stiletto, but the fort had been closed for weeks and there was nowhere for a thief to run. 'What do you want?' she called, walking towards the men at the front of the cart. They were standing side by side, dressed in black, their faces masked.

'I'm not carrying much money,' she cried. 'But you're welcome to what I have.'

The men behind caught up to her. Hands seized her shoulders. A palm closed around her mouth. She struggled and kicked backwards. The men in front rushed forward too, grabbing her legs and lifting her into the air. She kicked again, but the men held firm. A rope was thrown around her knees.

What were they doing? She twisted her head, trying to tear her mouth free, twisted her body like a landed fish. She felt her knees brought together and bound, a cloth being pulled over her face. With her knees bound, her struggles were useless. Swiftly her hands were bound too, and another rope fastened her hands to her body. Silent and helpless, she was lifted into the cart and put down on the floor. The men climbed in and the cart turned back towards the factory square.

She fought the instant panic. This was ridiculous. Why would anyone kidnap her? As head of da Soares someone might want to hold her to ransom. But in the middle of a besieged fort? Even a lunatic would have realized it would be impossible to get out or hide her within Madera.

The cart moved round the square. They seemed to be heading towards the gates, but they were closed, and the guards would examine a cart leaving the fort.

She held her breath as the cart stopped before the gate and she heard the measured tramp of a soldier's boots. There was a brief, indistinct exchange and the cart was moving again. Fool, she mumbled into her gag; stupid, careless, imbecile of a guard. Moments afterwards they were rattling across the Land Bridge on to the Kokinada Road.

Ten minutes later the cart stopped. She was carried from the cart into a tent. They rolled her on to the floor and she looked up into the face of a big, bearded man with a dent in his skull. 'Good evening, Mrs Darnell,' he said, speaking with a lisp that, because of his size, sounded sinister. 'It is good to meet you after all this time. I am Karel van Cuyler. As soon as I have settled matters with your husband and the English, you will be free to go.'

*   *   *

Darnell dismounted and led the horse to the edge of the grove to where the palms thinned out by the beach. Though it was night and cool, his body was covered with a fine patina of sweat and his clothes stiff and grainy with sweat and dust. He'd been riding steadily for five days, at first with Bharatya's troops, but since noon yesterday, ahead of them, alone. He had to get to Madera and arrange for a cannonade to soften up Railoo's army before Bharatya's troops arrived.

God's bones, he was tired! He found a tree by the beach and sat, leaning his back against it, holding the reins loosely in one hand. His body hadn't had time to recover from the fight with Railoo's soldiers. The right side of his forehead was still livid and though – because of the marvellous potions Bharatya had administered – the stab wound below his ribs was already scabbed over, it still hurt to breathe deeply or move quickly. After riding all day, he felt weak.

He rubbed his eyes, scolding himself. This was not the time to think of weakness. He had to get back to Madera, organize the cannonade and a supporting attack from within the fort. He had to help Bharatya and Seringa get rid of Railoo once and for all and secure Vaidya for the English.

He peered into the darkness. A quarter-moon illuminated a heaving silver-black sea, fringed with a dark strand of beach. He strained his eyes, looking for the figure of a man, for the low, black silhouette of a boat in the water. He saw nothing. Naidu hadn't come, or had come and gone. Darnell knew his journey had taken longer than they'd anticipated and he was hopelessly late.

He had a fleeting moment of worry as he wondered if Naidu had been prevented from coming because the fort had surrendered, then told himself that was not possible. Railoo's men did not have the force, and the da Soares ships would have kept the fort supplied. He looked again at the cove. Nothing in the water, nothing and no one on the beach. He got to his feet and stretched. Then, keeping to the shelter of the trees, began to make his way along the edge of the beach towards Madera.

Ynessa stared at van Cuyler, the hatred welling like blood from a wound. Her insides wrenched, her wrists and knees writhed against the bonds.

'It's no use, Mrs Darnell,' van Cuyler said with that sinister lisp. 'You're tied as tight as a chicken on its way to market.' He was watching her with a cold amusement that only increased her fury.

'Bastard!' she mumbled into the gag. His expression didn't change and she realized her struggles were only amusing him. She forced herself to stop and stared angrily at him, pulse pounding in her ears. She told herself she had to control her temper. There was nothing she could do to hurt van Cuyler now. She had to be calm and collected and then when she had a chance . . .

Van Cuyler ordered the soldiers to free her. She sat up, massaging her mouth and wrists, feeling the blood tingling through to her fingers. She made herself look carefully round the tent. Knowledge of her surroundings would be essential to her escape. The tent's interior was spartan, divided by a green canvas sheet into work and sleep areas. They were in the work area, which was simply furnished with a table and three folding chairs on a groundsheet covered with flecks of parched grass. The tent flap was open. In the circle of light beyond it were the boots and muskets of sentries.

'You're in the middle of an army camp, Mrs Darnell,' van Cuyler said. 'It would be foolish to even think of escaping.' He pointed through the flap. 'You may think that Madera is just across the road and only a quarter of an hour away. But between you and Madera, there are over a hundred soldiers.' He paused, his face twisting in a malicious grin. 'Men, who haven't been near a woman in weeks.

386

Men who right now would be prepared to kill for a bit of comely flesh.' He paused again, his eyes studying her. 'Or even stand in line for an hour . . .'

Despite herself Ynessa shuddered. There was a casual matter-of-factness in van Cuyler's tone that convinced her he was not bluffing. Ignoring his outstretched hand, she rolled on to her side then, bracing herself on all fours, stood up. Her legs trembled and she staggered. Van Cuyler caught her shoulder but she steadied herself and pushed his hand away. 'Why have you brought me here?' she demanded, walking unsteadily to a chair.

Van Cuyler followed her and sat across the table from her, leaning forward so that only one side of his face was illuminated by the lantern on the table. The discongruence made him look even more malicious and sinister. He said, 'With you out of the way, we'll secure peace.'

Ynessa swallowed to ease the dryness in her mouth and the fear that twisted her belly. She said, 'I have agreed to the peace. Your bringing me here by force will only hinder it.'

Van Cuyler clicked his tongue. 'Andrew Cogan has been very reasonable, so far.'

'Cowardly, you mean.' Anger flared through her as she realized Cogan was in league with van Cuyler, that Cogan wanted peace at any price and had arranged her abduction so he could get it.

'Reasonable,' van Cuyler repeated, and added, 'By noon today we will have settled the terms for ending the siege and be on our way out of Madera.'

So soon, she thought, the shortness of time making her feel desperate. 'I've agreed to the peace,' she repeated, thinking that if she were back in Madera she would find a way to prevent Seringa being surrendered. 'I promise I won't do anything to delay it.'

'There's nothing you can do,' he said and glared at her, the eyes small and reddened, a pulse beating beneath the dent in his skull. His voice became guttural, urgent. 'I want Mirza Baig's confession,' he said. 'I want it now.'

'Goddamn it, no!' Ynessa felt the anger again, raw and stinging. She'd never give van Cuyler the confession. That would resolve nothing and deprive her of her sole means of bringing him to justice.

'Don't fool with me, woman. Because of you and that confession I've had to kill de Groot. Because of that confession, Ali Baig is no longer Naik of Caliatoor and the nizam of Kokinada wants to expel me from Kokinada. Give me that confession!'

He'd killed de Groot. His words echoed in her ears, cold and terrifying. No wonder the confession had never reached Batavia. What was she to do? He'd killed before and wouldn't hesitate to kill her. She was trapped . . . She forced herself to think calmly. He needed the confession and, until he got it, he needed her. 'I don't have the confession,' she said. 'It is in San Thome.' Improvising quickly, she added, 'I've left it with the captain-general, who will return it only to me.'

There was a white flash and an explosion that sent her flying off the chair. She stared at van Cuyler jangle-eyed, her head ringing, her elbows smarting from her fall. Van Cuyler was standing over her, twisting a supple, elephant-skin rod between massive fists. 'Lie again,' he said hoarsely, 'and I'll flay your back open.'

Ynessa cowered. Jesus, Mary, Joseph help me, she prayed as she dragged herself on to all fours.

Boots vibrated along the groundsheet. Buckles and spurs jangled above her head. 'Mynheer Governor,' a voice cried out in Dutch, 'the raja's chief minister and army commander are here and want to see you at once.'

She heard van Cuyler's feet shuffle as he hesitated. Then his hand grasped her roughly by the back of her neck and dragged her upright. 'Show them in,' he said, pushing her towards the green canvas curtain. 'Get in and stay there,' he said gruffly to her. 'Railoo's people won't help you, so don't make a scene.' He pulled the sheet aside and shoved her into a dark, sloping corner of the tent. 'And don't try to escape.' He pulled the curtain down behind her, leaving her in semi-darkness.

Ynessa peered through the gloom, making out the shape of a narrow bed, the shadowy outline of a washstand and a jug of water and a large trunk. The area was dank with trapped air and the acrid odour of night sweat. She stood trembling, clenching and unclenching her fists. Oh God, what was she to do? She had to get back to Madera and warn Ravi. She had to save Seringa.

A high-pitched, whining voice carried from the work area: 'Mynheer van Cuyler, our scouts report that Bharatya's troops are only an hour away.'

Another deeper voice said, 'Darnell is with them and Bharatya has been joined by two companies of Marathas. He has nearly a thousand men.'

Ynessa's heart cartwheeled with joy. Darnell was coming back! Bharatya's troops and the English were about to attack Railoo and the Dutch. Her ordeal would soon be over.

'*Gott im Himmel!*' Van Cuyler sounded angry and surprised.

'Raja Railoo says you must attack the English now with your cannon, or have them make peace!'

Ynessa crept to the curtain and peered round its edge. Railoo's chief minister was speaking. The army commander beside him had a thick, grey-flecked beard held in place by a net attached to his turban. He whined, 'You must talk to the English now, Mynheer van Cuyler. You must stop them from using their cannon.'

Van Cuyler said, 'Don't worry, my friends. The English won't support Bharatya.'

'How can you say that?' The army commander's whine

was even more high-pitched. 'Darnell and Bharatya are both opposed to Railoo.'

Van Cuyler leaned across the table. 'If the English do not support Bharatya, can you defeat him?' He looked into the face of the army commander.

'We have more men than Bharatya,' the army commander said cautiously. 'But Bharatya's men and the Marathas are more experienced.'

As if making up his mind, van Cuyler said, 'Go and tell His Excellency he will have Bharatya's surrender by noon.'

'We must have certainty,' Dayal murmured. 'His Excellency is contemplating abandoning the siege.'

'He mustn't do that.' Van Cuyler sounded alarmed. Soothingly he added, 'Tell His Excellency I have something that Darnell will do anything to get. I promise you he will not only surrender Seringa and abandon Bharatya, he will also give up Madera!'

Ynessa retreated into the bedroom. Van Cuyler was going to use her to stop Darnell attacking Railoo. She ran to the space beside the washstand and pushed her fingers between the ground and the bottom of the tent. As she'd expected, the ground was soft from waste water. Her fingers gouged the earth and curled round the thick seam of the tent's edge. The rough fabric gave a good grip. She squatted down and heaved but the canvas hardly budged.

Fear lent her strength, but it was no use. The tent was pegged too firmly into the ground. Sweet God, she had to get out! She looked desperately for some implement. Raised voices came from the work area; they were still arguing but she didn't think it would last much longer.

She darted to the trunk and knelt by it, running her hands frantically along the sides, trying to lift its lid. No use. The trunk was locked, its lid firm and flush with the body. She went to the bed. Maybe if she could unscrew a leg she could burst the taut canvas. She knelt and groped.

Her fingers ran along the groundsheet and stopped. Her hand closed round a sheathed knife.

Heart beating rapidly, she pulled it out from under the bed and held it up. A cross-shaped hilt protruded from a leather scabbard. She drew it. Double-edged and tapering, the blade gleamed dully in the gloom. Almost bursting with excitement she strode up to the taut canvas and slashed it.

The canvas parted with a harsh, tearing sound. A whisper of breeze flitted through the gap. Behind her, the men were still arguing. She put her head through the gap.

The space in front of her was covered with sleeping bodies, small tents and the embers of scattered fires. Madera was to her right and van Cuyler's tent faced it. She recalled the north end of the garden hadn't been cultivated and was directly in front of her. If she could get there, she could slip into the river beyond the garden and wade or swim round to the Kokinada Road and the Land Bridge. Knife still in hand, she stepped quietly out into the soft pre-dawn light.

To her right, soldiers stood in the light from the open flap of van Cuyler's tent, but they stared straight ahead as she moved quietly away from the tent, walking quickly along the roughened grass. Her heart was beating uncomfortably fast and she kept her eyes fixed firmly in front of her. There was a clump of trees ahead; once there she'd be hidden from view. She wasn't conspicuous, she told herself. There were other people walking around the camp and dressed in pantaloons and boots. She could, in that light, be taken for just another restless soldier. She moved to the left to skirt a camp fire and heard a rustle behind her.

A man was walking a few feet away from her, looking at her. 'Hey, hey,' he hissed, clicking his fingers. 'Woman, come here.'

She ignored him, hurrying on.

'Hey, hey, woman!' It was another voice, behind her and to her left.

She turned, extending the knife in front of her. There were two of them, closing up to her. 'Come any closer,' she hissed, 'and I'll cut you.'

'Come on! If you put out for him, you can put out for us, right. Don't worry, we'll pay you.'

'Get away.' She had to walk sideways now, looking at the men, turning her head from side to side to see where she was going.

The first one raised his voice slightly. 'Come on, whore, do it with us and it'll be only two. You make a fuss and we'll wake the whole camp.'

'Leave me alone.' Ynessa felt the panic mounting within her. The men were close enough now that she could see the gleam of their eyes and teeth.

'We'll give you half a florin!' It was another voice. Two more men loomed out of the half-darkness to her right.

Suddenly the camp seemed to be full of moving figures. Panic filled her. She turned and ran. Once she got beyond the trees she'd be safe. She swerved round a sleeping figure, hearing boots thump on the grass behind her, the hurried breathing of men. She tightened her grip on the knife, trying to recall the layout of the garden. The trees, another open space, more trees, then the wild land and the river. She had nearly half a mile to go. It was hopeless. Someone grabbed her shoulders from behind. A knee jammed into her spine, throwing her into the air. 'My God,' she gasped, as the knife fell from her nerveless fingers. Then they were all over her, hands pawing at her breasts and shoulders, trying to seize her flailing legs.

'No!' she screamed. 'Let me go! Let me go!'

'Shut up whore! You do it for one, you do it for all.'

Her hands were grasped and raised above her head. Her blouse tore. Their bodies closed on her, filling her nostrils with the odour of stale sweat. Hands pulled at her breeches, closed around her mouth. They were pushing her to the ground, tearing her hands away from her body. 'No!' she screamed.

'Stop it, you fornicatin' bastards!' Van Cuyler's shout was accompanied by the swish and thwack of his *sjambok* smashing into flesh. Boots skidded and twisted on the grass as the men holding her tried to avoid the new assault. 'Get away from her, you muck-fickin' bastards! That's an order!'

The hands holding her were abruptly loosed. She rolled and scrambled to her feet and, as her attackers ran off into the darkness, van Cuyler grabbed her. 'I warned you, woman,' he said savagely, and slapped her open-handed across the face. 'They can have you later,' he sneered contemptuously, 'but for now I have other uses for you.'

Forty minutes later, Karel van Cuyler pounded the butt of his pistol on Madera's iron-banded Choultry Gate. Though he'd concealed it well, he was devastated by the news Railoo's people had brought. He hadn't expected Bharatya for another day, and now there was no time to turn his cannon and cover the route of Bharatya's advance. Worse, his guns were now vulnerable to the cannonade Darnell would undoubtedly order in support of Bharatya's attack. The Marathas too worried him. They were fierce warriors and with their support, Bharatya's combat-hardened veterans would decimate Railoo's ill-trained forces. Which meant that his plan to use Ynessa Darnell as a bargaining tool wouldn't work. With Bharatya's victory almost a certainty, Darnell would never honour any agreement he made over Ynessa.

Preceded by a creaking of bolts, Cogan came out of the fort. He looked about him nervously and spoke in a strained whisper. 'What's happened? Why have you come at this time?'

Van Cuyler said, 'Darnell is on his way here with Bharatya's army and two companies of Marathas. There's over a thousand of them and they will be here by dawn.'

Cogan swallowed noisily. 'You'll use Ynessa as a –'

'It means the end for Railoo and for us,' van Cuyler said. 'With your cannon, Bharatya's forces and the Marathas, Railoo is done for and without Railoo's soldiers, my people don't have a chance. By noon today, Darnell will be the most powerful man in Vaidya.' Van Cuyler shrugged. 'Perhaps even the most powerful man in India.'

He had to stop that, Cogan thought. In Java Darnell had been merely rich. Now he would have power one could only dream of. The entire Company would be beholden to Darnell. Darnell could have whatever he wanted: the agency of all Coromandel, the presidency, a directorship, not to mention whatever Seringa granted him for putting him on the throne of Vaidya. 'That is too much power for one man. Darnell must be stopped.'

'And you must do it. You must kill Darnell and become agent of Madera. Then you must join with Railoo, surrender Seringa and turn the English cannon on Bharatya!'

'I can't,' Cogan said, his voice trembling. 'I've never killed anybody before. If I tried to kill Darnell I'd fail.'

'If you don't kill Darnell and become agent of Madera, we're finished.'

Cogan looked down at his boots. 'There may be another way. Without Ynessa Darnell I have a majority on the council. We can vote to support Railoo against Bharatya.'

'Darnell wouldn't give a fig for your votes. He stands to gain too much, and if he takes Vaidya, no one is going to worry if it was done with the right number of votes.' He brought his head close to Cogan's and asked, hoarsely, 'What do you think Darnell will do to the man who betrayed his wife?'

'How will he know?' Cogan shuddered. 'You won't tell him, will you?'

'Of course not. But as Viceroy of Vaidya he must find out.'

Cogan's chin touched his chest. The stocking cap over the back of his head drooped. 'What – what do you want me to do? I'll never be able to kill Darnell.'

'Send word to me the minute Darnell reaches Madera. The password "Prinsen" will get your people in and out of my camp. Then have Darnell meet with me and persuade him to accept my peace offer.'

Cogan looked up. 'Peace offer?'

Van Cuyler smiled and nodded. 'The terms will be generous. But neither Darnell nor his wife will live to see them implemented.' He brought his face close to Cogan's. 'Whatever happens you must get Darnell to meet me. Do you understand?'

Chapter Thirty-Five

There was the faintest lightening of the sky when Darnell limped up to the southern gate of Madera. The journey from the rendezvous had taken him an hour of slipping and sliding along the beach, every sense strained for a sign of Railoo's patrols. His breeches were soaked and his boots filled with a soggy mixture of mud and sand. The barely healed stab-wound in his side throbbed. He drew his knife and pounded on the gate with its haft, the noise ridiculously faint against the crash and thump of the sea.

'Who's there?'

'Richard Darnell. And I don't know the bloody password.'

With a drawing of bolts, a slot in the gate opened. A soldier peered through it, then opened a narrow, man-high door. Darnell stepped through. A second soldier stood behind the first, a musket aimed at Darnell. 'You have a horse, sir? Luggage?'

'No. And put that bloody gun away.' Darnell squelched past them up St George Street. He hesitated momentarily as he came to his darkened bungalow. He wanted to see Ynessa and he wanted a clean pair of boots. He longed for *cha* and food, and would have given the world for a chance to stretch his body and sleep. But he had barely enough time to get Bharatya's support organized. He hurried on.

At the factory house he sent four of the guards to summon the rest of the council, then went into the committee room, sat at the head of the long, baize-covered table, took off his wet boots and socks and had a steward make him some *cha*.

The drink warmed him and its sweetness eased his fatigue. He was halfway through it when Cogan came in wearing a joinet and a stocking cap. Before Darnell could ask where he'd been, Johnson and Whiting appeared, doublets thrown hurriedly over open tunics and pantaloons. Ravi came immediately after them, skin-tight *salva* freshly creased, a scarf round his throat, his breeches neatly fastened.

'What the devil's going on?' Cogan grumbled. There was a tremulousness in his chest that made his voice waver. 'It's gone four in the morning.'

'Bharatya will be here by dawn,' Darnell told them. 'We're going to break out and drive Railoo from Madera.'

Eckaerts and Captain Martin came in, and Darnell repeated what he'd told the others. 'As soon as Bharatya's army is sighted,' he told them, 'I want a cannonade driving Railoo's troops from the garden to the island. The bombardment must be kept up till Bharatya's forces close with Railoo's. Then our men must go out and support Bharatya's.'

'This is wild and reckless, and will cost far too many lives,' Cogan cried. 'For heaven's sake, Richard, there are Dutch troops out there.'

'Dutch troops?' Darnell looked from Cogan to Captain Martin and Eckaerts. 'When did they come? How many are there? How are they armed?'

Eckaerts said, 'There's about a hundred of them, Mr Darnell. They came about two weeks ago, under the command of their governor, Karel van Cuyler. They brought five cannon with them which they've lined up covering the Land and Island Bridges and the beach.'

Darnell's mind reeled. 'How did van Cuyler become Governor of Pulicat?' he asked. 'What's happened to de Groot?'

'It seems he met with an accident,' Ravi said.

Accident or murder, Darnell wondered, thinking

that Ynessa's report on Rodrigo's murder would now never reach Batavia. 'What have the Dutch done?' he asked.

'Not much,' Captain Martin said. 'They've stayed outside and been as good as gold.'

'The only problem's been with their cannon covering the beach,' Eckaerts said. 'Because of that, we haven't been able to get any more supplies from San Thomé.'

'But we got most of the women and children off before the Dutch came,' Ravi said. 'Crispin's with Caddy and her children at Donna de Soares's.'

Darnell felt a flutter of relief at that news. He asked Eckaerts and Captain Martin about the Dutch cannon.

'They're fawcons, sir,' Eckaerts said.

Darnell relaxed. Though the fawcons were small, they each weighed around seven hundred pounds. Van Cuyler wouldn't be able to redeploy them before Bharatya's troops arrived. 'Are the Dutch cannon within range of ours?' he asked.

'Yes,' Captain Martin said.

'I want them destroyed before we begin our cannonade on Railoo.'

'Should be easy,' Eckaerts said. 'The only reason I haven't done it before is we weren't ready to break out.'

'We are now,' Darnell said, and waved them out of the room.

'Honestly, Richard, there's no need for any of this.' Cogan's throat was so tight the words were hardly more than a croak. 'I spent all yesterday with Railoo and the Dutch. We're on the verge of a settlement.'

'On what terms?'

Cogan's eyes slid about the room shiftily. 'We retain Madera and let the Dutch trade in Vaidya. We hand over Seringa but not his family or soldiers.'

'Unacceptable,' Darnell snapped.

'But nothing's final. I'm sure with the threat of Bharatya's approach, we'll find both Railoo and the Dutch very reasonable.'

'There's no time,' Darnell said. 'Bharatya's forces are on their way. They're outnumbered by Railoo's and need the advantage of surprise to succeed.'

'If we secure acceptable terms, we won't require Bharatya's army.' Cogan dragged his eyes round to face Darnell.

Darnell said, 'The only acceptable terms are an unconditional withdrawal beginning now.'

'No!' Cogan had to get Darnell to meet with van Cuyler. 'I say we should talk further. I vote against this premature attack. I vote we should continue negotiations with Railoo and the Dutch.' Cogan jerked his head at Johnson and Whiting. Immediately both of them raised their hands.

Ravi said, 'I'm with Richard, all the way.'

Darnell said, 'That's settled then. With Ynessa's and my vote and my casting vote, we agree to attack Railoo as soon as Bharatya gets here.'

Cogan said, 'Ynessa cannot vote unless she's here.'

'She'll be here in a mom –'

'The vote's been taken, Richard, and the result is a deadlock. Which means we maintain our position. There won't be any attack. Only negotiation.'

'The devil wi' that!' Darnell cried. 'And the devil take your vote! We'll vote again when Ynessa –'

A white-faced soldier burst into the room. 'Mrs Darnell is not in your house, sir,' he cried. 'The servants say she didn't return after the council meeting last night!' The soldier held out a single sheet of paper. 'This was nailed to your front door!'

Darnell took the paper with fingers that had suddenly gone cold. Mouth drying, heart pounding fearfully, he read:

> War will only ruin everyone. In order to bring this wasteful conflict to an end, we have taken Mrs

Darnell who, with her husband, has prevented us achieving peace.

Mrs Darnell will be released unharmed as soon as peace has been agreed.

We stand ready to meet with you at any time and negotiate that peace.

Karel van Cuyler

Darnell felt the blood drain down to his feet and put his hand on the table to steady himself. His breath came in short, sharp gasps. He couldn't lose Ynessa; the thought of her held by van Cuyler filled him with horror. Van Cuyler hated him. Van Cuyler believed Darnell had deliberately injured his wife by leaving them adrift on the *Prinsen*. Van Cuyler wanted revenge. There was nothing van Cuyler wouldn't do to Ynessa, Darnell thought. In fact there was a lot he would do to her simply because of whose wife she was. He flung the note down on the table, oblivious of the hands reaching for it, oblivious of everything except the single, stark fact that van Cuyler had Ynessa!

He had to get her out. There wasn't a moment to lose. He pulled on his wet boots. 'I'm going to have Captain Martin begin that cannonade now,' he announced. 'Then I'm going in with twenty men to bring my wife out – and Karel van Cuyler's head!'

'No!' Cogan and Ravi cried together.

'What the devil's wrong wi' you? I'm not leaving Ynessa with the Dutch a moment longer!' He stamped his heel on the floor to settle his foot in the boot and stood up.

'You're foolishly risking your life and that of twenty men!' Cogan cried. 'You'll never get her out!' He thought, if Darnell succeeded in killing van Cuyler, he was a dead man too.

Darnell pushed past Johnson and Whiting to the door. It was Ravi who rushed ahead of Darnell and stood with his back to the door. 'If yer does this, yer'll lose Ynessa, sure as hair will grow on yer face tomorrer,' he cried.

Darnell stopped in front of Ravi. 'The devil d'you mean, lose? I'm going to get her out of the Dutch camp!'

'Yer can't if yer doesn't know where she is. And whaddyer think the Dutch are goin' to do when you come stormin' in? Give you tea? Or shoot both of you? And then what'll 'appen to Bharatya and 'is flippin' army?'

Ravi was right. He couldn't just storm into the Dutch camp and expect to get Ynessa back. He had to have a plan. He snapped a fist into his palm. 'So how the devil do I get her out?'

'Yer talks,' Ravi said. 'Yer finds out what the Dutch want. And while yer doin' that, yer also finds out where Ynessa's bein' 'eld.' He turned to Cogan. 'Can you fix a meetin' with them Dutch bastards right now, Mr Cogan?'

'Of course I can!'

Darnell whirled on him. 'How can you do that?'

The sweat stood out on Cogan's cheek-bones. He wiped the crust from his mouth with the back of his hand. 'I . . . we . . . in case of emergency, van Cuyler and I arranged a password so we could contact each other. The password is "Prinsen".' He stood looking confusedly at Darnell, then added, 'I'll go to the Dutch camp myself now and tell van Cuyler we want a meeting at the Land Bridge at once.' Pulling his cloak around him, he hurried out.

The bungalow was large and empty without Ynessa and Crispin. Ravi had come back with him from the committee room and Darnell was glad of his company. While Ravi had the servants make *cha* and milk rice, Darnell washed and changed, checked the draw of his knives and reloaded his pistol.

They ate in the dining room by the light of lanterns, the servants scurrying silently in and out, as if at a funeral. Ravi told Darnell again about the committee meeting. 'I offered to walk Ynessa home, but she said she only had to go a few hundred yards and no one would be silly enough to try to rob her in the middle of a siege.'

'The Dutch must've been waiting,' Darnell said. 'How did they get in and out?'

'Using the password agreed with Cogan?'

Yes, van Cuyler would have had no hesitation about betraying Cogan's trust. 'But how could they have known about the meeting?'

'Maybe it was somethin' Cogan let slip. Or maybe they just got lucky. Maybe they would've snatched Ynessa from 'ere if they 'adn't spotted her leavin' the factory house.'

That too was possible. 'Arrest the sentries at the Choultry Gate,' Darnell told Ravi, 'and find out exactly what happened.'

'I'll do that now.' Ravi got to his feet and stood looking down at Darnell. 'What're you goin' to do about van Cuyler?'

'I don't know. I'm still thinking.'

Ravi clasped his shoulder. 'Give van Cuyler whatever yer has to, but get Ynessa back.' He walked to the door. 'I'll see you 'ere after the meeting.'

Darnell took a final swig of *cha*, buckled on his pistol and followed Ravi out. The street outside was still dark. He reckoned he had a little over an hour before Bharatya's troops arrived. From the factory square he could see lights flickering across the parade ground and along the West Wall as the soldiers prepared the cannon. He knew that whatever van Cuyler wanted in exchange for Ynessa would ruin him. Dutch supremacy in Vaidya would prevent Madera from becoming the most profitable fort in Coromandel and make his agency worthless. It would stop him becoming president and director, stop him from creating the Anglo-Indian partnership that was so necessary for both the English and the Indians. It would stop him rebuilding his fortune.

But Ynessa was worth all those things and more. He'd

give up those things a dozen times over just to have her safe with him right now. Goddamn it, he'd already sacrificed too much for his ambition. He wouldn't do it again. He would do whatever he must to save Ynessa.

Without realizing it he'd passed through the Choultry Gate and the Black Town. He started with shock as he saw the soldiers standing in the road opposite the Land Bridge. There were about a dozen of them, a mix of English and Dutchmen carrying lanterns and muskets. Van Cuyler's burly figure loomed above them. The men separated as Darnell approached; the soldiers, except for two lantern carriers, backed away to the edges of the road leaving van Cuyler, framed between Cogan and van Roon, turning to face him.

Hatred flared through Darnell. 'You blathering, scum-sucking lump of dog meat!' Darnell couldn't believe the voice was his. His arm was wrapped round van Cuyler's neck, his fist tight round the gun pressed against van Cuyler's cheek. 'Let her go, goddamn you, or by God I'll pull this trigger!'

Van Cuyler smelt of perfume and his face was red. His eyes swivelled round, their expression veiled but unperturbed. 'You kill me, Darnell,' he lisped throatily, 'and there will be no one to stop one hundred soldiers passing your lady wife one to the other and filling her every opening with their scum.'

The gun trembled against van Cuyler's head, then Darnell pulled it away to stop himself from pulling the trigger. 'Bastard,' he breathed, 'bastard. If she is touched by even one man, I'll kill you and your whole family – yes, even your wife in Holland.'

For a moment van Cuyler's eyes blazed. Then he stood away from Darnell and rubbed his neck. 'We will see,' he lisped, and repeated, 'that we will see. But for now, let us discuss how and on what terms Mrs Darnell will be released.'

Darnell stood back, wiping the sweat from his face with the back of his hand.

Van Cuyler cleared his throat and said, 'First, you will not build any more factories in Vaidya, nor will you interfere with Dutch factories or trade. Second, when Bharatya's soldiers come, you will make them surrender to Railoo. The same also for all Seringa's soldiers now in Madera. Railoo will not punish them if they are loyal to him. Third, Seringa and his immediate family will be banished from Vaidya, or, if you want, they can stay with you.' He paused and looked directly at Darnell. 'Last, you will give me the confession of Mirza Baig. When all this has been done, we will return your wife.'

'A pox on your conditions,' Darnell cried and heard Cogan gasp. He couldn't settle with van Cuyler. He was an Englishman and it was his *duty* to take Vaidya for the English, his *duty* not to lose Vaidya to the Dutch. He could not sacrifice so much to save Ynessa.

But he couldn't leave her to van Cuyler either; that was unthinkable. He had to find a way to save both Ynessa and England. Think! There *had* to be a way. A raid was out of the question. So he had to use stealth and deception. What would van Cuyler do in the same situation? Sign the agreements, of course, and then break them. Well, he would do the same. Agreements made under duress were neither morally nor legally binding. As soon as Ynessa was free, the attack would begin, Railoo would be forced to surrender, and van Cuyler and the Dutch decimated. Yes, that's what he would do. But careful now. If he gave in too easily, or was too eager to accept the terms, van Cuyler would be suspicious. He said, 'I will exchange Mirza Baig's confession for Ynessa.'

Van Cuyler shook his head. 'What about the English monopoly in Vaidya?'

'That stays.'

'The Dutch monopoly stays also.'

404

Cogan said, 'There is a truce between our Companies. Why don't we honour it and develop Vaidya together? Why don't we agree to trade in Vaidya on equal terms?'

That would reward the Dutch for extortion, Darnell thought, and still endanger the Company and England.

Van Cuyler turned and spoke softly with van Roon. Then he turned back to Cogan. 'We would accept this.'

Van Cuyler hadn't really accepted sharing Vaidya, Darnell knew. As soon as Bharatya's forces had surrendered, van Cuyler would prevail on Railoo to abrogate the agreement. But he had to move on from here and get Ynessa out of van Cuyler's hands. 'If I agree,' Darnell asked, 'will you release Ynessa?'

Van Cuyler stared into space, his fingers playing with the *sjambok* at his waist. Then he nodded and said, 'Yes. If Railoo agrees to all this. If we have signed agreements. If Bharatya's troops have surrendered.'

That wasn't going to work. Once Bharatya's troops had surrendered, his means of enforcing any agreement were gone. Darnell said, 'Why don't we draw up an agreement now, take it to Railoo, have everything signed and Ynessa released before Bharatya's troops come?'

'Because then you will have your wife and the power to overwhelm us. Until Bharatya's troops have actually surrendered, there is no guarantee that you will do what you say.'

Darnell thought there was another way. He said, 'If I agree to be a hostage, will you exchange my wife for me?'

Van Cuyler gave a slow smile. This was what he'd been waiting for.

'I will leave Mirza Baig's confession with our guards here,' Darnell said, 'and you will bring Ynessa to the Land Bridge. We will make the exchange and I will stay with you until Cogan has finalized the agreements with Railoo and brings them to your tent for signature. When the agreements are signed, I will return here and order our guns to stand down and Bharatya to surrender. Then Cogan will collect the confession from our border guard and give it to you, and I will walk across the road to Madera.'

'That is an excellent idea,' Cogan cried.

Van Cuyler's smile was beatific. 'I agree,' he said, 'I agree. Now, Darnell, you go and bring Mirza Baig's confession here. And I will go and get your wife.'

Darnell turned and hurried back across the Land Bridge.

Darnell rushed into the bungalow, shouting to the servant boy to bring him a lantern, and then to fetch Ravi. He took the lantern into the small room he used as an office, wrenched open the bureau and took the keys from the drawer beneath his account books. He opened the drawer that contained his and Ynessa's wills, marriage certificate and Mirza Baig's confession.

He would have Ravi come with him to the Land Bridge and leave the confession with him in case it should be needed. But he had no intention of handing over the confession. Once Ynessa was free, he would get as close to van Cuyler as he'd done at the meeting, stick a gun into him, walk him back to Madera and charge him under English law with kidnapping and extortion. If Ravi was at the Land Bridge he could organize any covering fire that was necessary.

Ravi came into the room. Before he could speak, Darnell handed him the confession.

'I want you to take this and come with me to the Land Bridge,' he cried. 'I've arranged for Ynessa to be set free!' Quickly he told Ravi how.

'Yer stark, starin' mad,' Ravi said. 'I won't let yer go!' He put the confession down on the bureau. 'Listen, I've talked with the guards. Cogan arranged for 'em to let the Dutch in and out of the fort. 'E ordered 'em not to check the cart. And Cogan 'ad a secret meetin' wi' van Cuyler outside the Choultry Gate just before you got here.' He flung the confession down. 'Now do you see why you can't go? Cogan isn't going to come back and get you. 'E's goin' to leave you with van Cuyler and 'e's goin' to become agent of Madera.'

Cogan was greedy, stupid and jealous, Darnell thought. And he would pay Cogan back as soon as all this was over. But first he had to get Ynessa back.

Ravi said quietly, 'You can't go back to van Cuyler.'

'I have to. If I don't they'll suspect something is wrong and hurt Ynessa.'

'Van Cuyler will kill both of you.'

Darnell stared at him. 'I'm going,' he said. He picked up his bullet-bag. 'With this and a slow-match, anyone who tries to attack me will be blown up.'

'Yer'll be blown up too,' Ravi said glumly. 'We 'ave to find another way, Richard.'

'There *is* no other way. At least not now. Look, I've got a gun, two knives and this. What I want you to do is to make sure Cogan cannot countermand my orders to Eck-aerts and Martin. As soon as Bharatya's forces are sighted, the cannonade is to start, whether I'm back or not. Is that clear?'

Seringa rushed into the room, briefly raising steepled palms to his face before bursting out, 'I've just heard about Ynessa. What are you going to do, Darnell?'

Rapidly, Ravi told him, and Seringa's face clouded. His eyes filled with apprehension. 'That won't save Ynessa.'

'Ynessa will be out of van Cuyler's hands in ten minutes. Now get out of my way – both of you!'

Seringa stiffened. 'I have a better idea,' he said.

Darnell stood beside the guards at the end of the Land Bridge, staring across the road at the Dutch encampment with its natural barricade of garden wall and trees. The Kokinada road, a faint lightness at his feet, was empty. There were figures gathered near the garden gate surrounding the dull metal of cannon and ammunition. Darnell stepped into the road. 'Mynheer van Cuyler,' he called. 'This is Richard Darnell. I am coming across now. Are you there?'

An answering voice came from the gate. 'Mynheer Darnell, come across whenever you are ready.'

Darnell took a slow-match from one of the guards and walked into the middle of the road, aware that he was an easy target for a good musketeer. A single figure moved from the Dutch guard-post and came up to him. 'Mynheer Darnell, it is I, van Roon.'

'Where's van Cuyler? Where's my wife?'

'She refused to come. She doesn't want to be exchanged. She says you are needed at Madera more than her.'

Darnell stared into van Roon's battered face. It was impossible to tell whether the man was lying or not. If it was a lie it was well chosen. Ynessa was proud enough to refuse the exchange. 'Bring her to your guard-post and let me talk to her,' Darnell said.

Van Roon looked up at the sky. 'She will not come. She fears that you might persuade her to accept the exchange.'

True or false? Either way, he had no choice. He couldn't leave Ynessa with van Cuyler. He had to go into the camp with van Roon. He said, 'I'll come. But remember this. Our attack starts in half an hour unless Ynessa or I are back in Madera.'

Van Roon looked at him blankly. 'No problem,' he said.

'And I won't surrender my gun or knife or this.' He waved the slow-match and patted the bullet-bag.

Van Roon looked at it carefully, then took two steps back. 'You have the confession?'

Darnell smiled tightly. 'Yes. If there's any attempt to disarm me or any attempt to stop my wife leaving your camp, this blows up.' He patted the bullet-bag again, and van Roon winced.

'Now let's go,' Darnell said. 'You walk in front of me.'

He took out his pistol and placed it against van Roon's back. 'Walk slowly. Don't do anything to make me suspicious or I'll blow away your spine.'

Darnell followed van Roon into the shadowy camp. They walked to the middle of the garden, where a row of small tents stood before a larger one. Lanterns cast a ghostly light on the path between them. Darnell walked carefully, taking care not to stumble. The entrance flap of the main tent was open and lights glowed inside. There were six sentries outside; all recognized van Roon and stared imperturbably ahead of them as he and Darnell went in.

The interior of the tent was large and sparse. Lanterns dangled from poles. A table and three chairs stood on a brown, grass-flecked groundsheet. A wide strip of green canvas separated the front of the tent from another area. 'Where the devil's van Cuyler?' Darnell demanded.

Abruptly the green canvas curtain was whipped back and Darnell froze with shock. In the gloomy space beyond, Ynessa lay racked up on a bed, her arms spread out and bound, her body covered with a sheet. Her face was swollen and bruised, and her eyes had the look of a trapped animal. Behind her, with a pistol pressed to the top of her head, stood Karel van Cuyler.

'So, Darnell. It is fool's mate,' he cried. 'Except that I do not care very much what happens to van Roon.'

Darnell held up the slow-match. 'I have enough powder in my bullet-bag to blow us all to hell,' he said. He quickly calculated the chances of shooting over van Roon's shoulder and hitting van Cuyler, and decided it was too much of a risk. 'We had an agreement,' he called. 'You were going to release my wife in exchange for me. You were going to release me for Bharatya's surrender and Mirza Baig's confession.'

'Yes,' van Cuyler laughed. 'But you weren't going to keep that agreement, were you, Darnell? As soon as your wife was free, you were going to find some way of breaking it. And if you didn't do it now, you'd have done it afterwards, isn't that so?'

'What about you?' Darnell asked. With Ynessa bound he couldn't hope to shoot van Cuyler and make a break for it. Now more than ever he needed to buy time. 'Did you mean to share Vaidya with us?'

'No more than you did, Darnell. No more than you did.' Van Cuyler stopped laughing and said, 'You see, we each tried to fool each other. But you are the one who got fooled. Because I have you *and* your lady wife. And neither of you are going to see this day's end.'

'You won't either,' Darnell called. 'If I'm not back in Madera in twenty minutes, the attack starts.'

Van Cuyler stopped laughing. 'There will be no attack,' he cried. 'As soon as Cogan has made peace with Railoo, he will return to Madera and turn the English cannon on Bharatya.'

'That's treachery! Cogan was coming here –'

'He's already been. Ask your wife. Cogan hates you almost as much as I do, and wants more than anything to be agent of Madera.'

Darnell said, 'Whatever happens, you will die, van Cuyler. My slow-match will kill us all. So what is it to be? Do we leave here to fight another day? Or do we all die now?' He stepped back, bringing the slow-match across his body so he could ignite the bullet-bag in an instant.

Van Cuyler's smile faded. He looked down at his pistol barrel buried in Ynessa's hair. Sweat trickled down his slab-like cheeks.

Suddenly Darnell saw Ynessa's eyes widen, felt a rush of air, heard something swish behind him and Ynessa's scream: 'Darnell, behi –' Then the water hit him in a chilling shock wave, jolting him sideways.

For a moment he lost all vision. He heard a sharp hiss as the slow-match went out and smelt the acridity of wet smoke. Then the pail crashed into the side of his head. Groping desperately for his pistol, he fired once, the sound deafening, the flash blinding. He saw van Roon turn and rush at him, and hurled the gun into his face. A massive weight descended on his shoulders. He swung round, trying to lose it; the old knife-wound in his side wrenched. Darnell couldn't move. He was wedged against bodies. Blows thudded into his chest and stomach as he struggled to get his hands free. There were five of them, hitting, pummelling, kicking. He felt his legs give. But they were holding him up; beating him again and again. Over the sound of their blows he heard Ynessa scream and felt the tent closing in on him, saw the twisted sweat-limned faces growing more indistinct, felt the blows receding . . .

When he woke he couldn't move. Every part of his body ached. There was a dullness in his head and blood filled his mouth. His body, clothes and hair were all wet. He tried to stand up but couldn't move; he realized his hands were fastened behind him, his ankles lashed to the legs of a chair. He opened his eyes.

Pain sliced his skull. He closed his eyes and tried again, more slowly this time, holding his breath against the pain, which was thick and sickening. He found himself staring at his thighs. His pantaloons were dirty and torn and splotched with blood. Slowly he raised his head.

He was in the middle of the tent, van Cuyler seated behind the table to his left, van Roon and five other men to his right. In front of him Ynessa was still racked to the bed, arms spread out and legs spreadeagled. She was completely naked. Her copper-brown skin gleamed with sweat. She was returning the lewd stares of the assembled men with an expression of defiance. Darnell felt an overpowering sense of shame and a flaming anger.

'Well, English, how do you feel now?' van Cuyler asked, lisping.

Darnell cursed loudly and fluently, tugging at his bonds. Where were Bharatya and Ravi and Seringa? They weren't coming. He had to break free and save Ynessa and himself.

A slight movement from Ynessa caught his attention. She was shaking her head, trying to convey something. Darnell looked round the tent again. The lantern's glow was feeble against the morning light. It wasn't yet dawn; it wasn't too late. He had to play for time. He stopped struggling and looked at van Cuyler. 'What are you going to do with us?' he asked.

Van Cuyler smiled smugly. 'I'm going to kill you, Darnell,' he said. 'And kill your wife also. But first I am going to watch you go crazy, do you understand? I'm going to drive you crazy just as you drove my Annatjie crazy. Do you know what it was like those days on the *Prinsen* with everyone around us dying, with no food, no water, and the sun drying us out like leather?'

Darnell said, 'I did not let you drift. I sent a Dutch caravel –'

Van Cuyler was staring at him, his gaze fixed and glowing. In a strangled voice he said, 'You drove my Annatjie mad. You forced her away from me.'

It was useless, Darnell knew. Van Cuyler was obsessed with what had happened in Java. But he had to be kept diverted, he had to be kept from doing anything until his time ran out. Darnell said, 'You'll never get away with this, even if your arrangement with Cogan works. If there is peace you can't explain away our deaths.'

'Peace or war, no one will be interested in your deaths,' van Cuyler said. 'After this, I return to Amsterdam. After I give Vaidya to the Compagnie, I become a member of the Lords XVII. I have got what I came for. But not you. You have failed, Darnell. You have lost and I have won.'

Van Cuyler was insane. But he had to be kept talking. Darnell wondered what was keeping Ravi and Seringa and why the attack hadn't started. Surely Bharatya's forces must be here by now? A chilling thought struck him. Had Cogan got back and countermanded the attack?

'Wait!' Darnell cried. 'Release us and I'll sign an agreement granting you Vaidya – all of Vaidya, without condition. You can build as many forts as you please, make as much money as you please. You can make the Dutch the supreme power in the East.'

So Darnell was a coward like everyone else. Van Cuyler shook with glee. This was delightful. It was so good to see Darnell crawl. 'I already have Vaidya,' van Cuyler said. 'Railoo is mine. Cogan is mine. There is nothing for you to give and nothing you can do to stop the Dutch taking Vaidya and becoming lords of the East.'

'All right,' Darnell said, desperately. 'Think about yourself. The da Soares are wealthy. We will give you any sum of money you ask, if you will release us.'

Van Cuyler laughed.

'And I swear I will not take revenge on you afterwards. I swear I will leave you and your family alone.' Darnell's voice broke.

Oh, it was good to hear him beg, good to hear him plead. Van Cuyler had never imagined it would be as satisfying as this. 'No, Darnell. You are offering me nothing I do not have.'

There was a commotion at the front of the tent, and they all turned to see one of van Cuyler's soldiers rush in.

'Excellency! Excellency!' he shouted. 'One of Railoo's commanders is outside with twenty men, demanding to see you.'

'Tell him –'

'Get out of my way!' another, deeper voice cried in Tamil. 'I am Commander Pillai and Raja Railoo has placed me in charge of this sector. What the devil is going on here? Why aren't you men preparing to defend us against the English?'

Chapter Thirty-Six

Van Cuyler turned to stare at the tall, imposing figure in the mottled green and brown uniform. His turban was pulled low over his head. He was armed with a sword and dagger. His assistant, an Indian, also in a mottled green and brown uniform, stood beside him, a musket over his shoulder and a pistol in his hand. Other men filed in behind.

A special unit of Railoo's army, van Cuyler thought. Then he thought, special unit or not Railoo had no business sending someone to take command of his sector. 'There's no need for you to trouble yourself about the English,' he said, curling his lips in contempt. 'Go back and tell Railoo I've made arrangements with the English. There will be no English attack. Tell him also that I do not need you to help defend my sector. Go instead and help Railoo defend himself against Bharatya.'

At a signal from the assistant, three men suddenly rushed forward. Darnell started, but the assistant – goddamnit! – had swung his pistol round and was aiming at van Cuyler, whilst three more of the intruders drew pistols against van Roon and the other Dutchmen.

Van Cuyler felt the breath seep out of him. 'Who are you?' he cried, fighting the sickening feeling that something terrible had happened. Eyes fixed on Commander Pillai, he took two steps forward. He'd seen that face before, but not in Railoo's camp. He stared at the cherry red mouth behind the heavy beard and the large almond eyes. 'By the Cross!' he cried. 'Prince Seringa!'

A seething wave of panic threatened to engulf him.

Seringa had used the password to bring English troops to rescue Darnell! He turned and shouted, 'These aren't Railoo's troops! They're muck-fickin' English!' He ran back to the table for his pistol and knife.

The shots made him leap. Acrid smoke filled the tent and stung his nostrils. Ahead of him men screamed in surprise and pain and fell to the ground still screaming, blood welling from huge wounds in their chests and faces. Over the sound of their moans he heard Seringa's assistant snap out an order: 'Get the sentries!'

Seringa's men rushed to the entrance flap. There was a rapid burst of pistol fire, followed by explosions as they flung their grenades. Then a louder, more distant explosion followed. The English cannonade had begun.

Seringa's assistant was shouting to van Cuyler as much as to Darnell. 'We've arrested Cogan, charged him with treason and flung him in jail!'

Van Cuyler couldn't believe it. Madera was lost! Vaidya was lost and Railoo finished! His chest felt tight. His head throbbed with a pulsing pain. Through the ringing in his ears he heard Darnell say, 'Karel van Cuyler, you have committed the crimes of kidnapping and extortion on English territory. I am placing you under arrest.'

Darnell was coming towards him, and Seringa's assistant was pointing his pistol at him. But if the English arrested him he'd be jailed for what he'd done to Ynessa Darnell, and then handed over to the Portuguese for Rodrigo's murder. If he survived that, the Dutch would get him for de Groot's death and breaching the truce. He was finished, unless he could get to Pulicat and hide.

Darnell was two feet away from him. Rushing at him, his shoulder caught Darnell in the chest and spun him away. Van Cuyler ran past the green curtain to the bed. A figure in green and brown moved to stop him and was shoved away by van Roon. A shot rang out and he heard van Roon gasp. Then he was past the bed and standing by the washbasin. He tore open the gash Ynessa Darnell had made and pushed himself through it. From behind him he heard Darnell cry, 'Stop him!'

A pall of smoke hung over the garden. There were two great, raw gashes of earth across the lawn between the tents and the river. Bodies lay scattered everywhere and two tents burned furiously. 'Help!' 'Water!' The cries came from all around the garden. By the gate, flames spread over a deformed cannon and the bodies lying around it. Van Cuyler began to run away from the English fort, towards the uncultivated area at the back of the garden where their horses were.

Goddamnit, he wished he hadn't stabled the horses so far away. The journey felt like an eternity. The smoke seared his lungs. His legs, pounding over the uneven grass, felt as if they were weighted. But he had to keep on.

He willed his body to keep moving. He heard the explosion of cannon a split second before the earth-shaking thump that almost threw him over. He staggered and turned to look at Madera. Darnell was only fifteen yards behind him and gaining.

The gap narrowed to a few yards. Van Cuyler heard Darnell call out, 'Stop, or I'll shoot.'

He turned. Goddamnit, Darnell was less than five yards away, and he had a pistol in his hand pointed straight at him. He swerved and ran up the hill to the trees that bordered the river. There was a group of Dutchmen running in the same direction; he used them as cover, then broke away and sped for the trees.

He swung his hands to give him more speed, and careless of the consequences flung away his doublet. But it was no help. He was slowing. He couldn't breathe. His legs were heavy and tired and slow and to move them was agony. He felt himself go splay-legged for balance, and pumped his arms. Three yards to go, two, he pressed himself into the slope, forced his legs to pound. A few more strides.

There, there, this was a race, just like in school and Uncle Hendrijk was waiting beyond the tape to applaud his victory. And he was winning! He had to win. Uncle Hendrijk would never forgive him if he lost. He darted into the gloom of the trees, breath sobbing.

Darnell's legs began to go halfway up the slope. His stride became uneven; his legs felt leaden. His racing heart couldn't pump enough air into his lungs. All of a sudden he felt exhausted. He couldn't run the hill. He couldn't beat van Cuyler to the forest beyond it.

The forest beyond! He'd be mad to follow van Cuyler into it. Running from light into darkness he'd be an easy target. But if he didn't go in after van Cuyler, he'd lose him. And once van Cuyler got back to Pulicat he'd be impossible to dislodge. Darnell told himself he had to go in. He couldn't lose van Cuyler now!

He willed his legs to move, breasted the slope, and ran across the two yards of flat ground before the forest. As he reached the edge of the forest, he hurled himself forward, forcing his body low and parallel to the ground, flying in like an arrow. Skimming an ugly nest of roots, he landed with a breath-jarring smash on the solid earth beyond. The fall smashed the breath out of him and knocked the gun from his grasp. He grabbed it again with both hands and looked round quickly. Van Cuyler was leaning out from behind a tree, his pistol trained on Darnell's head. Darnell fired.

A roar, a flash, and a watery van Cuyler dissolved into the trees. Darnell dragged his sleeve across his eyes. There was no hump of fallen body, no sound of someone wounded thrashing through the undergrowth. He'd missed and van Cuyler was gone!

So what was he still lying there for? He'd had only one shot and now van Cuyler had one shot and probably had him in his sights while he lay there as if it was *siesta*. The explosion startled him as he jumped off the path, rolling behind a tree as the ball smashed into the earth where he'd been lying. He saw van Cuyler step out from behind a tree, smoking gun dangling from his hand. Putting aside the useless pistol, van Cuyler took out his *sjambok* and charged.

His lips were drawn back from his teeth, his eyes bulging with fury. He raised the *sjambok* above his head for a blow that would smash bone.

Darnell pushed himself to his feet, thighs burning with the effort, and ran towards van Cuyler, flinging his pistol into van Cuyler's face before following up, fists swinging. Van Cuyler roared with pain and came forward, big, lumbering and dripping blood.

The *sjambok* flailed. Darnell danced back and jabbed van Cuyler twice in the face, then danced back again as van Cuyler swung wildly with the *sjambok*. It hissed past Darnell's face. Darnell moved in quickly before van Cuyler had time to recover from the swing, and jabbed van Cuyler twice more to the head. Van Cuyler swung again, back-handed this time. Darnell, moving in, stepped closer and smashed van Cuyler on the mouth and ribs and jumped back. His fists hurt. His arms were becoming heavy. But van Cuyler was strong. He was bleeding all over and still coming forward.

Darnell circled warily. Van Cuyler slowed, his face streaming blood, then swung once more. Darnell danced back. His foot caught a root and he staggered. He saw the look of triumph in van Cuyler's eyes as he swung the *sjambok* back-handed. It caught Darnell high on the shoulder; Darnell felt his boot catch, his body curl, and let himself go. He hit the ground and rolled with the force of his fall. Rolled once more so he could face van Cuyler.

With a roar van Cuyler was on him, the weight of his body smashing all the breath out of Darnell. Van Cuyler's fist pounded into his face. Darnell turned his head and tried to lift van Cuyler off, but van Cuyler had him firmly pinned. The next punch caught him high in the chest. Darnell couldn't breathe.

Darnell saw van Cuyler's bloodied lips break in a smile, saw the triumph in van Cuyler's eyes. 'Got you, Darnell,' he breathed, and raised the *sjambok* high.

Suddenly Ynessa's voice came high and strong above the sounds of carnage. 'Stop!' she cried.

Like hell he would, van Cuyler thought. He'd smash out Darnell's brains and then deal with her. He raised the *sjambok*. 'The devil take your soul,' he cursed.

Van Cuyler heard the muffled blast as he hit the grass with his shoulders, and found himself looking at the sky. The cannon, the blasted English cannon had fired again.

He couldn't sit up. He rolled on to his side. There was blood on his hands and on his sleeves. He wasn't hurt. It was just the blast of the cannon. He climbed on to all fours. He was bleeding from his chest. Shrapnel, no doubt. It was then that he saw Ynessa Darnell walking up to them, a smoking pistol in her hand.

The bitch had shot him! He tried to get to his feet. A knee collapsed. He stared at them, the hatred welling. Goddamn you, Darnell! May your soul rot in hell! An arm went and he fell face down into the ground. The earth was damp against his beard. Was it dew or was it blood? Was it his blood?

He suddenly realized he was not going home again, that he would never see Amsterdam or Uncle Hendrijk or become a member of the Lords XVII. Annatjie, he muttered, Annatjie, and felt his face fold into the earth.

Darnell dragged himself to his feet and draped an arm round Ynessa, who stood, white-faced, with lowered head, her hand still clutching the pistol. 'It's all right,' he said. 'It's all right. Thank God you came. You saved my life.' His arm still around her, he limped forward, stooped and pulled up van Cuyler's head. The sightless eyes stared into his, all enmity, all life gone. Slowly Darnell lowered him to the grass. It was over. He felt drained. The battlefield had gone strangely quiet.

The garden was littered with the bodies of men and the wreckage of tents and carts. Tents still flamed; smoke poured out of the shattered cannon near the gate. Through the dying smoke, men were shambling away from Madera, heads lowered, muskets trailing, some supporting wounded comrades. Darnell took Ynessa's hand. 'Come,' he said, softly. 'Let's go home.'

They went quickly past the tents and the shattered gate to the Kokinada Road. There were no Dutch guards; the English sentries, recognizing them, rushed them over. Darnell kept holding on to Ynessa's hand as they crossed the Land Bridge. 'Home,' he said. 'We're safe,' and took her in his arms and let her sob against his shoulder.

They were halfway through the Black Town when the cannon started again.

They went to the top of the north-west bastion. A faint haze hung over the garden, abandoned now to smouldering fires and the bodies of the dead. The Dutch cannon which had been hit first lay in twisted lumps before the Island and Land Bridges, bodies scattered about them. On the island, Railoo's forces were milling around anxiously, pulling down tents, loading carts and dragging wounded to the rear.

Captain Martin and a group of soldiers stood on the battlements, well back from five cannon standing on wooden platforms and pointing across the muddy silt of the river at the island.

The master-gunner called instructions to the matrosses.

A figure shambled on to the bastion and walked slowly up to Darnell. 'Richard!'

Darnell turned. Cogan still wore his joinet and his cheeks

were covered with a soft stubble that glinted in the sun. Behind him, two guards waited.

'I asked them to let me up here,' Cogan said. 'I had to ask your forgiveness. I had to tell you I was mistaken. I had to say I was sorry – to both of you.'

Darnell's eyes were hard and unforgiving. Cogan had nearly killed Ynessa and nearly killed him. Cogan had almost lost the Company and England their future. 'You will be charged with treason,' he said. 'If found guilty you will be stripped of your fortune and executed.'

'Richard, we were friends once. In Java. We looked after each other. We –'

Darnell picked up a pistol and gave it to Cogan. 'For your family's sake,' he said harshly before turning back to look at the fighting.

Cogan shambled back to where the guard waited.

Below them, streaming along the Mintoor road, came Bharatya's cavalry. The men came in orderly succession – spearmen, swordsmen, bowmen, pikes – riding fast and furiously for the bridge that joined the northern part of the mainland to the island.

Railoo's men saw the threat and charged for the bridge, but the cannon boomed and Railoo's first detachment exploded in a mixture of smoke and fire and dismembered limbs. A second detachment, running to their relief, turned and ran back.

Bharatya's cavalry streamed over the bridge, slashing, hacking, fighting. In no time at all they were mixing with Railoo's men at the back of the island. Railoo's tent and standard had fallen. The island was a mass of struggling, fleeing, fighting men and horses. Below them, the West Gates opened, and Seringa galloped out, followed by his men and a column of English infantry. They charged across the Island Bridge.

From behind them, the look-outs on the Sea Wall called, 'A ship! A ship!'

Darnell and Ynessa turned. A Company carrack was sailing into the roads, flags fluttering gaily from its mast. Ovington had arrived.

Chapter Thirty-Seven

Darnell sat with Ynessa, Ravi, Johnson and Whiting. They faced Ovington and his councillors across the green baize table in the committee room. The battle was over and Bharatya's men were tidying up. The speeches had been made and Ynessa and Darnell effusively congratulated and thanked. Now Ovington pushed four bags of coin across the table. He'd put on weight since Pettahpoli, and his pompadour was riffed with grey. During his journey from Surat, President Frederick Greenhill had died, and Ovington had become the new president. The chain of office gleamed brightly round his neck.

Ovington said, 'On behalf of the Honourable Company, I hereby formally adopt Fort St George, Madera, and appoint you, Richard Darnell, agent of Fort St George, Madera and principal agent of Coromandel.'

A ripple of applause crackled round the room. Ravi shouted ''ear, 'ear,' and Johnson cried, 'Speech!'

Ovington smiled and raised a temporizing hand. 'The future of the Company lies here in Madera,' he said. 'Mr Darnell, within six months, I want you to build me offices on St George Street, large enough to accommodate the presidency. I also want you to have someone ready to replace you as agent of Madera one year from now.'

Darnell felt a hot flush of anger. He opened his mouth to protest and saw Ovington was smiling.

'At the end of a year,' Ovington went on, 'I want you to join my council here in Madera as deputy president.'

Deputy president! Darnell felt Ynessa's hand quiver in his. That was a huge step; that would give him the power to reorganize the Company in India and power to get things done! In three or four years, Ovington would return to England and he would be president ... 'I agree,' he said, the words catching in his throat. 'Ravi Winter will be my successor.'

Ravi stood up and bowed to Ovington and the councillors. Everyone applauded. Ovington smiled and looked at Darnell. 'Well, Mr Darnell, have you got everything you wanted?'

'No,' Darnell said and stood.

Ovington and the councillors stared at him in surprise. Darnell cleared his throat and spoke. 'This is only the beginning,' he said. 'Our support of Seringa will set a precedent for all other *feringhi* in India. In future, Europeans will support princes in exchange for trade concessions. From now on, Eastern trade will not be about building factories, but about controlling provinces and ruling kingdoms.' He leaned on the table and looked directly at Ovington. 'In the end it will be about ruling India. Soon the Mughal will be finished; India will come apart unless someone holds it together. That someone must be us. And to do that we must become the strongest European power in India – *now*!' In a lower voice Darnell added, 'Through India we control the spice trade, and through the spice trade we become the wealthiest nation on earth.'

Ravi and Ynessa applauded as he sat; others joined in. Ovington looked thoughtfully at Darnell before he said, 'I share your views, Mr Darnell. The era of peaceful trade is over, and I see it as my function to adapt the Company to its new role.' He stroked his chin, the rubies on his fingers glinting dimly in the shade of the room. 'But it is a huge step for the Company. We must be careful not to change too much, too quickly.'

'Things have changed already,' Darnell said. 'The Company changes or it dies.'

A soldier entered the room and saluted. 'Beggin' your

pardon, Mr Darnell. His Excellency Raja Seringa of Vaidya and the Reverend Bharatya are outside and wish to speak with you.'

'Show them in.' Darnell walked to the door with Ynessa to greet them.

Seringa and Bharatya came in together. Seringa had changed into his customary white tunic and *dhoti*, and the tiger's eye glinted fiercely from the centre of his turban. Bharatya was bare-bodied, with a green and brown shawl beneath the prayer-beads round his neck.

Bharatya said formally, 'The war is over. Railoo has been executed and what remains of his army has sworn loyalty to us. Prince Seringa is the new Raja of Vaidya.'

Seringa came forward and bowed low before Darnell.

Darnell put his arms around Seringa and hugged him. 'Serai,' he said, softly. 'Ynessa and I owe you our lives. We thank you –'

Seringa hugged Darnell and Ynessa in turn and placed a hand on each of their shoulders. 'My family owes you our lives,' he said, 'and Vaidya owes you more than it can ever repay. Without you and your guns we would have lost, and Railoo would have ruined our country. You are the real ruler of Vaidya, Darnell. I ask for your guns and your soldiers to defend us against the Mughal and Kokinada. Without your help, Vaidya cannot survive. We will give you permission to build more factories and a right of exclusive trade. But we must have a formal defence alliance. From now on, our enemies must be your enemies. From now on, you must use your guns and soldiers for our defence.'

Darnell turned to Bharatya. 'What do you say, my friend?'

Bharatya smiled thinly. 'I say that neither a man nor a nation can fight its *karma*. I think, Darnell, that it is your *karma* to lead us and to change us.' He steepled his hands in front of him.

Darnell returned the greeting and turned to Ovington.

Ovington was looking at the island where Bharatya's men were wandering among the carnage, searching for lost comrades, tending to the wounded and corralling Railoo's soldiers into an enclosure by the Land Bridge. The English would witness many more scenes like this before they controlled India, he thought. He turned to face Darnell and the Indians. 'Carry on, Mr Darnell,' he said.

Darnell took Ynessa's hand and faced Seringa and Bharatya. 'On behalf of the Honourable Company, I agree,' he said solemnly. 'From now on, your enemies will be our enemies. Your friends, our friends.'

A new era was beginning, Darnell thought. They were embarking on something that would take generations to complete. He raised Ynessa's hand to his lips. Without meaning to, they were founding an empire, and only God knew how it would turn out.